Reflections
of Cherished Love

Darlene Davis

Reflections
of Cherished Love

*'To a best friend
from Charles'*

*Best Wishes,
Darlene J Davis* 2/23/05

Ⓘ ngenuity Publishing ™

This book is a work of fiction. Names, characters, places and incidents are either the product of the author's imagination or are used fictitiously.

Softcover: ISBN: 0-9718327-4-9

Hardcover: ISBN: 0-9718327-3-0

Library of Congress Control Number: 2002105046

First Printing November 2002

Published by
Ingenuity Publishing
P.O. Box 42055
Fredericksburg, Virginia 22404-2055
(540) 785-2441

www.IngenuityPublishing.com

Manufactured in the United States of America

10 9 8 7 6 5 4 3 2 1

Acknowledgments

Special thanks to the brilliant author Dr. Gary Woditsch for reviewing sections of the manuscript and coaching me in the craft of writing. I will always be grateful to you for seeing — from the first draft — my potential and encouraging me to keep writing.

Thanks to the Jarvis family for your strength, courage, common sense and compassion, and for sharing all of that with me. My gratitude also to you, my immediate family, as well as the family of Maxie and Reid Penn for always encouraging and believing in me.

Thanks to Judy Wigglesworth for consulting on the cover art concept, Bob Broomall for help during the copy editing process, Diane Parkinson for her reading and insightful comments on the manuscript, and Di Thompson for graphic design.

For

My parents, friends, relatives, Ricky, Jerry,
Stan, Victor, Leslie, Alex and Austin.

And for the readers.
Thank you for your support.

Reflections

of Cherished Love

One

*O*utside the Pentagon, Nathan and Brandi stopped and grinned at each other like a couple of mischievous kids. Their morning conference had broken up early on this beautiful April day. Savoring the fresh spring breeze, they got into Nathan's white BMW and curved away from the Pentagon lot for their offices at the U.S. Department of Interior.

Envious of the joggers and tourists strolling and taking advantage of the magnificent weather, Brandi sighed. "I wish we didn't have to go back to work yet."

"We don't," Nathan responded. He glanced playfully at Brandi and then out the window at the cherry blossoms in full bloom. He continued driving down the busy streets of downtown Washington.

Brandi gave Nathan a suspicious look. "What are you up to now?"

Nathan aimed for a parking spot that had just been vacated off Twentieth Street. "We're going for a walk."

"My wish precisely," Brandi said.

Nathan pulled his suit coat off and laid it across the back seat. Brandi sprang from the car as he opened her door. Her wavy brown hair pulled back into a ponytail showed off her pretty tan skin and emphasized her bright face. Though she was dressed comfortably, a professional appearance prevailed. She wore a navy double-breasted jacket with a white pleated skirt that hung above the knee, and a brick-and-white cotton blouse underneath. Her one-inch stacked-heel, navy-and-white Via Spiga loafers further polished her look.

As Nathan and Brandi strolled down Twentieth Street, they found themselves approaching the green-and-yellow sun umbrella of a vendor's cart. "Um, let's get a hot dog," Brandi said in her chipper voice.

Nathan led the way. "Let's see. Two Pepsi's and two hot dogs with the works, please," he said to the oriental lady as he reached into the right-hand pocket of his coffee-colored suit pants.

While standing on the sidewalk, eating, talking and laughing, Nathan dripped ketchup on the front of his crisp white dress shirt.

"Oh, Nathan," Brandi said, frowning. She took her napkin and wiped the stain. "You know, you need someone to take care of you."

"No, thank you." He gave her a sweet smile and nodded over his half-devoured hot dog. "I'm doing just fine all by myself."

"Yeah, I can tell." She pointed at the ketchup stain on his shirt. They laughed.

As they leaned against the granite wall along the sidewalk, Brandi raised her soda to eye level and seemed to study it seriously for a moment. "Nathan," she said. He glanced at her quizzically. "I'd like to make a toast!"

"What to?" He raised his bottle and tapped it against hers as he waited.

"To you." Her eyes shone with warmth. "Here's to the outstanding friendship of Nathan Whitaker, through one of the most difficult times in my life."

"Oh, that's sweet." He gazed fondly into her light-brown eyes.

"I know I've thanked you before, but if it weren't for you and your caring ways, I'd probably be divorced right now."

She looked solemnly at Nathan. She had thought that after her breast cancer surgery, her marriage would never be the same. Her husband, Justice, had tried to convince her of his undying love, but she didn't believe him. She thought he mostly felt pity for her. And when Justice couldn't make all their problems go away, he felt like he was failing Brandi. He started withdrawing from her.

When Nathan went out of his way to talk to Justice, Justice's entire attitude changed. He grew more patient with Brandi and her illness. Nathan told Justice to never give up on love, and that if he truly loved Brandi, he needed to stay strong. Justice and Brandi felt like Nathan had been sent to them for this special reason. He had been their anchor when their ship was drifting, their guide when grief and confusion blinded them. He saw their love for each other quite clearly, and he reminded them that it was far greater than the problems they were having. And so, the friendship and bond forged among the three of them was strengthened and had since never wavered.

"I don't know what you said to him, but I know what you said to me, and it sure worked miracles," Brandi continued. "He thinks very highly of you, Nathan." She stood on her tiptoes and kissed him on the cheek.

"Hey, the feeling's mutual. And it's not that hard to befriend the charming Brandi De Silva."

Brandi smiled. "Well, I have to tell you, Justice and I are happier than we've ever been. We know now what life is really all about, and we're so grateful for each other."

"You both have a good reason to be grateful for each other," Nathan replied, smiling warmly as the sun shone down on his smooth, dark skin. He took Brandi's elbow and hustled them both across Constitution Avenue.

They walked alongside Constitution Gardens. The immaculate greens and colorful flowers provided a fresh, wholesome fragrance to accent the cultivated beauty. Passing respectfully by the Vietnam Wall, they reached the Lincoln Memorial and stopped to enjoy its majestic structure. The Washington Monument was in full view and towering to their far left. They stood by the Reflecting Pool and watched a toddler toss bread in mashed handfuls to the sea gulls.

Suddenly, Nathan's senses seemed to sharpen. A warmth came over him. He looked up slowly. A short distance away stood a strikingly beautiful woman, staring at him as though hypnotized. He knew instantly who she was, although it had been ten years since he'd seen her last.

Brandi glanced at Nathan, then at the woman. "You know her?" she said.

"Yes," replied Nathan, never taking his eyes off the woman's face. His soul trembled as he moved gently away from Brandi and closer to the woman.

"Nathan," the woman said in a breathless voice.

"S- Serena," Nathan stammered.

Serena stepped forward with the grace of a swan. They stood in awe for a few moments before embracing shyly.

"God," Nathan said. "I wouldn't have believed you could get even more beautiful." His dark eyes gazed lovingly into hers. "You always were special, but now . . ." He studied her exquisite features. Her down-like curly brown hair lay softly against the flawless bronze skin on her face and neck.

"It's so good to see you," she said softly. Nathan almost melted, listening to the purr in her voice. She went on. "You haven't changed a bit. You look great."

She smiled, then glanced over his shoulder at Brandi who stood a few yards away. Brandi raised her eyebrows with interest as she smiled with her lips shut and waved timidly at Serena. Serena waved back. Then Brandi turned her attention to some tourist asking for directions.

Nathan looked over his shoulder. "Oh that's Brandi," he told

Serena. "We work together. She's a good friend."

"I see." Serena nodded, then briefly studied Nathan's strong, muscular physique.

"So, do you live here?" he asked, fighting the excitement in his voice.

"No," she said. "I've been here for the past two weeks, performing at the National Theater."

"Two weeks! You're kidding."

"No. I live in New York. Today is my last day here, so I'm touring the city with some fellow artists." She turned and pointed to a small group of people standing near the Washington Monument.

"I wish I had known you were here," he said. "Maybe we could have gone to dinner." She smiled tenderly. "I live here," he continued. "I work for the Department of Interior and also as a private engineering consultant."

Serena listened curiously. She knew how intelligent Nathan was, and she took great pleasure in guessing that he had completed his college education after all. Then she glanced over at her group and her eyes widened. "Oh, I have to go. They're leaving me."

"Wait, please!" Nathan's heart quickened. He had thought about Serena every day for the past ten years, and now she was about to walk away once again.

"Can I call you?" he asked.

"Yes." Serena reached into the small black handbag that hung against her black silk skirt. While she retrieved a pen and paper, Nathan surveyed her taut, delicate body. She leaned her hip out and used it, along with her pocketbook, to jot down her phone number. Her leg protruded through the slit on the right side of her skirt. Nathan fixed his eyes on the symmetry of her thigh, smiling when he noticed her small brown birthmark shaped like ocean waves. He recalled that Serena once thought that birthmark meant something, because she was a Pisces.

She looked up and handed him the paper. "This is my number in New York."

Nathan shifted his eyes and reached for the paper. For a few seconds, he cautiously held her hand in his before slowly and seductively easing the paper from her fingertips.

"I'm leaving for Africa in a few days," she said. "I'll be there for about a month. I'd love to hear from you when I get back."

"Great," he said. "Have a safe trip, and I hope you enjoy yourself."

"Thank you," she said. "Goodbye."

Brandi stood in the background, looking at Nathan while he watched Serena disappear from sight. She walked forward. "Don't tell me," Brandi said. Nathan turned to her, finally. "That was Serena, wasn't it?"

"Yes." He beamed with joy.

"I knew it! When I saw the way you looked at her, I was sure it could not be anyone else. You hadn't seen her in years, had you?"

"Ten years."

"That's incredible. They say it's a small world."

"Yes, it's a miracle." Nathan's voice was as mellow as the soft sound of a violin.

Brandi wrapped her arm around his. "Let's go. We need to get back to work."

As they headed back to the car, Nathan said, "I'm sorry I didn't introduce you. I . . . I was going to, but she left so fast."

"That's okay. When you saw her, you looked like you had been lost alone on a deserted island for years and she was the first person you had seen. I think you were in shock initially."

"I still am, my friend. I still am."

As the days passed for Nathan, every spare thought was with Serena. In the shower, he recalled the time they got caught in the rain at Riverdale Park in Georgia. She even made the rain lovely. In his car, he remembered Serena driving on the "London" side of the road in Georgia. Knowing she would need to make a quick left turn, she had driven up the lane designed for traffic coming from the opposite direction. All he had been able to do was cover his face and grimace for the few seconds until she had looked at him and realized her mistake. She had apologized passionately: "Oh, I'm so sorry, I'm so sorry." "It's okay," he had said, laughing at her embarrassment . . . . His work was seasoned with thoughts of how much she had always encouraged and believed in him.

But there were nagging thoughts as well.

Had she been wearing a ring when he saw her by the Reflecting Pool? He tried hard to revive a glimpse of her left hand. Was there a ring? If so, on which hand? Try as he would, nothing resolved the burning question.

Nathan's world had revolved around Serena from the time he first laid eyes on her thirteen years ago, until they painfully ended their dream three years later—a dream for which he now fanned a hope for revival.

❖

Two

A few days after her chance meeting with Nathan, Serena was preparing to leave for John F. Kennedy airport when the phone rang.

"Serena," Nikki said, in the slightly hoarse voice that men found so enticing, "I'm glad I caught you." Serena held the cordless telephone in one hand while she scanned the clothes in her bedroom closet. Ninety miles away, Nikki sat curled up on the green-and-blue plaid sofa in her Greenwich, Connecticut, condominium.

"I was just about to call you to say goodbye," Serena told her best friend.

"Oh, you were. Well, don't forget about us common folks while you're off seeing the world. Maybe you can bring me back a little magnet or something to go on my refrigerator."

Serena laughed. "Please."

"I still can't believe you're going by yourself. But I'm sure you'll have a good time. You deserve to."

"Thanks, Nikki."

"Be careful, Serena, and call me when you get back. I have an appointment, so I have to say goodbye now."

"Yeah," Serena said. "Shante should be here soon, and I need to call Julian before I leave. I'll talk to you when I get back."

Serena thought of Nikki Campbell and Shante Peyton as the sisters she never had. And as she said goodbye, she wished they were taking the trip with her. She slid a pair of tan cashmere pants off the hanger. Yes, these will be comfortable, she thought, pulling them on.

Looking at herself in the wall mirror of the walk-in closet, she decided to add a little eyeliner. She usually wore very little make-up—maybe lipstick, mascara and a dab of rouge. But some days—like today—she felt better, more confident, with eyeliner on, too. Other days she felt prettier wearing no make-up at all. Many people had told her—including Nikki—that she didn't need make-up, that it covered her natural beauty.

Serena took one last look in the mirror. Suddenly, she wondered if she had forgotten something. She walked down the wrought-iron and oak stairway and into the living room of her lavish Long Island home. She canvassed the room, trying to figure out what she could have missed. African American and European art graced the white walls, including paintings by two of her favorite artists—William R. Cantwell and Henry Sumpter. The white damask sofa, chair and ottoman, along with the glass and green wrought-iron tables, gave an air of sophistication to the room. Serena's white baby grand Steinway added still more elegance to the spacious, light-filled home.

She smiled as she ran her fingers down the keyboard, thinking of the day, three years ago, when she had walked into the store and bought it with her own money. She had taught herself how to play the piano by ear when she was a young girl. "I can't afford lessons," her father had told her. But Serena wasn't easily discouraged. She would walk a mile to her Aunt Lucy's house, savoring the smell of Georgia peaches that filled the air from the nearby orchards. Lucy had a dusty old piano that was never tuned.

But with that, and a twelve-dollar keyboard, Serena was soon playing her favorite tunes.

Serena tucked her long-sleeved white blouse into her pants and tightened her brown belt. "Oh, yes, I remember, my camera." She dashed across the polished oak floors to the marble fireplace and reached for her camera on the shelf. She unzipped her luggage and placed the camera inside. Then she used the phone on the end table by the sofa to dial her husband at work.

There was no answer. "Where is he?" she asked herself. She dialed his beeper number and left a message: "Hi, Julian. Give me a call, if you can. I'll be leaving any minute now. Don't forget, the cleaning service comes on Saturday mornings, so make sure you're here. Let them know the dates you won't need them. Um, goodbye."

Moments later the phone rang.

"Hi, Serena," Julian said. "We were in an important meeting. I'm glad I caught you, though."

"Me, too. I wish you were here. I wish . . . I'm glad you'll be joining me in a couple of weeks."

"Yeah," Julian said. "Serena, have a safe trip and call me as soon as you get there."

Serena began to feel lonely as she said goodbye. She didn't like traveling alone. In fact, the thought of it scared her and made her stomach cramp. But she reminded herself that she was taking this trip to help conquer her fear. She knew that she needed to do more things independently of others. Still, when she had called Julian to say goodbye, she had badly wanted him to say, "Don't leave without me. I don't want you to go alone." Then she thought about the conversation they'd had two weeks ago.

"Serena," Julian had said, "why don't you just wait and we can go together."

Serena knew that if she waited for Julian, she would probably never go. He was a pro at canceling their plans and changing his mind at the last minute. And so she said, "I've already planned everything. There's a lot I want to see, Julian. And I need to get over this fear I have . . . . You *will* be joining me, right?"

"Right," Julian had answered, reassuring her that he'd join her in two weeks.

Still feeling her fear, Serena tried to convince herself that taking this trip to Africa, alone, was not a totally ridiculous idea. I've been wanting to visit Africa for a couple of years, and now I'm finally going, she thought. Serena knew this would be a good experience. She really did need to get away. She needed this time to herself.

Serena looked out the open window beyond the lovely maple and white dogwood trees in her front yard. A soft breeze flowed through the window and she took the fresh air into her lungs. Shante should be here any minute, she thought.

Serena and Shante had met four years ago. Shante had taken her class to see an off-Broadway musical in which Serena was starring. After the play, Serena allowed Shante's class to come up onto the stage. Serena welcomed them with open arms, and Shante thanked Serena for being so helpful and friendly. They realized their compatibility almost immediately. Serena was impressed with the skillful manner in which Shante handled such a large group of children. They began talking and hadn't stopped since.

HONK! HONK! HONK! Serena heard the horn on Shante's Saturn. She opened the door and set her luggage on the cement steps.

Shante stepped out of the car and helped Serena load her luggage into the trunk. Shante's blue jeans showed off her tiny waistline and slender yet curvaceous figure. Her dark, short hair was cut in a sophisticated, low-maintenance style, and her caramel-colored skin glowed. Her big dark eyes and long lashes were the first things Serena and Nikki had noticed when they had met her—mainly because they resembled Halle Berry's. The happy bounce in her walk was all her own.

"Hey, girl, I wish I could go with you." Shante spoke with a youthful, but very feminine voice.

"I wish you could, too," Serena replied. "Maybe next time."

"I'm serious, Serena. The next time you or Marcus go, I'm going, too."

Serena smiled, thinking how nice it was to have a friend like Shante. Serena thought Shante was simply awesome on the inside and out. And so did everyone else who knew her. Whenever Shante walked into a room, tired faces lit up and caught a fresh breath of life. Shante was happy, outgoing, and had a contagious energy. Serena wasn't surprised when she opened Shante's high school yearbook and discovered that she had been homecoming queen. She was the first queen ever chosen from the basketball team at her school.

"We'll have to go shopping together when you get back," Shante said.

"Sure. Okay. But after this trip, we'll have to use your plastic."

On the way to the airport, Serena sat quietly, with her stomach in knots. She found herself trying to figure out what had possessed her to travel alone. Then she remembered, took a deep breath and thought, it's too late to turn back now. Shante was busy talking about her boyfriend Marcus, her third-grade class, and how she had noticed, while fueling her car and changing the oil, that gas prices had gone up. Serena glanced at her as she talked, recalling the time she, Shante and Nikki decided to go to Atlantic City three and a half years ago. They rode together in Nikki's car which—on the way—blew a tire as Nikki sped down I-95.

And Serena had asked, "What are we going to do?" And Nikki had answered, "Get somebody to change it." Serena had asked, "Who?" And Shante had said, "I guess me, ya dodo's."

Serena and Nikki had stood in the chilly wind with their arms folded while Shante insisted that they watch carefully. "Didn't your dads or anybody show ya'll how to change a tire?" And they had answered in unison "No-o-o."

Serena snapped back to the present as Shante pulled up to the airport curb. Minutes later, they hugged and waved goodbye.

As Shante drove back to her apartment in New Rochelle, Nikki, driving her dark blue Acura Integra, was nearing the Greenwich Shopping Plaza after having finished her earlier business.

"I have got to stop eating out so much," Nikki said to herself as she turned into the grocery store parking lot. She hardly ever cooked since she lived alone and hated taking the time to shop for groceries.

She saw an empty parking space and prepared to drive into it when a man in a black Mustang swerved in front of her and into the space. Nikki blew her horn, cursed under her breath, then rolled her eyes. "Of course it's a man," she said angrily as she found another parking space. "They are so selfish. He knew I was getting ready to pull into that space. No, just pretend that you don't even see him."

Nikki was comfortably dressed in a colorful wraparound skirt, sandals, and a simple white, short-sleeved body top. Her long silky black hair cascaded down her back. Her dark, exotic skin gave many people the impression that she was from a tropical island, at least until she spoke, for she was actually from Louisiana—Shreveport, to be exact.

Once inside, Nikki hurried down each aisle. She grabbed a head of lettuce, a bag of carrots, and some tomatoes, apples and bananas and raced ahead to the next aisle.

She spotted the same man with whom she'd had the parking lot encounter. "Oh, God," she said under her breath. "Now he's going to hog the aisle, too."

"So, what's your name?" the tall lanky man asked. He smiled, and all Nikki noticed was a gold tooth that seemed to sparkle in an unattractive way.

"Excuse me, you're crowding my space," she said impatiently.

"What?" the man asked.

Nikki said nothing. She continued loading her shopping cart with canned foods.

"I's just wonderin' if you'd like ta get togetha," the man said in a brassy and cocksure manner. He moved closer, until his face was only a few inches away from Nikki's.

She backed away from him. "Listen," she said, "you can hog the parking space, you can hog the aisle space, but you may not hog my personal space, *sir*!" She stressed the word "sir" and jerked her head.

"Damn," he said in surprise.

Damn you, she thought. She hurried up the aisle and to the checkout counter.

Another man bites the dust.

As Nikki loaded the groceries into the car and headed home, she glanced down at the frozen broccoli and green beans that had fallen to the floorboard, and her annoyed expression subsided ...

"Oh, I'm sorry," Nikki had said, searching her tray for something to wipe the broccoli and cheese sauce out of her hair. Nikki looked like an awkward freshman not yet used to her environment. Serena stared wide-eyed at Nikki, then handed her a napkin. She studied Nikki's vivid features and told her she was pretty. It was their freshman year at Clark Atlanta. Serena was sitting alone in the cafeteria when Nikki approached. Serena expected Nikki to say "Hello" or "Is anyone sitting here?" But Nikki didn't utter a word. Though there were other empty seats at the table, Nikki plopped down right next to Serena. When she did, her long hair grazed Serena's plate. "You can have my plate," Nikki had said.

"No, that's okay."

"But my hair got in yours."

Serena looked down at her plate of chicken, broccoli with cheese sauce, creamed potatoes and green beans. Then she lifted a piece of chicken into the air by a long, stiff hair which was protruding from it. "I didn't have much of an appetite anyway," she said.

Yuk!" They frowned. Then they smiled at each other ...

As Nikki neared her condominium, she reflected on last night's conversation with Serena. Serena had shared her encounter with Nathan at the Reflecting Pool, and how it had made her need to travel—to get away—even greater. But it bothered Nikki that Serena was traveling alone. It was so out of character. Nikki sensed that Serena's desire to confront her fear of traveling alone wasn't the only reason she was taking this trip. But why was she going to Africa? Was something wrong? Or was Serena in search of something she herself didn't fully understand?

Three

The next day during lunch, Nathan decided to get out of the building for some fresh air. He went for a walk and found himself near the Reflecting Pool again. Being there somehow made him feel close to Serena. He sat on the bench with his hands clasped together, envisioning that incredible moment when Serena had graced him with her presence just four days before. He replayed that day over and over in his mind. Then he thought about the years they had spent together and the events that had transpired. He smiled as he thought about the day that he first met Serena, thirteen years ago ...

It had been a hot summer day at Six Flags amusement park in Georgia. Seventeen-year-old Nathan and some friends had stopped to catch a musical stage show. They usually didn't do the shows, but this time they wavered from their usual hair-raising expeditions and ducked into the small, air-conditioned arena.

The curtains had just swung open when the most beautiful girl Nathan had ever seen stepped onstage. As she danced, he kept his eyes on her every move. Her fluffy brown hair bounced up and down as she kicked her long legs in the air. When she began to sing it was like the sweet melody of her voice caressed his body and mind. He was so overcome he could barely remain standing. The vibrations swept across his body like ocean waves. Her voice was like none he had heard before. It was soft and enchanting as she sang a sweet ballad. He was falling in love, right then and there.

The song that followed was very different. It was a fast-paced hillbilly song. Nathan laughed as Serena clogged around the stage. And when she began singing about having pig feet for dinner, he wasn't sure if he would be able to contain himself.

"Hey," his friend, Ron, called. "Lets go. I've heard enough."

"No way!" Nathan answered.

"We're gonna leave you, man," another friend, James, warned.

"Just wait a minute," Nathan pleaded. "I have *got* to talk to that girl!"

"Oh m-a-n." James slung his head to the side as if annoyed.

Nathan approached the stage immediately after the show. When his eyes met the girl's, it was electric. There was instant chemistry.

"Hi," she said, bending her head to the side and carefully looking him over. They smiled adoringly at one another.

She had taken off the cowboy hat but still had on the black cowboy boots. Her blue denim dress hung just above the knees and flared out at the hips.

"Can I call you?" Nathan asked bravely.

She said, "Yes," and he was both amazed and delighted when she agreed to see him.

After that day, they spent as much time together as they possibly could, laughing, loving and nurturing one another. They shared their very souls and pledged to be together "forever."

Nathan's thoughts were interrupted by a young woman who appeared to be in her early twenties. "Do you mind if I sit here?" she asked. "I'm waiting for my boyfriend. He's taking pictures over there." She pointed toward the Lincoln Memorial.

"Not at all," Nathan said, glancing at the girl as she sat next to him. Nathan focused his eyes momentarily on the girl's rose-colored top. It reminded him of the dress Serena wore when he took her to her high school prom. She had looked just like a princess, he thought. She wore an antique rose strapless dress with a sheer cover. As they slow-danced, he held her gently. She was so soft that he was afraid she might bruise if he touched her too hard. And the flowers in her hair smelled almost as good as she did.

He had a poem for her that night—one of many that he wrote for her. She was always so impressed with his romantic creative genius. His rhymes seemed to flow so easily and naturally, and when they did, so did Serena. She always said that Nathan's words warmed her body and filled her heart and mind with so much love that she felt like calm lava oozing downstream from a volcano. He made her feel like the most special woman on earth.

Nathan sometimes tried to hide his intelligence—his talent—from his friends and teachers. It wasn't always "cool" to be the way he was—so gifted and romantic. But when he was with Serena, he could be himself. And that meant more to him than Serena ever knew. "Serena," Nathan muttered under his breath.

"Excuse me," the young woman said. "Were you talking to me?"

"Oh, I was just thinking about someone," Nathan said.

"Someone special, right?" The girl turned to Nathan, waiting to hear more.

"I was here just the other day and I saw my high school girlfriend. I hadn't seen her since college." Nathan thought back ten years to when he had attended Clark Atlanta University, along with Serena. He majored in electrical and environmental engineering. Serena chose her two passions, music and theater. And she joined the dance company. Dancing was a natural talent for

Serena, much like her singing and Nathan's poetic gift. "It was incredible," he said.

"Really?" said the young woman.

"Yes. Back then, I had graduated from high school with honors, and had already been taking some college courses. I was proud of the fact that I would be able to finish college early, and all I could think about was how, and when, I would ask her to marry me."

The girl looked into Nathan's eyes and seemed to understand. "Ahh. But you didn't marry her."

"No," Nathan said. "We were happy for awhile. You couldn't separate us for anything in the world. But college life can be hard for a young couple." Nathan thought back to a time when there were pitfalls he and Serena could not foresee. A time when the pressures and curiosities of youth began to sway him to become involved in activities that weren't at all impressive to Serena.

"Yes, it can," the young woman said. "What happened, if you don't mind my asking."

"I was a little on the wild side back then," Nathan said. "I joined this group called the Crows." Nathan recalled the small, unsophisticated group of guys that used to party, hang out and make birdcalls. Serena had been annoyed, to say the least. She saw no sense in joining what she referred to as just a bunch of guys looking for an excuse to behave like juvenile delinquents. She was more concerned, however, that Nathan might somehow get into trouble. Nathan insisted that Serena was just trying to have her own way. He was not giving in. "This is something I want to do, and I'm gonna do it." Serena had to accept his decision. She told him that it was his life. Perhaps she knew in her heart that she could not, and should not decide this for him.

Nathan continued. "Serena thought it was a waste of time. And it was. But you couldn't tell me that, then. I was just having fun, right?"

The girl smiled.

"It wasn't a real fraternity," Nathan said, "but we held initiation night just the same . . ."

On Nathan's initiation night, Serena was back at the dorm, crying her eyes out from worry while Nathan was blindfolded and subjected to a number of immoral pranks. The next morning Nathan had a hangover. Rumors started flying and Serena found out that there were females involved in the pranks.

When Nathan learned that Serena had been crying the night before, he rushed to see her. Serena didn't ask him the details of what had happened. Perhaps she didn't want to know, or doubted if Nathan even knew. She pouted like a homeless baby. "Is this what I can expect from you in the future, Nathan?" she asked, wiping her eyes like a kitten. Then she pursed her lips and glared at him.

"I told Serena that people weren't perfect. She told me that was just an excuse for bad behavior. Despite our differences, I loved her so much . . . But a couple months later, Serena decided she'd had enough."

"Another girl?"

"Yeah," Nathan said looking sadly into the waters of the Reflecting Pool.

"Uh huh."

"But there wasn't anything to it." Nathan thought back to a warm evening while leaving the college football field after practice. He had been approached by Roxanne. She was a sassy girl with long thick hair and wide hips who often came around trying to seduce Nathan. Serena had told Nathan what she thought of Roxanne and why. She thought of her as a bit of a tramp—especially after overhearing Roxanne say one day at Burger King that if a guy treats her to McDonalds, she would give him some—sex, that is. She'd also heard a guy talking about how Roxanne had invited him over to her house only two weeks after he broke his leg. She became angry when he was unable to perform sexually. The cast came all the way up his thigh and was obviously interfering with his ability to maintain an erection.

"Hi, baby, you look so hot. You really turn me on," Roxanne said to Nathan. She put her arms around him. He quickly removed them. But he thought it was rather comical, and it fed his ego, too.

As he tried to walk past her, she stood in front of him, leaned forward, and kissed him smack on the lips. At that instant, Serena walked up. The look on her face revealed her anger. She stared at Roxanne's short skirt and high-heels. She was certain that Nathan was enjoying himself more than a little.

When Nathan saw Serena, he felt like he was standing on a railroad track and a train appeared from out of nowhere.

"Why'd you do that, Roxanne?" Nathan said angrily.

Roxanne shrugged her shoulders, looked at Serena, then excused herself—a few minutes too late. Serena walked off.

"Serena wait a minute!" Nathan yelled. He ran to catch up with her. "Serena, I wasn't doing anything. I didn't know she was gonna do that."

"It didn't look that way to me. Why were you even talking to her? You know I can't stand Roxanne." Serena was fuming and Nathan was scared.

"Serena. I'm sorry."

"Nathan, this isn't working." Serena shook her head and moved away from him.

No matter what Nathan said to try and convince Serena that he was not enjoying himself, it didn't register in Serena's mind. She could not get that picture out of her head.

"I would have never allowed something like that to happen," she scolded. She decided that they needed some time apart. "I need some space. Nathan we're too young to be so serious. I think we need to date other people for a while." She explained to Nathan that their problems would only continue and damage their love for one another.

She was saying the words, but Nathan couldn't believe he was hearing them. He didn't believe she meant them. Maybe she didn't. But Nathan knew she was hurting inside, and sensed she was afraid of being hurt further.

"No, Serena. I don't want this. I can't even imagine you with anybody else." The very thought of it nearly drove him mad. He pleaded with her. "Don't do this, Serena." It was as though his soul was bleeding, and only Serena could stop it. He felt like the very ground he walked on had suddenly vanished.

She offered Nathan a friendship. Nathan would not compromise. He wanted it all, and that was not in Serena's plans at the time. As the tears rolled down their faces, she told him that the separation didn't have to be forever.

The young woman spoke. "You still love her, don't you?"

"Yes, I do," Nathan said in a low voice.

"Well," the girl said as her boyfriend approached, "I hope it works out for you."

"Thank you," Nathan said. As he watched the couple walk away arm in arm, his thoughts shifted back in time, again...

They had promised always to be together. Now it seemed as if Serena was throwing all their dreams away. Nathan still did not believe it. But he knew somewhere deep inside that he had to honor her wishes, or he was going to make matters worse.

Nathan was brilliant and at the top of his class academically. The dean of engineering invited him to events and career fairs where prominent corporate heads looked for new talent. When these scouts heard about Nathan and saw his résumé—which was better than many who had already graduated because he had worked on a community project with a professor—they were highly impressed. Nathan received several job offers and decided to sign a multi-year contract with a firm in Boston. Though he'd have to relocate, he'd be able to complete his education when he was ready, and the firm would pay for it. He didn't discuss this with Serena first. When he told her, she was stunned to find out that he was dropping out of school and leaving.

Nathan thought that if he left, she would miss him and want to be with him. He was so afraid of losing her that he wasn't thinking clearly. He bought her a ring and asked her to marry

him. Nathan just wanted to get both of them out of the college
social environment. He thought, even if she stays, at least she
will be my wife. I can provide for her now.

Serena told him that marriage would not solve their problems, and she wasn't about to get married on a whim. In addition, she wasn't ready to become engaged at such a young age.
She didn't want to end up like her parents—divorced—and she
was determined to complete her education without any interfer-
ence. Nathan was not about to stay there and watch Serena become involved—no matter how superficially—with other guys.

In Boston, Nathan worked as a programmer/systems ana-
lyst. He still believed that he and Serena were going to be together eventually. He worked long days and often had to get up
in the wee hours of the morning when he was called to do trouble-
shooting. He would normally rise before six o'clock in order to
get to work on time. Sometimes he'd ask himself why he left
Serena. "How could I have been so foolish? Why would I think
she would marry me when I knew we were having problems? It
was selfish of me to leave her, but there was no way I could stay
there and not be with her." He was sabotaged by his own imma-
turity and passion.

Nathan learned that Serena was making new friends. He
guessed that she was trying to bury her feelings for him. Maybe
it was easier for her that way. She told him that there was too
much tension and drama between them, and that it had become
difficult for her to concentrate on what she had gone there to do,
and that was to finish school.

"This is for the best," she added.

Nathan, on the other hand, prayed for the Lord to help him
and Serena work out their differences. "Please, God, give us
strength to get through this, and never let Serena forget our
love. I know I won't. I couldn't possibly forget, even if I wanted
to."

His mother always told him that "God works in mysterious
ways." She would say, "He may not be there when you want Him,
but He's always right on time." Nathan took these words to mean

that when things weren't going well, there was an angel watching over him and that there was hope.

How ironic, he thought. Hope is Serena's middle name. Serena Hope Taylor. My shining star.

As the days passed, Nathan began to realize that, by leaving school, he was in part rebelling like a stubborn child in order to get Serena's attention. This ridiculous notion backfired. He learned from others that Serena was getting along just fine without him. When he called, she was hardly ever in her dorm room. When he did make contact with her, he insisted that they still belonged together. This drove Serena further away, as she could not handle the tension.

As Nathan matured, he at last realized the mistakes he had made. He could see how stubborn and hot-headed he had been. The Whitakers were known for being hot-headed at times, and he was no exception. This experience granted him that wisdom.

He knew that he needed to stay strong. He wrote Serena almost every night. She wrote him often, but no longer acknowledged that they were a couple. Her letters, however, remained a constant source of inspiration for him, even without the red lipstick imprint on them. One thing he did appreciate was the sweet, fresh, exotic smell of her perfume that the letters bore—like yellow roses on a breezy, Indian summer morning.

Nathan soon found out that Serena had begun dating other guys—no one intimately, he hoped. Serena's parents had raised her to believe that she should remain a virgin until she married.

Nathan could not believe it was over. He called her often but she still offered only a friendship. Nathan thought this was the ultimate betrayal. But he saw that the pressure was getting to be too much. Their love was becoming too intense.

"I can't just be your friend," he had said. "My whole world is you."

If Nathan could have walked away from his job and the contract he had signed and back into Serena's arms, he certainly would have. The reality, however, was that he could not force himself upon her. After all, his erratic, hard-nosed behavior was probably a factor in the destruction of the relationship. He was finally mature enough to realize that. He didn't need any more strikes against him. The pain in his heart was staggering.

How will I go on? he thought. How will I survive without my Serena Hope?

One day, while at work in Boston, Nathan reached inside his briefcase to read one of Serena's letters. As he perused it, he began to realize that her letters were far less affectionate than they had once been. Before, he had not given it much thought. He was just happy whenever he heard from her.

Tears streamed down his face.

A colleague named Dean saw what he was doing and yelled, "What's that, a Dear John letter?" Then Dean laughed. All of the anger Nathan had been holding inside was about to explode. He felt like he was having a nightmare. In the nightmare, he was being stoned, for no reason, and people were angry at him and some were laughing. But it wasn't a nightmare, it was real.

Nathan glared at the smirk on Dean's face. Then he bolted from his chair, knocking it to the floor as he did. He lunged forward with his fist balled.

"Hey!" Chase, another coworker, dived forward and held him back. "Come on, you know you're better than this, Nathan. It's not worth it."

"I know you don't want any of this," Dean said smugly as he stuck out his chest.

"Just let it go," Chase said, still holding Nathan's arm. Nathan pressed his lips together and stared crossly. Then he did let it go. He let Serena go.

Later that night, he stood alone on the cold shores of Cape Cod. The bitter January winds blew hard as the tears of pain rolled down his cheeks. His jacket rippled in the wind as he stared at the dark ocean. He could not feel his frostbitten hands and face. He could only feel the pain of losing Serena. He fell to his knees. With the gritty sand blowing in his face he closed his eyes and vowed that night, on that lonely shore, no one would ever hurt him again.

Nothing seemed to matter to him anymore. He felt ugly and undesirable. His heart was like icy flesh. For a while, he let no one near him physically or emotionally. Then he felt the need to prove to himself that he was worthy of love. Many months of partying, women and drinking followed. He was willing to do almost anything to keep his mind off Serena . . .

Nathan's cell phone rang, bringing him back to the present. It was his attorney, Alonso Cruz. "Nathan, where are you? I tried to call you at the office."

"I'm at the Reflecting Pool. I went for a walk on my lunch break."

"I know you have a lot on your mind, that's why I'm calling. I spoke with Alysse's attorney and I want to make sure you aren't having any second thoughts before I talk to the judge again. Nathan, I'm going to suggest that you—like I do all my clients— think back to when you first met Alysse. Think about the good times . . ."

Nathan thought back to the day he met Alysse Carter at a local movie theater in Boston. She was an attractive woman. Her hair was cut in a neat, close-cropped style. There was something about her clothes and the way she sat in the theater that convinced Nathan that she was a nurse. She wore a thin sweater with tiny buttons up the front and a pair of neatly pressed black pants. She was serious, yet mellow-looking. His guess was basically right. She was a nursing student in her last year at Tufts University. They were the only two people in the theater and she waved and smiled. He noticed a small gap between her teeth that reminded him of his cousin Brenda. He thought she was cute. He smiled back.

"Looks like we're the only ones in here," he said. He walked over to her and sat in the end seat along the aisle, leaving one seat empty between them.

Nathan had never been to a movie alone before. But that day he had been walking along idly when he came upon the theater. With nothing else to do but feel sorry for himself, he went inside. He was so depressed over losing Serena that he didn't want to be around anyone. But what he wanted and what he needed were two entirely different things. When he saw Alysse, he began to realize that.

He and Alysse got acquainted before the movie started. It turned out that they both needed some company, since Alysse had just gotten out of a bad relationship.

After the movie, Alysse and Nathan exchanged numbers. They became friends. They confided in each other. He told her about Serena and she comforted him. He was impressed with the concern she showed, and she found him to be a nice guy and very "fine looking," as she put it.

"We really did have some good times," Nathan said to his attorney. "But—"

"Nathan," his attorney interrupted, "I'll have to get back to you. I have another call."

Nathan said goodbye and his thoughts drifted back to a night, six months after he and Alysse had met ...

"I want to get married. We've done everything else and we're good for each other," Alysse had said.

Caught up in the moment, Nathan agreed. They went to a Justice of the Peace and were married.

It didn't take Nathan long to realize that marrying Alysse was another immature move on his part. To top it off, they had made an agreement: after their marriage, they would no longer discuss their past loves. The reality was, however, that they had come together mostly because of their ability to communicate compassionately about their pasts. Now the question was: would there be enough left to talk about? Did they have anything in common other than their broken hearts?

One year after Nathan's marriage, Alysse gave birth to an

adorable baby boy. His face and body were full and round. He had big, beautiful brown eyes and long eyelashes. His creamy mocha-colored skin was similar to Alysse's. He looked a little like both Alysse and Nathan, but mostly like himself. They named him Devan.

Fortunately, Alysse graduated from Tufts before Devan was born. She certainly had her hands full after his birth. Nathan thought she was a terrific mother. He would watch proudly as Alysse held and fed their son. Devan gave Nathan something to believe in again. Nathan became stronger, more mature, and determined to set a positive example for his son. Life was no longer about himself and his self-pity. He began to ponder the future and how he could go about making it better for Devan.

Nathan applied to, and was accepted at, the Massachusetts Institute of Technology. He worked and went to classes, and time flew by. He majored in both environmental and electrical engineering, just as he had at Clark Atlanta. Soon he graduated with honors and was finally the double engineer he had always wanted to be.

After graduation, Nathan accepted a job in Washington with the Department of Interior. Alysse had no objections to moving to the District of Columbia. She was very much in love with Nathan and was prepared to follow his lead wherever it took her.

As Nathan walked back to his office, he thought about the past four years spent in Washington, and how unhappy he and Alysse had been. Our divorce should be final any day now, he thought. At least Devan's happy, and has lots of friends.

Nathan loved Alysse, but he was not in love with her. He never had been. And she knew it. But she wanted him so badly, she had fallen in love with him. But after a few years of marriage, reality set in for Nathan. "This was a mistake, Alysse," he said. "I was not completely myself when we married. I had been hurt so badly. And you, you needed someone, too. We didn't stop to think about what we were doing. We just got married. Like that was going to solve all our problems."

"Stop it, Nathan! I hate you."

"No, you don't," he had whispered, all choked up. "But you will if we stay like this. And I can't let that happen, because I care about you. I can't let Devan see us at war. It's time for me to finish growing up."

Alysse had practically smothered Nathan to death in the marriage. She had to know his whereabouts at all times. Nathan had always been faithful to Alysse, but that wasn't enough for her. And as Nathan grew, he began to realize why. Alysse had never been secure in the marriage. She knew that the marriage probably shouldn't have happened the way that it did, if at all. But she was going to make Nathan love her the way she loved him. Nathan grew to realize that love would never happen. He could not stay and give her false hope. She deserved better than that.

Alysse had not been very cooperative with the divorce, and today, Nathan wondered, would Alysse finally accept the fact that their marriage was ending?

Four

It was a frosty spring morning. Dew was still on the windshield of Nathan's car as he approached the concrete and granite Department of Interior building. Nathan entered the outer office area with his brown leather briefcase in hand. He greeted Brandi with his usual, "Hello, you," as he brushed by the big Dracaena Marginata plants placed near the entrance.

"You're here early this morning," Brandi said from her desk. She pushed up the sleeve on her gray-and-white pinstriped pantsuit and glanced down at her watch.

"I have a long day ahead of me," he replied, strolling past her desk with its fresh assortment of roses. "I really need to work on the water supply project this morning."

He entered his office, laid his briefcase on his rosewood desk and sat down in the burgundy leather chair. Contemplating where to begin, he scanned the few paintings on the wall. Then he looked at the framed picture of Devan that he kept on his desk. He smiled proudly before noticing the many papers stacked nearby. Then he got down to business, sending e-mails to a few clients.

Nathan was working on several different projects. In addition, he had just invented a sophisticated piece of equipment he named the Whitaker Enviro/Safe. It would become instrumental in detecting various types of pollution, and for conducting experiments.

Nathan had been concerned since childhood about the effect pollution had on the environment and human health. When he was growing up, his mother often complained about the water. She always told Nathan that pollution was the reason her sister Helen died of leukemia. "This water doesn't taste right," she would say. "The environment is so polluted, the water probably is, too."

The water tasted fine to everyone else, but these words were indelibly printed on Nathan's mind. As a young boy, Nathan was always inventing something. He would use any materials he could find—wood scraps, old pieces of metal, twigs, moss, algae, buttons, yarn, glue, wires, clay, golf tees. His father even let him use his hammer and nails. Afterwards Nathan would proudly show the project to his mother, explaining to her exactly what it was. It was usually something to help purify the water, or clean up the environment.

Brandi stood in the doorway to Nathan's office. "If you need anything, just yell."

"Thanks, Brandi. You know I will," he said. Brandi was the best assistant anyone could ask for, Nathan thought. Even when she was sick, she somehow managed to make it to work every day—except when she was having reconstructive breast surgery. Nathan could tell whenever Brandi wasn't feeling well. She'd have dark circles under her eyes and her skin would turn pale. But her work never suffered.

Later that morning, Brandi knocked on the door to Nathan's office. "Come on in," he said.

"How's it going?" she asked, handing him some memorandums.

"Actually, I need to leave. I have to be in court in one hour. You know, Brandi, I think Alysse wants everything, including my behind," he said, shoving some memos inside his briefcase.

"We know she wants your behind," Brandi said in her chirpy voice. Nathan looked up at her. "That's why she's been so angry. She had it once, and now it's hard to let it go." She playfully looked down at Nathan's firm, well-sculpted buttocks.

Nathan laughed softly at the joke, then sighed. "I just want to settle this peacefully, for Devan's sake."

Brandi studied him a moment, then blurted out, "Why won't you let me fix you up with someone?"

Nathan shook his head. "I don't have time.

"Nathan, you're making too many excuses. This time," she said, in a very determined way, "I'm insisting." Her eyes widened. She knew she was being bold. Nathan looked at her impatiently. "Oh, come on, Nathan, please. I think it's just what you need."

Nathan smiled as if to surrender. He had put this off as long as he could, and he wasn't getting out of it.

"I'm having a social at my house in a few weeks." Brandi walked back to her desk, then re-entered Nathan's office. She handed him a card with the name "Monique Samuels" on it, along with an address and a phone number. "I'll tell her you'll pick her up around seven."

Nathan politely accepted the card. "I've got to go. I won't be back this afternoon, so if I get any important calls, tell them they can reach me at home around five o'clock."

"See you in the morning, and good luck!"

Nathan grabbed his jacket, gathered his briefcase and car keys and headed toward the door.

"Thanks Brandi," he said. Grinning shyly, he rushed out.

Due to traffic caused by construction work on the roads, Nathan arrived at the courthouse barely on time. Judge Cochran, an attractive lady who wore her hair in a neat, short Afro, was eager to settle his divorce and custody case once and for all. The stern judge allowed no time for petty squabbles in her courtroom, and she'd had just about all she was going to take from Nathan and Alysse. She had heard arguments several times from both their lawyers, and her patience was wearing thin.

Nathan's attorney, Alonso Cruz, a bald, ginger-skinned man, was waiting for him when he arrived. "Hello. I was beginning to wonder if you were going to show up," he joked in a bass voice. Nathan took a deep breath and shook his hand. Alonso Cruz patted him on the shoulder. Nathan glanced over at Alysse, who was whispering with her lawyer.

Judge Cochran took off her glasses and cleared her throat before speaking. "I'm awarding joint custody of Devan," she said. Then she ruled that Alysse, now a nurse at Georgetown Hospital, would be able to keep their home in a quiet Northwest neighborhood.

Nathan was satisfied with the financial settlement. The house was fully paid for, and he wanted Alysse to have it, especially since he was the one who had asked for the divorce. Also, Devan liked the neighborhood and had several friends his age on the same block. Nathan didn't want him to move.

Nathan volunteered to pay Alysse full support for Devan even though he would have joint physical custody. In return, alimony payments were limited by the judge to a token amount. "Your salary as a registered nurse will provide a decent income," the Judge told Alysse.

Alysse accepted the ruling with a nod. She was Devan's mother and Nathan had told her how important that was to him. "I'll help you if you need it," he had said.

Judge Cochran spoke again. "If either of you, Nathan or Alysse, move further than a sixty-mile radius from downtown Washington, full custody of Devan will be automatically awarded to the person staying in the area. The only exception would be if you two happen to agree in writing to something else."

This ruling was certainly in Nathan's favor. He breathed a huge sigh of relief. His biggest fear was that Alysse would take Devan and move back to her home of Newark like she had threatened.

Alysse and Nathan thanked their attorneys and Judge Cochran. Judge Cochran wished them well before imparting a few words of wisdom: "You are two blessed individuals. You're healthy. You're both well educated. You have good careers and a fine son to finish raising. Don't take any of this for granted—not for one second."

As they were leaving the courtroom, Nathan walked up to Alysse and spoke sincerely. "Alysse. Well, I guess this settles it."

She looked at his face and spoke in a monotone. "Yeah, I guess it does. It's over."

Nathan returned her look with genuine compassion and feeling. "Alysse, we had some good times together. I want to thank you for those times, and for our son. You, um, you know we were young and—"

Alysse interrupted. "You don't have to say any more, Nathan. Besides, I'm not in the mood."

Nathan sighed sadly and Alysse turned to walk away. Then she turned back. "You were right. I can finally admit it. This is so . . ." She sighed. "It's hard for me right now, but I hope in the future we can be friends." She looked into his eyes as though she were reflecting on the past.

Nathan said, "I don't think we ever truly stopped being friends. It was the marriage that didn't work." He gave her a warm hug. She closed her eyes tightly as he squeezed her. And she believed him. She had a friend in Nathan.

Five

As the day of the party approached, Brandi made it a point to remind Nathan of his promise to bring Monique. He was seriously dreading the whole blind date thing. "I just want to get this over with," he muttered while on his way to Monique's home in Potomac, Maryland. He knew that Brandi was concerned about him and that she wanted him to be happy. "Ahh, it can't hurt to go to this party with Monique. You can never have too many friends, and Brandi's parties are always fun," he reminded himself.

Nathan found Monique's townhouse and parked. The door opened almost before the doorbell stopped ringing. Monique's eyes danced as she studied Nathan's handsome face and well-built body.

"Nathan Whitaker, I presume," she said, smiling broadly.

"Yes, and you're Monique?"

She nodded, blushing as they exchanged pleasantries.

"Come on in and have a seat over there." She pointed to the burgundy-and-tan striped sofa. "I'm almost ready," she said as she walked toward the garage door.

"Don't rush, I'm fine," he responded.

You're right about that, she thought, you are fine!

Nathan had to admit that Monique was attractive. She was slender with thick black bobbed hair, a pug nose and soft café au lait-colored skin. She wore three gold earrings in each ear, three bracelets on one arm, and three gold chains around her neck.

Monique went in the garage and came back to the living room with a big brown-and-white Saint Bernard by her side. "This is Bailey. Would you like a cookie?" She lifted a plate of cookies from the table and held it in front of Nathan. Bailey ignored the cookies, but kept his eyes on Nathan.

"No, thank you," Nathan answered, holding up his hands. "I'm going to wait until we get to Brandi's house before I eat anything." He glanced at Bailey with raised eyebrows. "Big dog ya got there."

"Yep, he is. He helps me feel safe." Monique patted Bailey, then tugged on his collar. "Come on, boy. Come on, Bailey. Time to go outside." Monique pulled and tugged on Bailey's collar with all her might, grunting. Nathan's eyes widened with concern as he watched Monique struggle with the dog. He leaned forward on the sofa and watched carefully. Finally Monique started dragging the dog out the back door.

Nathan stood. "Do you need some help?" Bailey growled.

"Nope," Monique insisted. "He's not usually this rebellious. He doesn't know you so he's being stubborn. If that cute little bulldog is near, he'll go out in a heartbeat. I don't have any problems then. I told him he better stay away from that dog—she might be a little femme fatale."

Nathan smiled. Monique finally succeeded in getting Bailey outside. Then she went into the bathroom and washed her hands before sitting on the sofa next to Nathan. As he turned his body to face Monique, she looked him up and down.

"Any friend of Brandi's is sure 'nuff welcome in my home," she said, still admiring his body.

Nathan smiled. "By the way, how do you know Brandi?"

"We go to the same health spa down on Blueford Street. Brandi told me all about you. She told me about your career and your son, and that you went to Clark Atlanta. I have a nephew that goes there . . ."

Nathan nodded as he listened to Monique talk for five minutes non-stop. She talked so fast that he was barely able to get a word in. Finally, he managed to say, "We can talk on the way to Brandi's house. I think we should get going. You look very nice," he added.

"Thank you. So do you." She brightened as she found her purse and they headed out the door.

Brandi's house was in an upper-class neighborhood in Potomac, Maryland, only a few miles from Monique's home. During the ride, Monique talked constantly. In fact, she talked so much that Nathan passed the exit to Brandi's house and had to turn around. She talked mostly about her job as a court clerk for Montgomery County.

It was 7:15 p.m. when Nathan pulled his BMW alongside the curb in front of Justice's and Brandi's large brick house. Nathan got out of the car and walked around to the passenger's side door. "Brandi's flower garden is as beautiful as ever," he remarked, nodding toward the perfusion of coralbells, roses, lilies, azaleas, and pansies in the front yard. Gardening was obviously one of Brandi's talents.

Brandi opened the door smiling and looking lovely in a loose-fitting, periwinkle blue, long-sleeved tunic and black knit, ankle-length skirt. "Welcome! I was wondering where you two were."

"Hello, you," Nathan said to Brandi as he hugged her. "How are you?"

"I'm fine, particularly now that I see you. Hi, Monique."

Monique and Brandi touched cheeks together.

Nathan joined the other guests in the living room while Monique stood at the edge of the foyer talking to Brandi.

Brandi's home was decorated along classic lines with antique furniture and soft prints. The pale yellow walls, spacious rooms, flowers, and colorful art added light to the home.

Nathan saw his buddy James sitting by the fireplace talking to two of Brandi's female guests. "James!" Nathan said.

"My man Nathan." James, a sort of heavy-set guy, cute according to many women, rose to his feet and walked to greet him. His chubbiness was as natural on him as the tall muscular build was on Nathan. He extended his hand and gave Nathan a firm handshake. "So, what's up, Nate? I haven't seen you in a good while. Brandi called me and told me you would be here. So I thought, free food and my buddy Nate. Yeah, I think I'll take time out of my busy schedule to engage in a leisurely evening with my main man—you." He squeezed Nathan's shoulder.

Nathan clapped his hands three times. "That was pretty good, man. Are you sure you didn't get in some acting classes while you were training to be a plumber?" They laughed.

"So, how have you been?" James asked.

"Busy, man, busy," Nathan answered.

"Yeah, I heard about the divorce. I hope you're happy now, 'cause you were messed up. You were *not* happy in that marriage."

"I'm better now that the whole thing is over," Nathan said. "I don't have anything against Alysse, but we ... well, you know."

"You can't keep a good man down," James said. He smiled and gestured with his head at Monique, who was still talking to Brandi. "She's cute."

Nathan shook his head. "It's not like that. I'm only with her tonight because Brandi insisted on fixing us up."

James chuckled. "Come on, Nate, ya talkin to James."

"No, seriously," Nathan said, "I'm not joking. Brandi set this whole thing up."

"Brandi acts like she's your mother." James smiled.

"I know, but it's just because she doesn't like seeing me alone. I'm not interested in anything with Monique other than a friendship."

"Is that right?" James said. "Well, pass her number my way."

"Hey, that's on you. Tell Brandi you're interested in Monique. Better yet, tell Monique. But what about Matilda?"

"Matilda and I are free to see other people," James said.

"Since when?"

James looked at his watch and then at Monique. "Since about two minutes ago."

Nathan smiled shyly and shook his head.

Across the room, Brandi looked at Nathan. "So what do you think?" she asked Monique.

"He is *fine*, just gorgeous," Monique responded.

Brandi looked at Nathan with admiration.

"I've never wanted to sleep with a man on the first date," Monique went on, "but I could definitely spend the night with him tonight. I mean the entire night."

Brandi giggled, surprised to hear Monique talk this way about any man. She gave Monique a tight smile.

"Don't look so shocked," Monique said. "It's been a long time."

"Longer than I had realized," Brandi said playfully.

"Well, you know I haven't been involved in a serious relationship in over a year," Monique said. "You're lucky. You got a good man."

"Yes, I am fortunate, I know." Brandi remembered when she had met Justice. They had married two years later.

Monique spoke again. "The few men I've dated weren't worth my time."

"Yes, you told me about Jim," Brandi said. "The handsome one."

"Yep," Monique said, "he was handsome but incredibly conceited. Then there was Joey. I don't think he said more than five words the entire time we dated, and you know how I like to talk! And Cory, that no-good slacker. All he wanted to do was party, party, party. He partied his way into someone else's life, and I was happy about that."

"Well," Brandi said, "Nathan didn't date the whole time he was separated from Alysse. You're his first date. Maybe you two can have some fun together."

"Ummmhu," Monique said, looking up and down at Nathan. "I sure hope so."

"All right, everyone. It's time for dinner," Brandi said to her eleven guests. She had prepared a buffet-style dinner of soul food, lasagna, baked skinless chicken and steamed vegetables. "I hope you can find something you like."

Justice strolled down the spiral staircase impeccably dressed in a tan, lightweight, single-breasted suit. His luscious deep tan skin and handsome features captured the best of his Egyptian father and African-American mother. Justice walked over to Nathan and shook his hand. "Hey, pal. Thanks for coming."

"Thanks for having me," Nathan said.

"Anytime. Hey, is everything working out okay for you?" Justice asked, referring to Nathan's divorce.

"Yeah, looks like the rough part is over, finally," Nathan said.

Justice gave a charming grin, then patted Nathan on the shoulder. "Let's go eat."

Everyone gathered in the elegant dining room with its large crystal chandelier, antique table, and Queen Anne-style chairs. Justice had his favorite classical music playing softly and Brandi's finest porcelain adorned the table.

"I don't know if I want to eat from this china or not," Nathan said to everyone gathering around the table as he looked down at the fancy floral designs on the plates.

"Me, either," James mumbled.

"It's pretty," said a guest.

Nathan said, "I remember when Brandi bought this china. She talked about it for a week at work."

Everyone laughed, including Brandi.

"Stop trying to embarrass me, Nathan," Brandi said.

"I guess the only thing that could destroy our friendship is if I break a piece of this china," Nathan joked to more laughs.

Monique sat at the head of the table and Nathan took the corner seat next to her. Even as he gazed at Monique, his thoughts were with Serena. As he thought of Serena, he smiled unconsciously at Monique, who was staring at him.

Then Brandi spoke. "Now that we are all at the table together, I want to ask for all of your prayers and good wishes . . ."

She must be going to announce that she's pregnant, Nathan thought. A few months back, Brandi had told him she wanted to try and have a baby, even though she knew it could be dangerous for her because she'd had cancer.

"Justice is about to open his own private practice out in Rockville," she declared.

Everyone gave their sincere congratulations.

Justice, a surgeon, had been voluntarily taking a great deal of emergency room duty for five years now. He enjoyed helping people in emergency situations, but the unpredictable work hours were beginning to wear him down. "I've been working some long hours with no flexibility in my schedule," he said. "Now, my main desire is to spend more time with Brandi, doing the things we like to do most, the things that makes us feel good—you know, like tennis, gardening, and . . ." He kissed her lips.

"Well now," she said softly as she blushed.

Everyone smiled warmly. Then he continued. "Still, I will always value the experience and knowledge that this kind of work has afforded me . . ."

Things are really looking up for them, Nathan thought as he watched the happy couple.

"Here's to new beginnings," Brandi said. They all lifted their glasses.

Nathan's thoughts shifted back to Serena. *I wish we were toasting our own new beginning, Serena. If only you were here, or I was there . . .*

❖

Six

It was Serena's last night in Africa. The sunset was exquisite that evening as she attended a traditional dance ceremony. She wore a colorful cloth tied around her body, the tradition in rural Kenya.

She watched, excited, as the drummers played and the dancers began to circle.

"Serena," Zawadi called, with a delightful accent.

"Yes?" she answered.

"My name, Zawadi, means 'gift.' Did you know that, Serena?"

"No, I didn't." Serena smiled.

Zawadi sat on a stump with a drum between his thighs. There was a box on the ground beside him. He opened the box and took out a colorful, beaded African necklace and matching earrings "Yes, I like to give gifts to my friends," he said. "These are my gifts to you. I hand-made them." He smiled and his pearly white teeth lit up the dusk. He stood and draped the necklace around her neck. As he did, she put on the earrings.

"Thank you so much. They're beautiful." Serena was deeply touched and she found Zawadi to be quite charming. She gave him a hug. They smiled at one another. Then Zawadi started playing along with the other drummers.

Serena continued to enjoy the music and dancing, though the crowd was becoming sparse. At this point, Zawadi was the only one left playing the talking drum. Serena paid close attention, noticing that as Zawadi squeezed the drum its pitch varied.

Serena began to move to the drum's rhythm. She felt a new-found freedom and courage that was spiritual in nature. She had done it. She had taken the trip, alone. Now, it was ending. Yet somehow, somewhere deep inside, it felt more like . . . a beginning.

The next morning Zawadi took Serena to Nairobi International Airport. "You must come see us in New York," she said as they stood inside the airport.

"I must," he agreed.

"I've enjoyed myself tremendously," Serena said. "I won't forget you, or the beauty of the people, the land, and the culture of Africa. I will be back."

Zawadi grinned. "I'll see you"

She smiled and then spoke in Swahili. *"Kwaheri-Rafiki-Yangu."*

"Oh, yes. Goodbye, my friend," he said, returning her fare-well phrase. Before she turned to walk away, they touched hands. Still adorned in the beautiful jewelry he had made, Serena waved an emotional goodbye as she boarded her flight.

On Serena's flight to Europe, she thought about how spec-tacular her trip had been, even though she had been ill with anxiety the first few nights she was there. She had sat in a small motel room along the Ivory Coast and worried about anything and everything that could possibly go wrong. But when she be-gan to realize that she was scaring herself with her own thoughts, God spoke to her. He told her that she was never alone—that He was with her and that there were angels on earth watching over her. So she began to relax and enjoy her trip, blocking out all negative thoughts. And the longer she stayed, the more fun she had, even though Julian had not joined her as he promised.

❖

Seven

On Friday evening, Nathan and James got together to play a few games of basketball. They met at Bryant Park, near Nathan's Arlington apartment.

While Nathan took pride in staying physically fit, he had not been getting enough sleep. Between working overtime, being an active parent, and lying awake thinking of Serena, he was already fairly exhausted before they began playing. He had thought about going home instead of meeting James. Then he realized that the exercise would probably help him sleep better.

By the middle of the third game, both men were gasping for air. It was about eighty-five degrees outside, and the sun had not fully descended behind the clouds. The humidity was high and Nathan felt like he was in a sauna. He bent over with his hands placed on his slippery knees. His shorts were wet with sweat.

"Man." Nathan groaned as James dribbled the ball. "We're getting too old for this."

"You're getting too old, not me. Watch this." James faked left, then right. Dripping with perspiration, he spun around before taking the ball to the hoop. "Swoosh," he said as the ball went through the net. "See, I've still got it. Matilda said I am the man." He stuck out his chest, his ego strong as a bull's, and patted it three times with his right hand. "It doesn't get any better than this."

Nathan started laughing.

James smacked his lips together and frowned. "Why ya laughing? Okay, okay, look at this." Nathan watched as James sucked in his stomach and held out his arms. He flexed his muscles, but not much showed through the layer of fat. Nathan's laughter increased. He thought James looked like the Tasmanian Devil cartoon caricature.

"O-o-h," Nathan moaned and held the right side of his stomach.

James smacked his lips together again. "Forget it. Just come on. I'm tired."

"No-o, you're the man," Nathan said. He was still chuckling as they walked over to the bench and used their towels to dry off. James glanced at Nathan and smiled before they sat down to rest.

Nathan's laughter slowly died. He glanced at James. "You'll never believe who I saw last month."

"Who?"

"Serena." Nathan felt exhilarated just mentioning her name.

"Naw!" James said. "Get out of here. Where was she?"

"Here in Washington."

"Is she married? I hope not, because if she is, there's gon' be trouble."

Nathan gave a deflated look. "She was wearing a ring."

"Yep! *TROUBLE!*" James shook his head from side to side.

"But I don't remember if it was on her left hand or her right hand."

"You probably don't *wanna* remember if it was on her *left* hand."

"I hadn't seen her in ten years, and there she was, standing near the Reflecting Pool. At first, it was like a mirage. I lay awake at night thinking of that day over and over again. James, it was like I was out there in mid-air floating, like a heat wave. Every part of me was ready to surrender to the energy she possessed."

James listened intensely. Oh, man has he got it bad, he thought. He almost laughed, but he realized that Nathan was serious.

Nathan continued. "I thought I was being summoned by the most pleasant spirit." He shook his head to clear his mind. "She's just as beautiful as before. Seeing her again was truly a gift from God."

"Where does she live?" James asked

"New York. When I saw her she was about to take a trip to Africa. She should be back in New York now."

"Did you get her number? Wait a minute, don't even answer. I can't believe I just asked that question."

Nathan laughed softly.

"I never believed you two would break up. People were so jealous of ya'll." James shook his head as he thought back. "Yeah, ya'll were in love. 'Serena, Serena,' that's all I heard. I remember when I used to try to get you to hang out more with the fellas. I used to tell you that all you wanted to do was be up under Serena, remember that?" James chuckled.

"Oh, yeah, I remember. You used to give me hell," Nathan said, a mock scowl on his face.

James glanced at his watch. "Well, I got to go. I'm gon' catch hell if I don't get over to Matilda's."

"Yeah," Nathan said, "it's getting late." They stood and shook hands.

"I wish you luck, Nate," James said.

"Thanks," said Nathan.

Serena listened as the flight attendant announced that the plane was nearing John F. Kennedy Airport. Good, she thought, we'll be landing soon. She sighed and twirled a finger through a curl in her hair. *I know I have to go back. One month just wasn't enough*. She could think of only one thing that had happened recently that topped her trip to Africa, and that was seeing Nathan after so many years.

Serena thought back to the day she and Nathan first met and how they had immediately connected. She had never been instantly attracted to anyone before. It seemed to her like stars were twinkling brilliantly just above his head and in his eyes. Yes, his shimmering eyes magnetized her and she knew it would be almost impossible to say no to whatever he suggested.

When Serena thought about how she had been clogging around the stage and singing some song about pig feet, she started giggling. "Oops," she said before using her hand to cover her mouth. She noticed a pretty, fair-skinned, elderly lady with gray hair smiling at her. She's probably wondering why I'm sitting here by myself laughing, Serena thought, embarrassed.

Serena's thoughts were interrupted as the plane began its descent. She sighed. "We were so naive."

Julian was waiting for her as she stepped off the plane. He held his hand up to get her attention and they embraced. "I'm glad you're back," he said.

On the ride home, they were silent. He just looked at her and smiled as she sat with her head resting against the gray leather seat.

"It seems like we were just at the airport a few seconds ago," Serena said as Julian pulled into the driveway. She didn't even remember the ride home because she was so tired.

Once inside, they set the luggage down and Julian drew Serena close for a long embrace. "Give me a kiss," he said. Their lips met for a short kiss. "I'm sorry I couldn't make it, Serena. I thought you would come back home after I told you I couldn't join you."

That had been one reason why Serena didn't come back. For years, Julian had backed out of things at the last minute. And she would cancel her plans too. But now Serena was beginning to learn that she could not lean on Julian for emotional support. She would have to stand on her own two feet and take responsibility for her happiness. She would have to toughen up.

"Well," Serena said, sighing in fatigue. "I was disappointed at first, but I had the best time."

Julian raised an eyebrow. "Oh, you did, huh?"

"I'll tell you all about it, but first I want to show you something." Serena unzipped her luggage and pulled out a ceremonial wooden mask. "Isn't this impressive? This will look perfect right over here." She placed the mask on the shelf above the fireplace.

Julian smiled. "That's nice."

"There's more on the way," Serena said. "It was really great to get away. I'm still on a spiritual high. I can't believe I traveled alone."

She took off her loafers and plopped down on the sofa. "Everybody was so nice to me." She yawned.

Julian sat beside her and put his arms around her. "Let's go upstairs," he whispered. "It's been too long since we've been together."

She slid her feet back into her loafers and followed him upstairs. Her big, oak-framed bed looked so inviting that she didn't even take the time to shower or undress. While Julian was in the bathroom, Serena curled on top of the ivory damask comforter. She grabbed a fluffy pillow from Julian's side of the bed and stuck it between her thighs. Ah, this is so comfortable, she thought. Within minutes, she was asleep.

Julian came out of the bathroom to find Serena sleeping peacefully. He smiled at her, then began undressing her. He pulled off her loafers, unfastened her belt and un-tucked her blouse. He admired her beauty as he unbuttoned the blouse. He caressed her breast and began kissing her all over. None of this seemed to affect Serena. He slid her pants off before turning out the lights.

She feels so good, he thought, as he held her close. I'm so glad she's home.

❖

Eight

On Sunday morning, Nathan went for his usual 6:00 a.m. jog around the apartment complex. Staying physically fit was one of his top priorities. His treadmill, weights and other exercise equipment sat in the corner of his living room. The black leather sofa and chair, along with the royal blue, red and yellow rug gave his apartment some style, especially since there were no pictures on the wall.

Returning from his jog, he picked up the newspaper that lay on the ground by his front door. He went inside, showered and fixed a light breakfast of cereal and orange juice. As he ate, he sat in his small white kitchen and read the newspaper. He saw an article about a local singer who had recently recorded a hit song. Then he thought of Serena. He looked down at his watch, wanting to call her, but it was too early.

Nathan went to church at eleven o'clock in the morning. When he returned home, he removed his tie and retrieved the remote control from the coffee table. He sat on the couch watching

"CNN" for a few minutes before his thoughts once again shifted to Serena.

"I can't wait one more minute," he said, feeling his heart skip a beat. "I'm going to call her right now." He reached in his pocket and took out his wallet. The paper with Serena's number on it was crinkled and folded, but safely tucked inside.

A man answered. "Hello?"

Nathan looked at the paper. "Is this Serena's residence?"

"Hold on," said the man.

After a short silence, Nathan heard the most pleasant "Hello." It was like Serena's voice was singing as she spoke that one word. Nathan had been without her for so long, her voice was enough to make him happy—at least for now. He felt like he could do or be anything in the world.

They exchanged brief pleasantries before Nathan asked, "How was Africa?"

"I had a wonderful time there. I could go on about it forever. It was so good to see you in Washington."

"Can I see you again?" he asked, praying she would say yes. "I'm going to be in New York on business in a couple of weeks. I'd love to take you to dinner or lunch."

"I'd like that very much," she said.

"Serena!" Julian called from his office in the stern tone that sometimes made her tense.

"I'm still on the phone, Julian," Serena said, raising her voice. "I have to go now, Nathan."

"I'll talk to you soon," Nathan said.

Serena joined Julian in his office. He sat at his computer, checking the market for land for sale.

"Who was that on the phone?" he said.

"You won't believe this," she replied.

"Try me."

"I ran into Nathan when I was in Washington."

Julian looked up at Serena, then back down at the computer. "You're telling me you just happened to run into him?"

"Yes. I hadn't seen him in ten years." When she said those words, chills ran up her neck.

"Where does he live?"

"In Washington. I was so surprised to see him after so long. I mean, could you imagine seeing your ex-girlfriend, Vicky, after all these years?"

"No." Julian answered in a dull voice. He was focused on his own agenda and didn't notice how thrilled Serena was to have seen Nathan.

Serena stood next to Julian and put her hand on his shoulder. "Guess what? I'm going to write a musical about life on the continent of Africa. I was thinking about it before my trip, but now I'm sure I can do it. I have some excellent ideas."

Julian gave her a preoccupied glance. "Good."

"You want to hear some of my ideas?" Serena pulled up a chair and sat next to him. "I was thinking—"

Julian interrupted. "I'm busy right now, Serena."

"It won't take but a few minutes," she said. Half of her enthusiasm evaporated. He never wants to talk, she thought. Serena felt like she was living with a statue. When she married him, she thought he would be her friend for life. She couldn't understand why he ignored her most of the time. He wouldn't even talk about his job, or anything.

She walked over to the office mirror and looked in it—scrutinizing her face, hair, and the sleeveless beige sweater and short black skirt she was wearing. She felt unattractive, unwomanly. More importantly, she didn't feel validated at all when she was with Julian. Being around him sucked the life out of her. People told her she was pretty. Julian even told her that she was pretty—usually just before he kissed her and asked for sex.

When Serena walked out the door each day, she put on a happy face. She was beautiful, talented, friendly, and no one would have guessed that she ever felt otherwise. And she didn't want to let people down. They expected her to shine always. So she did, on the outside.

"Julian," she turned the mirror and walked back to him, "are you angry with me about something?"

"No. Where did that come from?" he asked dully.

"You never talk." She frowned. "Let's talk."

"About what, Serena?"

"Why do we have to know what we're going to talk about? Anything. Let's talk the way we did in the beginning."

Julian threw his hands in the air and smacked them on his thighs. He pushed himself away from his desk. "Okay," he said, "I'm waiting."

"Forget it," Serena said in disgust. She folded her arms and turned away from him.

"Make up your mind, Serena!"

She turned back. "Why is it that almost every time I try to talk to you, you're either not interested, busy, or you cut me off and shut me out?"

"You never talk about anything important," Julian said.

"So then why are we together?"

"Because I love you." He looked and sounded sincere for about a half a second. "I just don't have time to sit around and talk about nothing."

"Neither do I, Julian. Nor would I, or could I if I had time."

Visibly frustrated, Julian took a deep breath and released it slowly.

"I feel like you must want a divorce." She sighed and looked sadly into his eyes. Or was that what she really wanted deep down inside?

Julian stood and put his arms around Serena's waist. She held him, too. "I don't want a divorce," he said.

"Okay," she said, feeling a tad better.

"I just want you to stop talking so much when I'm busy."

That better feeling quickly vanished. She sighed inwardly as Julian sat back at his desk. She sat next to him again. She thought, first he tells me that he can't join me in Africa after I'm already there; then, when I get back, he tells me I talk too much. "Julian."

"What."

"You know, I have a lot of different interests and ideas and it's important for me to share them with the people in my life."

"Serena we've had this conversation at least twenty times before. Just give it up, please." She knows I love her, Julian thought as he stared at his computer. Everybody praises her all the time. I shouldn't have to praise her all the time, too. I'm busy with my own work. I don't bother her with my issues. Julian thought of the awards Serena had received over the years, and how her friends, their acquaintances, and her audiences always praised her for her talent.

"You sound like you're angry with me."

"I told you, I'm not." Julian spoke in the slightly high-pitched voice he'd get whenever he was annoyed.

A silence stretched between them.

Serena left the office and sat on the living room sofa. She crossed her arms over the top of it and peered into the office, watching Julian while he worked. She looked at his handsome, chiseled features and deep bronze skin. "The only thing Julian has time to talk about is antique cars," she muttered. "He laughs and talks and carries on with people in public and at work, then he comes home and treats me like this."

Serena knew that she had to accept Julian the way he was and stop trying to change him. But she felt so empty sometimes. She couldn't even cry about it. The tears were trapped inside her. Why was she so needy? She shook her head violently. No. She wasn't asking for much. A meaningful conversation every once in a while was surely not too much to ask for in a marriage. He has no idea how insensitive he's being, she thought.

Serena realized that Julian wasn't really interested in her ideas no matter how successful she was. This thought shocked her. She recalled two years ago, when she wrote some jingles for the Warner Advertising Company. She had been excited about the fact that they had asked her to sing them in their television commercials. But Julian had hardly said anything when she told him. And when she told him about her first leading role in a Broadway musical, he barely responded. Serena thought that Julian felt like he was in competition with her. He seemed to want all the credit, and if he didn't get it, he'd either play down, or ignore her successes.

Serena sighed and then reached onto the coffee table for some photographs she had recently developed. She flipped through them, pausing and looking thoughtfully when she came to a photograph of Julian and his family.

She looked at his older brother, Earl, now divorced twice, retired from the military and living alone in Hawaii. Serena wondered if he was happy living alone. Then she looked at his parents, Joyce and Lester. She shook her head, thinking of how odd their relationship seemed to be. She found them to be nice folks, but quite stuffy and stiff. Joyce and Lester only talked when absolutely necessary. And they appeared to like it that way. Serena shifted her eyes to Julian. Julian was taller than his older brother and more handsome, but Earl was more athletic. While Earl was on the wrestling team in high school, Julian was on the golf team. It was a game he had enjoyed with his father ever since he was a young boy. Some of his peers thought he was a nerd at first because he didn't play football or basketball. And she knew he had felt awkward at times. He was the first black guy to ever play golf at this school, and the only one on the team. But he loved the game just the same, and he really didn't care what others thought of him.

Serena put the photo album down only to glance up at another framed picture on the table of her and Julian. It was a wedding photograph. The two of them stood smiling and holding each other close. Serena wore a white, knee-length dress with a sheer bodice; Julian wore a black suit. Serena's hair hung down against her neck, and her hand on Julian's arm revealed a delicate, diamond wrap ring. Their wedding, over six years ago, had been small. Serena had been twenty-three and Julian, twenty-nine. Serena's career as a performer was starting to take off and Julian's real estate development business was growing even faster. They didn't have time to plan a big wedding, nor did they care to have one. They spent the extra time they had enjoying each other. Julian liked taking Serena to all the finest restaurants in New York, and along on some of his business trips. He would go see some of her performances, and he went with her to see some of her favorite Broadway shows. "Oh, happy days," Serena said as she looked at the picture.

Serena had spent the last six years making sure Julian was comfortable and being a loving wife to him. She learned how to cook early in the marriage, preparing delicious meals and sometimes entertaining Julian's business colleagues. And even though Julian's and Serena's schedules often conflicted, they usually managed to eat dinner together at least three nights a week.

Feeling a slight headache, Serena massaged her temples. She glanced at Julian again, then thought about his good points. He was committed to his work, and he was a smooth talker when it came to financial dealings. Serena had the utmost respect for the way he had worked his way up the ladder as a real estate developer. But it had gone straight to his head. He was arrogant, and he expected her to support his arrogant ways.

Julian wasn't a bad person, but he wasn't the man Serena thought he was when she married him. Was it just a game to him? she wondered. Maybe he wasn't so much interested in what she said or did as he was getting her in bed. But she did believe he loved her, in his own way.

Serena didn't see much use in arguing with Julian at this stage in their marriage. They had spent years doing that, and their conversations would accomplish nothing but fatigue and dizziness. Now, instead of trying to reason with Julian, she would usually just study his personality and try to stay optimistic about their relationship. Perhaps if she always approached him in an upbeat way, he would eventually behave the way he had in the beginning of their relationship. She saw no reason why he shouldn't. Yes, she would keep trying, even with the questioning thoughts she was having.

Serena went back into the office.

"Julian. I can't believe we've been married for six years. Time really does fly, doesn't it."

"Yes, it does."

"We haven't discussed having children lately," she said. "I really do want the responsibility of raising and nurturing a child of our own. I have a lot of love to give a child. I think I'd be a good mother. I'm ready to have a baby."

Julian stopped working. Serena sat in the chair next to him.

"You are?" he asked.

"Yes, but I think having a baby right now would be selfish. We need to be able to communicate better before we bring a life into this world."

"I agree."

"I just need you to listen to me, Julian. It hurts me when you don't listen." She reached out and touched his hand.

"I don't mean to ignore you," he said kindly. He stood and took hold of Serena's hand, helping her up. They held each other closely.

"I know." Serena thought of the way Julian's parents had raised him and realized that much of his attitude was learned behavior.

"I need you to try not to make derogatory remarks about me." Then she realized she said *try not to*. Her self-esteem had obviously been damaged. It was as if she thought an attempt was good enough. Or was it that she just didn't have much confidence in Julian? "I mean don't."

"I'll try," he said. "But I think we should wait a while before we have children. We still have some things to work on."

"You're right." Is this progress? she wondered.

"I love you," he said. Then he kissed her lips.

"So, tell me," she said, looking into his eyes, "What do you think we need to work on? What do you need?"

"If you come upstairs, I'll show you what I need," he said.

"Julian, I'm talking about from the marriage—emotionally or otherwise."

"You're everything I need, Serena."

Okay, she thought, so the only thing Julian needs is to be married to someone who never has anything important to say. Serena kissed his cheek and moved out of his arms. "Go ahead and finish your work. I have some things to do myself."

Serena went upstairs and crawled onto the bed with an *Essence* magazine. She looked through the magazine briefly before dialing Shante's number.

"Serena!" Shante said. "You're back. Marcus—it's Serena. She's back."

Marcus jogged up to the phone and put his mouth next to Shante's. He had a steak sub in one hand and his mouth was half full. "Hey baby!" he said with a cheery grin on his face.

"Hey, honey!" Serena returned.

Marcus started laughing and Serena joined in. Shante smiled. Marcus went back into the kitchen and Shante shook her head as her gaze followed him there. "I wish you could see him, Serena. He's cramming a steak sandwich in his mouth and drinking red Kool-Aid. We just got back from the gym and he's already shoving it in."

Serena laughed. "That's Marcus."

"No doubt," Shante agreed. "He's my heart, though."

Serena smiled tenderly.

"How was your trip?" Shante asked.

"It was fabulous," Serena said. "Why don't we get together for lunch and shopping tomorrow, and I'll tell you all about it."

"Yeah, let's do that."

❖

Nine

The following morning, Serena met Shante in Garden City, at Roosevelt Field Mall. Serena was waiting in front of Bloomindales when Shante arrived.

"Shante," Serena called, waving her hand. "Over here! Hi! You look so good."

"Hi, Serena." Shante struck a pose. "You like it?"

Serena admired Shante's yellow and white backless halter dress. "I love it. It looks great on you."

"Thanks. It's such a beautiful warm day, and I couldn't wait to wear it. It's been in my closet since last fall." Shante studied Serena's short sleeve, lilac crepe dress with a bow at the breast. "You look good, too."

"You think so?"

"Oh, girl, yes. Serena, you know you always got it going on! I called Nikki to see if she wanted to meet us, but she wasn't at home." Shante said as they headed to Bloomindales shoe department.

Shante and Serena enjoyed shopping together on weekends. They couldn't resist a good bargain. Whenever Nikki went shopping, it was usually to buy a new suit to wear to work. Nikki would join them from time to time, though. That's how she met Shante. "Let's go shopping Saturday. I want you to meet Shante." Serena had told her. Shante and Nikki got along well. Serena thought they would. They were all originally from the south and shared similar philosophies and core values. But the strong southern accents they had once shared were now soft whispers of their native drawl.

After a couple hours of shopping, they decided to grab some lunch at Panino's. With their shopping bags in tow, they settled at a table and ordered.

Shante took a gold watch with a white leather band from its box and placed it on her wrist. "I'm so tickled with my watch."

"That *was* a great buy," Serena said.

Ten minutes later, their lunch was served. Shante tasted her pasta. "This is really good. The sauce is delicious." She glanced at Serena. "You sure are quiet today. What are you thinking about?"

"I was thinking about the divorce rate," Serena answered.

"Yeah, it's high."

"I was thinking about all the people who must be in unhappy marriages."

Including yourself, Shante thought. Julian thinks you're privileged to have him because he's nice-looking and makes good money. He never thinks about the fact that he might be the lucky one. Shante didn't want to be rude so she kept her opinions to herself, but she couldn't help feeling that Julian took Serena for granted. And a few months back she'd said to Serena, "I think I'd slip into a coma if I was married to Julian." Then she had pondered: "Why would someone as together as Serena stay in that situation day after day? Why would she stay? It wasn't for financial reasons, Serena could make it on her own. It couldn't be out of a desperate need for love and companionship; Serena was an attractive woman and men didn't seem to notice the wedding ring on her finger. Was love keeping her there? Shante was beginning to doubt even that notion. She had not been a witness to much, if any, affection between Serena and Julian.

Serena said, "I think people get married in a hurry, before they've had a chance to really get to know each other."

"Ummhu," Shante said with food in her mouth. She chewed, swallowed, and then added, "People believe that their life is complete once those vows have been taken. They are sure, totally convinced, that they are going to be smitten with that person *for a lifetime.*" Shante's eyes widened at the thought.

Serena nodded in agreement. "That's a rare thing."

"No doubt."

"Yesterday I was thinking about how I met Julian in Macy's, a few months after I moved to New York. He was being fitted for a suit, and I was trying to find a birthday present for my father."

"Yeah. I remember you told me he couldn't keep his eyes off you," Shante said.

"I wasn't really interested at first, but he was so persistent." Since Serena hadn't known very many people in New York at the time, she had agreed to accept his business card. She had called him ten days later. She told him she was a performer, and it wasn't hard for him to locate her after that. "You know, Shante, Julian used to be so attentive and sensitive."

"That was about five or six years ago, wasn't it?" Shante asked. Shante was trying to make a point and Serena knew it.

"Yes, six years we've been married. The first year wasn't bad. He seemed interested in what I had to say. The most important thing was that he loved me so much. I really thought we would be happy together. I loved him, too. I wanted to make him happy. I've come to the conclusion that, in most cases, it takes more than a few years to fully get to know someone—especially when you marry young, because people change so much. I think with true love the more you get to know someone, the more you love them. At least that's the way it should be. Ten or twenty years down the road, you should be able to look at that person and love them more than you did in the beginning, or at least just as much." Both women sat in silence for a few moments, thinking about Serena's idea of love.

"Nowadays people are so quick to say, 'This is not working and goodbye,' " Serena said, raising her right hand and waving to illustrate her point. "I don't want to be like those people."

"Serena, you're not like those people," Shante said sympathetically. "You're not giving up without trying to make it work. You haven't been happy for years now."

"Yes. True. But I made a vow for better or for worse."

"Yeah, Serena, but you were young, and in my opinion, you got shammed."

Serena looked surprised. Shante could be quite blunt in giving her opinion. Serena appreciated her frankness, though. It made her think, even if she didn't always agree. She knew Shante was sincere.

Shante added, "As Maya Angelou put it, you did what you knew how to do then." She's listening to me, Shante thought, but I can tell it's not sinking in. "I can still hear my parents' voices ringing in my ears. They would tell me to be independent and not to marry anybody until I was absolutely sure he was sent from God."

"The only thing I remember my mom telling me is, 'Marriage is what you make it,' " Serena said.

Shante thought about how Serena always aimed to please everybody, how she hated disappointing anyone. Shante decided to give her a few words of encouragement, realizing after the fact, as usual, that she had been quite blunt. "You have a good head on your shoulders, Serena. You've always had enough confidence in yourself to know that you're a very good decision maker. I don't always make good decisions."

"Hmph! You're the confident one. And you did pretty good when you chose Marcus," Serena said. "How's he doing?"

"You know how the life of an activist can be. He's been speaking here and there and organizing and leading debates at various colleges. You know, the usual. He's been keeping a journal of his activities and discoveries. He hopes to get it published eventually. And he's going to be on C-Span next month."

"That's terrific! I'll make sure I tune in. What will he speak about?"

"He's going to give his analysis on economic and social issues in America and abroad. I think he mentioned something about sanctions and world hunger. I'm not sure, though. I know he did some research and he's going to present some new statistics."

"Oh, it sounds interesting."

"He's my heart," Shante said. "I'm so proud of him."

"You should be," Serena said. She felt proud of him, too.

"He really cares about people, Serena—all people, from all walks of life. He has the biggest heart. I think that's what I love the most about him. It's really such a turn on to see him concerned about the welfare of others. It's incredible. He feels so deeply. And he's so sensitive, not about himself and his feelings, like so many people, but towards others." Shante's eyes glowed whenever she talked about Marcus. Serena smiled and they continued eating their salads.

"Tell him I said thanks for contacting his friends in Africa and letting them know about me. They were all so nice. Zawadi and I hit it off rather well. He treated me just like family. And since Julian didn't come, it meant that much more to have—"

"What! Julian didn't meet you there?"

"No."

"Why am I not surprised?" Shante said.

"Actually, Shante, I thought about it afterwards, and I probably wouldn't have enjoyed myself as much if he had come with me."

"Ouch!" Shante turned her lips downwards. Then she gave a wee smile.

Minutes passed before Shante spoke again. "Serena, Marcus is the best thing that has ever happened to me in my entire life. We are so in love." Shante suddenly looked concerned. "But there is a problem."

Serena leaned forward, thinking she might have heard wrong. She thought about how Marcus and Shante's relationship had always been a symbol of hope for her. Whenever she saw Marcus and Shante together, she felt like fairy tales really do come true. Seeing them happy made her feel better about love and life itself.

"He's not being honest with me," Shante said.

Serena looked worried. "About what?" She stopped eating and patted her lips with her napkin.

"Some nights, when he's supposed to come to my apartment, he doesn't get there until way past dinner. He always says he was in a meeting and it ran over."

"You don't believe him?" Serena asked.

Shante smiled half-heartedly. "Serena, he couldn't lie if he studied how to do it for four years at Columbia University. No, I don't believe him. I know better. He comes over in a taxi cab."

"He does?" Serena frowned, not sure if she was hearing Shante clearly over the rattling dishes and the other diners' conversations.

"He gives me some bogus excuse about why he's riding in a taxi, like, 'I was tired,' or 'My eyes were bothering me.' I guess his eyes *were* bothering him. He couldn't keep them all the way open if he wanted to. I'm relieved that he always calls a taxi, though. I told him that, too."

"What exactly is he doing?" Serena didn't want to believe what she was hearing. And she was surprised to hear Shante talking this way about Marcus.

"He's been drinking," Shante said.

Serena gasped.

"Please, Serena. I have to stay calm about this or I'll lose it." Shante took a deep breath as things in the restaurant quieted down. "I can tell he's been drinking because I can smell it on his breath. And it doesn't matter how many breath mints he pops before he gets there. He's usually crunching on a peppermint as he's coming through the door."

"How long has this been going on?"

"For a few months." I told Nikki about it while you were in Africa. She told me he should join Alcoholics Anonymous. But he doesn't consider himself an alcoholic. So, I haven't suggested that—*yet.*"

Serena's stomach began to burn with worry. "What . . . what are you going to do?"

"I've tried to talk to him, but he insists that everything is just fine."

"Of course he does."

"I know what you're thinking, Serena. If he admits he has a problem, he'll have to get help. Last year he started doing the same thing. I was so hurt. I told him that if he didn't stop, the relationship was over."

"Oh, Shante." Serena's heart was breaking. Her eyes were moist and a lump formed in her throat.

"He stopped, but now he's doing it again." There was a look of dismay on Shante's face and her eyes began to tear. She swallowed hard.

"Did he get treatment?"

"No. I thought everything was okay."

"I know you did." Serena reached out and touched Shante's hand. Her mind was already scrambling for ways to help.

"Serena, I would never leave him. I knew that when I told him I would leave. I love him so much. Why doesn't he just stop? He has so much to offer. Why is he trying to ruin everything?"

"It sounds like you're angry with him."

Shante's expression changed as she thought hard. "Maybe, a little. It just scares me practically to death." Shante had never been afraid of anything in her life, except maybe violent criminals. Unlike Nikki and Serena, her well-balanced emotions were never a front. "We have the most powerful love. When he makes love to me I'm paralyzed with pleasure. Once I closed my eyes and tried to imagine what would be better than loving Marcus and having him love me the way he does . . . And you know,

Serena, there was nothing that would appear in my mind. Only Marcus, his love, our life together, and all of our good times growing up together. I could welcome death if I could take a little bit of Marcus's love on the journey to my new life. It would be the most remarkably peaceful journey . . ."

As Serena listened to Shante, visions of Nathan emerged in her mind.

Shante's mood changed, snapping Serena out of her trance-like state. "I'm just so frustrated. This threatens everything. This could get even worse." Shante thought of Marcus's five-year-old daughter, Ashley, and how inconsistent Ashley's mother, Cindy, was. "I'm concerned about Ashley, too. Cindy's mainly worried about her own agenda. And her daughter's not at the top of it. Ashley needs Marcus to remain the constant source of stability that he's always been."

"Maybe he's trying much harder than you or I can under-stand," Serena said. "This is a serious illness."

"I realize that. But if anyone knows better, it's Marcus."

"It's not a matter of knowing better," Serena said softly. "He needs help, and unconditional love and support. He's probably far more disappointed in himself than you are in him. He probably feels terrible about this. Sometimes men don't always open up. You know how they do. They keep things inside and try to be macho."

Shante said, "Marcus has a strong mind. I just want him to get control of this and say: I'm not going to let this destroy my life."

"Even strong minds suffer from illnesses," Serena responded. "But I know how you feel, Shante. Sometimes I can't understand for the life of me why people do the things they do. I think to myself, they know their behavior is hurting themselves and the ones who love them, so why don't they stop? Whatever it takes, just do it?"

"Marcus needs to get control of this," Shante said with a fear-ful look in her eyes.

"He will. Just talk to him, without threatening to leave him."

"You're right," Shante said, suddenly sounding hopeful.

"I know a place where he can get help," Serena said. "A good acquaintance of mine is a doctor there. Call me when he's ready. Make sure Marcus knows he has your unconditional support."

"Thanks. You always manage to open my eyes a little bit wider."

They sat quietly for a few minutes, then Shante said, "Ya know, it really saddens me to see so many young people in prisons." In the back of her mind, she was afraid of losing Marcus to alcoholism. And she knew that a lot of alcoholics end up in jail. "Some of them are there because their addiction to drugs or alcohol has affected their ability to function as law-abiding citizens—which is exactly what they would be, if they weren't addicted."

"I know," Serena sighed. "I think many of them need to be in some sort of high-tech hospital instead of prisons. After their release, a lot of them just pick right up where they left off. Those who do get treatment aren't there long enough to get well and stay that way—mainly because of inadequate insurance and outrageous medical bills. I mean, come on, really, everybody knows the average family can't afford to pay those costs."

"Yeah. And in the meantime, families are being destroyed, children are left without fathers, and people wonder why society has gotten so bad. What are we going to do? Build fifty thousand more prisons over the next ten years? Or are we going to make some common-sense changes in the way we operate as a society?"

"That's true, Shante. Next you'll be telling me that you're going to run for congress."

"Not unless you do, Serena," Shante teased.

"Maybe later in life—much, much later. Right now, I enjoy what privacy I do have."

Shante smiled fondly at Serena and thought, Serena's such a good friend. She's a real person, even though she has that glamorous career. Shante appreciated the fact that Serena cared and would talk about the issues she found important, issues on behalf of which Marcus sometimes demonstrated. Some people thought Serena was aloof because she held her chin up slightly when she walked. But Shante and so many others saw Serena as simply graceful. Shante thought, if they only knew her. If they had a friend like Serena, they wouldn't need another.

They both sat deep in thought, then Shante added, "That's one reason why I love teaching. I make it a point to tell my children about the hazards of using drugs. I tell them to recognize anyone who offers them drugs as someone who cares absolutely nothing about them or their future."

"We need more people like you," Serena said.

"Thank you. I just want them to believe in themselves enough to make positive choices and feel good about those choices."

"Speaking about feeling good, you'll never believe who I saw when I was in Washington."

"Who?" Shante asked, her big ebony eyes shining with curiosity.

Serena grinned. "Nathan."

"What! Are you serious?"

"Yes, I am. He lives there, and I had no idea."

"Tell me what happened," Shante said, eager to hear all about it. Serena had told her about Nathan years before, and she knew he held a special place in Serena's heart.

"It was my last day there. I was sightseeing and enjoying the perfect spring weather when I saw him at the Reflecting Pool. I hadn't seen him in ten years. It was totally thrilling! I can't eee-ven begin to tell you how unbelievable the whole thing was."

"Whew." Shante took a deep breath and fanned herself.

Serena giggled. "I was just standing there, staring at him, speechless, like I was hallucinating. Then . . ."

"Yeah?" Shante leaned forward on the edge of her seat.

"Then he just looked over at me, as if he felt me staring at him."

"Wow!"

"I gave him my phone number."

"Is he married?" Shante asked.

"I didn't see a ring on his finger, but I think so. I heard he had gotten married not too long after he quit school. Anyway, he called me."

Shante looked surprised. "He called you? At the house?"

Serena nodded.

"How'd you get away with that?"

"Oh, it was totally innocent. Besides, Julian doesn't pay much attention to what I do, anyway. He knows how strongly I feel about keeping a marriage intact, and I've never given him any reason not to trust me."

"So, what did Nathan say?" There were moments of silence as Serena sat starry eyed. Shante wiggled in her chair, then blurted, "Serena, hurry up and tell me what the man said!" Shante didn't have nearly as much patience with adults as she had with children.

"He's coming to New York on business, and we're going to have lunch together."

"*Ummmmm*. This should be interesting," Shante said.

Serena giggled faintly. "What?"

"You come back from Africa, and Nathan just happens to have business in New York. My, my, my," Shante said, before laughing.

"Shante, stop. I knew you were gonna act like this. What are you saying?"

Shante grinned from ear to ear and pushed her plate to the side. "I'm saying that I think the only business he has in New York is coming to see you. Now I don't know if you can call that business or not, because I don't know what he has planned."

"I think you over ate again," Serena said. Shante had a tendency to act a little silly and giggly whenever she ate too much.

"No, that's what I believe—he's just coming here to see you."

Serena shook her head insistently. "Naah, I don't think so."

"Okay, okay—maybe you're right." Shante kept grinning.

Serena looked at her watch. "I've got to go."

Shante looked at her watch, too. "Gosh! Me, too. I'm supposed to meet Marcus at his place."

They paid the waitress, giving her a gracious tip before gathering their shopping bags and leaving the mall.

Ten

"Marvelous, Serena," Ollie said as Serena finished practicing her solo song. "That was perfect. You're a director's dream!"

Serena had arrived at work early today so she could practice for her leading role in the musical *One Perfect Man*. It was a comedy about three women who get together and compare qualities of different men, wishing they could make one perfect man. Serena's character "Jamilla," was the only one of the three women who still had hope. The other women laughed at Jamilla and told her she was living in a fantasy world. Still, Jamilla kept the faith, and in the end her character found true love.

Serena's director, Olivier Reneau, had performed on stage in France for ten years before coming to America fourteen years ago. In France, he had met and fallen madly in love with a pretty fair-skinned brunette. They married, but eight months later she was killed when the train she was on derailed. Heartbroken, Ollie left Europe at the first opportunity. He had poured himself into his work and soon became an award-winning director.

Serena's and Ollie's working relationship turned into friendship shortly after they met. They both enjoyed occasional moments of innocent flirting. He'd refer to her sometimes as Aphrodite and she'd compliment him on his olive skin, hazel eyes, and sexy French accent. Performing and meeting a diversity of people, like Ollie, was what Serena liked most about New York. And Ollie had invited Serena to an event a few years ago where he introduced her to Mikhail Baryshnikov and Debbie Allen. Since Serena was a young girl, she had been inspired by and fascinated with Baryshnikov's brilliance as a classical dancer and was thrilled to meet him at Ollie's party, as well as Allen, whom she also admired for her talent as a dancer.

Serena stepped down from the stage. "Thanks, Ollie," she said reaching for his hands and holding them. He kissed her on the forehead. "You make me feel good about what I do."

His voice was seductive. "You always work so hard to get it right the first time, Serena."

"I don't always succeed," she said.

"You're the best, kid. I'm glad I found you." They smiled.

As Serena walked backstage, Ollie thought about how well liked she was amongst her fellow artists. But Ollie was unaware that there was one employee who didn't like Serena—Nadine Frye.

Nadine was a tall brown-skinned woman in her late forties who assisted the cast members before, during, and after performances. She never gave Serena much assistance. In fact, she often tried to make things more difficult for her.

A few months ago, Serena had noticed that her costume was mysteriously missing. It was later found crammed in a drawer in the dressing room. Serena suspected Nadine but she never confronted her. A few days later, Serena walked into the dressing room to find soda spilled all over her cosmetics. "I did it," Nadine had admitted in a defensive voice, "but it was an accident." Serena chose to believe her, even though she wondered why Nadine had not come to tell her on her own.

Serena knew that if she had told Ollie how Nadine was acting, Nadinc would be out the door in a matter of seconds. But
Serena felt she should continue to be nice to Nadine and ignore
her negative behavior. Serena was the type of person who never
wanted to hurt anyone—even if they were deliberately hurting
her.

Later that day, Serena was in the dressing room laughing
and talking with two other cast members, Candace and Zoe. She
tried on a blue satin dress she had designed herself.

"Do you like my dress?" she asked her friends.

"I don't."

It was Nadine. She stood in the doorway with her long arms
folded across her tall narrow body. The lenses on her glasses
seemed thick with fog.

"She didn't ask you," Candace told Nadine in her strong New
York accent. She popped her chewing gum.

"You're always lying to her," Nadine said in her harsh voice.
"I thought I'd tell the truth."

Serena's jaw dropped.

"Well, I like it. It's very pretty," Candice said.

"I like it too," said Zoe in her mousy voice.

Nadine rolled her eyes.

"She's just jealous," Candace whispered to Serena. "It's so
obvious."

Jealous of what? Serena thought. There's nothing to be jealous about. I guess people don't actually need a reason to be jealous. All they have to do is think they have a reason. It's all in
the head. Then Serena faced the fact that Nadine might be jealous of her career, her looks. But inside, Serena didn't feel like
she was any better than Nadine—or anybody else, for that matter. Serena knew that everybody had various strengths and weak-
nesses. She knew people whom she admired and aspired to be
more like. So why couldn't Nadine just admire her? She had always been nice to Nadine—extra nice, because she sensed that
Nadine didn't like her and she wanted the woman to know that

she was a down-to-earth person who didn't think she was more special than anyone else. "I don't understand," Serena said.

"Serena, you're a nice person, but you have a tendency to believe everybody else is nice, too," Candace said.

"This time, I'm speaking up." Serena turned and faced Nadine.

Zoe and Candace looked at each other and then at Serena.

"Nadine," Serena said, have I done something to offend you? Because if I have, I'd like to know."

"Look. I just said I don't like ya dress. What . . . you think everybody's supposed to like everything you do?"

"What?" Serena couldn't believe what she was hearing.

"You think you're supposed to have everything your way," Nadine said.

"That's not true," Serena said. "I come here and do the job that I've been hired to do. I've never asked for any special treatment. Please explain to me what you're talking about."

The silence was deafening.

"You're not willing to, are you?" Serena said.

Nadine rolled her eyes. "Whatever." She tossed her head and exited the room.

Serena turned back toward her dresser and looked at herself in the mirror. This was so strange to her because she knew she had not done anything to Nadine.

"Don't worry about it Serena," Zoe said. "Let's get back to work."

That evening, Serena and Julian sat in silence at the dinner table. Julian had a fork in one hand and an antique car magazine in the other. Serena, still upset about what had happened earlier with Nadine, was very quiet. Julian didn't seem to notice. He was happy that he wasn't having to say anything unless he wanted to. He got up, went to the refrigerator and looked in. Then suddenly he spoke. "Serena, why'd you put the mayonnaise on the shelf?"

"I know it goes in the doorway, Julian, but I was in a hurry yesterday. The door was full and I didn't have time to rear-range things."

Julian put the mayonnaise in the doorway, poured himself more tea, and sat back down.

Serena scanned the long white counters. Everything was put away except the cappuccino maker. Julian didn't mind if that sat on the counter. Serena liked to keep things a certain way, but she wasn't zealous about what she thought were "small" matters. These were important issues to Julian, though, and for the most part Serena respected that. She knew—though it annoyed her at times and she told him so—it was just his particular way of doing things. But she had never known anyone who had to have their shorts dry-cleaned. She'd made the mistake of washing Julian's shorts in the washing machine shortly after they were married.

"Serena, why'd you wash my shorts?" He'd asked.

"Because they were dirty."

"They shrink in the washing machine. I like them dry-cleaned."

"I was careful not to shrink them," she'd said. Then she ironed and ironed the shorts, making sure they were perfectly creased. She probably did a better job than the dry cleaners could have. "Here, Julian," she said proudly handing him the shorts.

"Next time don't wash my shorts in the machine," he responded with a forced smile, still annoyed. Then he'd kissed her.

"So, how was your day?" Serena asked Julian halfway through dinner.

"It was the same, nothing different," he said.

There were a few more moments of silence, then Serena said, "My day was fair."

"Just fair?"

"To tell the truth, I'm a little upset. I was in the dressing room in pretty high spirits, and you know that dress I designed—the blue one?"

"Uh huh." Julian was still looking at the magazine.

"Nadine said she didn't like it."

Julian chuckled softly. "Oka-a-y."

"No. It was the way she said it. She said, 'I don't like it.' " Serena wiggled her neck and tossed her head to show how Nadine had acted.

"Here we go," Julian said. He took a deep breath. "See, that's the difference between you and me, Serena. I don't have time to worry about whether or not someone likes my suit."

Serena frowned. "That's different, and you know it, Julian,"

"Okay, why do you care what she thinks?"

"I don't understand how people can justify mistreating you when you haven't done anything to them. It's so incredibly rude. It seems to me that no matter how nice you are to some people, they still may not like you."

"That's right. So why worry about it? Nadine's not paying your bills for you."

Julian's response was typical, but not what Serena was hoping for, nor what she felt she needed. She needed compassion and understanding, or at least an intelligent conversation about some people's psychological rationale.

She said, I'm not going to dwell on it—"

"Thank you," he said.

"I guess it just boils down to the fact that when people aren't happy with themselves, they sometimes take their problems and frustrations out on others." She began clearing the table and washing the dishes. "But I'm still curious about what it is, exactly, that makes them tick. Aren't you?"

Julian said nothing. Serena looked over at him. He was reading the magazine again. He had completely tuned her out. She sighed in disappointment as Julian got up and went to the garage to be with his cars. She finished washing the dishes and went upstairs to choose an outfit to wear to lunch the next day with Nathan.

The big closet was what Serena liked best about the design of the house, which she and Julian had bought five years ago. Before, they had lived in an apartment. There, the closets were tiny and she often found herself cramming clothes inside. She called that closet a hole in the wall, and she never understood why anybody would build such a minuscule area in which to keep clothes and shoes.

The size of her closet and the clothes in it reflected the fact that Serena liked shopping. She had everything from expensive designer suits, glamorous dresses, and shoes in every color and style to overalls, Levis, and other casual clothes. She didn't care what store it came from—a thrift shop or Macy's—if she liked it, she bought it. But she did care about the price. She had purchased most of her wardrobe for less than half the original prices.

Serena took a black suit off the hanger and held it against her. She looked in the mirror, then hung the suit back up, thinking it too conservative. Next she held up a lavender tank dress. "I don't feel like wearing lavender," she said to herself.

Remembering that it was supposed to be a nice day tomorrow, she decided she would wear something pretty. June had rolled around and the weather had been very warm all week long. She decided to wear a sleeveless black dress that hit a couple of inches above her knees, with a short slit in the right front. Tiny cream and pink silk roses bordered the square neckline and a cream ribbon tied around the waist. Then she tried on a pair of black high-heeled sandals. She smiled as she looked down at the shoes, thinking that they were made just for her. She also thought she couldn't wait to see Nathan. She had so much to say. Tomorrow she would finally get the chance.

❖

Eleven

*N*athan strolled into the revolving dining room in the Marriott Marquis at exactly one-fifteen—fifteen minutes earlier than he and Serena had agreed upon. He couldn't believe he was about to have lunch with Serena. It felt surreal to him. He sat nervously rubbing the back of his neck with his left hand as he peered at the restaurant's entrance. Now anxiously rubbing his red silk tie, he glanced down at his dark gray Gucci suit. He thought he looked sharp, which was what he wanted for this important meeting.

When Serena entered the restaurant, Nathan immediately felt her presence. He stood quickly.

She saw him standing. She smiled as she was escorted to the table.

Dear God, let this dream last forever, Nathan thought. He couldn't hide what was obvious—he was wholly enamored of her. Their embrace was quick, but filled with warmth. Nathan enjoyed the feel of Serena's soft fresh-smelling hair against his face. He closed his eyes and inhaled.

He pulled her chair out for her and sat back down. "Thanks for coming, Serena," he said as she hung her black purse on the chair.

"It's really nice to see you." Serena was tingling all over, and she could tell Nathan was, too, by the look on his face.

"You look so beautiful," he said in his soft, yet masculine voice.

"Thank you. You look very handsome yourself."

Nathan smiled as he handed her a menu from his side of the table. Serena's soft brown eyes twinkled as she reached out to receive the menu. She felt like she was twenty again. She thought of a song by Teven Campbell—"I'm Ready." That song always made her feel happy and very young. Serena was only thirty, but she sometimes felt like ninety.

The waiter approached to take their order. Serena was so excited to see Nathan that she had little appetite. Nevertheless, she ordered chicken, penne pasta and a salad. Nathan ordered the swordfish special.

Still smiling, Serena admired how handsomely dressed Nathan was. "I have so much to say to you that I don't know if I'll be able to eat anything."

"I don't know about you, but I have all afternoon, and evening, and night and . . ," he said. They laughed. "God, I can't believe I'm here with you," he said.

She smiled. "So, tell me, what have you been doing all this time?"

"I got married a couple of years after we broke up."

"Yes, I heard about that."

"I was so lonely after we broke up." He suddenly looked sad. He took in a deep breath and pulled himself together. "I made a stupid mistake, something I did quite often back then. I thought that by marrying Alysse, the pain of losing you would go away."

Serena looked down in sorrow.

"I'm sorry," he said. "I didn't come here to upset you, or for your sympathy. It was just a foolish thing to do."

"I'm sure you weren't the first person to make that mistake."

She thought of her own marriage, even though it wasn't as hastily done as Nathan's. "I remember when you got married. It did seem awfully sudden."

"I was so immature, Serena. When you told me it was over, I couldn't handle it. You did the right thing. I wasn't good for anybody at that time. But I did learn from my mistakes. I pray that no man ever makes the mistakes I made if he has to feel the kind of pain I felt over losing you."

Serena was touched. "Before you got married, I heard you were in Macon visiting your family. I got upset because you didn't call me. Then I realized that I had pushed you away. I was the one that ended the relationship."

"I knew you were seeing someone. Practically everyone I knew told me."

"That ended rather quickly, Nathan. It wasn't serious at all."

"I was so messed up. I just kept making mistake after mistake after mistake. It was like I was constantly tripping over myself."

Serena smiled. "We were just young and naive."

Nathan nodded in agreement. "There were so many negative influences, and I know now that I didn't fully understand what was happening to us. I felt like we were being chewed up and spit out. Then I was crawling around trying to figure out what to do next. Yeah, we fell prey to it all."

"You always did have an interesting way of putting things, Nathan."

Nathan laughed softly, showing his perfectly straight teeth. "You were far more mature than I was."

"I was naive, though." Serena recalled that she had wanted things to be like a happy fairy tale *all* the time. "And I used to get upset over the slightest thing. And, to tell the truth, I still do sometimes."

They laughed together.

"If I hadn't been so hot-headed, maybe I never would have lost you," he said.

Serena was suddenly warm all over. The fact that he realized his mistakes charmed her immensely. She saw how much he had matured.

Nathan recognized the look on Serena's face—the one she used to get when she was hot and wanting him. She's so beautiful, so enchanting, he thought. I want to hold her forever.

Serena reached for her glass of water and took a hefty gulp.

"Anyway, I'm divorced now," Nathan said."

"Oh, I'm sorry."

"Don't be. I was never in love with her, but she was a special friend to me, and I to her, after she'd gotten out of a bad relationship. We came together out of loneliness." He looked down in a moment of distress. Then he proudly raised his head. "I have a son."

Serena grinned from ear to ear. "Oh. Do you have a picture?"

"I just happen to have one right here," They laughed, and he reached inside his suit coat and took out his wallet.

"He's so cute," she said as she studied the picture.

"Thank you."

"How old is he?"

"Seven."

Serena smiled as she handed him the picture and he put it back inside his wallet. "You are very blessed," Serena said. Then she moved to study the view of Manhattan. "The view is magnificent, isn't it?"

"Yes, it is," he answered, looking at the view of Serena. He found her profile to be exquisite.

"I've never eaten here before," she said. Nathan was staring so attentively at her that she thought he must have spoken and perhaps she had not heard what he said. She leaned forward. "Excuse me, what did you say?"

"I'm sorry, I didn't say anything. And I don't mean to stare, but you are so beautiful." He shook his head from side to side as he said the words.

Serena shyly looked away and he glanced at her soft, firm cleavage. She looked at him again.

"I remember everything, Serena," he said. "I remember what you smell like. I remember how soft you were, how soft your hair was." She's got that look on her face again, he thought.

Serena gazed into his eyes and her body tingled. "I remember all the beautiful poetry you used to write for me."

"You do?" he said.

"Oh, definitely. I even have some of it memorized—"

Serena was interrupted by a slender waiter. "Your meals will be out momentarily," he said with a British accent.

"Thank you," they said in unison.

Nathan reached across the table and held Serena's hand. He looked painfully at the diamond on her finger.

"You're married."

"Yes."

"Do you have children?"

"Not yet. But we hope to start a family soon."

Nathan hid a look of disgust. Even after all this time, he still could not bear the thought of another man touching Serena.

"I've been married for six years," she said. She told Nathan about her career and how she usually performed four nights a week.

Their meals arrived and Nathan thanked the waiter.

"How's your family?" Serena asked him.

"Good, good. My sisters are fine, and my parents are doing well. But, my grandfather died a few years ago."

"I'm sorry." She reached out and held his hand. "I know how close you two were."

"Thank you," he said softly.

"Remember how he used to run us off the telephone?" Serena asked.

They both laughed and Nathan nodded. "I used to fall asleep talking to you," he said. "I'd come home from football practice and I'd be so tired. I would tell you that I had to go, and you'd insist that I wasn't really tired. I remember Granddad would come and hang up the telephone after I'd fallen asleep. You'd still be on the phone talking. 'Hello . . . hello . . . Nathan,' you'd say as Granddad was hanging up."

"That was embarrassing," she said.

Nathan laughed softly. Even his laugh was sexy, she thought.

"How's Mom?" Nathan asked.

Serena was surprised that Nathan referred to her mother as "Mom." Nathan could tell what she was thinking. "She always did treat me like a son," he added.

"She's very happy with John," said Serena. "They've been together for ten years now. They got married about eight years ago. They do a lot of traveling and are very active in the church."

"Oh, that's good. She's so sweet." Nathan thought back to the day Serena ended their relationship. He had begun to suspect that Serena's parents' divorce was part of the reason why Serena pushed him away. And he had been right. Caroline left Lou the same week Serena graduated from high school. Serena was devastated. She didn't understand. It had always been the three of them, and she had never seen them have a serious argument. She knew her dad had been insensitive at times. She knew her parents had disagreements. Still, she thought their marriage was basically good and she had told Nathan this. "I know your parents' divorce hurt you."

"Yes, it did. You were really there for me. You were my light on foggy days. I used to tell you that, remember?" Nathan nodded as Serena thought about her parents' divorce and how it eventually affected her relationship with Nathan. When Serena broke up with Nathan, she was still grieving about the divorce, though she had started keeping her feelings to herself. Keeping her grief inside affected the way she viewed her problems with Nathan. The problems seemed *bigger* than they were because they were *harder* for her to cope with. Nathan had been so wonderfully supportive and she didn't want to burden him any longer. Besides, she was a little ashamed of her feelings. Were they normal? Wasn't she too old to feel that way? Shouldn't she have gotten over the divorce sooner? Nobody had bothered to explain—

much—why the divorce was necessary. In Serena's mind, one day her parents were happily married, and the next day they were separated. She believed if it could happen to her parents, it could happen to anyone—including her and Nathan.

Nathan spoke again. "Your mom used to cook the best food." Nathan recalled how the smell and sight of meatloaf, baked bread, and fresh strawberry cobbler always made his mouth water. "One time she asked me to stay for dinner. She had cooked squash and I told her I didn't like squash. She said, 'You don't say you don't like somethin', you just eat it.' She had the sweetest voice."

Serena smiled and said, "Mom was thinking about her own life growing up in a family of ten. She'd talk about how they often made a meal out of biscuits and gravy."

"I couldn't believe the squash actually tasted good."

"She still cooks like that. It's delicious."

Moments later Nathan said, "Tell me about your trip to Africa."

"Oh, I had the best time I could have ever imagined. But I tried to do too much in too little time. I wore myself out. I couldn't be still. I visited the Ivory Coast for a few days before traveling to Egypt and finally Kenya."

"You went on an adventure," Nathan said.

"It felt like one sometimes. While I was in Nairobi, I did a lot of shopping—mostly for art. In Egypt, I sailed the Nile River and toured various temples and pyramids by camel. When I got home, I was numb! Oh, I also visited a school while I was in Kenya. My friend Shante suggested that. I'm glad she did."

"Does she live here?" he asked.

"She lives in New Rochelle. I talked to the students there about my Broadway career. I sang a song for them and they sang one for me, in Swahili. It was so moving." She remembered that she had a few photographs in her handbag. She showed Nathan a photo of her dancing in a Kenyan village, another of her on a camel, and one of a pyramid.

"Can I have one?" Nathan asked.

"Sure." She handed him the picture of her dancing in the village.

"I think what fascinated me most was rural Kenya," she said.

"Why is that?" Nathan asked.

"Because there, I was at the center of culture and learning. I went on a safari. The wildlife was incredible. I felt like my camera wouldn't snap pictures fast enough."

Nathan smiled as he visualized Serena in a jeep in the countryside, snapping pictures.

"I took pictures of birds, giraffes, elephants and lions. I saw some of the prettiest emerald cuckoos, and hundreds of pink flamingos. I felt like spreading my wings and flying, too. I just kept staring at them. I didn't want it to end." Suddenly Serena giggled.

"What?" Nathan said, grinning.

"I thought the animals were funny at times. The way they interacted with each other. The mating process of the lion and the lioness was interesting. The lioness sat on the ground and moved her body from side to side. Then the male came along and took care of business." Serena frowned a tad. "That process was rather lengthy."

Nathan laughed. "That was quite a trip. You didn't go alone, did you?"

"Yes, I did," she said proudly.

Nathan was surprised. He knew Serena had never liked traveling alone. If she went outside her normal routine and surroundings, she had to have someone by her side. He recalled the time in high school when she was chosen by the principal to go to Europe as a foreign exchange student. She didn't go because no one else from her school was going. He also remembered that when she worked at Six Flags she was asked by a talent scout to travel abroad. She declined for the same reason.

"It was good for me to get away by myself. I had never done that before," she said.

"I'm glad you enjoyed yourself."

"In fact, I'm writing a musical about life on the continent of

Africa. I want this musical to show people the problems and concerns, such as poverty and disease, but also the beauty of Africa, and its various cultures."

"That sounds great! Serena, you are so talented."

"Thank you." She blushed. "I plan on going back in the near future. I want to visit South Africa. I'd like to invest in Africa and keep the hopes of Mandela and so many others alive. My friend Marcus is looking into investment opportunities there. He has lots of friends in Africa. In fact, I stayed with some of them while I was in Kenya."

"You did? So you got a true sense of life there, more than the average tourist."

"Yes. They were so gracious."

Nathan was listening so carefully that it almost scared Serena. She never got that much attention from Julian.

"I'd like to go to Africa myself," he said. "In all my traveling—and I've been a few places—I've never been to Africa."

"You have to go. It's so wonderful."

"I will."

"Marcus suggested that I travel somewhere alone. He travels by himself a lot, and I told him I didn't like doing things by myself—especially traveling alone. I told him I was afraid. He said that was exactly why I should do it."

"He sounds like a nice guy."

"He is."

They sat there eating, smiling, and gazing warmly into one another's eyes for a few minutes before Serena spoke again. "So, tell me about your career—or should I say careers?"

"I went back to school while I was in Boston. I graduated from M.I.T."

"Oh, Nathan! That is wonderful. I'm so impressed."

"Thanks. I got both my degrees, then moved to Washington to work for the Department of Interior. I got better job offers, but I wanted to work there, for a while anyway, on environmental projects and issues. I started my own business on the side two years ago. So I use both majors. I also invented a device that helps detect pollution levels. My patent request has been approved."

"That's fantastic. And I'm so happy you went back to school," she said. "You were so brilliant."

"Thank you, Serena. You always told me that, too. You made me believe in myself. I could have told you that I was going to climb the Eiffel Tower, and you would have believed in me."

The waiter approached and asked if they wanted dessert. They said "No thank you" and he excused himself.

Serena's and Nathan's conversation shifted to poetry, music, and other mutual interests. They talked for a long time about their beliefs and their individual plans for the future. They were both romantics. Even though Nathan had a brilliant technical mind, he enjoyed and appreciated the arts just as much as Serena. And Serena was delighted to realize that they had more in common than just their past.

"Well, it's getting late," she said, disappointed at the thought of having to leave. "I have to go." She reached for her purse.

Nathan felt a bit of panic. He spoke quickly. "Can I see you again before I leave New York?" He was afraid she might say no.

"Yes," she said. Nathan stood and pulled out her chair and she gave him another quick hug.

"Let me walk you down," he said.

"No, no," she said, and she hurried off.

They waved goodbye until she was out of sight.

On the drive home, Serena's thoughts were all of Nathan and how much fun she had being with him. She definitely wanted to see him again.

Twelve

"Good morning," Serena said, tossing back the covers and sitting up in bed. Julian yawned and stretched as Serena looked on.

"Ya love me?" he asked, with his eyes still half shut and a smug look on his face.

"Yeah," Serena answered halfheartedly. Julian didn't notice Serena's lack of enthusiasm.

He got up and started getting ready for work.

While he was in the shower the telephone rang. It was Nathan. "I know it was just yesterday, but I want to see you again today if I can." Serena remained silent. "Can you talk?" Nathan said.

"Sure."

"I'm only going to be here for a few more days, and then I'll be out of your way. I promise," he said.

"Actually, I have to work all day and evening. I'll be rehearsing at the theater all morning. If you want to stop by, maybe we can talk for a few minutes. I have to go now."

"Thank you," he said. "Goodbye."

Shante returned home from her doctor's appointment. She had gone there to renew her prescription for Claritin—something she did every spring because of her allergy to pollen. She sneezed as she opened the door to her apartment, hitting her head against the doorframe. "Great," she muttered as she went inside, rubbing her head. Fortunately, she didn't feel a knot, just a dull ache and a little idiotic.

Shante liked her apartment. It was small, but warm and cozy. She had decorated it with earth tones and lots of plants. On her way home, she had stopped and picked up a ceramic vase she had ordered. Now she stood with it in her arms, trying to decide on the best spot for it. She walked over to the sliding glass door, set the vase down, and lifted the corn plant by the door into the vase. She nodded her approval. Then she walked over to the cherry-wood desk that sat in a corner of the living room and started straightening everything on it. I smell a rat and I think her name is Ashley, Shante thought. She shook her head and smiled. Ashley had knocked over the apple-shaped pencil holder—a gift Shante had received from one of her students. Ashley had also left markers all over the desk and a few papers scattered.

After Shante finished straightening up, she took an allergy pill, then fed her tropical fish. She went into her bedroom and changed into navy pinstriped overalls and a white T-shirt. Comfortable, she picked up a small stack of school papers from the floor beside her bed, thinking that she might as well grade these now. She read the first paper, smiling softly as a lump formed in her throat.

WHY I LIKE SCHOL
I like schol becus my teacher always ask me where is my homwork. She maks me think about what is inportent. We play outside. My teacher's name is Miss Peyton. She is nice to me. She said I'm speshul. That is why I like schol.
Kyle

Shante sniffed, but not because of her allergies. This letter, like so many others, touched her deeply. She thought, my job doesn't pay much, but it's the best job in the world. Then she frowned at Kyle's spelling. Well, he was improving, she grinned.

When she finished grading the papers, Shante found her knitting basket and went back into the living room. She sat on the brown leather sofa and started knitting a sweater for Ashley.

Shante first tried knitting two years ago. To her surprise, she liked it. "Gee, have I changed," she had said to Marcus. She found that knitting helped her relax. She had a tendency to keep going sometimes when her body was tired and telling her to slow down. She also liked knitting because it reminded her of her life growing up in Pinnacle, North Carolina. Her mother, Viola, was a seamstress who also knitted quilts and sweaters for people in the community. Shante had been indifferent to knitting growing up. It just looked so boring to her. On the other hand, she was always very interested in her father's hobby—motorcycles.

She'd jump on the back of her father's Honda motorcycle and they'd take off. "Hold on tight, Shante," Jimmy would say. "Now you know you have to lean with me in the curves, so I don't wreck this thang." And he'd rev up the engine.

"I know, Daddy! Burn rubber!"

Jimmy raced motorcycles as a hobby. Shante and Viola went to many of his races. "I want a motorcycle, Daddy," Shante had said when she was nine. He bought her a mini bike instead, and she spent many hours speeding along the dirt trail up the street from their house. Viola had learned when Shante was three to keep a jar of cocoa butter handy at all times for minor scrapes and cuts. Shante still carried a couple of scars on her legs and one in her eyebrow from the daredevil stunts she had performed as a child.

Shante smiled as she sat knitting and thinking of her childhood, and how her parents had always behaved like happy newlyweds. Jimmy would come home from a long day's work to find Viola at the door wearing a low-cut dress and her hair hanging down to her shoulders. Viola had said to her friends, "That's

how I get Jimmy to come straight home from work every day."
Jimmy and Viola always kissed hello while Shante giggled.
Then she'd run and jump into Jimmy's arms.

Shante was an only child for nine years, until her twin brothers were born. Her parents tried for years to have more children.
When Viola found out she was finally pregnant, she and Jimmy
went all over town telling people the good news. But it would be
years before the twins would be able to keep up with Jimmy and
Shante.

The doorbell rang. Shante knew it was Marcus, returning
from giving a speech at a middle school in the Bronx. She put
her knitting materials away and eagerly opened the door.

"Hey, darlin'," he said playfully, with a big grin on his face.

"Hey, honey."

He leaned forward and puckered up. "Give me some suga."
He stressed the word "suga." His cheery smiling eyes, handsome
face and slanted dimples inspired Shante to pucker up quickly.

Shante closed the door behind him. Then she wrapped her
arms around his neck and they kissed again. Marcus held a bag
in one hand and gently placed his other hand on Shante's tiny
waist.

"I brought us some lunch," he said.

"I thought we could go out for lunch," she said. "What did
you get?" Marcus smiled and headed for the kitchen.

When Shante saw him smile, she knew what was in the bag.
"Not Chinese food again," she said.

"Chinese food is good," he said, bursting into laughter.

"It's too early for Chinese food," she grumbled, following him
into the kitchen.

"What difference does it make what time you eat it?"

"Well, thank you for bringing it," Shante lied.

They sat at the table in the small kitchen and began to eat.
Shante put a fork full of rice in her mouth. "Tell me about your
speech. How did things go? I bet you were eloquent."

"That's what they told me," Marcus bragged half-jokingly, as
he stuffed his cheeks with pepper steak.

Shante smiled and looked at him out of the corner of her eye. "What was the title again?"

"Integrating Racism. I spoke about why it was important for all people to receive equal opportunities and how it would benefit the entire society. Once people are afforded opportunities, it's up to them what they do with them. They can either move ahead or they can waste them. And we know there are plenty of ways to ruin a good opportunity. But I told the kids that if they make a mistake—like dropping out of school, for example—to keep trying."

"That sounds great," Shante said, leaning across the table. They kissed.

Marcus blushed. He liked impressing Shante. "Thanks, Shante. You know how much I value your opinion. Don't get me wrong, but you don't give out compliments unless you really, really, really mean it."

"That's the way it *should* be," she said.

"Yeah, but most people will tell a little white lie every now and then, just to make people feel better. But not you. You tell it like it is—don't you, honey pie?"

They laughed.

"Getting back on the subject, I talked briefly about how important it is to vote and about reaching out into the community to help others, especially children, make a better life for themselves."

"There you go again," Shante teased. "Caring about people; making people realize that they're just as good as anybody else and that they can do or be anything that they want as long as they believe in themselves. Aren't you ashamed of yourself?" Marcus smiled. Then she said, "How did you come up with the title?"

"Well, the title is open to interpretation. I can think of several very different ways it could be interpreted. You know, there is a big debate on affirmative action. Some people believe in it, and some people don't. So I thought, both sides need to be listened to and understood before anyone can agree on any type of action. Respect is a key word. People need to have genuine concern for others and not always think of themselves first. I thought, how can I look at this issue objectively? I asked myself, how do I feel about it?"

"Okay." Shante listened attentively.

"Now, you know me, Shante. I'm the type of person that can give my opinion, but at the same time keep my mind open to others' opinions and grievances."

"That's the way I am, too," Shante said.

"That's the only way to be," Marcus said. "That's how you learn and gain respect and valuable insight into people's minds, and into social issues that perhaps haven't been discussed thoroughly. If you don't keep an open mind, you simply close the door. I don't ever want to close the door to my mind."

"Amen to that," Shante said. "I know exactly where you're going with this. It happens all the time, not just in politics, but in everyday life. You could be sitting there with a friend, and all of a sudden you're discussing a subject that you largely disagree on. Then you get uncomfortable. People get offended. Either you start arguing, or you just shut up and let the other person think that you agree with them, or maybe you just agree to disagree."

"Yeah," Marcus said with a smile. "What I usually say to avoid exhausting the issue is, 'I don't necessarily agree with you, but I hear what you're saying, and I'll think more in depth about it in the future.' "

"I wish everybody had that attitude," Shante said.

"But, getting back to what I was saying about my title. Some people believe that the playing field is level in terms of opportunities. One main question came to my mind. Do discrimination and racism exist? If they do, how and where do they exist? And what are their effects? I thought about something I saw on the news about a school out west. Some parents and community members objected to naming the school after Dr. Martin Luther King. Because of his race, some were afraid that their children wouldn't get into certain colleges if they came from a high school named after Dr. King. Now, to me, that spoke volumes."

Shante nodded as she added more soy sauce to her rice. Marcus went on. "Then I thought about integration, and how the schools were integrated to help level the playing field academically. But once we integrated the school system, there was no integration of the society at large. Nobody integrated the banks, the government, the judicial system, the corporate world. We all know that integrating the schools didn't solve the problems. Some people silently rebelled against it and adversely affected the students in terms of their self-esteem and education. And some of those who didn't intentionally rebel continued to feel as though they were superior, because that was what they were accustomed to believing."

"I know *that's* right," Shante said. Shante and Marcus were including some of their own experiences as black children growing up in the seventies and eighties. "Those misguided people went into the classrooms and taught the children according to what they believed the children were capable of learning. Often times, if you were from a low-income or minority family, you weren't given the same opportunities early on."

"It still happens," Marcus said. Then he smiled as he recalled how Shante used to pretend to be a schoolteacher when they were little. She used to be so bossy, but she sure was cute.

"I know it still happens," Shante said. "And what's so sad about it is that it hurts the children. They're smart enough to recognize these beliefs that others have about their abilities."

"That's why," he said, "it's so important for parents to play an active role at their children's school. I just like to sit back and visualize the world as one big family working together to support one another."

Shante smiled as she thought of the strong passion they shared for the welfare of children. She knew it had been hard for Marcus growing up without a father around. And now he was concerned about Ashley, and the fact that Cindy didn't pay her enough attention.

"If I adopted three children," he said, "one black, one white, and one Asian, I would want all three of my children to have equal opportunities."

"I understand," Shante said. "If you had two pieces of bread, or two apples or whatever, and three equally hungry children, you would divide the bread evenly."

"Right! It's that simple." He sat up taller in the chair. "There was a minority professor, Conrad, who was busy working to end affirmative action, even though he himself had benefited from it." Shante nodded as she ate. "He's entitled to his opinion, but some minorities became angry with him and said he was discriminating against his own race. He was against admitting a small percentage of women and minorities into prestigious universities unless their test scores were in the top five percentile. To me, test scores often measure exposure of the person taking the test, not intelligence, potential, compassion, patience, common sense. The person with the lower score might be the very one who has the mental capacity, determination, insight, creativity, or whatever, to discover a cure for a deadly disease, or a plan to help save the earth from destruction by man."

"Testing is important, though," Shante said.

"I know. It's often necessary, but intelligence can't be determined by test scores alone. Intelligence is something much broader than any test."

"True." Shante nodded.

"So, after thinking about all that, I tried to look at this subject from all angles. And that's how I came up with the title, 'Integrating Racism.' I thought about how discrimination really knows no boundaries. Racism is an integral part of the society, existing not only among people of different races and religions, but also among people of the same race. I thought of the fighting between races all over the world. I thought that if we all step back and take a look at this, maybe we can begin to see how, as individuals, we might be contributing to this chaos. Then, hopefully, with love in our hearts and respect for differences, we can learn to live side by side in harmony and begin to combat these problems. I mean, we all have the same basic needs."

"No doubt." Shante liked seeing Marcus so excited about his projects. She hoped his drinking had subsided.

Marcus sighed. "Well, we know there are no easy answers. We just need to work together to extinguish the flames of racism and discrimination that people from all races have been a victim of. And as long as that's the case, we need to prepare all children, all races, from all walks of life, to succeed in the face of these problems and to know how to help make the world a better place for everybody."

"Yes," Shante agreed. "I think the best way to do that is to guide them in a positive way to have high self-esteem and believe in themselves. We need to educate them about all the people—Black, White, Native American—all the people that have worked hard, and even died, to make a positive difference. They can learn from these people. I think schools are making good progress in this area."

They looked at each other and suddenly had the same thought. Shante came out of her seat and Marcus pushed his chair away from the table. He reached out to her as she sat on his lap. "I love you," he whispered just before their lips met.

Serena was in the middle of her solo rehearsal when Nathan walked into the theater. As he stood in the dark aisle, he was overcome by her. Her voice was so enchanting, almost as pleasing as her beauty. A fascinating woman, he thought. No one had a greater wish than he. "I wish I had one more chance with Serena," he said under this breath. "I wouldn't blow it this time. I'd spend the rest of my life making her happy."

Nathan became aroused as he listened to the sweet sound of Serena's voice. How lovely, he thought, admiring her sheer, sleeveless, light purple dress with the sweetheart neckline. She was perched on a stool and leaning forward slightly—intent on the song. He listened carefully to the words in the ballad:

You're the one for me.
You are the one that I've been waiting for.
All my life, I searched for something real,
Wanting more, needing more.
Suddenly, there you were before my eyes.
Magic man, I'll never leave this magic ride,
Filled with love,
And I'll always want you by my side.
You and I, together as one.
You and I together as one.

As Serena sang the final note, Nathan walked a few steps closer and into the light from the stage. Serena couldn't help but notice him.

Ollie stood in the aisle next to Nathan. "Marvelous," he said.

Nathan extended his hand toward Ollie. "Hello, I'm Nathan Whitaker."

Ollie shook Nathan's hand. "Olivier Reneau. Just call me Ollie, everyone else does. Serena told me you might stop by."

"Serena and I go way back," Nathan said.

"She's fabulous. We met five years ago on *A Woman's Reign*," Ollie said. "This play is a spin-off of *A Woman's Reign*, so I had to have her back."

Nathan nodded.

"Again, it was a pleasure," Ollie said before going backstage. Ollie watched as Serena stepped down from the stage and approached Nathan.

Serena was radiant. She took a deep breath. "Hi."

"Hello," said Nathan, gazing lovingly into her eyes. "That was beautiful!"

"Thank you," she said.

Then he started laughing softly.

"What is it?" She looked curiously at him. She thought she might have something on her face or maybe her hair was messed up.

"I was remembering when we first met. You were singing

that cowboy song. What was it? Something about having hog for dinner."

"Pig feet." Serena corrected him. She smiled. "Well, it was a job."

"Yeah, and you were great at it. And what was that dance you were doing?"

"It's called clogging," she said.

"Yeah that's it."

Their expressions turned serious and they were once again transfixed by one another.

Ollie interrupted from backstage. "Serena! Someone's on the telephone for you."

"I have to go now, but I'll call you." Serena backed away and waved goodbye before turning and heading backstage.

It was Julian on the telephone. "Hi, Serena. I have to go out of town on business for a few days."

"Again?"

"Yeah, again, Serena."

"When are you leaving?"

"In about an hour."

"An hour!" she said.

"Yes, I got a chance to get a good deal on some land. If I don't act quickly, it could be gone."

"I had something I wanted to talk to you about," she said.

"Can't it wait?"

"Yes, I suppose so. Where are you going?" she asked.

"Chicago. I'll call you tonight and let you know where I'm staying."

"Okay, Julian. Take care."

Ollie approached the dressing room. "Serena?"

She raised her brows. "Yes?"

"I want to talk to you," he said, placing his hands on her shoulders. "I know all about Nadine. I know how she's been treating you. Why didn't you tell me?"

"It's really no big deal," Serena responded. "It's probably just her personality."

"She's creating a hostile work environment, and I'm prepared to fire her. Nadine is apparently more malicious than you real-ize."

"I think she needs this job," Serena said.

"Well, if she does, she needs to start acting like it."

"Don't fire her because of me. Talk to her first, and see if she's willing to be fair."

"Kid, Nadine's overall attitude is a problem. None of us need this around here. I've talked to some of the others and they agree. I'm going to talk to Nadine about it, and if it continues, she's out the door."

Serena looked concerned. "Okay, Ollie."

Serena returned home from work at nine-thirty that night. She went in the kitchen and fixed herself a salad. The salad wasn't very tasty because she was out of everything except lettuce and carrots. She took two bites and tossed it in the trash can.

She went upstairs and ran a hot bubble bath. Afterwards she toweled dry and opened a jar of Venenzia body cream. She thought it smelled so incredibly good as she rubbed it all over her body.

As Serena rubbed the cream over her feet, she thought back in time. She had to wear orthopedic shoes when she was little, because of low arches. She thought that she would never be able to dance professionally, for she could sometimes feel the pain of her arches slipping more. But in college, whenever Serena slid her tired feet out of her shoes, Nathan would instinctively take hold of them and massage them gently. Serena smiled as she re-membered this. Then she climbed into bed, enjoying the feel of the soft sheets against her nude body. She lay there, still think-ing of Nathan. She thought about the first time they had held hands and kissed. To be so deeply and completely in love was something that had been missing in her life for many years. See-ing Nathan had made her realize this even more.

When the phone rang, Serena was already half asleep. "Hello," she whispered into the receiver.

"Oh, you're in bed," Julian said.

"Uh huh."

"Write this down."

"Write what down?" she said.

"Where I'm staying."

"That's okay, I can remember. Just tell me."

"I'm staying at the Hyatt, on Wacker."

"The Hyatt, on Wacker," she mumbled. "Okay."

"What did you want to tell me earlier?" Julian asked.

"It's not important." Serena yawned. "I'll tell ya la—"

Julian interrupted, "I'll see you in a few days," he said, then he hung up.

Marcus was late getting to Shante's apartment. He used the key Shante had given him and quietly entered. Shante was lying awake in bed when she heard the door creak. She got up and walked to the bedroom window. There was a glare on the pane. The street light was shining and there were drops of rain still on the window from an earlier drizzle. Beyond the glare she saw a black-and-white taxicab pulling away. She got back into bed, but anger got the best of her.

"This has got to stop," she said to herself. She got up and went in the living room. "Where have you been?" she asked loudly. "And if you tell me, 'in a meeting,' I'm going to scream."

"Shante, I'm fine," Marcus mumbled. "Please go back to bed."

"No! You're not fine! And neither am I! I can't, and I won't, take these excuses anymore. You've been drinking! This has to stop!"

Marcus sat on the sofa. He held his face in his hands and began sobbing.

Shante's heart sank as she watched him break down.

"I'm sorry, I'm so sorry," he said in a slurred voice.

Shante sat beside him. She took his hands from his face and placed them around her body. Then she laid his head on her breast and held it there. Her ivory gown was wet from his tears.

"First thing tomorrow we're going to get you some help," she said. Her voice trembled with fear—fear of losing the Marcus she had always known and loved.

"You don't deserve this," he hiccupped. "Hell, nobody deserves this. You, deserve the world. I'd give it to you if I could. You know that, don't you, Shante?"

"Marcus, you are my world," she said.

Marcus raised his head and looked into her eyes. He ran a hand down the side of her face. "My pretty angel. I love you Shante, for always."

Shante looked worried as they held each other. "For always, Marcus."

"Please," he said, "go back to bed. I'll be there soon."

Shante went into the bedroom and called Serena, waking her up for the second time that evening. Serena agreed to meet Shante and Marcus early the next morning at Shante's apartment. Then Serena called Dr. Bradford's answering service and left a message, asking for an emergency appointment the next day.

Marcus sat alone for a long while in the den, then staggered to the hall closet. He knew there was a loaded Colt .22 caliber semi-automatic pistol in a box on the top shelf. Shante's father had given her the handgun for protection.

"I might as well do it," he mumbled. "I might as well kill myself. I'm a loser, always frontin' a winner. What do I know about anything? All I do is hurt Shante. It's just a matter of time before she leaves me."

He reached up on the shelf to retrieve the box. Piles of clothes tumbled down on his head. He swung his arms wildly, freeing himself from the clothes.

In his drunken state he tried to neatly fold the clothes back. After a few unsuccessful attempts, he gave up and left the clothes piled on the floor. Then he spotted the box with the handgun inside. For a brief moment, visions of his father's face flashed before him. He blinked hard. Then he took the box down and opened it. He looked at the gun. "One second and it will all be over," he said.

"What's taking him so long?" Shante said as she lay in bed.

"Marcus!" she called. "What are you doing? I'm waiting for you."

"Marcus's eyes widened like he had just stuck his finger in an electrical socket. He felt his heart leap into his throat. Quickly he put the top back on the shoebox and the gun back on the shelf. "I'll be right there," he yelled. Hearing Shante's call had literally sobered him.

"God, what was I thinking?" he asked himself as he entered the bathroom. He brushed his teeth, undressed, and climbed into bed. He caressed Shante delicately and kissed the back of her neck. "I'm the biggest fool," he said.

Shante patted his hand as he wrapped his arm around her waist.

"I have to quit this shit," he said to himself. "I can't ever let this happen again. God help me."

❖

Thirteen

*W*hen Serena arrived at Shante's place the next morning, it was barely daylight. The sky was gray with a fine mist. But the birds were whistling and chirping, and their merry sounds gave Serena a positive boost as she watched the paperboy delivering newspapers.

Shante and Marcus were waiting for her. After hugs, they all settled in the den with steaming cups of coffee. Serena told Shante and Marcus about Dr. Bradford and the treatment center. "I met Dr. Bradford at a fund raiser for the performing arts. He explained his work and his role at the center. He told me that his wife was a theater lover, so I arranged for them to get VIP passes, and we've gotten to know each other pretty well. He told me that if I ever need his services, or anything, to let him know. I think he can be a real help to you, Marcus."

Marcus seemed uneasy as he listened. His hands trembled and he squeezed them.

"He's a nice guy," Serena assured him. "You'll like him. I

checked with his office this morning. He can see you first thing today."

"Well," Marcus said, "let's go."

Serena drove her Lexus, with Marcus and Shante following in his Jeep. An hour later, they arrived at the treatment center in the New Jersey suburbs. It was a beautifully designed brick, two-story building, surrounded by trees and a large lawn. Behind the building were picnic tables and a walking trail that led to a small lake.

Shante and Serena sat tense and quiet outside Dr. Bradford's office. "He's been in there for over an hour," Shante said looking at Serena with concern.

"Dr. Bradford is a very thorough," Serena responded. "I recommended him to a colleague of mine who became addicted to pain killers. She praised him. She said he spent a lot of time with her."

Marcus sat in Dr. Bradford's office, listening carefully. The portly doctor talked to Marcus about how alcohol acts as a depressant in the body. "Alcoholism is a disease, and it should be treated as such," Dr. Bradford said in a gravelly voice. "Understand, Marcus, that you have to give this the same care you would if you were suffering from any other disease."

"I want to get well, and I want to stay well," Marcus said.

"That's just what I wanted to hear. Think of it this way—if you had heart disease, would you turn down life-saving treatment? Would you hesitate to save your life?"

"No," Marcus answered.

"No, you wouldn't. You would follow the recommendations of the medical staff and cooperate fully in order to get and stay well. That's what is needed for your recovery. It's a life-long commitment. I want to keep you here for at least a few weeks. While you're here, you'll undergo medical and psychological treatment. There will be holistic therapy and spiritual meetings every night. I'll also want to schedule a substantial amount of cognitive therapy. We're going to try to find out what treatment works best for you. You need to be able to recognize the warning signals that could be indicative of a possible relapse . . ."

Marcus's mind was racing. How am I going to tell him I can't stay, he thought. He started fidgeting, then he spoke. "I can't stay, but I'll come back every day. I have responsibilities. I have a daughter and I . . ."

Dr. Bradford stood and walked to the door. He opened it and motioned Shante to come inside, then closed the door behind her. He returned to his desk. "Have a seat, Miss . . ."

"Peyton. Shante Peyton."

"Yes, Miss Peyton. Have a seat next to Marcus. I've told Marcus that he needs to remain here at the center for two, three weeks, maybe longer . . ."

While Dr. Bradford talked, Marcus stared straight ahead, like a scared little boy. He sat with his hands tucked in the tight pockets of his blue jeans.

"Your first responsibility has to be getting well," Dr. Bradford said. "You must take care of yourself before you can properly care for your daughter or anyone else. Maybe you'd like to make some phone calls to get your affairs in order."

"I can help take care of everything," Shante said.

"Very good," said Dr. Bradford.

They returned to the waiting room, where Serena was half-heartedly flipping through a magazine. She stood slowly as Marcus approached. He kissed her cheek. "Thank you, Serena."

Serena looked into his eyes and held his hands. "You know how much you both mean to me. Everything will be fine, don't worry."

Marcus glanced over at Shante, who was still talking to Dr. Bradford. "Take care of her while I'm in here," he told Serena. "She's really hurting. She's scared. She's trying to be strong for me."

"I will," Serena said. "You just focus on taking care of yourself."

Marcus nodded and walked toward the lobby to make his arrangements. Serena thanked Dr. Bradford before he left the waiting area, then she hugged Shante.

"Thank you for always being here when I need you," Shante said.

Serena felt like she had known Shante and Marcus her entire life. "You and Marcus mean so much to me. I'm just glad you realized that I would want to be here for you."

Anxiety overwhelmed Marcus as he approached the arc-shaped information desk. He used the telephone to call his mother, Lillie Mae, in Brooklyn. She was shocked to hear her only child calling her from a treatment center. After reassuring her as best he could, he explained everything that had happened to him. "If you need help with Ashley, call Shante," he said.

"We'll work it out, son. Please take care of yourself."

"I will, Mama. Goodbye."

Lillie Mae sat down at her kitchen table, still dressed in her robe and drinking a cup of coffee, though it was late afternoon. Her dark hair was graying and pulled back in a bun. She had a hard time accepting that Marcus was in trouble. She thought of Shante. "That girl is one more sweet child," she said to herself stressing almost every word with her southern accent. "And she's so loyal to my son." Lillie Mae shook her head as the steam from her coffee rose against her high cheekbones and dark skin. She took a few sips and her thoughts turned to Ashley's mother Cindy, and how Cindy had been in and out of Ashley's life since she was born. At least Marcus didn't have to worry about fighting for custody, she thought. And Cindy *does* keep Ashley one night a week when she's in town. But her top priority seems to be herself, and chasing behind whatever man she gets involved with. She can't seem to handle more than a few minutes without a man. Yes, Lord. Thank God for Shante.

When Shante returned home that evening, she took out a small photo album. In the album, she kept pictures of only herself and Marcus. She focused her attention on a picture of them as children standing in front of a church, and she smiled softly.

Shante and Marcus had attended Mount Moriah Baptist Church together as children. The small white wooden structure had no air conditioning, but it was a cherished place of worship nevertheless. Mount Pilot towered over the church and their hometown. Shante often told stories about how she and Marcus used to sneak out of church to play and to admire the spectacular mountain.

Shante let out a little laugh as she thought of some of her and Marcus's other experiences. They used to play in the dirt and make mud pies. A few times they actually put the mixture inside their bottom lips, pretending to be like Teets Sersy, their mutual baby sitter, who always had snuff in her mouth. By putting the mud inside their lower lips, she and Marcus could spit the dirt out a little at a time, just the way Teets did her snuff.

Every summer, both children would wake up to the smell of honeysuckle and the sound of the whippoorwill. Outside, they'd imitate the whippoorwill, suck the juice from the honeysuckle, play in the creeks and navigate the woods behind their homes—discovering the many wonders of the forest.

Whenever they got tired or hungry, they'd run to Shante's seventy-five year old grandmother's house for water and candy. Maxine always kept a can of hard candy under her bed. Maxine was concerned about Marcus and Shante roaming around and getting into seemingly everything both in and out of sight. "Stay out of those woods with that boy!" she'd yell. "And get some pants on!"

Maxine was an able, determined woman who did everything for herself, including chopping her own firewood. Shante and Marcus learned a lot from her strong personality. She'd had several strokes, and her right hand was stuck in a fist position. She had no feeling in that hand, so she used it as a switch to hit Shante and Marcus on the head. Ducked low and running past her as fast as they could, the two would race into the kitchen for water, then straight into the bedroom for candy, and out the door they'd go. "Come back here," Maxine would yell. The doctors had told Maxine that she would never walk again after her last stroke, but she recovered almost completely. The exception was that right hand, and she had even found a way to put it to use.

Shante's smile twisted as she thought of the time she and Marcus had decided to pick some flowers for their mothers. They proudly and concurrently entered their side by side homes with fresh bundles of chiggers—yes, chiggers. Their mothers screamed simultaneously as Marcus and Shante set foot inside.

Shante had bites all over her back. Marcus wasn't as lucky—he had some on his privates. Shante had a sick frown on her face. Marcus cried to no one in particular as his mother doused him with alcohol.

Shante and Marcus remained very close over the next six years, until Shante's family moved to San Francisco. They kept in touch for a while through letters. But they lost contact when Lillie Mae and Marcus moved to Brooklyn, three years later. They lived with Lillie Mae's older sister, who was a widow and quite ill. Lillie Mae was a housekeeper, and she always had to struggle to take care of Marcus. Living with her sister meant no mortgage or rent payment. This enabled her to save money for Marcus's education.

Marcus's father, Ralph, had gotten Lillie Mae and another woman pregnant around the same time. He married the other woman, leaving Lillie Mae alone to care for her baby. Ralph didn't take much interest in Marcus when Marcus was growing up. In addition, Ralph's wife didn't want him to communicate too often with Lillie Mae, so Marcus only got to see his father and his half-siblings occasionally.

After Lillie Mae moved to Brooklyn, when Marcus was sixteen, she frequently thought of Shante. She had always been fond of her and began to wonder where she was and what she was doing. When Marcus got involved with Cindy and Cindy got pregnant with Ashley out of wedlock during his senior year of college, Lillie Mae began to think even more about Shante. "Cindy is so trifling," she would say. "Why couldn't he have found someone nice like Shante?"

So in 1991, Lillie Mae called around until she found Shante. Shante was twenty-four and had just graduated from San Francisco State with a degree in education and a minor in mechanical engineering. Lillie Mae was delighted to find out that Shante wasn't married. She told Shante that she had been thinking about her over the years and she also told her about Cindy.

Meanwhile, Marcus was in jail in South Africa. He had been arrested for participating in a non-violent protest against the apartheid government. He had gone there with some classmates from New York University and members of a peace movement. Marcus was also twenty-four. He and Shante had both worked part time to help pay their way through school; so as a result, it had taken them longer than the usual four years to finish.

After Marcus returned from South Africa, Lillie Mae told him that she had found Shante. Marcus was on a plane the next week, heading to California to see his childhood friend. Shante greeted him with a big smile. "Marcus, you look almost the same, except you're taller, of course."

Marcus answered slowly. "Well, you don't look the same at all," he said, with amazed eyes. She laughed at him as he looked her up and down with his mouth open. She was proud of her figure and he was obviously pleased at how she had turned out.

"Close your mouth," she said.

"Yes, ma'am," he said, pressing his lips together. They both grinned.

Marcus traveled to California to see Shante several times over the next year. They discovered that their friendship was as strong as ever. He told her all about New York, and how exciting he found it to be. He suggested that she come and visit, and if she liked it, she could move. He told her she could stay with Lillie Mae in Brooklyn until she found a job and saved some money.

After visiting New York one time, Shante was ready to move to the East Coast. Shante's father helped her get settled into an apartment in New Rochelle, not too far from Marcus's place in Mount Vernon.

It didn't take Shante long to find work. She got a job teaching school in White Plains. It was her first permanent teaching position and Shante was elated when she was hired. She had been a substitute teacher in California and had been waiting for a permanent position there.

In New York, Shante began spending more than she could afford of her own pay check to buy school supplies. She wanted the children to have the equipment she felt they needed, so she used her own money. When she expressed her concern about the lack of funding in her school, Marcus helped her organize a demonstration for equal funding for all public schools.

A year later, Marcus's and Shante's friendship began to grow into a romantic love neither of them could deny. Their souls seemed to be naturally connected. There was never any effort to establish or maintain a loving relationship. It was just there. What they had was unique. No matter what the problem, they had each other to count on.

Marcus and Shante slowly realized how effortless their affection for one another was. And their enduring friendship blossomed into a deep and abiding love.

When Serena returned home from the treatment center, she sat at her piano and played out some of her worry. She let her mind wander over all that had happened that day. She thought about how close Marcus and Shante had always been. "Please let him get well," she prayed as she pulled herself out of her reverie. Her thoughts shifted to Nathan, suddenly remembering that she had told him she would call.

Fourteen

athan was in his room at the Marriott, watching reruns of The Cosby Show and glancing off and on at the telephone, hoping it would ring. When it did, he struggled to let it ring twice. One-and-a half rings were all he could stand.

"Hello," Serena said softly.

Nathan was filled with joy the second he heard her voice. His body was as light and free as a bird. "I'm so glad you called. What are you doing right now?"

"I'm getting ready to cook dinner." She took some canned foods down from the kitchen cabinets. She still had not gone to the grocery store. She held the cordless telephone between her shoulder and cheek as she grabbed a dishrag and wiped the tops of the cans. "I just called to tell you that I'm sorry I didn't have more time to talk yesterday. Today I was with some friends who are having some problems, which kept me quite busy."

"Are they okay?" Nathan asked.

"Yes, I think everything will be fine. Thank you for asking."

"Are you eating alone?"

"Yes. Julian's out of town."

Nathan cringed at the mention of Julian's name. "Would you like company?"

There was silence as Serena looked wide-eyed around the big, quiet house. She thought, he wants to come here.

"Uh, you could come here," he said. "I'll come get you. We can have dinner together."

"Okay," she agreed, "but you don't need to come here. I'll drive myself. I can be there in about an hour."

"Great! I'll be waiting—and thank you."

Nathan stood in front of the mirror, surveying himself carefully before deciding to shower and change his clothes.

Serena entered the fancy hotel looking absolutely stunning. It was a warm evening and she wore a long silk dress with a faint floral pattern and matching high-heeled silk mules. Heads turned as she elegantly crossed the lobby. It was obvious to Nathan that he wasn't the only one who found her beauty exceptional. Like a fairy princess, she commanded everyone's attention in the room. He knew it would be unusual for anyone not to notice her. He thought, it really doesn't matter much what she wears. She could have on old blue jeans and a rag on her head and she'd still be the most beautiful woman there is to me. It isn't just her outer beauty. If it were to fade for some reason, it would still be there in my eyes. She's the sweetest, most loving person, I've ever known.

He knew thirteen years ago that she was the woman he wanted to spend the rest of his life with. He knew, deep in his heart, that nothing had changed.

They greeted each other before taking the elevator to the Encore Restaurant on the eighth floor. Serena was ravenous. The only thing she had eaten all day was some chocolate from a vending machine at the treatment center. As the hostess seated them, a tiny wrinkle appeared in Serena's forehead. *He's so sexy. And what kind of cologne is he wearing? He smells so delicious.* She looked down at the menu.

Then she glanced up at Nathan, noticing that he had been staring at her. *The way he's looking at me makes me feel so beautiful—the way I felt years ago, when we first met.* She felt like she had just found a treasure chest filled with love, peace, and happiness.

"Remember the first time I broke up with you, in high school?" she asked.

"I recall every time you broke up with me." They laughed.

"Actually, I'm talking about the time I told you that I'd been sneaking out."

"Yes, I do. Lou wouldn't let you date."

"I was seventeen and he told me to wait until I was eighteen. He said, 'Look at all these young girls having babies.' I started crying and he said, 'See how mature you are, and you want to date.' I felt so humiliated and confined. To be honest with you, Nathan, I think that was one reason why I pushed you away. When I told you I needed space, I was starting to feel like I did when my dad wouldn't let go." Nathan listened with interest and Serena went on. "Mom tried to reason with him. He said to her, 'I don't want to hear it, Caroline.' She knew you were special because I'd never asked to date before. She helped me sneak out. But I got tired of keeping secrets and I didn't want to cause problems for Mom. When I finally confessed to you that I had been seeing you without my father's permission, you promised to wait for me, and you did. That was so sweet."

Nathan nodded and recalled that when their paths met again four months later, Serena was a cheerleader at Hardaway High School in her hometown of Columbus, Georgia. He was on the football team at Warner Robins—a rival school. He made three touchdowns on that crisp autumn night in Macon. He was trying hard to impress Serena. The football field was covered with mud and so was he. The smell of hot cocoa filled the air as the band played and the crowd cheered.

"Remember when I was playing football and I was covered in mud?" he asked. "I mean, mud was everywhere, and I asked you for a date. I had no idea I had that much mud on me. When I went in the locker room and saw myself in the mirror, I was so embarrassed."

Serena giggled. "You were totally saturated. I just saw these white eyeballs."

"I couldn't believe I asked you out looking like that, and you said, yes."

"Only you could do that," Serena said, rendering him helpless with a warm smile.

There she goes again, he thought, making me feel like a king, just the way she used to.

"We thought we were hot stuff at the prom, didn't we?" she said.

"We were," Nathan bragged. "I'll never forget that gown you wore. It was a dark pink color."

"Yes, you're right! It was rose colored. I was so skinny that if the wind had blown hard, I would have vanished. Pouf, I would have disappeared into the night."

They laughed.

"I remember breaking up with you two weeks before the prom because I'd heard that you had been seen with someone else," she said.

"What you heard wasn't true. Just jealous people trying to come between us."

"I didn't eat for two weeks," she said, before laughing at the thought of starving herself for any reason.

Nathan didn't laugh. "Two weeks is a long time, Serena." He looked concerned.

"Oh, but it's true. The only thing I ate was a small bite of a Baby Ruth bar. I simply could not eat anything, no matter how hard I tried. I had absolutely no appetite."

"You called me and said—loudly and angrily—'I've already got my dress, and it's too late to find another date, so we're going!' "

"Serena placed her hand on her left cheek, looking slightly

embarrassed. It's a good thing you agreed to go. I would have starved myself to death, I guess."

"Caroline had mentioned that you could be quite dramatic at times," Nathan said, smiling.

"I'm not surprised. She used to tell people that I was going to be an actor because I was *so* dramatic. I must admit, the stage is a good place to release my drama."

They were still smiling at each other when their dinner arrived. The pianist played soft romantic music as they ate.

"I remember everything," Nathan said, reaching across the table and holding Serena's hand.

Already full after eating a third of her meal, Serena pushed her plate to the side.

"Thank you for inviting me," Serena said. "I really didn't want to eat alone, and I can't think of any better company than you. To me this is a blessing, a miracle, that we're sitting here together, after so long."

Hearing her say those words was a complete turn-on for Nathan. He felt himself become aroused. He, too, believed that it was a miracle that they were spending an evening together. "If I could only choose one person in the world to hear say that, I'd choose you, Serena. Thank you."

After a few moments of glowing smiles, Serena said, "I have to go now. It's getting late."

"Let me follow you home."

Serena looked a little surprised. "Oh, no, thank you. There's no need for that, really."

"It's dark, and I don't want you entering your house alone," Nathan said.

"I do it all the time."

"Please," he insisted. "You were nice enough to come here, and I'd just feel better if you let me follow you home. It's the least I can do."

Serena accepted, appreciative of his concern.

Minutes later they were crossing the Queensborough Bridge.

Serena pulled her car into her driveway, with Nathan right behind her in the Cadillac he had rented. He jumped out of his car and was opening Serena's car door before she had time to take the keys out of the ignition.

He walked her to the door. As she clicked the key in the lock, he said, "Tomorrow is my last day here." Serena turned and looked at him with curious eyes. He went on. "I know it's asking a lot, and I'll understand if the answer is no."

Is he going to ask me if he can come inside? If he is, the answer will be no. Serena was tempted to invite Nathan in. But she thought it would be wrong, or improper, because of her strict upbringing and the obvious feelings they shared for each other.

"Can I see you tomorrow?" Nathan asked. "I know someone in Queens who owns a boat. I thought it would be fun to go for a ride. We could meet at the pier in the morning." He reached in his pocket, pulled out a piece of paper with an address on it, and handed it to her. "Say you'll come, please."

"I'll bring lunch," she said, opening the door.

Nathan wanted to hold her so badly. But he knew the kind of woman she was, and he didn't want to scare her away. He held back his temptations.

"I'll see you in the morning," she said.

"I'll see you in the morning," he said.

She wiggled her fingers at him before closing the door. Nathan took a deep breath and looked up at the stars. He drove away a happy man, knowing he would see Serena in just a few hours.

As soon as Nathan pulled away from the driveway, Serena went back out to the grocery store. She stayed up until midnight cooking for the picnic. But she still looked fresh the next morning when she met Nathan at the pier. Her flowery, short-sleeved sun dress rustled in the breeze, while her dark shades gave her an exotic look.

Serena watched Nathan standing on the pier. As the wind blew, his clothes whipped around him giving her a good view of his muscular physique. She studied his sharp facial features, mahogany skin, and strong jaw line. She thought he looked like a beautiful piece of art.

"Hi," she said, waving as she approached the pier.

As they left the dock, Serena marveled at the grand view of Manhattan. It was a warm morning and the sun peeped eagerly from behind the clouds. Serena liked the feel of the wind blowing against her skin.

"Go faster," she said as she looked out at the Atlantic.

While Serena watched the ocean, Nathan surreptitiously studied her graceful legs where they protruded through the slits in her dress. He visualized touching her and holding her in his arms the way he once had. If I ever get the chance to pleasure her, she will be mine forever, he thought.

They spent most of the morning on the Atlantic before heading back to the pier. It was now much warmer and Serena's once perfect hair had become tousled in the wind. Nathan wanted to touch it as he studied the outline of her oval face. As the sun shone down it brought the few light-brown freckles on her slightly upturned nose into clear view. Nathan smiled as he watched her remove the food from the basket.

Serena had grilled a marinated chicken, baked some fresh bread, tossed a pasta salad, and even made fresh-squeezed lemonade. For desert, she had brought peanut butter cookies. She remembered that peanut butter cookies used to be Nathan's favorite. The picnic table grew crowded with all the food.

"You didn't have to cook all of this, Serena. I would have gladly taken you out. I thought you were going to make sandwiches," Nathan said.

Serena smiled as she removed the paper plates and plastic forks from the basket and placed them on the wooden picnic table.

"Remember, you used to say, 'Nathan, you eat like a pig,' " he said, moving his head from side to side and speaking in a girlish voice.

"Of course I remember," she said with a giggle. "Why do you think I brought all of this food?"

Nathan laughed. "This is delicious, Serena."

"Good."

He found himself staring again. He couldn't take his eyes off of her. He was afraid that if he did, she would be gone.

As they were finishing their lunch, Nathan suddenly said, "I still love you."

"Nathan, I'm married."

"Are you happy with him? It doesn't matter how long you've been with him, nobody knows you as well as I do."

"I . . . I, I'm committed to my marriage, of course . . . I'm very lucky. I have everything." Her voice quivered and her eyes grew misty. "I have to go now." She was afraid that if she stayed any longer, her feelings would become all too obvious. "Thank you so much for today." She turned to walk away, leaving her picnic basket behind.

"Wait!" he said.

She stopped, but didn't turn to face him. He moved closer until his hard throbbing body pressed against her. He placed his face against her soft hair. She turned around and they held each other closely.

"Do you really have everything?" he whispered.

"We can't have everything we want." She backed away from him. "We can be friends." She smiled with teary eyes.

"Okay, Serena. But I have this funny feeling that no matter what you give, I'll always want more."

"I'm so sorry, Nathan. That's all I can give you." She turned and walked away.

Nathan choked back his tears. His emotions twisted and tangled. *How could this be happening?* As he watched her walk away, he felt like he was losing her all over again.

Fifteen

The next morning Nathan was back in Washington sitting at his desk in the Department of Interior. He appeared to be in a hypnotic state. "It's my fault," he muttered.

"What's your fault?" Brandi asked as she approached. She leaned against the chair in front of Nathan's desk.

"I knew she was married, but I thought I could handle it," he said, staring blankly ahead.

"You can't stay away from her, can you?"

He looked at Brandi. "It's hard, but I have to. If I push her too far, she won't ever see me again. I continuously ask myself, how can I have these feelings for her after all this time."

"True love abides, remember? That's what you told me and Justice."

"That's it," Nathan responded. "Even when I was working in Boston and traveling all over, she was on my mind and in my heart. It didn't matter where I went or who I met along the way, she was with me. And in the back of my mind, I always believed we'd be together one day. I prayed to God that one day she'd need me again."

Nathan thought back to that day in Boston when he finally realized that Serena was not coming back to him. He reminisced about the months that followed and how he had turned to partying and other women in a futile attempt to try to stop thinking about her. Those wild nights didn't change anything. It wasn't long before he realized that, no matter what he did to try to forget Serena, it was an impossible task.

How could I forget the most fascinating person on earth, he had thought. It doesn't matter where I go or what I do. There will always be Serena.

Her image remained fundamental in his mind. He realized that his involvement with other women was a vain attempt to find another Serena Hope Taylor. It was as though she had poured the very foundation upon which his mind was built. She and only she had the formula, the blueprint, yes, the key to his heart and soul. More and more he learned that the memories and love would never fade. Serena was to Nathan as the sunrise is to daylight. She was his everything. He believed in his heart that one day they would be together; until then, he would have to go on without her, somehow.

Nathan's thoughts forwarded to shortly after he'd met and married Alysee, and he said, "Whenever I went to Georgia to visit my parents, I'd ride by Serena's house, hoping to get a glimpse of her. I knew she was involved with someone, and I was married, but I hoped for the chance to see her face. Seeing her at the Reflecting Pool was more than a coincidence. I believe it was God answering my prayers. We were meant to be together."

"Don't obsess about this, Nathan. It's a beautiful story, but you just got out of an unhappy marriage. You don't need any more problems."

"You're right, Brandi. She's married, and I have to respect her marriage." He put his hands over his face in a moment of distress. "I have to be reasonable."

"If it's meant for you to be with Serena, you will be. She knows how you feel, and where you are. Any woman would be lucky to have you."

"Thank you," he said, smiling faintly. "But I know the way she thinks. I'm afraid she will stay with him out of obligation, rather than love." He thought about her parents' divorce and the powerful affect it had on her. He knew it would be extremely difficult for her to leave her marriage, even if she was unhappy in it. "I know she still loves me. I can see it in her eyes."

"Just be careful," Brandi warned. "I don't want to see you get hurt."

"It's too late. I'm already hurting. But, as the saying goes, it's better to have loved and lost, than never to have loved at all."

Brandi put her hands on his shoulders and squeezed firmly. "Ah," Nathan said, "that feels good."

She patted his shoulder. "Let's get to work now. You need to keep busy."

Later that morning, General Saxon stopped by Nathan's office. The first thing Nathan noticed was the shine on the General's shoes. General Saxon's presence was powerful and charismatic and he proudly wore numerous ribbons as well as the one star insignia on his crisp green uniform. "Nathan Whitaker," the brown-skinned curly headed general said in a husky voice as he extended his hand.

Nathan stood and shook General Saxon's hand. "Please sit down," Nathan said. "What brings you here?"

"I only have a few minutes, Nathan. I have to be at a meeting at the Pentagon in twenty minutes. I came to ask you a big favor. I need you to join a team of engineers on a trip to the Middle East. We need you in Saudi Arabia and Kuwait to help assess the damage to the environment caused by the Gulf War." General Saxon went on to name some engineers from the Environmental Protection Agency, the Pentagon, and the Department of Agriculture who would be taking the trip too.

Nathan frowned. "That war was over years ago. It's a shame that the environment is still suffering."

"We need you to help determine what techniques should be used at this stage of the disaster, and to develop a plan to help clean up the mess. You'll need to spend a week or two over there initially."

"I'll be glad to help in any way I can," Nathan said. "When do I leave?"

"In a few days. And I apologize for the short notice." General Saxon handed Nathan a list of names to contact once in Saudi Arabia and promised to touch base the next day.

Nathan called his son, Devan, as soon as he arrived home that evening.

"Daddy! Daddy!" Devan cried. "Mommy—it's Daddy on the phone."

"How's my little strong man?" Nathan asked joyfully.

"F-i-i-i-ne," Devan answered. He liked being called little strong man. It made him feel special—young, but strong like his daddy. "I just got back from soccer practice."

Nathan thought how sweet and innocent Devan's voice sounded. "Good for you! Devan. I need to talk to your mother for a minute, okay?"

Nathan explained to Alysse that he had to take a trip to Saudi Arabia in a couple of days. Then he asked, "Can I come and get Devan? I know this is not the regular schedule, but I'd like to spend time with him before I leave."

She hesitated before finally agreeing. "I'll be there in about an hour," Nathan said.

When Nathan arrived, he greeted Alysse with a friendly hug, as he usually did. It was important to both him and Alysse that Devan see with his own eyes that they cared about one another, even though they were no longer married. In fact, after the divorce, Nathan and Alysse had taken great care in explaining to Devan that they would always be a family who cared about each other, and that their divorce was in no way his fault. Devan seemed happy that his parents were often in the same room, yet no longer arguing.

"Hey, Daddy!" Devan said.

Nathan hugged Devan and rubbed the top of his head. Devan rushed out the door past Nathan and jumped in the car. Nathan arched his eyebrows as he watched Devan run past him. Then he looked at Alysse. Alysse smiled and shook her head as Nathan waved goodbye to her.

Nathan and Devan talked and laughed in the car. They started playing video games as soon as they arrived at his apartment. Nathan let Devan win once before beating him twice.

"You look cool, Devan," Nathan said. "Is that a new outfit?"

Devan pushed the buttons on the Nintendo and stared at the screen. "Yeah, Mom got it for me,"

Devan was always dressed neatly in designer clothes. Alysse often dressed him in suspenders, a neat shirt and slacks. But today he was wearing a casual denim outfit from the Gap.

"Son, you need to brush your teeth and get ready for bed."

"Can I have a snack first?" Devan jumped up from the floor and ran into the kitchen.

"Yes." Nathan shook his head. That's my boy, he thought.

Devan opened the refrigerator and grabbed three slices of cheese. Then he reached up into the cabinet and knocked down a box of crackers.

Nathan followed him into the kitchen. "Devan, put back a slice of that cheese. If you're still hungry, you can have some fruit."

"Okay, Dad."

After the snack, Nathan read Devan a bedtime story, just as he always did when they were together. Then Nathan gave the boy a goodnight hug before turning off the light.

In a tiny voice, Devan called out, "Daddy, do you have a girl-friend?"

Nathan turned the light back on. "No."

"Mommy had a date," Devan said. He lay in bed, propped on his elbow with his hand on his cheek. He looked at Nathan with wide eyes.

Nathan sat on the bed next to the boy. "How do you feel about that, Devan?"

"How do you feel about it, Daddy?" Devan shot back.

"I just want your mother to be happy."

"Me too." Devan smiled, relaxed his arm, and pulled the covers up to his chin. "Are you happy, Daddy?"

"I'm just fine, little strong man."

"I'm happy, too."

"Good. I'm happy you're happy."

"But at first I was afraid I wasn't going to see you anymore," Devan said.

Nathan was surprised. "Why did you think that? Because of the divorce?"

"One time I heard Mommy tell you that she was moving back to Newark. You told her that it would be difficult to see me if I was in New Jersey."

Nathan's heart foundered at the thought of Devan believing this for one moment. "That would never happen. I told you that I will always be with you. Devan, listen carefully, son. If she had taken you to the moon, I would have traveled there to see you. I would have built the spaceship myself, if I had to."

Devan laughed as he pictured Nathan in a self-made spaceship.

"I'm sorry you overheard that conversation," Nathan went on. "All of that has been permanently settled, so please don't ever worry about it again. Okay?"

"Okay, Daddy."

Nathan turned out the light.

The following evening, Devan had a soccer game at Lincoln Multi-Cultural Center. As Nathan found a seat on the bench, he peered at the overcast skies. It looked as if it was going to rain, and Nathan hoped that it would hold off until after the game.

The game began and Nathan watched calmly. Some of the parents sitting near him weren't so calm. They cheered and yelled loudly. Some were angry because the other team scored three goals in the first quarter.

Nathan sat on the bench wondering if Devan's team had enough time to catch up. "Go Hurricanes!" he yelled. "*GO, GO, GO*—a-ah darn." He glanced up at the scoreboard. Five to one, in favor of the Blazers. Devan's team just can't seem to get going, he thought. They're getting their tails kicked. "Man," he said under his breath, "this is messed up."

A few minutes later, Devan scored. Nathan rose to his feet. "He's pretty good at this game," he said to a man sitting next to him. Then he thrust a fist into the air. "Way to go Devan!" he yelled.

Devan looked over at Nathan. "Yes!" he said, with his arms in the air and his fists clenched.

The game was over a few minutes later. Devan's team shook hands with the winning team. Then Devan got his water bottle from the bench and ran across the field toward Nathan.

Nathan patted him on the shoulder. "Great game, son."

"We lost. I wish we had won," Devan said, as they headed toward the car.

"We would all like to win every game, but that would be unrealistic."

"The Blazers win all the time."

"It seems that way, son. It seems that way. But even the Blazers lose every now and then."

"Daddy?"

"Yeah, little strong man."

"We've lost every game."

"I'm sorry, Devan. But what's important is that, as a team, you guys worked together and did the best you could. You guys were great. You didn't give up. You fought to the very end. I like that. I believe that's just as important as winning. Things will get better. Just do your best and have fun. I really enjoyed watching you play."

Devan smiled in relief. He felt happy that Nathan wasn't disappointed.

"Let's get some ice cream," Nathan said.

"Yeah, Daddy, lets!"

Nathan drove to Carl's ice cream parlor. "I have to go out of town early in the morning," Nathan said as he parked the car.

"Where you going, Daddy?" Devan asked. He looked long-ingly at the people coming out of Carl's, licking their ice cream. Then he unbuckled his seat belt and gazed up at Nathan with his big, chestnut-brown eyes.

"Saudi Arabia," Nathan said. "I'll be over there for a week or two. I'll try to call you every night, but if I don't, it's because it's a long way away, and I'm going to be very busy."

"Okay. Come on, Daddy, let's go get the ice cream." Nathan smiled as he watched Devan eagerly get out of the car.

Since Nathan had to get up early the next morning, they chose to eat their ice cream on the ride home. Nathan got strawberry. Chocolate was Devan's choice and you could tell by the evidence all around his mouth. Nathan dripped ice cream on his shirt, and wondered why he ever wore white. Devan licked his ice-cream and a scoop fell onto the seat. Like father like son.

"Uh oh," he said, looking up at Nathan.

"That's okay. It was just an accident," Nathan said. He reached on the dash and handed Devan some more napkins. "We probably should have eaten in the restaurant."

"Yeah, that would have been best," Devan agreed, still lick-ing his ice cream vigorously.

Nathan rubbed Devan's head. "You're so smart."

Minutes later, they arrived at Nathan's apartment. "Devan, you need to shower, do your homework, and then go to bed. Your mother will be here early in the morning to take you to school. When I get back, I'm going to take you to the go-cart-track."

"Wow, that rules, Dad! We haven't done that in a long time. I like go-carts."

The following morning, Brandi drove up to Nathan's apart-ment in her candy apple red Jaguar, just as Alysse was backing away. Alysse blew her horn and Brandi waved as she walked to-ward Nathan's apartment. She knocked three times and Nathan opened the door.

"I'm ready," Nathan said. "I just need to get my wallet from the bedroom."

Brandi looked at the bare walls in Nathan's apartment. "When are you going to put some pictures on these walls?" she yelled into the bedroom.

"I plan on buying a house whenever I get the time to look for one," Nathan said as he came out of the room. "I'm just not much interested in decorating right now. I plan on hiring an interior decorator whenever I do buy a house."

"Oh. You all set?" she asked.

"Yeah, let's ride," he said.

Nathan loaded his luggage into Brandi's car and they left for Dulles airport. Rush hour traffic seemed heavier that morning. Nathan was glad they had left early because Brandi was patiently allowing other cars to cut in front of them.

"Make sure you call me as soon as you get to Saudi Arabia," Brandi said as she pulled in front of the busy airport terminal.

"I certainly will, Brandi." Nathan reached in her trunk to retrieve his luggage.

Brandi adjusted her ponytail, then slid her shades on top of her head. "The breeze is really picking up out here." She suddenly felt chilly as the wind rippled her white cotton, tie-front blouse.

"Yeah, woman. You better watch that skirt." As Nathan said that, a gust of wind lifted Brandi's skirt into the air, revealing her panties. They laughed as Brandi held down the pleated black skirt that stopped just above her knees.

"Tell Justice that I said we need to get together again real soon," Nathan said.

"Okay," Brandi said cheerfully as Nathan gathered his luggage and jacket. "We can double date. There's a comedy show in town called 'Defending The Caveman.' I'll see if I can get some tickets. Or maybe we can go see *Chicago*. Blues Alley would be nice. I'll call Monique."

"That's not necessary," Nathan said. "I appreciate it, though."

"It's no problem at all. She's been talking about you ever since my party."

Nathan listened, but it was obvious by his slight frown that he was only tolerating Brandi's zeal over fixing him up with Monique again. He couldn't discuss the matter right then, so he just smiled tiredly as a man pulled his car behind Brandi's and blew the horn. They waved goodbye.

During his flight to Saudi Arabia, Nathan fell asleep. He had a dream about Serena. In his dream, he and Serena were happily married. They lived in a big house. He was playing soccer in the yard with Devan. Serena was sitting on a blanket with a picnic basket and a pitcher of lemonade, watching. She was pregnant. They were happy.

"Sir. Sir." The flight attendant tapped him on his shoulder.

"Oh," he said, rubbing a hand down his face. "It was just a dream."

"Sir, you need to buckle up. We'll be landing shortly."

Sixteen

It was thundering, raining, and for June, unseasonably cold, as Julian pulled into the driveway. He had arrived back from Chicago earlier that day, but had stopped by his office first.

Serena stood by the window, looking out, as he entered the house. "Hi, Julian." She came over to him and greeted him with a kiss. The pink knit sweater and blue jeans she wore got wet and she caught a chill from their embrace.

"Hi. It's bad out there," Julian said.

"Yes, it is," she agreed. "It was lightning hard here earlier. The wind was howling ferociously. Come sit down."

Julian hung his black all-weather coat on the rack by the door, then sat next to Serena on the sofa. Serena reached for the flashlight on the coffee table. She flicked the on\off switch several times.

"Serena, I *like* for my flashlight to stay in my office," Julian said.

"I was afraid the power would go out," she said.

"Use the candles."

"I prefer the flashlight. But it's not working." She flicked the switch again.

"Did you check the batteries?" he asked.

"No."

Julian went into his office and came back with a pack of batteries. He sat in the chair across from Serena. "Give me the flashlight."

"That's okay. I'll do it," she said confidently, but she couldn't get the battery compartment open.

Julian gave her a dead look and held out his hand for the flashlight.

"It sounded like there was a tornado earlier. I started to go in the basement," she said as Julian put in the batteries.

"That's not very smart, Serena."

"What! That's what you're supposed to do."

"No, it's not. The house would fall down on top of you."

Serena looked stunned. "Well, what would you do?"

"I'd go outside."

"You would go outside?"

"Yeah, I'd go outside," he said.

"You'd run out in the middle of a tornado?"

"No!" he said angrily. "I'd go outside and run *from* the tornado."

"You can't run from a tornado," she said.

"Yeah you can. What do you think those tornado-chasing people do?"

"I think they chase tornados." Serena shook her head in disbelief at what Julian was saying. "And then of course they run from them because they've been chasing them. I wasn't speaking in terms of *chasing* tornados."

"There's lots of things I'd do," Julian said arrogantly.

"Like what?" she asked.

"I'd open up all the windows."

"I'd get away from the windows while you were standing there opening them."

Julian frowned. "When you open the windows, ya see, the

wind blows through and takes some of the pressure off the house."

"That makes *some* sense," she said.

"It makes more sense than going down into the basement."

Serena looked at him with a fake smile on her face. How can anyone . . . be . . . so stupid, she thought.

Boy she's dumb, he thought, returning her phony smile.

Maybe he's suffering from jet lag, or fatigue, she thought. He does work a lot. She decided to change the subject. "So how was your trip?"

"I bought some land on the South Side. I got an even better deal than I thought I was going to get. I'll show you all the paperwork tonight in my office. Did you miss me?"

"Yes," she said, fairly sincerely.

She stood, walked over to the stereo and turned on some music by Luther Vandross. She massaged Julian's shoulders while they listened to the music and Julian closed his eyes, moaning. "That feels good," he said. She did this for a while, then she began telling Julian everything that had happened concerning Shante and Marcus. He listened to less than half of what she said. Then she peered out the window. She was glad to see that the storm had ceased. "I'm going to call Shante and see how Marcus is doing."

Julian went into the office and began reading some real estate documents.

Shante told Serena that Marcus was doing well. "He is so courageous, Serena. Matter of fact, I just left him. I just walked through the door." She pulled off her black rain jacket. Raindrops dotted her face.

"I've been praying for you and Marcus," Serena said.

"We appreciate that. He's trying to adjust to being in a controlled environment. But he was in good spirits when I left him. Ashley and Lillie Mae were still there."

"I was getting ready to call him, but I think I'll wait till the morning," Serena said.

"It's best if you call him right before lunch, around eleven-thirty, or after one o'clock," Shante suggested. "He's usually in therapy between nine and eleven-thirty."

"Shante, why don't you come over for dinner?"

"I don't want to impose. Didn't Julian just get back from Chicago? Or is he back yet?"

"Julian," Serena called, "Will Shante be intruding on anything if she comes over?"

Julian walked out of the office. He nodded "yes" and yelled "no!" at the same time.

"See," Serena said.

"Serena," Shante said in a low voice. "Why did you do that? Of course he's going to say no."

"I really would like for you to come over. Come on."

Shante perked up. "Well, if you're sure."

They agreed on seven o'clock before saying goodbye.

"Julian, what would you like for dinner?"

"I just got home. I would like to spend some time alone this evening."

"Why didn't you say that earlier?"

"It should've been obvious, Serena."

"I'm sorry," she said. But she knew he wasn't going to say anything, so what was the point in being alone? And it wasn't obvious at all to Serena—not at this stage in the marriage. She thought spending time together to Julian meant being in the same house at the same time, saying nothing to each other, or satisfying his sexual desires. She felt that his real concern was that he might not have full control of her attention and emotions. *I think he feels powerful when he knows that, if he doesn't talk to me, I'll have no one else to talk to.*

She said, "We'll have some time together later on tonight, and next week." Julian didn't respond, and Serena went on. "I'm gonna fix smoked trout cakes with horseradish cream. It's Shante's favorite."

Julian brought his laptop computer from his office into the living room. He searched the Internet for land options while Serena prepared dinner.

The doorbell rang just as Serena was finishing up in the

kitchen. It was Shante and Ashley.

"Hi, Ashley." Serena bent and gave the girl a gentle squeeze. "What a pretty dress."

"Thank you," Ashley said. "My daddy likes it, too."

"I'm sure he does," Serena said.

Ashley skipped through the doorway, her pigtails flopping happily. She's such a pretty little girl, Serena thought.

Shante bounced in wearing a suede jacket, a long bone-colored skirt, and bone-colored mesh sling back pumps. Serena had managed to freshen up a bit before Shante arrived and was now wearing a long-sleeved blue and white space-dyed tee, and some comfortable black full-legged pants.

"Hi, Shante," Julian said. He sat his laptop on the coffee table, then stood and hugged her. "How is Marcus?"

"He's doing much better, thank you."

"Good."

"I'm glad that storm is over," Shante said as she pulled off her jacket and handed it to Julian.

"So am I," Serena said.

"That's one thing I don't like about my apartment—I don't have a basement."

Julian and Serena looked at each other.

Julian went back to scanning the Internet. He looked annoyed when Ashley ran over to the white sofa and put her feet up on it.

"She's so cute," Serena said to Shante.

"Isn't she? I know she's not mine, but she's a tomboy just like I used to be when I was little. She acts a lot like I used to." They smiled and Serena tapped Shante's arm. "So tell me about Marcus."

"Dr. Bradford said that Marcus's drinking problem was triggered by stress rather than a chemical imbalance," Shante said. "He said that Marcus worries about people more than he should. The doctor told him to slow down. He said one man can't save the world. He suggested that Marcus keep doing the work that makes him feel good, but he said that, emotionally, Marcus will have to back away some. He also told him that he needs to confront the issues involving his father."

Serena listened carefully as Shante continued talking. Meanwhile, Ashley had a small toy truck in her hand and she was making motor sounds as she drove it through the air. Ashley glanced over at Julian. Julian frowned, pointed to her feet, and then down to the floor. Ashley looked hard at Julian and took her feet halfway off the sofa.

A few minutes later, Ashley jumped up and ran over to Serena and Shante. "Shante, why won't the wheels roll on this truck?" She held the truck in the air. She used her hand to push against the wheels so that Shante could see what she meant.

"That's the way they made it, sweetheart." Shante was trying to continue her conversation with Serena.

"Why?" Ashley asked. "I want the wheels to roll."

"Uh, honey, they probably just want you to use your imagination. Anyway, Serena, what was I saying?"

"I don't want to use my imagination," Ashley said, looking sadly at the truck. "I want the wheels to roll."

"Well Ashley, that's the best that truck can do," Shante said. It was a little plastic truck that probably cost a dollar. Ashley's friend Jason had given it to her. Ashley put the truck down and leaned on Serena's lap.

Shante began telling Serena about Marcus's demeanor. "He's a little grouchy at times, but that's to be expected."

"That's right, it sure is," Serena agreed.

Ashley interrupted. "Watch this, Serena. Daddy had a plane, and his went: Ummmm errrr ummmm errrrr." Ashley's hand was stiff and her fingers were together as she moved her hand through the air.

Serena looked at Ashley for a few moments. "Yeah!" she said. Then she turned back toward Shante and continued their conversation about Marcus.

Ashley pushed on Serena's thigh. "Serena, you're not paying attention."

Shante corrected Ashley. "Say Mrs. Avery."

"I'm sorry, sweetie," Serena said. "Go ahead."

"Daddy's plane said: Ummmm errrr ummmm errrr . . ."

Ashley's hand was still traveling through the air like an airplane. Serena wondered if Daddy's plane was ever going to come in for a landing.

Serena's eyes widened as she struggled to keep them firmly on the plane. It continued.

"Ummmm, errrr, ummmm, unnnn . . . ."

"*Wow! That's neat!*" Serena exclaimed.

Ashley stopped flying the plane. She smiled and blushed.

"I have to ask Shante something now," Serena said. "Okay sweetie?"

Ashley was happy. She felt like she had just done a remarkable thing. She said, "Okay." Then she ran up to Julian and watched as he worked on his laptop.

Julian looked up at her. She stared at him. When he looked up again a few minutes later, she was still staring. "Mr. Avery, are you plugged into your computer?" she asked.

Julian looked puzzled. "Am I plugged into it?"

"Yeah."

Julian smiled. "No, I'm just busy."

Ashley ran back to her truck and decided to use her imagination as she pushed it across the carpet.

"I've never seen Marcus this determined," Shante said. "And we know how resolved and motivated he is in his work. He's cooperating fully with the doctors, and talking openly and honestly about his problem for the first time."

"This is great news," Serena said. "I'm so happy to hear it."

"What's that delicious aroma coming from the kitchen?" Shante asked.

"It's your favorite."

"No. You didn't, Serena."

"Yes, I did." Serena smiled.

"I thought I recognized that aroma. You are so good to me, girl."

In the middle of dinner, Shante asked, "How's your writing

coming along, Serena?"

"I haven't had much time to write lately, but my trip to Africa certainly broadened my vision. Speaking of Africa . . ."

Serena excused herself momentarily, then came back to the table with an Egyptian painting of Nefertiti and a carved African mask.

"I got these for you and Marcus." Shante said.

"You're giving these to us?"

"Yeah."

"Thanks, Serena. I can't wait to show these to Marcus."

Julian smiled as he looked on.

Shante put the gifts in the corner and they resumed eating. Ashley hadn't looked at the gifts. She was busy eating, sucking on lemon slices and drinking punch.

"How's your family, Shante?" Serena asked.

"They're doing well, thank you. Still acting like lovebirds. Mom recovered quickly from her hip surgery. I'm going home for Thanksgiving this year."

"So am I," Serena said. "Last year we spent Thanksgiving with Julian's family."

"How's your mom and dad?" Shante asked Serena.

"They're happy, as long as they are not together. Last year I invited them both to one of my performances. They were still uncomfortable around each other after all these years."

"Is anyone going to ask me how my family is?" Julian asked, making the conversation awkward.

"Ye-e-s Julian, I was getting ready to," Shante said. "How is your family?"

"They're fine, thank you."

"Good."

After dinner, Ashley ran over to Serena's piano and started playing—off key. Serena sat next to her and Shante followed, leaning against the piano. Serena showed Ashley how to place her hands in the middle C position. She demonstrated how to play legato, staccato and allegro. Ashley interrupted, smiling, "How did you do that?" Serena told Ashley how she had learned to play the piano. Then she and Shante left Ashley downstairs while they went upstairs to look at Serena's new clothes.

"I have one like this," Shante said, holding up a black short-sleeved dress. "Marcus bought it for me last year . . . I miss him so much. I visit him every day, but it's not the same."

Serena smiled. "He'll be out before you know it."

At the same time, in the suburbs of New Jersey, Marcus was in his room at the treatment center. He stood staring blankly out the window, into the dark woods behind his room. As he stared, he thought, maybe Dr. Bradford was right. Maybe he *should* call his dad.

❖

Seventeen

"**S**he got the job with WOZN!" Serena said to herself. She sat on her living room sofa watching Nikki report from downtown Manhattan. Nikki had spent years reporting for a small television station outside Stamford, Connecticut. For a year now, she had been trying to land a job with WOZN, a larger station.

"You go, girl," Serena said, as she thought back over the past eleven years. She and Nikki became close after they met at Clark Atlanta University, attracted by their many differences. Serena was an artistic dreamer, a visionary who had an idea for everything. "I'm following my dream," she'd say. Nikki believed that in order to obtain success, "You must get a good education, find a good job, and work hard."

They agreed that they were both right. They remained best friends during their four years at Clark Atlanta. When they came to New York more than seven years ago, they were young, excited and ready to take on the world. Serena came to fulfill her dream of becoming a Broadway performer. Nikki's desire was to establish a successful career in journalism as a reporter and anchor woman.

They rented a studio apartment in the village and within weeks they had both found jobs in their fields of study. Being both savvy and driven, they used each other's career to enhance their own. Serena gained a helpful amount of publicity from Nikki's stories about her career. In turn, when Serena became well known and admired for her talent, Nikki's earlier interviews of Serena gained more respect. In addition, Serena secured for Nikki several interviews with famous performers whom Serena had come to know.

Serena looked at the television screen and said, "I feel awful. I told her I would call her when I got back from Africa."

"Nicole, tell us exactly what happened," the blonde-haired, blue-eyed anchor said.

Nikki looked into the camera. "Apparently, Ken, the foundation simply collapsed. Three men were buried by the rubble. Wet cement covered their bodies. The ambulance just arrived a few minutes ago. I saw two men being rolled out on stretchers. The ambulance is pulling away as we speak."

"Two men, Nicole?" Ken said.

A bulldozer started in the background and dust flew through the air. "Excuse me, Ken, I'm having some difficulty hearing you."

"You said two men were on stretchers?"

"Yes, that's right, Ken."

"What about the third man, how is he faring in all of this?"

"I understand that he refused to be taken to the hospital by ambulance," Nikki answered. "I saw him limping, but he was able to walk away from this horrible tragedy, knowing that he will live to tell about it. The others aren't as fortunate. I'm Nicole Campbell, reporting live from downtown Manhattan. Back to you, Ken."

"We'll keep you informed about the conditions of the other two men as we uncover more details about this unfortunate accident," Ken said to the television audience.

Serena turned off the television set and went into the kitchen to make dinner.

At the construction site, the camera crew loaded the equipment into the white WOZN van while Nikki talked briefly to the supervisor there. Then she started toward the van. She was unaware of the fact that she had some admirers watching her.

Malik and Jazz, construction workers, had been near the accident when it happened. "Who is that fine reporter in the light blue suit?" Malik said to Jazz. Malik walked slowly toward Nikki. Look at that voluptuous body and that beautiful skin and hair, he thought.

"Hello," Malik said. He took his hard hat off and held it under his arm.

Nikki backed away from the man. *Where did he come from?* She glanced at the dirt on the man's face, then up at the dark clouds nearing.

"I'm Malik. Malik Jordan," he said with a boyish confidence as he extended his hand. Nikki hesitated, extending only her fingertips. Malik looked into Nikki's dark, almond-shaped eyes and thought, the more I look at this woman, the prettier she gets.

Nikki continued walking toward the van. Malik admired her derriere for a few seconds, then jogged to catch up with her. Nikki had a sexy twist to her walk, but she often complained that her rounded butt was the reason she had to wear a size ten jeans. She had told Shante and Serena that she could wear a size seven if her butt wasn't so big. Nikki had no idea how nice her figure was, even though men often complimented her on it. She thought they were just being lustful men who would look at anybody in a skirt.

Malik said, "I watch WOZN all the time and I haven't seen you before. You must be new."

Nikki looked gingerly at the cinnamon-skinned guy with the

wavy hair, thick eyelashes and three-day stubble. "I am," she said.

"Well, they definitely needed some new talent. You did a hell of a job on this story. I mean, I like the way you covered it. It was so . . ." Malik held his fist to his heart, "sincere. And it was accurate, too. Thanks for getting the truth out about that foundation collapsing. You—"

"Thank you," Nikki interrupted. "I have to go."

Malik was turned on by the slight hoarseness in her voice. "Can we finish this conversation over lunch sometime? I'd really like to get to know you better." His voice was sort of deep and it had a calm, friendly tone to it.

"I don't think so," she said with a bit of a snobbish attitude before climbing into the van.

Malik stood staring at Nikki like a heartbroken adolescent.

"In fact . . . no," she said, looking him up and down. She closed the door and the van pulled away.

"Man, that was cold," Malik said under his breath.

He stood there momentarily, looking at his soiled clothing. Rain suddenly fell from the sky. With his head down, he walked back to the site.

Eighteen

he following morning Nikki's alarm clock went off at 5:45, as usual. The white walls, curtains and yellow comforter on the bed gave the room a look of spring, her favorite season. She had been born in April, 1967. As a child she had wished that her mom had named her April. But as she got older, she liked the name her mother had given her better. Nicole Rochelle Campbell.

Nikki slowly sat up in bed. She yawned, rubbed her eyes, and pushed her long hair away from her face. Then she noticed a letter on her night table that she had yet to mail to her sister Kileigh in Louisiana. She picked it up and read it.

> *Hi Sis,*
> *I'm sorry I didn't write sooner. You know I'm still concerned about you going with Tony. He doesn't seem to have any direction. What does he plan on doing with his life? He's ten years older than you. He should be doing something by now. Is he going to live with his mother forever?*

*It's best if you don't get involved with anyone
seriously until you've completed your doctor-
ate. Now I realize that you didn't plan on
getting a PhD or a Master's either. But it takes
that long to figure out who you are and what
you want in life. Don't let some guy get in your
way. You can learn a lot from my mistakes.*

Love, Nikki

Nikki put the letter in a stamped envelope, addressed it,
then put it in her pocketbook. She walked over to the golden
oak dresser, took a pair of blue silk shorts out and put them on
over her panties. She left on the teddy bear t-shirt she usually
slept in.

She stretched at the foot of her bed before putting a Richard
Simmons exercise tape into her VCR. She worked out three mornings a week for forty-five minutes. Exercise wasn't something
she looked forward to, but she was disciplined enough to do it.
And she always felt better afterwards.

After her workout, she went in the bathroom to shower. Everything in the room was white except for the wallpaper, which
had a bright floral pattern. Afterwards she dressed, put on a
thin layer of foundation, lipstick, a little rouge and some false
eyelashes. And as she did every morning lately, she brushed on
a fresh coat of Nail Biter. Nail Biter was the only thing keeping
her fingers out of her mouth. It was a habit Nikki had only
intermittently conquered—one she had developed as a child.
She bit them when her cat got lost, when she was cramming for
a test, when her parents argued, whenever she felt like she was
not in control.

She went into the kitchen and popped two pieces of bread
into the toaster and fixed herself a cup of coffee as she did every morning. Minutes later, she served herself the hot buttery
toast with apple jelly as she watched the sun come out and shine
through the window and yellow curtains over the sink. Another

sunny June day, she thought. Then she grimaced and covered her eyes with her arm. The bright June sun brought back memories she tried with all her might to block out. "Ahh get a grip," she said, lowering her arm. Then she bolted from the chair and left for work.

Later that morning, Nikki was busy at her desk at WOZN. The pale yellow suit she wore made her look like a beautiful flower in motion. She was well organized and her office was as neat as a pin. She had everything filed away and she knew just where to locate information when she needed it. Compared to everyone else's desk, Nikki's looked like no one was using it, though she probably worked harder than anyone in the building. Nikki liked hard work. Working hard made her feel strong and in control. And she needed to be in control. It was a habit she had formed as a child. She felt powerful whenever she put a smile on her parents' faces. Getting terrific grades, helping with chores and keeping her room perfectly clean always seemed to do just that. In high school she enjoyed being lead majorette, but she was more proud of being voted most studious by her fellow classmates.

"That's not my problem, sir," she said into the telephone. "Yes. I understand sir. You need to speak . . . ask for Ken Monroe when you call." Nikki looked up and saw Malik standing near the entrance to her office. "Ask for extension 3885. He should be able to help you. Goodbye now."

Malik knocked on the open door. He approached confidently, wiggling his fingers with boyish charm. Nikki thought he was cute, but she wasn't about to let him know it. She noticed a small dimple in his chin and she thought he looked more like a soap opera hunk than a construction worker.

"Remember me?" he asked grinning widely. His grin looked a little like Will Smith's.

"How could I forget," she said sarcastically.

Malik was impeccably dressed in a brown suit and cream shirt with a button collar. He rarely wore suits, but he put on his Sunday best to impress Nikki. "I realize I was a bit untidy yestaday," he said.

"That's a bit of an understatement," she said.

"Well, anyway, I thought I'd try again."

"Did you?" She raised her eyebrows.

"Yeah."

"Even after I told you, no?" She rolled her eyes. "Don't you think that's rude? You know, disrespectful?"

"Maybe," he said. Nikki looked interested.

"Maybe it's a little selfish too," he added.

"Yeah," she agreed with a slightly puzzled look on her face.

"The audacity!" he said, lifting his chin and shaking his head from side to side.

Nikki hid a smile and managed to refrain from laughing. Then she fixed her eyes on the gold looped earring in Malik's ear. He noticed her looking at it. He raised his hand to his ear and touched his earring. He's a player, she thought.

"Oh, you like my earring," he said, still grinning.

"I don't need a man who's trying to be prettier than I am."

Nikki watched as Malik appeared to be adjusting his earring. Malik took the earring off, glanced at it, and threw it to his right, across Nikki's office.

Nikki's surprised eyes followed the earring through the air. She heard it jingle as it hit the floor. With her mouth wide open, she looked at Malik. When she saw the goofy grin on his face, she swiveled her chair around, turning her back to him. Her shoulders were trembling. Still she managed not to make a sound as she pressed her lips together.

"I know you're laughing," Malik said. "You can't hide it. Your shoulders are jumping all over the place."

A few quiet giggles burst through, even though she had fought hard to control them. Then, she regained her composure. "This is ridiculous. I don't have time for this nonsense." She swiveled her chair back around and looked seriously at Malik. "Yes, I laughed . . . a little," she said snobbishly. "But only because it was so . . . unusual."

"Well," Malik said. "If a man dudn't try, a man won't know."

"You tried already . . . remember . . . yesterday." She frowned. "You know, you men think it's all about you and how you want to feel, don't you?"

"No-o-o," he said. "It's all about yo-u-u-u-u, women."

Nikki's lips twitched.

"Is that a smile I see on your face?" he asked.

"I've got a job to do here," she snapped.

"Now you're too pretty to be acting so ugly," he said as if to say 'shame on you.'

"Uh, I believe you came here to impress me, Mister, Malik . . . and your effort is lousy."

"I was just kidding," he said.

"How did you get in here anyway?"

"I explained that I was employed by the construction company that you reported from. I showed my work ID and told them that I had spoken with you about the accident, and that I needed to talk to you again . . ."

Nikki listened suspiciously. "Well, kid yourself right on out the door." She raised her right arm and tossed her hand as she motioned for him to exit her office.

"I won't bother you again. But if you need anything or change your mind, here's my card."

When Nikki failed to extend her hand, he laid the card on her desk. It read: Malik Jordan. Chavis Construction Co. Beeper# 2124854657, with a Bronx address.

"Goodbye, now," she said sternly.

Whoa, she's hell, he thought as he left her office. Then he smiled to himself.

On his way out, he stopped at the desk of a female employee. The employee blushed, as she found him to be quite handsome. He instructed her to write down his name and number and said, "Could you please give that to Nikki tomorrow?" The blushing smile on the employee's face disappeared, but she was still willing to help. Malik had a feeling that Nikki might conveniently lose or throw away the card he had given her.

Nikki saw him talking to her co-worker. She shook her head and rolled her eyes, thinking he was now trying to hit on the co-worker. When he left the building, she picked up the card and tossed it in the trash can beside her desk. "That guy has some nerve coming to my job like this," she said to herself. "He's probably some nut."

At one o'clock in the afternoon that same day, Nikki had just gotten back from her lunch break when someone knocked on her door again. The door was ajar and Serena entered, holding a large box under her arm.

"Congratulations. You got the job," Serena said.

"Hi, Serena! You're back!" Nikki jumped out of her seat and went around her desk to greet her. They hugged and Serena handed Nikki the gift. "What's this?" Nikki asked. She held the box in front of her.

"I bought it while I was in Africa. It's art."

"For me? Thank you." Nikki unwrapped the gift. It was a colorful painting, with faces representing members of different African tribes.

"I like it, Serena. I think I'm going to put it in my office at home. I've never seen anything quite like this."

"I hadn't either. That's why I bought it. I'm glad you like it."

"So, how was Africa?" Nikki sat back down. "Have a seat."

Serena sat on the edge of the chair in front of Nikki's desk. "I had a great time. It was beautiful. But if I get started, it'll be some time before I'm finished talking. I'll tell you all about it later. I just came to congratulate you and invite you to a pool party that I'm having at the house next Saturday. We can celebrate your new job. You can bring someone. Are you dating now?"

"Serena, you know me better than that. Nothing's changed. I find men to be useless in my life. I mean in terms of any personal relationship. They are all the same to me."

"Those are strong words, Nikki."

"I know they are. That's the way I feel."

"I'm sorry you feel that way," Serena said. "I know you've been hurt terribly, but you need to learn to trust again."

"They can't be trusted," Nikki said, frowning. "They put on these enormous acts when they want something—especially in the beginning. When they get what they want, they change like a chameleon. I choose to avoid the whole mess. I don't have time for it."

The phone rang. Serena motioned that she was leaving. "I'll see you next Saturday," she whispered. Nikki nodded and waved goodbye, then picked up the phone.

Before leaving work that evening, Nikki looked down at the trash can, thinking of Malik and the card she had thrown away. She noticed that the trash had already been taken out. She shook her head. "What was I thinking?" she said to herself. A small part of her had wanted to keep the card.

Nineteen

When Nikki got to work the next morning, she headed for the ladies room. She pulled, twisted and tugged on her light green suit skirt as she looked in the mirror. Then, she reached into her pocketbook and took out her false eyelashes. She rushed and couldn't get the lashes on correctly. She looked in the mirror, thinking her eyes looked like a vacuum cleaner brush. She tried again.

"Why do men always get the eyelashes? Even that Malik guy has long eyelashes. God, we'll trade some of our brain power for some of their eyelashes." She looked up at the ceiling. "I know you know they can use it, because you created them." She snatched the eyelashes off and threw them in the trash.

Nikki heard her telephone ringing as she approached her office.

"Nicole Campbell speaking."

It was Logan Rinehart, a co-worker from a previous job and now her boss. "Mr. Collins told me to tell you, as soon as you walk through the door, that he needs the Jenkins story completed within the hour."

"I have it ready, it's right here on my desk."

"You've been taking work home again, haven't you?" Logan asked.

"Well," Nikki responded.

"Nikki, you have no social life."

"I do, Logan."

"I suppose you're going to tell me how you spend time with Serena and Shante. And how you enjoy occasional visits with your family. You need more, Nikki—more."

"I've got you, Logan," Nikki teased, as she thought about the fact that she had known Logan for three years now.

"I knew you were fond of me, Nikki," Logan returned.

"I didn't say I was fond of you. I said I got you. I was referring to our decent working relationship."

"You can't fool me. I know the feeling's mutual. But, because of my gender you're just not willing to admit it."

Nikki smiled agreeingly, recalling the day she finally admitted to him that she thought he was handsome. And he had been thrilled to receive a compliment from her, because he knew it was a rare thing for Nikki to complement any man. She also thought about the fun she'd had when he talked her into going scuba diving with him and two other divers. Nikki had never been diving before and she'd had a great time.

"Goodbye now, Logan." Click. Moments later, the phone started ringing again.

"Hello, this is Malik."

Nikki blew hard. "Are you stalking me?"

"No-o," he assured her.

"Then prove it," she snapped.

There were a few moments of silence.

"H-e-l-l-o-o-o," she said sarcastically.

Malik was stunned silent. He took a deep breath.

"You find it hard to believe that a woman may actually not be interested in you, don't you?" she asked.

There was no answer from Malik.

"Let me clear that up for you right now. You men think you're doing women a favor whenever you're interested in us. When you're really only interested in yourselves and what we can do to help swell your already mountain-like heads and blow your egos through the roof."

That answers my question, Malik thought. He wanted to ask Nikki if she was involved in a relationship. "Like I said before, I'm here if you need me." His usual confident voice sounded weary.

"You don't even know me," she said.

"I think I know you better than you know you," he responded. "Goodbye."

Malik sat on his bed inside his small Bronx condominium. "She's really been hurt," he said to himself. "I understand how she feels." He stared straight ahead at the empty wall in his room.

Nikki sat at her desk, puzzled. She had been trying to provoke Malik into showing his "true self." She had turned off many men over the years with her icy words. This time, it didn't seem to be working.

She immediately got on the telephone and called Lonny Russo, a private investigator. "I want him followed," she told him. "I want you to probe his past. Christ, this guy came to my job."

❖

Twenty

Everyone seemed to be enjoying themselves at Serena's party. There were cliques of people around the living room and kitchen. Some of the men were in the den, huddled around the television, laughing, talking, and watching the Braves game. Most of the other guests were in the living room, listening to music and chatting. Serena and Julian were in and out as they grilled salmon, steak, and chicken. Marcus was just out of the treatment center and he looked great. The slanted dimples in his cheeks lit up his milk chocolate face. His eyes sparkled, and he delighted everybody in the living room with his jovial personality.

Marcus jogged over to Nikki who sat in a slouched position on the sofa. "Hey, Nikki, Nikki," he said, rubbing his hand in a circular motion on top of her head.

"He-e-y Marcus," Nikki said, with a slight smile as she glanced up at him. Shante joined them and they chatted a bit about the children's center that Shante and Marcus had founded. It was a non-profit center that provided a place for latchkey children, help with homework, and workshops on child development for the children's parents and others.

"Will you come and talk to the children about your career?" Shante asked Nikki.

"Sure, I'll come."

"Great. Thanks, Nikki," Shante followed Marcus back to the sofa chair. She sat next to him, leaning against him.

"I'm ready for some grub," Marcus said loudly. "Hey, where are the plates?"

Everyone chuckled. They all thought Marcus was funny because he would say the things they would only think.

Shante blushed with embarrassment and nudged his arm. "We just got here," she whispered.

Moments later the doorbell rang. It was Ollie, with a fair-skinned brunette with dark eyes and a nose like Meryl Streep's.

"Hi, Ollie. Thanks for coming."

"Hi, Serena—or should I say Aphrodite?" They hugged.

"Serena will do just fine," she said, smiling.

"Serena, this is Daria. Daria, meet Serena."

"I've heard so much about you," Daria said. "Nice to meet you."

"Nice to meet you, too." Serena said. "Come on in and get comfortable, Daria." This was the first time Serena had ever seen Ollie with a brunette. Ollie had dated more than a few women over the years Serena had known him, and all of them had been blondes.

Serena made it a point to tell everyone beforehand that there would be no alcohol served. She had bought a variety of non-alcoholic beverages and had made some delicious exotic drinks from pureed blackberries and other fruits.

Serena went into the kitchen and put a stack of plates and silverware on the table. "Marcus, the food is ready," she yelled from the kitchen. Everyone laughed. "Just help yourselves, everyone," she added.

Serena wasn't aware that Marcus already had a piece of steak on a napkin and was happily gnawing on it. Shante looked at him, smiled and shook her head.

The song "Open Arms" by Tracy Chapman played on the stereo and a few guests started dancing. It was one of Serena's favorite songs so she took Julian's hand and led him from the kitchen into the living room. "Come on let's dance," she said, pulling on his hand.

He pulled back. He wasn't big on dancing.

"Come on," she insisted.

Giving in, Julian started to move a little. He watched as Serena undulated to the rhythm of the music. Serena spun around and swayed her hips back and forth. She moved her head from side to side and closed her eyes. When she opened them, Julian was stomping like the Tin Man from the *Wizard of Oz*, and snapping his fingers off beat. Nikki looked on like she wanted to get up and give him some dance lessons, but she just didn't have enough enthusiasm.

He can't dance, Serena thought. She was losing her rhythm watching him. But at least he was trying. She smiled and gave him a hug.

Then he spoke. "I have to leave for a while."

"Where are you going?"

"I have to go by the office. But I'll be back shortly."

"On a Saturday, and during the party?"

"Yeah. I won't be long. I left some important papers I need to pick up. I want to read over them tonight." He kissed her on the cheek and left.

Serena looked around the room. Everyone except Nikki was eating and socializing. Nikki was on the sofa with a drink in her hand. She appeared to be daydreaming. Serena could tell something was bothering her because of the distant look in her eyes. Serena shook her head as she thought back to their college days and how Nikki had been the life of the party. "Let's get this party started," Nikki would yell, and she'd be the first one on the dance floor. "There's a party over here! Is there a party over there?" And soon she'd have everyone in the building jamming to the music. But even back then, whenever Serena looked into Nikki's eyes she sensed someone who had not always been in control, someone who needed to feel secure. She sensed a gentleness within Nikki that wasn't visible from the outside.

Serena went and sat next to Nikki.

"What's on your mind, Nik? What are you thinking about?"

"Ahh, I was thinking about something that happened recently," Nikki said. "I feel bad about something, and I probably shouldn't."

"Okay. What?" Serena asked.

"I met this construction worker when I was reporting on an accident in downtown Manhattan."

"Yeah." Serena nodded. "I saw you on television. That's how I learned you got the job."

"He was pretending to be this nice guy, you know." Nikki took a deep breath. "Well anyway, I wasn't very nice to him. As a matter of fact, when he tried to talk to me, I was sort of harsh. I don't even know him."

"If he was just pretending to be a nice guy, then why is this bothering you?"

"I don't know. Yes I do. I mean . . . I don't know." Nikki leaned forward and set her drink on the table.

Some of the guests began changing into their swimsuits. Nikki had been one of the first to arrive at the party and she and Serena already had on their swimsuits and cover-ups. More and more people gravitated outside to the pool as the sun came out and the temperature grew warmer. Nikki and Serena continued their conversation as they joined the others at poolside. "You know how they pretend to be nice in the beginning," Nikki said.

"Well, men have times when they feel unhappy or angry, just like we do. It doesn't mean they're always pretending when they're being nice. Now, I can relate to what you say about men, to some degree. And I understand why you feel the way you do. You've been hurt deeply. But all men are not like that. And, believe it or not, all men don't lie." Serena thought for a few moments. "A lot of them do, but you need to distinguish between some, and all."

"Good try, Serena," Nikki said. "The guy came to my job without being invited. I said, who in the world does he think he is?" Nikki stared into the sparkling blue pool water, then she looked at Serena. "That was so bold. I'm having him investigated."

"What!"

"Yeah," Nikki said.

"If you like him as much as I think you do, you should call him and at least apologize," Serena said.

"*Apologize!* At least! Isn't that going to extremes?"

"You met him, what do you think?" Serena asked in a gentle voice.

"I don't know." Nikki did respect Serena's opinions. In some strange way, they comforted her. She had been drawn to Serena, in part, for the strength she saw in her. Serena possessed a wealth of compassion, and Nikki drew from it whenever she needed to forgive someone or forget something. The occasional person considered it a weakness. "You're too nice, Serena," they'd say. Nikki saw it as a strength. She thought it took a strong person not to react in kind to the sometimes negative personalities around them.

Serena spoke again. "Nikki, you know this is yet another situation where you're letting your past control you. You're allowing the bad actions of a few people to rule your life."

"I don't have time for it, really. I just like being alone," Nikki responded.

"Is tha true? I mean, is that really true? I just think you're cheating yourself by shutting out so many interesting people. "Whoa!" Serena said, as a volleyball landed in her lap. She tossed it back to Marcus.

"I'm afraid," Nikki said.

"You should talk to a professional about this. As soon as possible," Serena suggested. "I'll be there for you." She thought of Michael Jackson's recording of 'I'll Be There.' Serena, Nikki, and Shante had been big fans of Michael Jackson when they were little.

Serena began singing the words to the song. "I'll be theeeeere, I'll be theeeeeere . . ."

Nikki joined in off key.

Serena managed not to lose her key when Shante joined in and drowned out Nikki. The three of them swayed back and forth.

"Just call my name and I'll be theeerre . . . ."

Everybody that wanted to started singing along with them. Serena's guests started jumping into the pool. Shante jumped in, wearing a purple and black bikini. Serena took off her cover-up, revealing her gold-colored bikini. She tugged on Nikki's hand. Since Nikki wouldn't go willingly, Serena pushed her in with her pink cover-up on.

Meanwhile, Serena's phone was ringing. It was Nathan. He had just arrived back from Saudi Arabia.

Where is she? He just needed to hear her voice again.

Twenty-one

"Julian, hon, you need to get up now," Serena said.

"I'm tired." Julian rolled over in bed.

It was a Sunday morning two weeks after Serena's party. Serena was looking through her closet, trying to decide on what to wear to church.

"You stayed at the office too long last night," she said.

"It was business. You know, real work."

There he goes again, implying that my career isn't important, she thought. "You promised, Julian. We haven't been to church together in a long time." Julian used to go to church with Serena every Sunday before they got married. "You can go back to bed after church, and I'll drive."

"Okay." He laid in bed for a few more minutes before getting up. "I don't want to be in church long, because I'm going to play golf."

As Serena drove to church, she glanced at Julian. "It's such a pretty day isn't it?"

"Yeah," he muttered.

Serena and Julian entered the church and sat beside Marcus. Serena was happy that she had been able to persuade Julian to come with her that morning. She had talked to Reverend Alexander about her marital problems after church the Sunday before. "Bring him to church with you on Sunday," he had told her. The handsome, reverend in his early forties didn't say what he was going to speak about, but Serena had a feeling he might say something about marriage.

Reverend Alexander started the service with a song entitled "I Can't Complain." Then he spoke about how a man and woman should treat one another according to the Bible. "Husbands, love your wives even as Christ also loved the church, and gave himself for it—Ephesians, 5:25." Serena glanced over at Julian to make sure he was paying attention. Good, he's listening, she thought.

It was one of the best sermons Serena had ever heard. She felt so inspired. Toward the end of the sermon, Serena looked at Julian again, sure he would be as inspired as she was.

Julian was asleep.

"I can't believe this," she said under her breath.

After church, many people, including Serena and Shante, gathered outside to shake hands. But Julian headed straight for the car.

"Guess what?" Shante said. She held her left hand out to Serena, showing a beautiful, pear-shaped diamond sparkling on her finger.

"Oh, my goodness," Serena said.

"Marcus surprised me. Last week he took me to the Poconos. We stayed at this really fancy lodge. He arranged for me to have a massage, manicure, and pedicure. I enjoyed the finest dining I have ever experienced. I was thinking, this is so *sweet* of him. Girl, it was such a nice departure from his usual bag of Chinese food."

Serena's cheeks turned rosy with laughter.

"During our dinner, he suddenly got down on his knees and said, 'Shante, if you will marry me, this is the way I'll treat you for the rest of our lives, darlin'.' You know how silly Marcus can be. He said, 'darrrrlin'.' "

Serena's and Shante's eyes were luminous and their hearts were filled with joy.

"I love him so much," Shante said. "I am so happy."

"Have you set a date?" Serena asked.

"Not yet. But we don't wanna wait too long. Serena, every day he thanks me for sticking by him. Of course, I feel like I'm the lucky one. We'll be together forever—through thick and thin."

Serena hugged and congratulated Shante as Marcus was coming out of the church. He had been inside talking to Reverend Alexander about his desire to become a Deacon.

Julian drove up in front of the church and blew the horn. "Come on, Serena!" he yelled.

"Hey, Marcus," Serena said.

"Hey, Serena-a-a," Marcus said. They laughed and hugged. "Congratulations!"

"Thanks." Marcus hugged his arm around Shante's shoulders. "This is my honey pie." Shante smiled and blushed.

"Let me go before Julian blows that horn again," Serena said.

Serena's heals made a clicking sound as she crossed the concrete sidewalk. She got into the passenger's side of the car and Julian pulled away before she could get her seat belt on.

"Julian, please don't blow the horn and yell out the window," Serena said with a frown.

"I didn't want to come in the first place," he said. "I told you I was tired."

❖

Twenty-two

*B*ANG. BANG. BANG.

It was Monday morning. Nikki was hitting the stapler as hard as she could. Logan's office was right next to hers and the banging sound annoyed him, because it seemed to go on and on. Nikki had a stack of papers she was trying to staple together.

She opened the stapler, hoping to find the problem and solve it. Everything looked okay. She closed the stapler. She tried again and again, tossing the bent staples into the trash can. "This stapler isn't worth two cents," she said. As Logan entered her office, Nikki realized that maybe the stack of papers was simply too thick.

He walked in and leaned over Nikki, his palms firmly on her desk. A forelock of his brown hair fell forward on one side as he did. His piercing blue eyes stared straight through her dark ones.

"Nikki, did it ever cross your mind that you might be sexually frustrated?"

"Uh. That's a man thang." Nikki wouldn't allow just anybody to speak to her that way. And Logan himself would never talk about this subject unless it was with someone he trusted. They had known each other for a long time, and Nikki knew that his strange comments were only harmless attempts to get her to consider his advice.

"You know better than that, Nikki. Everybody needs love."

"And it's just like a man to think love means sex. Why am I not surprised that you think this way? And how do you know if I'm getting love or not?"

Logan pulled up a chair and sat down. He spoke in a smooth voice. "Come on. You've made it clear around here how you feel about men. Plus, you work all the time, and you even take work home. You've been alone for years. That's a long time."

"Not long enough," she said. "And the more I talk to men, the more I'm convinced of that. Ya know, Logan, I sort of like you."

"Why only 'sort of' Nikki? How can you sort of like someone? Either you like me or you don't. Just admit that you like me."

"Don't press it, Logan. You're the luckiest man I know. Well, maybe there's one other exception "

"May I ask who the lucky man is?"

"No, you may not." She was thinking about Marcus. "Like I was saying before, I sort of like you, but you don't know whether I'm sexually active or not."

"Nikki, you wouldn't make time for sex if it was staring you in the face."

Nikki frowned. "Do you realize that comment is senseless? It's absolutely ridiculous."

"It's no more ridiculous than you banging on that stapler over and over again. You see it's not working."

Nikki frowned as Logan left her office. He turned and looked at her mischievously. "Later, doll," he said.

Nikki was usually successful at hiding her vulnerable side. She could fool most of the people most of the time. But she couldn't fool her friends.

Twenty-three

In late August, Nikki had made up her mind to take Serena's advice and seek counseling. She scheduled an appointment with Dr. Rosa Purcey.

Nikki arrived at her appointment wearing a black pantsuit, sunglasses, and a black hat, looking like she was going to a funeral. She was afraid someone might recognize her because of her profession. She knew all too well how stories sometimes got misrepresented. Stepping inside the red brick building, she tugged the front brim of her hat to make sure it shadowed her face.

The receptionists instructed her to go on back. Nikki hesitated before knocking twice on the door.

"Come on in." The doctor was an attractive, heavy-set woman, who wore her long hair in braids. "Nice to meet you," she added, extending her hand and shaking Nikki's. "Have a seat in the green chair."

The next week Nikki was back in Dr. Purcey's office for her third visit. Dr. Purcey believed that she had a good idea who Nikki was on the inside. She had also helped Nikki bring some subconscious fears to the surface.

"Nikki, tell me about your family."

"They're fine," Nikki said, looking like she didn't have much to say.

"When you think about your childhood, what's the first thing that comes to mind?"

"My father, Gerald," she said. "He used to come home some evenings and pick a fight with my mother. It was as though he wanted to hurt her and he was looking for any excuse.

"My mom worked hard in a nursing home. My dad was a truck driver. I think he took out his frustrations from being on the road on my mom. He used to smoke a lot. Mom didn't want him to smoke around me. One night my mom asked him not to smoke at the dinner table. He got so mad, he yelled, 'Damn it, Olivia!' and banged his fist on the table and stormed out. I ran in my room and hid in the corner. I used to hate it when he raised his voice. I remember I used to ask my mother every day before he would get home . . ."

"What, Nikki? What would you ask your mother?"

"I would ask her if the cabinet doors were closed." Nikki's eyes began to tear. "I would get a chair. I'd climb up and close all of the doors. If they were open, my father would fly into a rage. I'd say . . ," Her voice cracked, ". . . 'Mommy, are the cabinet doors closed?' "

Dr. Purcey nodded sympathetically.

Nikki's sad expression turned cold and solemn. "I remember praying every night for him to change. He never did. My Uncle Fritz promised to help my mother. He was going to help my mother get out of the marriage. He was always nice to me and my mother."

"That's something positive," Dr. Purcey said.

"It was positive briefly," Nikki said. "One summer evening he took me and my mother to the county fair in his 1968 Ford. I was so excited. We all got out of the car and headed for the concession stand. My mom and I got ice cream while Uncle Fritz went back to the car to get something. After I got my ice cream cone, I turned around and saw Uncle Fritz in the parking lot talking to a man. My mom was paying the cashier. I watched as I licked my ice cream. It was a hot day and I was licking fast, because the chocolate ice cream was melting on my hands."

Nikki's face suddenly filled with fear.

"He was arguing with a man by the name of Plug. Plug pulled out a gun and shot Uncle Fritz over and over again. I screamed and dropped my ice cream. My mother fainted. People went running in different directions. I saw people's candy apples and hot dogs lying in the dirt. A few people scurried by me and knocked me down on top of my mother."

Nikki sighed. "My mother never really got over it. She sometimes has a faraway look in her eyes, and I can tell she's recalling that tragic day.

"It turned out that the two of them were arguing over money. Uncle Fritz said Plug owed him money. So Plug shot him. How dumb is that? Why was Uncle Fritz even associating with someone like Plug? I never really found out all the details. I could only imagine.

"At that time I was an only child. Later on, my mother had two more girls. She was trying to give my father a son. My sisters and I are close." Nikki smiled a little. "They come to see me twice a year. I go visit them and my mother once a year, sometimes twice. That's a positive thing."

"How are your parents doing now?" Dr. Purcey asked.

"My father died a few years ago. He had a brain tumor. I feel like I never really had a father. I don't talk about him too much. I realize that things could have been worse. There are so many children in worse family situations than I was in."

"That's a very good observation, Nikki, but your feelings are important. They deserve to be validated. They need to be expressed."

☙❧

The next week Dr. Purcey picked up where they had left off. She asked Nikki about her adult relationships with men.

"I'm not seeing anyone right now," Nikki told her. "To tell the truth, I haven't dated in five years. Years ago, when I first started dating, I fell in love with a guy I thought was perfect."

Dr. Purcey leaned forward. "There are no perfect men. In fact, there are no perfect women, either."

"Anyway," Nikki said, "he was cheating on me."

"How old were you then, Nikki?"

"Nineteen. I think if he had been honest with me about it, I could have handled it much better. Sometimes I think there is nothing worse than a liar."

"How did you handle it?" Dr. Purcey asked.

"When I confronted him about it, he was like an entirely different person than what I had known. He acted so cold and unfeeling. So I yelled at him, and cried frantically."

Nikki seemed haunted by the memories. "It was like he was angry with me for finding out the truth—like I had done something wrong." She looked at Dr. Purcey. "Isn't that strange? I mean, it's just unbelievable."

Dr. Purcey raised her eyebrows. "It's believable. That experience is very common, especially considering your age at the time."

"That's when I learned about the double standard," Nikki said. "You know, men are just being men when they do such things. Women, on the other hand, are whorish if they conduct themselves in the same way. I think men should be held to the same standard as women."

"I'd like that too. But things aren't always as they should be in this world. You, Nikki, in your own way and perhaps the only way you know how, are trying to make that a reality in your own life. You have the right idea, you're just going about it the wrong way. It wasn't so much the other girl he was involved with, because I assume he was young, too—not that that's an excuse for his behavior. Instead, it was the fact that he showed such a callous disregard for you and your feelings. You trusted him, and he was dishonest. He knew he wasn't ready for a serious commitment. He selfishly led you to believe in him, for his own self gratification." Dr. Purcey thought about it further, then added, "Now of course there could have been other reasons for his actions. Like I said before, people aren't perfect. Perhaps he had strong feelings for this other girl, and didn't intend to hurt you. But the fact that you said he acted cold and unfeeling tells me something about his character."

Dr. Purcey paused, rubbing her forefinger across her lips. Then she continued speaking. "Nikki, often two people start a relationship not fully aware of their moral differences. They fall in love thinking everything else will fall into place. When they begin to learn more about the character of the person they have become involved with, they feel disappointed, hurt, shocked, sometimes even repulsed. All too often, they don't learn these things until they've gotten seriously involved, or even married to the person. When you realize you didn't know the person as well as you thought you did, you don't want to believe it. It's too shocking—too painful. Especially if you think you're in love. The reality is, you're in love with someone you don't know. You can't be in love with someone you don't know."

Dr. Purcey took a deep breath and continued. "You thought you knew this person. You must realize that you never knew him. Realizing this should be the first step in moving forward with your life independent of him, but in a healthy way. Staying true to yourself, and your morals and beliefs is the best way to do that. No matter how painful the journey. Don't lose yourself in the pain, or in someone else's character flaws. Don't be guided by the negative values and actions of others. You have the power in your mind to control the way you process information. Again, let your thoughts and responses be true to who you are. Who are you, Nikki?"

There was silence. Then Dr. Purcey continued. "Granted, your experiences help shape who you are, but when you're controlled by the negative ones, you become a stranger to yourself. You lose yourself. The result is a substantial amount of pain and fear. After all, a stranger lives inside of you. Don't let that stranger run your life."

Nikki listened, thoughtfully nodding her head as if she understood. "Well," she said, "I got over it a lot sooner than I thought I would. There were plenty of guys asking me out. I knew I couldn't trust any of them so I refused to commit to any one guy. Until . . ."

"Yes? Until what?"

"Wait a minute," Nikki said. "You're asking all the questions. Don't I get to ask you a question every now and then?" A part of Nikki wanted an excuse to leave, to avoid discussing her painful past. She wondered if Dr. Purcey really cared, or if it was all about getting paid. She didn't know Dr. Purcey from Adam, and here she was telling her everything.

"Sure, Nikki, ask away," Dr. Purcey said.

"Why are men such jerks?" Nikki asked.

"I know some women who are jerks," Dr. Purcey responded. "Have you only met nice women in your life, Nikki? If you have, I'd like to know exactly where you've been."

"Well, that's something I never thought about. I would say the women who act like jerks are probably suffering from being involved with a male jerk, but I'm more intelligent than that, so I won't claim that to be true."

Nikki hesitated, then asked, "How do you feel about men?"

"I like men, in general," Dr. Purcey said. "Men are quite different from women, not just physically, but emotionally, too."

"You got that right, they're all bald-faced liars."

"Do you actually believe that, Nikki?"

"Yes, I believe it. Sometimes I wonder if reverends lie. Maybe they don't, but I wouldn't be surprised if they do."

Oh, my, Dr. Purcey thought, she should have gotten some help a long time ago. "If you're not ready to talk about it today, I can reschedule you for later this week," Dr. Purcey said.

"I'm paying for the whole hour, I might as well use it." Nikki was thinking about how expensive therapy was, and how, years before, she wouldn't have been able to afford it. But she knew that was just the way things worked. At least Dr. Purcey was giving her some feedback, and not just asking questions, so she gave Dr. Purcey a little smile.

"Okay . . . okay," Dr. Purcey nodded. "Until what, Nikki? You were saying you refused to commit to any guy until . . ."

Nikki breathed deeply. "Until I met an older man. I was twenty-four and he was thirty-eight. I began to believe that I should give love a try again. He was so nice to me. He was all over me. He showered me with gifts and flowers—anything I asked for, he would give it to me. His name was Dallas. He used to wear a lot of different hats and a gold ring on his pinkie. At the time, I thought he was handsome. He owned a barbecue restaurant. We used to go there for dinner sometimes. I thought, yes, an older man is the answer."

Nikki sighed and continued. "We both talked about what we wanted in a marriage. He promised never to lie to me. He said he would always love me. We dated for nine months. Then we got married."

Nikki paused again as Dr. Purcey studied the pain on her face. "Five months after our wedding, I found out I was pregnant. I remember that day. It was a sunny June morning and I had a feeling I might be pregnant. After my doctor's appointment that evening, I rushed home. I couldn't wait for Dallas to get home so I could tell him. But he had started staying gone longer and longer each evening. That particular evening I noticed it more. I was so anxious to see him that I kept looking down at my watch and out the window of our condominium. I looked out until it was pitch dark and I couldn't see anything. But I kept staring out as if I could.

"Dallas didn't come home at all that night. He didn't even call. I felt like somebody had just ripped my heart out and stomped on it. I was sick with worry, but I didn't call the police. I knew somewhere in the back of my mind that he was safe. Safe in someone else's arms. I had suspected something weeks before, but I think I had blocked it out of my head. As long as I kept it at bay, I didn't have to confront it. I just didn't want to know for certain. I still thought we could work through it. I thought we could get past whatever it was and go on with our lives. I told myself, as long as this doesn't happen again, I will try to forget about it. Even though the pain was killing me.

"The next morning he called me. He was crying. 'Nikki,' he said to me, 'I won't be home. I need some time to think.'

"It was unreal what I was hearing. I don't know if I can accurately describe the feeling. I just know it was horrible. It was like I was standing outside myself. I called a friend of his and begged him to tell me what was going on, because Dallas wouldn't. All he did was cry and tell me he needed some time.

"His friend finally told me that Dallas had a mistress and four kids in Bridgeport." Nikki's eyes began to tear. "I barely got the phone back on the hook before the room started spinning. My legs collapsed. I fell to the floor. I tried to get up, but my legs wouldn't move no matter how hard I tried. So I just lay there for hours, bawling. Finally I got the strength to crawl to the phone. I called my friend Serena. She took me to the hospital. I lost the baby."

Nikki burst into tears. Dr. Purcey pulled a few tissues from the box and handed them to her.

"I thought I was going to die at first. Then I changed completely. I became so bitter." Nikki stared coldly into the air. She sniffled and wiped her nose. "Get this, he called me three months later, saying he'd had enough time and was ready to come back. He said that he still loved me.

" 'Please, Nikki.' he begged me, 'Please take me back.' He knew not to come in person. If he had, I probably would have half killed him." Nikki said.

"See," said Dr. Purcey. "You can always find something positive if you look at things hard enough."

"What do you mean?" Nikki asked.

"Well, think of it this way. You're not doing hard time for malicious wounding or attempted murder."

They looked at each other, and then burst into laughter. Nikki wiped her swollen eyes.

"This is what it's all about, isn't it?" Dr. Purcey said.

"What?" said Nikki, still giggling and wiping her tears.

"Laughter. We have to find a way to keep laughing. When life treats you cruelly, and things don't happen the way you'd hoped, reach within yourself to the heart of the woman you really are. Use your strength, courage, and compassion in the right way to move on and better your life. After you've cried and mourned over something that has happened in your life, pick your true self up and keep going. Try not to wallow in it. These experiences, though painful and sometimes tragic, can be of priceless value in terms of learning and giving insight that would have otherwise not existed. There are different lessons in life. Sometimes we learn humility. We can either let it bring us down or we can use what we've learned to grow within and help other people. Nikki, I suggest that you give love to others in the way you know how, and watch those good feelings come back to you. In time, you'll heal. You're smart, you're strong. You have managed, in the way you knew how, to survive and succeed. You're a good person. You have so much to give. Think of a way you can reach out to others. That's where you'll find your peace. Think positively, okay?"

"I will," Nikki said with a smile. "Thank you."

Nikki left Dr. Purcey's office and got into her car. A man in a black Mercury Marquis was parked a few car lengths behind her. She was unaware that the man had been following her. He snapped a few pictures before she drove away.

❖

Twenty-four

One late September evening, Nikki sat on her sofa with a glass of iced tea, after having retrieved her newspaper from her front steps. She read the front page, then started scanning the pages for interesting titles. To her surprise, she discovered a piece about herself. According to someone named Sandy Lovell, Nikki had suffered a nervous breakdown and was seeking psychiatric care.

Nikki immediately called Logan.

"Nikki!" Logan said.

"I take it you've read or heard about the story in the paper."

"I saw it with my own eyes. Are you okay? Where are you?"

"I'm at home. Relax, it's not true."

"Nikki, you know you can tell me anything. I've noticed that you've been a little uptight lately."

"Logan . . ," Nikki said.

"Yes, Nikki."

"I'm always uptight."

"Yeah, that's true," he said, now realizing that Nikki was telling him the truth.

"I just needed a professional opinion. I went to see Dr. Purcey to discuss some issues that had been bothering me."

"Oh." Logan suspected he knew exactly what issues she was talking about.

The more Nikki thought about the false statements in the newspaper, the angrier she became. "The next thing you know, they'll be saying I killed someone. And some people will believe it, because it was reported in the paper or on television. It won't matter what I say, that image will be firmly planted in their minds."

"You're going overboard, Nikki," Logan said.

"Maybe I am, but this kind of irresponsible journalism needs to cease. These are people's lives they're messing with. I'm going to call that newspaper and tell them to print a retraction."

"Are you going to tell them or ask them?"

"I'm going to tell them . . . very nicely."

"Good luck, doll."

Nikki tossed and turned that night, but she eagerly walked into work the next morning. Everybody expected her to do the opposite—if she showed up at all. She knew everyone would be gossiping and watching with curious eyes. She looked great in her black suit and white blouse with French cuffs.

Nikki heard a few people whisper as she walked toward her office. "Now I know why she wouldn't go out with me," Travis said to Sidney.

Sidney shook her head and looked at Travis like he was foolish. Travis was a tall, skinny, light-skinned guy with glasses. Sidney thought he was goofy looking. "Maybe she just didn't want to go out with you," she said.

"It's possible, I guess," Travis replied.

Nikki could feel everyone staring. Before she entered her office, she turned and faced them. "It's not true," she said. Then she went in her office.

"I knew that," Travis said. "I was just going along with ya'll—just trying to see what ya'll were thinking."

"Travis," Sidney said.

"What?"

"Shut up."

Logan followed Nikki into her office.

"I've already talked to the editor-in-chief of the newspaper and the writer responsible for the piece," he said. "They're sticking by their story, Nikki. They have pictures too."

"Pictures," Nikki muttered. "Somebody's been following me?"

"And guess what else?"

"What?"

"Our former boss had something to do with it, because the reporter let his name slip out when I confronted her about the story. You know he felt slighted when he asked you out and you said no. And he got angry when you told him you were leaving."

"Yeah. Uh huh, I gave that brute a month's notice, and this is the thanks I get?"

"Well, I guessed from my conversation with the reporter that he just happened to see you going in for your appointment one day and he couldn't resist. Although, I suppose he may have followed you to some degree after he spotted you going in."

"This is unconscionable. Logan, I've always taken great pride in the honesty and sincerity of my journalism."

"Yes, you have," Logan agreed. "I know how hard you work to ensure complete accuracy in your reports."

She thought about the seven years she had spent developing her career. She couldn't think of one complaint with her name on it. "My stories aren't always pleasant for everyone, but they're at least honest," she said. "One time I made a mistake. I reported something that wasn't accurate in its entirety—remember?"

"Yes, I remember. And you corrected it immediately, without being asked to do so."

"Right. I did. Thanks, Logan, but I'm going to call those people myself. Excuse me. I need to be alone for a few minutes. I'll give you a buzz when I'm done."

Nikki spoke with an inexperienced reporter named Sandy Lovell. "I expect a retraction to be printed in the paper tomorrow. I suggest that you make sure your story is completely correct before you print it."

"My story is correct," Ms. Lovell said with a slightly nasty attitude.

"Ms. Lovell, you wrote the story about me. Are you telling me that you know more about me than I do?" Nikki asked.

"No, I'm saying that maybe you don't want the truth to be reported, so you're saying it's not true. I have every reason to believe that this story is true," Ms. Lovell said.

"If I don't see a retraction in tomorrow's paper, the next person you'll be hearing from is my lawyer, and you definitely have every reason to believe that," Nikki said. "Hold on please, I have another call."

Ms. Lovell rolled her eyes and blew into the telephone as she waited.

Lonny Russo was on the other line. He told Nikki that he had found nothing scandalous about Malik so far. Then he told her that he had to do an investigation out of town and promised to contact her with more information later.

Nikki returned to Ms. Lovell. "Allow me to give you a few words of wisdom, Ms. Lovell. Honesty and integrity will take you higher, if that's where you want to go."

The following day the retraction was printed.

But Nikki felt like she needed to do more to make the truth known, and to help protect others from this kind of journalism. She appeared on the "Agnus Floyd Show," a small local talk show. Like the "Oprah Winfrey Show," it had a good reputation. Though the "Agnus Floyd Show" was not taped live, it had an excellent record for airing the subject matter in its proper context, and with accuracy and class. The title of Nikki's episode was "Lies, Spies, and Video ties."

"So tell me," Agnus said. "Is it true that you had a nervous breakdown?"

"That's absolutely not true. That did not happen," Nikki said. "I do want to say, however, that there is nothing shameful about having a breakdown. I realize that there are many people out there, sick or hurting inside for various reasons. It could happen to almost anyone."

"Do you really believe that?" Agnus asked.

"Yes I do. The problem I have with this rumor is that it's not true. So I thought it was important for me to come here today and correct the record. There was a retraction printed in the paper, and of course that helps, but as the saying goes, it was a day late and a dollar short.

"This inaccurate journalism is simply wrong and should not be tolerated by anyone," Nikki went on. "If we continue to accept it, it will never end, and get worse. Demand quality and accuracy. You, the consumer, are the ones paying for this. People should conduct themselves with sensitivity when they are delving into and reporting about people's private lives."

"That's why I like to do this show," Agnus said. "You really can't believe everything you hear or read."

"I always try to give the public a story without sensationalism," Nikki said. "I make a conscious effort to avoid this. I do this by getting to the heart of the story, rather than to the hype of the story. I like to use my intelligence to reach people. I believe that when journalists put negative spins on stories, they're not using their heads. Or perhaps they need to be retaught. If I make a mistake or get a story wrong, I won't hesitate to correct it. I challenge other journalists to do the same. You may not make it to the top as fast—but you'll make it, and you'll sleep better in the meantime. And when you get to the top, you'll stand there tall, distinguished and proud. Having compassion is so important. A dear friend of mine helped me see that years ago. And believe it or not, people like to hear the truth. They like good news. Too many people get caught up in thinking that the only thing the public wants to hear is scandal or bad news. It's not true."

"That's what I tell people," Agnus said. "Thank you for sharing your viewpoint."

Twenty-five

*N*athan had been called to Tranilla's Dump Site. He had no other plans this Saturday morning, so he had agreed to help check for leaking and hazardous waste. Before leaving home, he put on his Tyvek protective suit. Then he retrieved from his office the special detection device he had invented.

Nathan parked his car a distance from the site, so that it would not become contaminated. He put on his face respirator and walked to the site where he met up with the other workers.

At Shante's apartment, Marcus sat at the desk, writing a speech and waiting for Shante and Serena to return from the beauty parlor. Nearby, Ashley was using Legos to build a house for her dolls.

"Daddy, can I ride my bike with Jason today?" she asked.

"No. Not today, Ashley. It's raining. Maybe tomorrow." Marcus looked up and smiled at her. His thoughts drifted back in time to his childhood ...

❦

It had been a warm summer day. Shante and Marcus were riding their bikes up and down the road on which they'd lived.

"I'm goin' to see my daddy," Marcus said.

"That's all the way across town. We're not supposed to ride that far," said Shante.

"I'm goin' by myself." He peddled ahead of Shante. "I'll be back soon."

"Wait for me, Marcus!" Shante yelled.

They stopped when they reached the yellow field of grass across the street from Marcus's father's house. Straddling their bikes, they watched as Ralph entered the white wooden house with Marcus's half-sister in his arms and Marcus's half brother by his side.

Shante looked at Marcus. "Ain't you gon' say hello?"

"No," Marcus had said, and his little bottom lip trembled with emotion . . . "I just wanted to see him . . . Let's go home."

Marcus looked at the telephone, contemplating whether or not to call his dad. He had not spoken to him in ten years. Marcus now realized that his father's lack of interest in him had hurt him more than he had ever been willing to admit—to Lillie Mae, Shante, or, more importantly, to himself. He put his hand on the receiver for a few minutes. A wave of heat rushed through his body, tingling when it reached his fingertips. He took a deep breath, then lifted the receiver and dialed the number. He still had it memorized after all those years. It rang six times, and with each ring Marcus's stomach twisted into knots that made him hunch forward. He put the receiver back on the hook, feeling both disappointment and relief. He sighed. Then he tore a blank sheet of paper off his note pad and began writing.

> *Dear Ralph,*
>   *Or can I call you Dad? It's been a while,*
> *hasn't it? I hope all is well with you. I'm doing*
> *very well. Shante and I are getting married soon.*

Do you remember Shante? I have a five-year-old daughter. Her name is Ashley.

Ralph, I want you to know that there have been times over the years when I have resented you for not wanting to be in my life. But I felt more hurt than resentment. I now realize that we are two entirely different people. Mama raised me with a lot of love and that has made me who I am today. I don't know how you were raised, or if it has anything to do with the way you feel about me, I just know that I haven't walked in your shoes. And you wouldn't know how to walk in mine. People grow at different times, in different ways, and as individuals. We all have faults. Sometimes I think I'm a better person because of yours. I don't know for sure, though. I just know that I'm determined to be a good father, because I know what it feels like not to have one around.

The fact that you raised Lashawn and Bryce gives me a warm feeling about you. I want to thank you for that.

With love, Marcus

P.S. If you would like to come to the wedding, let us know.

He opened the drawer and took out a stamp and a business size envelope. He addressed the envelope and put the letter inside. Then he continued his work.

Ashley cleaned up the Legos and ran up to Marcus. "Daddy?" she said.

"Yeah, Ashley," he said, still writing.

"Put the pencil down. I'm going to plug you in." Ashley had a small toy airplane and a small remote control truck with a cord attached to it. Marcus put his pencil down—though he was busy and anxious to pick it back up.

Ashley placed the airplane on top of his head.

"Ashley, honey, Daddy's busy," Marcus said.

"You don't get it, do you, Daddy?"

Marcus smiled. And so, he sat there with the airplane on top of his head.

"Okay, Daddy, I'm getting ready to plug you in."

"Okay, honey."

"Hurry and pick up your pencil, Daddy! I'm getting ready to plug you in. When I plug, you write."

"Juuuuuuuuuuu," she said, and Marcus started writing again.

Then he said, "Okay, Ashley, Daddy can't play any more right now. I'm going to take the airplane off my head."

"Wait, Daddy. Juuuuuuuuuuuuu. Okay."

Ashley removed the airplane from his head. Then she took a letter-size piece of paper from his desk. There was typing on one side. She showed him the paper. "Is this important?" she asked.

He put down the pencil and read the paper. "No. It's okay. You can have it."

She turned the paper over and handed it to him. "Here, Daddy, I want you to write something for me. I want you to write four things you're getting for my birthday."

"Okay," he said.

"A camera," she said.

He wrote the word "camera."

"Daddy," she said.

"Yes, Ashley."

"You have to write: 'A camera for my birthday'!"

He wrote the entire sentence.

"Promise," she said.

"Yeah, I promise," he said.

"Write, 'promise,' Daddy."

"Oh, you want me to write 'promise'."

"Yeah. Write 'A camera for my birthday promise'."

"Okay, I got it," he said.

"Okay. Write, 'Two cupcakes for my birthday'."

He wrote the entire sentence because she was watching carefully.

" 'Two glues for my birthday'."

"Okay," he said.

"And, 'Take me to Fun Land for my birthday'."

"Okay," he said as he wrote.

"That was the longest sentence," she noticed.

"Yeah, it was. Now I need to finish my work. Go play with your toys, honey."

Shante and Serena arrived a few minutes later.

"Hi, ladies," Marcus said as they walked in. They both wore denim outfits.

"Hi, Marcus," said Serena.

"It started raining right after we got our hair done," Shante said. "We got caught in it."

"Oh, I'm sorry," said Marcus. "Ya'll still look beautiful."

"You're so kind, honey," Shante said. "It seems like every time we get our hair done, it rains."

Serena said, "There was a bad wreck out there. I think someone died."

"When I die, I want to be cremated, Shante said."

"You too?" Serena said in a surprised voice. "I think I do, too."

Marcus listened as he sat back down at the desk.

Shante said, "I want Marcus to keep my ashes with him, on a shelf."

"I want mine thrown into the ocean," said Serena. With a confused look on her face, she added, "I think." She began to feel tense. She started to hyperventilate. Marcus and Shante were talking and didn't notice Serena's excessive breathing.

At the dumpsite, the red warning light on Nathan's device was blinking on and off, but he wasn't paying attention. He was never this careless, but his mind had shifted to thoughts of

Serena. Moments later, there was an explosion. Nathan lay face down on the ground, unconscious.

Serena went in the kitchen. Taking a deep breath, she leaned into the sink for support. Then she drank a glass of water, wiping her face as some of the liquid trickled down her chin. She began to relax. As the tension subsided, her unconscious thoughts about her marriage came forth, revealing to her that she didn't want to be in an unhappy marriage for the rest of her life.

When Nathan regained consciousness, it took him a few minutes to focus his eyes. He was in a hospital. Everything looked blurry. He had a terrible headache. Then he saw Brandi's face. She was standing beside his bed.

"What happened?" he asked her.

"There was an explosion near where you were standing. The impact of the explosion lifted you off your feet and you hit your head against a rock. I don't know all of the details. I'm just happy to hear you talking. They found my number in your wallet."

Brandi held his hand until the nurse instructed her that visiting hours were over. She kissed him on the cheek before saying goodbye.

Nathan was bruised and groggy. He reached for the telephone. He was barely able to dial Serena's number. There was no answer.

The nurse came in and took the phone from his hands. "You're lucky to be alive," she said. "You need to rest." Within seconds, Nathan was asleep.

At the same time, Serena was saying goodbye to Shante, Marcus, and Ashley.

After Serena left, Shante went into the bedroom to match some outfits to wear to work the next few days. Ashley took the chess set out of the entertainment cabinet. Marcus agreed to play one game with her.

They played for a while, and as the game ended, Marcus said "You won."

"I don't want you to let me win, Daddy. Let's play again."

"I didn't let you win," Marcus said.

"Yes you did, Daddy. Be honest. Let's play again."

"Okay Ashley, one more game." He felt bad for lying.

The game was almost over and Ashley was losing. "I . . . want to win," she said firmly.

"Hey Shante-e-e," Marcus called.

"Yeah?" she yelled from the bedroom.

"Do you want to play chess with Ashley?"

Ashley pursed her lips and gave Marcus a mean look. Shante didn't answer.

Ashley put the chess set away. "Let's play a different game, Daddy."

"Okay, I'm ready," said Marcus.

"I say something weird, and you have to guess what it is," Ashley said.

"Okay."

"You," she said.

"You," he repeated.

"No. You have to guess what it is, Daddy. Like . . . you." She held out her hands, with no words to explain what she meant.

"Oh. Like finishing your sentence?" Marcus asked.

"Yes." Ashley nodded and smiled happily.

"Okay," he said, "we'll start over."

"You," she said.

"You are silly," he said.

"N-o-o-o-o-o," she said.

"You like pizza."

"N-o-o-o-o-o."

"I don't know what it is," Marcus said.

"U Turn," she said.

"Oh, that's very good, Ashley. I would have never guessed that." She grinned, and he smiled back at her.

"Let me get some construction paper so you can draw pictures," he said.

He gave Ashley enough paper to keep her busy for a good while. Then he went into the kitchen to have a snack.

Ashley cut the construction paper into strips. She glued bits of paper in various shapes onto the strips and designed a colorful hat for Marcus. She ran into the kitchen and put a strip of paper around his head in order to get an accurate measurement. She ran back and forth until she was certain her measurements were perfect. The result was a very interesting looking hat. She placed the hat on his head.

"You look like a mailbox," she laughed.

Marcus sat there looking like a big kid while eating chocolate Jell-O pudding.

Ashley took the hat off his head and worked on it some more. "Now," she said. She put the hat back on his head. "Now you look like an elf." She smiled. "You can be an elf for Halloween. Come look in the mirror, Daddy."

She grabbed his hand and led him to the mirror in the living room. Marcus cracked up laughing.

Shante finally came out of hiding. "What's so funny?" They all laughed.

"Ashley, you're so creative!" Shante said.

"Thank you, Ashley," Marcus said still laughing. "I love it."

Ashley blushed with confidence.

Twenty-six

When Serena got home, she turned on the television set and sat on the sofa. She scanned the stations, stopping when she saw John Gray. He was talking about his book *Men Are From Mars, Women Are From Venus.* She listened carefully, then she began to laugh. "This man knows what he's talking about," she muttered. "And it's *clear* that he knows what he's talking about—unlike some of the other experts."

Julian came home a few minutes later.

"Hi, Julian. Come here. This is interesting."

Julian walked over to Serena and glanced at the television. "Yeah," he said. "I'm sure it's good, but I don't want to watch it. What's for dinner?"

"Nothing yet," Serena said. "I just got here myself. Shante and I went to get our hair done and then it rained on us."

Julian looked at Serena's hair, which lay flat. "I don't understand why you even go get your hair done. Whenever you do, you come home and comb it out anyway."

Later, as they were getting ready for bed, Serena took a thick pair of thermal socks out of the drawer. She put on an oyster-colored satin nightgown. Then she put on the socks.

Julian Frowned. "Why are you wearing those thick socks, Serena? It's not cold."

"I like to sleep in socks sometimes, and your feet scratch me when you put them on my side of the bed," she answered.

"No, they don't."

I'm not going to argue, Serena thought. I'm just keeping my socks on. She turned off the light. "Goodnight," she said.

Before Serena could get comfortable in bed, Julian was already snoring very loudly.

"Honey," she whispered, patting him gently on the shoulder. "Will you please turn over? You're snoring."

Julian started mumbling. Serena didn't know which was worse—until he started snoring again. It sounded like a bull-dozer digging up the bed.

She thought she might as well get up. She wasn't sleepy anyway. It was a little chilly, so she found her matching robe and slid it on, feeling the softness of the silk.

She went downstairs and played music by some of her favorite artists—Whitney Houston, Pattie LaBelle, Celine Dion, and Julia Fordham. So as not to disturb Julian's sleep, she turned the music down low. She started singing "Porcelain, porcelain, treat my skin like porcelain." Then she went into the kitchen. The fresh smell of blueberry muffins brought back memories of her childhood. She thought about the elderly people she and her mother used to visit on Sundays, after church. One of them would always give her a batch of blueberry muffins to take home with her.

She poured a glass of orange juice, sat at the glass and marble breakfast table, and served herself a muffin. As she ate, she began thinking about Nathan and the time he was covered with mud. She started giggling.

"Serena!" a loud voice called.

She looked up. Julian stood in the doorway, rubbing his eyes. "What are you doing? Come back to bed."

"I'm coming soon," she said.

"No, I want you to come now."

"Okay, okay. I'll be there in a minute." He treats me like a child, she thought as she put her glass in the sink. Anything to keep him quiet. She stuffed the last bit of muffin in her mouth, turned off the music and marched up the stairs.

Twenty-seven

The first week in October felt like perfect Indian Summer to Serena. Autumn was her favorite season. She slowly inhaled the fresh, crisp air as she stepped outside her home to meet Shante and Nikki.

Serena and Nikki had made plans to take Shante to lunch and to look at wedding dresses. After lunch, they stopped at Baskin Robbins for ice cream. There were so many choices that Shante couldn't make up her mind which kind to get—as usual. Nikki usually could make up her mind fairly quickly. But one thing that amazed Shante about Serena, was that Serena would always get vanilla. "How can you walk in here, and see all these different flavors, and choose vanilla so easily every time?" Shante asked.

Serena laughed at Shante. It was simple to her. "I like other ice creams, but I like vanilla the best," she answered.

"But you haven't tasted them," Shante said.

"I can imagine what they taste like," Serena explained.

After they left Baskin Robbins, they went to a small bridal boutique that had just opened up in downtown Manhattan. When Shante stepped inside and saw all the beautiful gowns, she felt like a princess in a fairy-tale.

"Look Shante," Serena said, "this one is so beautiful."

"Oh, yes, it is," Shante agreed.

"It's exquisite," Serena added.

Shante said, "Serena, I do love this gown."

Nikki looked on with her arms folded as she studied the dress. "I like it, too," she said.

"Try it on," Serena said enthusiastically.

Shante went into the dressing room and put on the gown. It was elegant white satin with short sleeves. It was cut low and had satin roses around the neckline. The entire back of the dress was open—all the way to the hips.

"Oh," Shante said when she looked in the mirror, "I think I'm going to start bawling here in a minute." Shante's eyes sparkled like black pearls in crystal waters.

"Me, too," Serena said, her eyes aglow as well.

"Save that for the wedding," Nikki said. Or maybe after the wedding, she thought. Nikki liked Marcus, but she didn't think he and Shante should get married just yet. Even though she was getting better, she still had some doubts about a man's ability to commit to one woman.

As Serena and Shante continued admiring the dress, Nikki walked slowly around the store, surveying the various wedding gift ideas. She saw an antique clock in the window. How pretty, she thought. Then she peered out the window and down the street at the people passing by. She saw Malik standing at a distance. He was talking to a man in a suit and pointing at the top of a building.

"Why do I keep seeing this guy?" she asked herself. Then she realized that she wasn't far from the construction site between Fifth and Madison. It was the same site from which she had reported on the accident.

"I'll be right back," Nikki said.

"Where is she going?" Serena asked. Shante and Serena walked over to the window and stared out.

Shante shrugged her shoulders. "I don't know." They walked back to the gowns and continued looking at them.

Nikki crossed the busy, noisy street and walked toward Malik. She stopped abruptly. "What am I doing?" she asked herself. She wanted to say something to him, but she didn't know what to say or how to go about saying it. She took a deep breath. "I'm so confused," she said under her breath. "No, I'm not. I know what I want to say." She felt nervous. She started rehearsing one-liners. "Malik, I'm sorry for . . . No. That's no good. Malik, I want to apologize . . . No way. I was just down the street at the boutique and I saw . . . No, that is so corny. Oh, no. He's getting ready to leave. I'd better hurry. I'll just say, hi."

Malik heard footsteps coming towards him. When he saw who it was, he could feel his heart thumping.

"Hi," Nikki said.

"Hello," said Malik.

"Hello-o-o," said the man in the suit.

Nikki glanced at the man and said, "Hi." Then she focused her attention on Malik.

"Could you excuse us for a minute?" Malik said.

"Yeah," said the man. "But I need you to get back to work soon."

Since Nikki didn't show any interest in the man, the man seemed to feel the need to let Nikki know that he was in charge of Malik. He looked at Nikki, but she completely ignored him. The man excused himself.

Nikki took a deep breath, then spoke. "I just wanted to tell you . . ." She paused.

"Yeah?" Malik said, leaning his head forward expectantly.

"I saw you from the bridal boutique up the street," she said.

"The bridal boutique." Malik glanced toward the store.

"Yes. A friend of mine is looking for a gown."

"Oh," said Malik. He felt like he was having a fascinating dream. He could not believe he was actually standing there talking to Nikki and having a civilized conversation. He felt like he could conquer any battle.

"I want to apologize for some of the things I said." Nikki frowned, unsure if Malik would accept her apology.

"Hey, you don't have to apologize. I'm the one who should be apologizing. I'm sorry for coming to your job the way I did without asking."

"I forgive you. But, do you make a habit of doing that sort of thing?" she asked.

"No, no. I guess I just got excited and I wanted to show you that I don't always look . . . Well, like this." He looked down at his grubby construction clothes.

Nikki smiled. "Are you involved with anyone?" she asked. "You don't have to answer," she added quickly.

"No, I'm not," he said.

"Maybe you can come over for dinner sometime," she said.

"Maybe." He nodded, yes. Malik enjoyed seeing a different side of Nikki. He was both mentally and physically turned on by everything he was hearing and seeing.

Nikki felt like a load had been lifted off her chest as she said goodbye. Still blushing and looking at Malik, Nikki stepped backwards off the sidewalk into the street. At the same time, a man was backing his car into the space where Nikki stepped. The man blew his horn loudly.

Before Nikki was fully aware of what was happening, she had been lifted from the curb and was safely back on the sidewalk, wrapped in Malik's arms. She gasped for air. Then she looked into Malik's eyes and all her fear subsided. Their warm bodies grew weak and tingly. She felt so protected, and Malik didn't want to let go of her.

"Is tomorrow okay?" he asked still holding her close.

"Yes, tomorrow's perfect," she said.

Nikki straightened her short black skirt, smiling bashfully.

"Goodbye now," she said.

"Be careful," he said. Then he grinned like a young boy who had just traded a patch at the Boy Scout Jamboree.

Nikki went back to the boutique, where Serena and Shante were still concentrating on wedding gowns. "Where'd you go?" Shante asked Nikki.

"I saw Malik. You know, that guy I told you about, Serena."

Serena's and Shante's eyebrows went up at the same time, amazed that Nikki had approached Malik, and delighted to see the radiant look on her face. "Don't look at me like that," Nikki said. "I'm just taking my doctor's advice. She told me to reach out to people." Nikki thrust her hands into the air. "I'm just reaching out."

Shante and Serena grinned broadly.

Nikki thought about Malik all the way home that evening. "I can't believe I invited him to dinner," she said to herself as she entered her home. But she felt safe enough, since Lonny Russo had finished part of the investigation. Then she realized something else. "What was I thinking?" she asked herself. "I can't cook!"

She grabbed her keys and rushed back out to buy a cookbook and a few groceries. She came home and practiced making tuna casserole. She sampled it. She wasn't sure whether it tasted good or not. If I can't tell whether or not it tastes good, it must not taste good, she thought. She blew air through her lips in exasperation. She couldn't practice and learn how to cook in one day. She'd seen that happen to people too many times. She thought they'd usually overcook the food, undercook it, or make mush. She tasted the casserole again. Sometimes they downright burn the food, she thought further. Then she had a brainstorm. "That's it!" she said to herself. Tomorrow she would go to that deli down the street and buy dinner. She took a deep breath and smiled with relief.

Later that night, Nikki got a call from Lonny Russo—the private investigator. He was ready to tell her everything that he had found out about Malik.

She couldn't believe she had hired the investigator. But she had to listen to what he had learned. "Go ahead," she said. "Tell me what you know."

"Na, let's see," the pot-bellied investigator said as he talked from the cellular telephone in his Lincoln Towncar. "This Malik Jordan has been married once. Looks like it didn't last very long. He divorced a couple of years ago. He was born in August, 1968. "Ah," he said, looking at his notes, his voice hoarse and raspy. "Damn!"

"What!" she said.

"Ah shit . . . nothing . . . I just . . . excuse my language. I just spilled coke all over my seats and I don't have nothing to wipe it up with. He finished high school in the Bronx. No college. Let's see, Malik has no children and he's been working for Chavis Construction Company for eight years. He was raised by his grandparents. The only thing I've seen this guy doing is working, going to the grocery store, and taking his wheelchair-bound grandfather to his doctor's appointment."

Lonny Russo paused for a minute to clear his throat, then he continued. "Malik's parents were killed in a house fire when he was a baby." Nikki gasped and a lump formed in her throat. "Apparently, Malik's father removed him from his crib, rushed him outside, and laid him in the grass. When his father went back inside to get his mother, she was trapped in a smoke-filled room. When he got to her, she was lying on the floor unconscious. Then the floor collapsed. They both fell to their deaths. The sharp blades of grass left scratches on Malik's face, but other than that he wasn't injured." The investigator had been reading from an old newspaper article he had located.

Nikki sat teary eyed as she listened. She started feeling guilty about not giving Malik a chance to tell her himself, over time, and when he was ready. "I won't tell him that I know," she said to herself. "But that's lying. I hate lying, remember."

One thing she still did not know was why Malik's marriage

had ended, but she refused to let Lonny Russo tell her anything else. "Thank you for your services," she said. "I won't be
needing them any longer."

❖

Twenty-eight

*I*t was 5:50 p.m. Malik had arrived at Nikki's house ten minutes early, carrying an armful of long-stemmed red, pink, yellow, and white roses. One stem was stuck between his teeth and he wore a silly grin. He rang the doorbell with his elbow.

When Nikki opened the door and saw Malik standing there with the flowers, and one stem in his mouth, she laughed. When he came inside Nikki noticed that he smelled even better than the flowers. He was wearing Quarum cologne.

"Thank you," she said reaching out for the flowers. "There are so many of them. You didn't have to do this."

Malik still couldn't believe that he was standing in Nikki's home—and she had invited him. It was like a dream come true. "Thanks for inviting me," he said.

"I'm glad you came. Have a seat, I'll be right back." When Nikki turned to walk away, Malik found himself staring at her behind.

Nikki went into the kitchen. She had to use two vases because there were so many flowers. Malik canvassed her south-

ern, traditionally styled furnishings. He noticed the brown teddy
bears scattered around the apartment. One sat on a shelf, two
were hugging a lamppost, and another had glasses and was
propped against the window seal. Still another sat in a hand-
made antique stroller. He smiled warmly.

Nikki returned to the living room and sat on the opposite
end of the sofa. She wore a champagne-colored, long-sleeved silk
blouse and a matching above-the-knee skirt.

"You look beautiful," Malik told her. "I can't believe I'm here."

"Neither can I," she said.

There were a few moments of awkward silence. "How are
things going at your job?" Malik asked at last.

"Everything's going well," she answered. "When will you finish your work downtown?"

"We would be done by now, but when the accident happened,
it slowed us down."

"Ah, I can imagine."

"It shouldn't take much longer, though," he said. "Are you
from here?"

"No. I'm from Louisiana—Shreveport. I've been here for
seven years."

More silence lingered between them.

"Do you want to know where I'm from?" Malik said.

"Uh," Nikki said. "I think I already know."

"You do?"

"Uh, your accent! Yeah. Your accent tells me that you're from
this area." Nikki was really thinking about the investigation.
She wanted to tell him the truth, but wasn't ready.

"Oh, yeah," he said. "Most people can't tell because I talk
sorta slow."

"Ahem," she cleared her throat and stood. "Are you ready to
eat?"

"Sure," he said, rising slowly.

She glanced at his tan jacket and matching slacks. "I like
your suit. You look good."

"Thanks," he said confidently, nodding his head.

She led him into the kitchen where she served roast beef, green beans, potato salad, corn bread and iced tea. As they sat at the golden oak table, she nibbled on her dinner and watched happily as Malik seemed to be enjoying his. "That sure was good," he said.

"I'm glad you liked it," she said, as she put some dishes in the sink.

"I really liked those green beans. How do you season yours?"

Nikki quickly turned toward Malik. *"What was that?"* She looked toward the living room.

"What!" Malik's eyes popped with surprise.

"Did you hear something?" she asked.

"I didn't hear anything," he said. But he went and peered into the other room.

"Oh, it was probably nothing," she said.

Malik looked confused.

Nikki turned around and started washing the dishes. I hope he doesn't ask me how I seasoned those green beans again, she thought. She couldn't imagine how to change the subject *again*.

"Let me wash them," he said, moving to the sink.

"You can take off your blazer and hang it over the chair."

"Okay," he said.

Malik took off his jacket. He wore a black T-shirt underneath and Nikki noticed the sexy muscles in his arms and chest. She handed him a drying cloth. "I'll wash, and you can dry." They smiled, acting like fifteen year olds on a first date.

Then Malik broke the awkward silence. "I saw you on the 'Agnus Floyd Show.' I thought you were great! I said she'll get um straight."

"Thanks," Nikki said. Then she told him about her experiences as a journalist.

Afterwards, they talked for hours in the living room. Nikki told Malik about her sisters and her mother. Malik talked about his grandparents and his job. They didn't realize how late it was getting. They enjoyed each other's company and were very comfortable with one another.

"So, what do you like to do for fun? I mean, when you're not working," Malik asked.

"I either spend time with my friends, or I watch movies. I have a great collection of videos," she answered.

"You, too! I love movies, all kinds. I usually go to the theater, but a collection is a good idea."

They sat for a few minutes naming some of their favorite actors. "I like Cecily Tyson, Meryl Streep, Danny Glover and Anthony Hopkins," Nikki said. "Oh, and Denzel Washington. I thought his performance in *A Soldier's Story* was outstanding, and in *Glory.*"

"Yeah, all of his performances are great," Malik said. "I like Samuel L. Jackson, Whoopi Goldberg and Morgan Freeman. Robert Duvall and Sidney Poitier, too."

"There are so many great actors," she said. "My mom, my sisters and I used to stay up real late on Friday nights. We'd eat peanuts, drink soda, and watch scary movies."

Nikki showed him her video collection, and he picked an action movie starring John Travolta for them to watch. Nikki put the movie in the VCR, and they sat close together on the sofa.

They laughed and talked off and on as they watched the movie. It was now 11:55 p.m. Both of them had to be at work early the next morning, but that didn't seem to matter. They were having so much fun that they decided to skip a good night's sleep—at least for tonight.

Nikki looked at Malik as the movie was ending. He's beginning to look a little strange, she thought. His face—it's turning red, deep red.

"Malik, are you okay?"

"Uh, I . . . I'm okay."

It was late, she thought. Maybe he was just tired. She looked at her watch. It was now 1:00 a.m.

Malik began to feel dizzy. He blinked his eyes and shook his head. Then he started seeing light dots and black spots. He began to feel as if he might vomit, but nothing came up, fortunately, because he was too sick to make it to the bathroom.

"Malik," Nikki said. "Something's wrong! I'm calling 911!"

Still conscious, Malik slumped over on the sofa.

The ambulance arrived minutes later and Nikki climbed in the back.

"Can you tell us anything else?" one of the paramedics asked Nikki on the way to the hospital.

"No. Like I said before, we were just sitting there, and all of a sudden he turned sort of a reddish-purple color."

When they arrived at the hospital, Dr. Rhodes ran blood tests. Nikki was standing by Malik's bedside when the doctor said, "You have food poisoning, Mr. Jordan."

Nikki's eyes popped like a cork from a wine bottle.

Nikki told the doctor what she had served for dinner. The doctor said, "It was more than likely the potato salad that caused his illness." Nikki realized that was probably true, since she had not eaten any of the potato salad, and she wasn't sick.

This has to be the most embarrassing moment of my life, she thought. She confessed to Malik that she bought the food at a deli.

"I saw it in your pots and pans," he said.

"I'm telling you the truth," she said, her eyes teary. "I put it in the pots and pans after I bought it already cooked. The truth is I can't cook. I wanted to do something special for you. When I invited you to dinner, I wasn't thinking about the fact that I've never cooked for anyone before. I'm so sorry."

Malik was still in pain, but when he looked up at Nikki, he felt sorrier for her than he did for himself. A-a-a-h, he thought, as he looked at her eyes. She looks like a sad little puppy. "It's not your fault Nikki, you didn't know the food was bad," he said.

"I should have just taken you out to dinner or something," she said.

"Stop blaming yourself, okay? If getting food poisoning is the only way I can be with you, then I'll get it again if I have to."

Nikki smiled and wiped her tear-filled eyes.

"I had the best time I have ever had in my life. O-o-o-o-h, and I'm the sickest I've ever been in my life."

Nikki laughed softly.

"That's what I wanted to see," he said. "It was a privilege to be able to spend time with you, and having you here next to me right now makes it all the more worth while."

Malik was so sweet that Nikki felt like climbing up onto the bed, lying down beside him and holding him.

"I can cook," he said. "My grandma taught me how when I was little. My parents died when I was a baby."

"I'm so sorry," Nikki said.

"It's okay. Grandma was always afraid she might not be around and that I might have to take care of myself. Next time, let me do the cooking."

Nikki smiled. "Hey, whatever you say."

The doctor came in and explained the results of the test. "It is a fairly bad case of food poisoning, but it could have been much worse."

"Can I go home?" Malik asked.

"No, not yet. We want to keep a close eye on you for the next . . . twelve to twenty-four hours. When you're released depends largely on how you feel in the morning."

Twenty-nine

*M*alik kept his promise to do the cooking on their next date. In fact, over the next two weeks, he insisted on bringing groceries to Nikki's condo and cooking several nights a week. One evening when Malik pulled up in his older model Ford Explorer truck, Nikki did the insisting. She insisted on taking him out to dinner.

"I'll drive," he said.

Malik held the door open for Nikki and she climbed in, wearing a linen, cement-colored pantsuit. Malik couldn't think of a time in his life when he had been happier.

After five years of celibacy and not trusting men, Nikki now knew one man that she wanted more than anything in the world to trust.

Thirty minutes later, Nikki and Malik entered the dimly lit restaurant, which had a small dance floor. The band stopped to take a break just as Nikki and Malik sat down at their table. They studied the menu and then a waiter approached and took their order. As they sat waiting for the band to start again, Malik couldn't take his eyes off Nikki. Nikki noticed how intently he was staring at her.

Malik suddenly burst into song. "Am I dre-e-e-m-min-in-in-in. Am I just imagin-in' you're here." He flashed Nikki a silly grin.

Nikki looked wide-eyed at Malik. Okay, she thought, you never know what this guy is going to do from one minute to the next. Then she burst into soft giggles.

Minutes later, their dinner was served. As they ate, Nikki began to open up about her past. She told Malik about her marriage to Dallas. Malik was brought almost to tears.

"That son of a . . ," he said. Then he thought, I don't want to curse. This night is too special. Nikki is too special. "Gun," he said. "You did the right thing, by not giving him another chance. He didn't deserve the first chance." Malik felt angry. "My grandparents always taught me to treat people the way you want to be treated. And if you want to be lied to and treated badly, then you need to get some help."

Nikki started feeling uncomfortable. She thought about how she would feel if Malik had hired an investigator to find out about her and her painful past. She felt guilty, especially now that he seemed like such a kind and sincere person. She had not expected him to be genuine. She debated whether she should tell him what she had done. But then she concluded that she still wasn't sure if he was really sincere. So she told herself that she probably did the right thing. He could still be hiding something.

Malik told Nikki that he, too, had been hurt before.

Nikki listened.

"I divorced a couple of years ago. Actually, she left me," he said.

"What happened?" she asked. "I mean, you don't have to talk about it if you don't want to."

"I want to," he said. "I thought everything was fine. About a year after we got married, she started complaining a lot. I didn't understand it because I wasn't doing anything different. I was the same man she married. One day she said, 'Malik, you act like an old man.' "

"Really!" Nikki looked surprised.

"Yeah. I didn't understand that because I—"

"I know, you were the same man she married," Nikki said.

"Right. She said I spent too much time taking care of my grandfather, and not enough time with her. My grandfather was very sick at the time. He had just had heart surgery. He was supposed to take it easy. I wanted to be there for him and my grandma the way they were always there for me."

"Of course, you love them," Nikki said.

"She'd say, 'You don't have to go over there every day do you?' Anyway, he's much better now." Malik smiled.

"I'm glad to hear that," she said.

"Thanks."

"But, that caused your divorce?"

"Not exactly, but that hurt me a lot," Malik said, tapping his chest with his fist. "I felt like she didn't have a heart. I wondered how in the world could I have married someone so damn selfish? That's why, when I saw the way you reported that story, I knew you had a heart."

Nikki eyes sparkled. She thought that was the most romantic thing she had ever heard.

"I knew you had been hurt," he said, "because I saw your heart and there was nothing that could make me believe what I saw was a lie. I felt your spirit, too. I've never felt anything like that before."

Malik took a deep breath. Then he continued telling Nikki about his ex-wife. "One night when I got home from work, she announced that she was tired of being poor. She was a cashier, and . . . well . . . you know what I do. I make pretty good money, but it wudn't enough for her. Hell, sometimes it's not enough for me, but you do the best you can. She wanted to shop everyday, and she wanted a new car—a red convertible. I couldn't afford it. I bought her some diamond earrings. They weren't big enough for her. I have to admit, they were tiny."

"Tiny earrings are cute," Nikki said consolingly. "Besides, it's the thought."

Malik smiled. "Well, she met someone else—some lawyer cat. She left me."

"Oh. That son of a . . . gun," she said. She reached out and held Malik's hand.

"I never thought I was poor," he said. "My grandparents always told me that if you work hard, and if you're a good and honest person, you can always hold your head up high."

"And your grandparents were exactly right, Malik. Do you still love her?"

"No, not at all. She did me a favor by leaving. About six months after she left, she tried to come back to me—when her rich lawyer wudn't everything she thought he'd be. She was sure I would take her back. And I probably would have, if she'd come back sooner. After a few months it was too late. I learned that we were too different to make it work. When I refused to allow her to waltz back into my life, she got angry. She even tried to get my grandparents to talk to me."

"The very people she didn't want you to spend too much time helping," Nikki said.

"Right, right," he said.

"Selfish, indeed."

"They told me to do what I wanted to do. They knew I'd make the right choice, and I did."

Malik and Nikki chatted through the rest of their meal. When they were both finished, he reached for her hand and led her to the dance floor. They held each other close as they slow danced.

I love him, she thought.

"I love you," he said.

Nikki wanted to say the words, but she couldn't. "I'm afraid," she said.

"Say it with your heart," he said softly.

"I love you," she said, suddenly without difficulty. The words flew from her lips before she could think.

Nikki had not been held by a man in years. She realized that she had never been held in the arms of a real man, until now.

"You can trust me," he said. "I'll never hurt you. I promise you that."

"I can't believe that. It's not safe for me to believe that." Her eyes welled with tears.

"Nikki, you're safe," he whispered, holding her close. "You'll always be safe with me."

"How do you know you can keep your promise?" she asked.

"Because you've become my life support, Nikki—the air that fills my lungs," he said, in a deep seductive whisper. "I need you. I need you, Nikki."

Their lips met with a desire so strong, that they both trembled like the strings on a harp.

When they returned to Nikki's house, she asked Malik to come in for a few minutes. "I want to talk to you about something. Please, sit down. There's something I need to tell you." She had no idea where to begin.

"Okay, tell me." Malik creased a brow.

She sat next to him. "I've done something that I wish I hadn't."

"What?"

"I hired a private investigator to follow you and, probe into your past."

Malik was stunned. "What do you mean?"

"Remember when you called me at my job, after I'd already told you that I wasn't interested?"

"Uh, yeah."

"That's when I did it. I got curious. I didn't know who you were—if you were sincere. I'm so used to being lied to. I . . . I wanted to find out if you were seeing someone."

"Did you find out everything you needed to know?" he said sadly. He stood up. "I mean, is there anything I can tell you about myself that you don't already know?"

There was silence. "Was I able to go to the bathroom in private," Malik said, "or were they looking there, too?"

"I didn't let him tell me everything," she said, ashamed.

"Do you know everything about my parents, Nikki?"

"Yes. I'm sorry, Malik. I'm sorry about your parents, and I'm sorry about what I've done."

"All you had to do was ask me. I would have told you everything you wanted to know."

"I didn't know that then, but I do now."

Malik still grieved for the loss of his parents, and he felt robbed of the chance to express his grief to Nikki when he was ready. But then he thought about how Nikki had been lied to in her past. "Nikki, babe, you can't judge all men by what those bums did to you. I'm not like them. They were fools to even think about hurting you."

Malik looked wearily down at the floor. He's never going to speak to me again, she thought.

"I'd better go now," he said. "It's getting late, and I have to work early tomorrow morning."

I don't want him to go, she thought as she walked him to the door.

"I'll call you, okay?" he said.

"Okay." She didn't believe him. She swallowed hard to hide her emotions. "Goodbye now."

He opened the door and walked out. She closed the door behind him. Tears streamed down her face. The innermost part of her was crying.

Then she heard a knock. She turned around. "Did he forget something?" She wiped her red eyes until they were free from tears. Then she opened the door.

Malik stood in the doorway. "I just want you to know that I understand why you did it," he said. "I don't want you to think about it any more. It's over. And, I want to ask you if you'll go to church with me on Sunday."

Nikki was deeply touched. She stared at him for a few minutes. Then she spoke. "Only if you'll come back inside, and make love to me."

"Oh, boy," he said, his eyes widening. His heart skipped a couple of beats as he grabbed his chest. He took a deep breath and relaxed.

She gently tugged on the front of his shirt as she backed into the house. She held his hand and led him toward the bedroom.

"Hey," he said. "I'm not that easy."

"You are tonight," she said.

The charming grin on Malik's face let Nikki know that he wouldn't resist. She opened the bedroom door and they entered. The light of the full moon came through the window, casting a silvery glow over the room, much like the glow in Malik's eyes. Nikki fell back onto the bed, stretching her arms out and knocking the biggest teddy bear in her collection onto the floor. Malik rid himself of his shirt, then leaned over her, rapidly unbuckling his pants and kissing her lips. She leaned in to taste the taut and pulsating muscles of his chest. But Malik backed away, a frown of intense desire on his face.

"What is it?" she asked with concern as she unbuttoned her jacket, revealing her red satin bra.

He swallowed at the sight of her and Nikki could hear the moisture in his throat. "Let's go slow. We have all night."

Nikki's mouth parted in sweet anticipation. But she was glad *he* had some control, because for the first time in a long time, she didn't. And she too wanted this to last, and last, and last.

He slowly unbuttoned her pants and slid them off. With Malik's help, Nikki wiggled out of her jacket, her bra, her red satin panties. Malik gripped the panties, rubbed them between his fingers, then playfully tossed them on the floor.

He let his pants drop to the floor and Nikki smiled at him— a big smile. She pushed back the covers and lay against the soft sheets. She raised her neck to pull her long hair out from under her. It glistened in the moonlight. Still more light crept in from the living room.

She looked like heaven on earth to him, a vision too good to be true. A quiet peace filled the room as Malik studied her from head to toe. Nikki pulled the sheets up to her waist, suddenly feeling a little shy. Malik noticed her modesty and said, "Nikki, you're the sexiest woman alive, trust me."

She caught her breath, closed her eyes, as her body tingled from the top of her head to the tips of her toes. Malik watched her dark nipples protrude further. He leaned against her and his chest brushed against them. He trembled. His breath caught in his throat as Nikki softly ran her hands up and down his backside.

He moved to taste her lips, gently sucking the top one, and then the bottom. His manly scent and warm, moist lips nearly drove her over the edge as she moaned. He blew on and kissed her ear, then licked behind it, trembling again and grimacing when he caught the scent of her light, intoxicating perfume. He buried his head in her silky hair and she could feel his hard arousal.

Conscious of the fact that his hands were a little work-roughened, he was extra gentle as he slowly ran them down her neck, her arms, her thigh and then back up to her breast where they lingered . . . and lingered. Malik had never heard anything quite as sexy as Nikki's delicate moans. And her chocolate skin was so soft and beautiful that he wanted to devour every inch of her. He bent to taste her, to feel her all over before finally easing deep inside her tightness. Simultaneously, they gasped and Nikki arched back, gripping the hair on the back of his head. She leaned in to taste his lips again as they moved rhythmically against each other, feeling their love for each other growing stronger by the minute. Nikki's eyes watered and Malik kissed them gently as a lump formed in his throat. "I love you," he said deep in his throat. Nikki whimpered as her body tingled. Malik slowly and softly licked her cheek and they kissed each other passionately.

When it was over, they lay in awe of the pleasure they had just experienced. Neither of them had ever imagined that there could be this much love between two people.

Malik was the most gentle man Nikki had ever known. And as far as she was concerned, he was the only man she'd ever known—in this way, at least. "That was perfection," she said, dozing off. He smiled.

Malik held Nikki in his strong muscular arms and stroked her long silky hair as she slept. He thought about how good it had felt to be inside her and how he wanted to make love to her again. But she's sleeping so peacefully, he thought as he lay awake hard and holding her.

But minutes later, Nikki awoke . . . .

"Oh . . . I get it," he said, nodding his head. "You just took a power nap. You think you're slick, don't you?"

Nikki giggled. She lifted her head off his chest and looked into his beautiful dark eyes. Then she crawled on top of him, blushing when she felt him ready for her again.

She tenderly caressed the damp skin of his chest, stroking her fingers along the silky, dark hair that ran down the center of it. She kissed him, then moved to help him inside. They were in complete ecstasy as they made love again. Malik had never imagined that life could be this good. He held her face in his hands, kissing it over and over again . . . Afterwards, they both fell asleep.

"He awakened to see the sun rising through the sheer white curtains. Minutes later, Nikki opened her eyes and smiled at him. "Good morning," she said.

"Better than good," Malik said. "It's the best morning of my life."

❖

Thirty

It was a cold October Sunday in Washington. Nathan and Devan were enjoying a Redskins versus Dallas Cowboys game. Devan attentively watched the game while he ate popcorn and drank soda. Nathan sat stone-faced with his hands in his pockets. With the sounds of cheering and the band playing in the background, he began to think about that game some twelve years before when Serena was a cheerleader, and he was covered in mud. I would do anything just to hold her right now, he thought. He looked over at Devan and imagined Serena sitting on the other side of him, cheering. He smiled. Then he blinked.

Devan was excited that the Redskins won by seven points. He talked about it all the way home. As they entered the apartment, Nathan heard his phone ringing. He hurried to answer it. Devan rushed just as quickly over to his box of Star Wars toys that sat in the corner of the room.

It was Monique wanting to know if she could bring dinner over to Nathan.

"I, I just walked in the door," he said. He scratched his head. "We've been snacking on popcorn and hot dogs and we're really not hungry."

"I'm hungry, Daddy!" Devan yelled.

"I heard that," Monique said. "Why don't I just bring it over, and you can have it for dinner tomorrow."

"Okay," he said, not wanting to seem unappreciative. "That's so nice. I'll see you soon, goodbye."

A few minutes later, the phone rang again. It was Brandi. She called to tell Nathan that she'd be a little late for work the next morning because her parents were in town. "They're leaving in the morning, and I'd like to be here when they leave."

"Sure, no problem," Nathan said. "Give them my best. Oh, Brandi, did you ever tell Monique that I wasn't interested in a serious relationship with her?"

"No. I haven't seen her this week."

"She's on her way over here right now," he said, and added that he was going to tell Monique that he was only interested in a friendship. "She's nice, but I just don't feel the same way she does."

Brandi agreed that he should go ahead and tell Monique how he felt so that he didn't have to feel uneasy anymore.

One hour later, Nathan looked out the window and saw Monique approaching. Her hands were full and she was wearing a cream blouse and a short sage green skirt and matching jacket. Nathan, still wearing the jeans and sweatshirt he had worn to the game, quickly opened the door.

"Hello," he said. He took the bag from her and put it on the end tabie near the door. "Thank you. This is so nice."

"Oh, you're welcome," she said. Anything for you, she thought.

After a few moments of awkwardness and hesitation, Nathan said, "Come on in."

Monique smiled bashfully. "Are you sure?"

"Yeah . . . really, sure. It's okay."

Inside, he introduced her to Devan. Then he invited her to stay for dinner. He thought that was the least he could do. After dinner, Devan went into his room and started playing video games while Nathan and Monique sat at the kitchen table.

"The dinner was very good," Nathan said. "Thanks again."

Monique blushed. "I'm glad you enjoyed it."

Nathan gave a fake yawn and stretched, hoping it would signal Monique to leave.

"Oh, you're tired," she said. She got up and started massaging his shoulders.

Nathan looked left and right with startled eyes. Then the telephone rang. Thank God, he thought, saved by the bell. "Excuse me while I answer that." Nathan didn't see anything wrong with a nice massage, but he could tell Monique was thinking of taking it further. He also had a list of things he had to do before work the next morning.

While Nathan was on the phone, Monique started washing the dishes. After his phone conversation, he stopped by Devan's room. He laid a towel and a washcloth on the edge of Devan's red and blue soccer ball comforter and turned the shower on for him. "I won't be able to read you a story tonight son, but I want you to shower and get into bed, okay?"

"Okay, Daddy, Goodnight."

"I'll read you two stories next time. Okay, little strong man?"

"D-a-a-a-d."

"Yeah Dev?"

"I can read myself a story."

Nathan looked surprised. "I know you can, but . . . I—"

"It's okay, Daddy," Devan giggled. "You can read me two stories next time."

"Good night," Nathan said, smiling and shaking his head. I can't believe how much he has grown, he thought on his way back to the kitchen.

"No, no, no—I'm not letting you wash the dishes, too," he told Monique. "I'll finish them later." He handed her a towel so she could dry her hands.

She turned toward him, tossing the towel on the kitchen counter. "Are you ever going to make a move on me?"

Nathan was speechless. "I . . . I."

She leaned forward and planted a big kiss on his lips.

He put his hands on her shoulders and pushed back gently. "That was very nice, Monique. But I don't want to lead you on."

"I'll lead, you don't have to worry about a thing." She leaned forward to kiss him again.

He turned his head away and took a step back, his hands still on her shoulders. "I'm sorry," he said.

"So am I."

"It's getting late and I have some work to do. Let me walk you to the door."

"I'm just curious . . . are you seeing someone?" she asked.

"No," he answered, helping her with her jacket.

"Then, why not?" she said. "If you don't mind my asking."

He sighed. "The woman I'm in love with can't be with me. But, she's always had my heart, and . . . I'm just not ready to forget that."

"I wish someone like you felt that way about me."

"You're a very attractive woman, Monique. You're going to make someone very happy. I'm just not that man. Okay? Friends?" he said extending his hand.

"Why not." She gave a disappointed smile. Then he walked her to her car.

When Nathan got back inside, he dialed Serena's number. He had been wanting to call her all day. Her answering machine didn't pick up and the phone rang twenty times before he accepted the fact that she wasn't there.

Thirty-one

hat same night Marcus and Shante went dancing. Shante was a good dancer, but Marcus out-danced everybody in the room. While she sashayed in one small area wearing a little black dress, he bounced and whirled all around her. Shante always had a blast dancing with Marcus, and tonight was no different. He was so lively and she laughed at some of his zany moves.

"I'm getting tired," she said, her skin glowing with perspiration. Marcus couldn't hear her over the loud pop music.

They had danced through four songs straight and Marcus was still bouncing around like a slinky. Shante leaned forward and tapped him on the shoulder. "I'm tired," she said, louder this time. She started fanning herself with her hands.

"My baby's tired, ain't she?" Marcus held her hand and led her through the crowd, back to their table.

Shante took a deep breath as they sat down. "Let's just enjoy the band—while sitting—don't you get any ideas." She looked at him with narrowed eyes.

He laughed as Shante picked up her water and drank the

entire glass. Shante looked around at some of the outfits people were wearing. A lot of the women wore skimpy dresses and most of the men had on tight body shirts. Some of the partygoers were talking and smoking cigarettes and others were having drinks and enjoying the free chicken wings and drumsticks.

"They don't have any collard greens tonight," Marcus noticed.

"I know. Maybe they ran out."

Marcus leaned forward and kissed Shante on the lips. "Let's go home."

"Sounds good to me," she said.

They grabbed their coats and left in Marcus's jeep. When they reached Shante's apartment, she didn't wait for Marcus to open her door. She jumped out of the jeep before he could turn off the engine.

She ran into the apartment giggling like a little girl. Marcus wasn't far behind her. "I'm first," Shante said. "I've been sweating." She flicked on the light and scurried further into the living room.

"I've been sweatin' too! You think you're the only one who's been sweatin'." He laughed.

"Ladies first, Marcus." She pulled off her little black dress in one fluid motion and threw it on the couch.

"Not if I can get there first," he teased.

She laughed as she watched him try to get his clothes off as fast as she did hers. She ran into the bathroom and turned on the shower.

"Wait for me," he yelled playfully.

"You better hurry, slowpoke." A small amount of light from the den penetrated into the bathroom.

Marcus hopped toward the bathroom with one foot in his hand—trying to get the shoe off it. He pulled on it and flung it across the room, knocking the lamp onto the sofa. Then he went into the bathroom, pulled back the curtains and stepped into the shower. Shante looked down and saw he still had a sock and shoe on one foot.

"Marcus, take that shoe off! It's getting wet!" She shook her head while he bent down to remove the shoe. He laughed. Then he straightened, grinning at her. When she looked into his sparkling eyes and at his sexy slanted dimples, she smiled back at him. She used the soap to lather his arms, his neck, his muscular chest, watching with hazy eyes as the water rinsed the soap away. He looked down at her beautiful breasts and hard nipples, and back up into her dark eyes. "Oh Marcus," she whispered as he wrapped his strong arms around her and kissed her. The tight curly hair on his chest softened under the water, massaging her breast as she moved closer to him. The street light outside the bathroom illuminated the shower and their mingled figures.

"I love you, baby," he said, as the warm water flowed down their hot bodies—flattening Shante's short permed hair and making her pretty face stand out even more.

"I love you so much," she said, taking in the fresh scent of soap behind his ears.

"Forever," she added as he caressed her body all over. Shante moaned when Marcus bent to taste her.

"Forever," he said, as he groaned and entered her gently.

As they made love, Shante cleaved to him as if she couldn't get close enough. "Oh yes," she said, her fingers pressing into his back. When Marcus's love landed in every crease of her body, she was once again paralyzed with pleasure—so much so that tears filled her eyes as he carried her weakened body into the bedroom, where he pulled back the covers and laid her softly on the bed.

He turned on a tall lamp that stood in the corner of the room. It provided just enough light for him to view her exquisite form, but not enough to shine in her eyes and disturb her sleep. Shante was already in heaven from their love-making. But Marcus always had to go that extra mile. Nothing else would ever do, he relished every second of it. He patted her glowing skin dry with the towel as she moaned softly. He leaned in to smell the fresh, lightly perfumed scent of her body. Then he kissed the back of her neck, the inside of her wrist. Chills ran across her body. With his strong softened hands, he massaged her shoulders, her arms, her back, her tiny waist, her buttocks. He wanted to enter her again, but he held back, knowing that at this point it couldn't get any better for her—pleasing her beyond all expectations was what it was all about.

His hands stroked down her thighs as she moaned louder. He bent to kiss the three inch long scar on the inside of her knee and the smaller one on her calf—remembering how sorry he had felt for her when they were little and she had to have stitches. She had been a tomboy and a delicate flower at the same time. And he wanted to protect her as much then as he did now. He wished he could have taken the falls for her.

He continued massaging . . . kissing her from her head to the soft curves of her delicate feet and toes until she was in a deep, dream-like sleep. He held her close all night long.

At three p.m. the next day, Shante and Marcus arrived at Hastings Elementary School for the kindergarteners' fall play. Ashley's part was to recite a poem.

As Shante and Marcus sat in the dark auditorium, Marcus seemed eager to see Ashley perform. Look at him, Shante thought. He's so proud, and handsome too. He wore a button-down collared shirt and a brown tweed blazer and matching slacks. Shante wore a winter-white pantsuit.

"There's Ashley," he said. "She's beautiful, isn't she?"

"Yes, she is," Shante agreed. Ashley had on a dress with gold, yellow, and red leaf designs on it.

She's next," he said and Ashley began:

> *"Autumn"*
>
> *"Autumn leaves are all around."*
> (Ashley turned around.)
> *"Autumn leaves touch the ground"*
> (She touched the ground.)

"Yellow, Red and Orange and Brown,"
(She grinned.)
"Autumn leaves are falling, falling down."

Ashley crumpled to the ground on the last verse of the poem.

Marcus rose to his feet and clapped loudly. Shante joined him. He glanced at Shante and then back at Ashley. "She was great, wasn't she!" he said.

"Yes. She was very eloquent, just like her father," Shante said.

Marcus felt uplifted with pride. After the play was over, he and Shante praised Ashley as they stood in front of the school. "Ashley, you were outstanding," he said.

"Yes, you did so well," Shante said.

"I've got an idea," Marcus said. "Why don't I take my little lady and my big lady out to celebrate?"

"Yeah!" Ashley said.

"Where would you like to go?" he asked.

"I want to go to Fun Land," Shante said, as she privately winked at Marcus.

"Yeah—me too, Daddy."

"Fun Land, Fun Land, here we come," Marcus sang, marching to his jeep.

"Can I have a lollipop, Daddy?"

"Sure, girlie," he said with a silly slur of the tongue.

After they left Fun Land, they drove straight to Lillie Mae's house. Lillie Mae heard Marcus pull up. She opened the door and waved for them to come in.

Ashley ran under Lillie Mae's arm, straight to the sofa. Discarding her coat, she began bouncing up and down on her bottom.

"Hey, Grandma," she said as she bounced.

"Hey, Ashley," Lillie Mae said.

Marcus and Shante came in and kissed Lillie Mae on the cheeks. Then Marcus picked up Ashley's coat. "Ashley, what did I tell you about throwing your coat on the floor?"

"Sorry, Daddy," she said, still bouncing from all the sugar she had at Fun Land.

"What time is Cindy coming to get Ashley?" Marcus asked.

"I have no idea," Lillie Mae replied. "She said six o'clock. But you know how that girl is. She might come, she might not." Lillie Mae wore her signature navy blue housecoat and her coffee was well within reach.

"When she comes, tell her to make sure Ashley goes to bed no later than eight-thirty. That's thirty minutes past her bedtime," Marcus said.

"Daddy," Ashley said, still bouncing up and down on the sofa.

"Yeah, Ashley."

"Can I stay up until ten-thirty and watch the Rug Rats special?"

"No. People don't stay up that late. I mean, children need to go to bed earlier than that, so they can get a good night's sleep."

"Some people do stay up until ten-thirty. Some people stay up until twelve," Ashley said. Her big, pretty eyes widened. "Some people even stay up until . . . twenty." She held out her chubby little hands in expression.

Marcus laughed. "I think the special is coming on at ten-thirty in the morning, not at night, so I don't think you'll miss anything. I promise."

"Boy, you're bouncy," Shante said as she joined Ashley on the sofa.

Marcus went over to his mother's old radio and turned on some music. Shante jumped up and took hold of Ashley's hands. Marcus, Shante, and Ashley started dancing around in a circle.

Lillie Mae took a seat next to her coffee. *Just watching them makes me tired,* she thought as she slid her foot out of her shoe and glanced down at her bunion. *Where do they find all that energy? They are so happy.* She sipped her coffee and looked on.

Minutes later Shante and Marcus left Lillie Mae's house. "Do you want to go to my place or yours," Marcus asked.

"My place," she answered, as they climbed into his jeep and

drove away. "You never have any food in your refrigerator," she added.

Marcus chuckled. "I have some food in my refrigerator. I went to the grocery store the other day, thank you."

"Wow, you did?"

"Yes, I did. I told you I'm serious about this marriage thing. I know I'm gonna have to go grocery shopping sometimes when we get married—especially when we start having little babies."

"Babies?" she said.

"I was thinking we could have a few sets of twins. You know they run in your family."

"Yeah, right." Shante knew he was just kidding. They had discussed the subject and agreed that one or two more children would be enough.

"Let's just go to my place," she said. "Most of your things are there anyway . . . Your oil light's on."

"I'll check it in the morning," he said.

"Your engine might freeze."

"Yeah, you're right. I'll check it tonight."

On the ride home, Shante fell asleep.

Marcus glanced over at her. She looks so sweet, like an angel, he thought. Sometimes when he looked at her, he saw the little girl he had grown up with. The friend who was always there for him. Her childhood voice flashed through his mind: "Marcus, you will not go across town without me." He smiled, realizing that her voice hadn't changed much. Then he recalled the time she took ill when she was eleven. Her white blood count was too high and she had to stay in the hospital for a week. Marcus had missed her so badly. Each day, he'd get a stick and write in the sand behind his house: "God, please let Shante get well soon . . ." And she did.

Shante awakened just as they were pulling into the parking lot. It had been a long and exhausting day, but they had promised each other that they would sit down that night and decide on a date to get married. They agreed on the second weekend in December.

"That gives us exactly two months to get everything done," she said. Shante told Marcus that she didn't want a big, pretentious wedding with a lot of curious people there, just to get gifts and make it look good. "I want the people that have meant the most to us throughout our lives. The people who've been there for us when the going got tough. People like Serena and Nikki."

Marcus felt the same way. "I want the people that volunteer at the children's center, their families, and a few others to come, too," he said.

But Shante's feelings didn't stop her from wanting to look good. She had already bought the expensive gown she and Serena liked so much.

"Marcus," Shante said, giving him a serious look.

"Yes de-e-e-e-a-r-r," he said in a playful voice.

"I've been thinking," she said.

"About what?"

"I don't want to sleep together anymore until we're married."

This was the last thing Marcus expected to hear. "We've been sleeping together for three years," he said.

"I'm serious, Marcus."

"Well," he chuckled, "it's a little too late for that isn't it?" Shante wasn't laughing.

Marcus stopped laughing. "You're serious, aren't you?"

"Yes, I am."

"Is something wrong?"

"No. I just want to wait until we're married."

This must be a woman thing, Marcus thought. He knew he'd better be understanding and go along with this. He didn't want her angry with him.

"If you can wait, so can I." He smiled softly and they hugged.

"I get the bed," he said. "That means you have to sleep on the couch."

Shante threw a pillow from the sofa at him. He dodged it, ran over to the sofa, straddled his legs over her and started tickling her. "Stop," she said, laughing.

"Say you're sorry," he said.

"*I'm sorry!*" she gasped through her laughter. "Now please, stop tickling me!"

Thirty-two

A week later, Shante and Marcus were at the children's center giving a workshop on positive guidance. Shante had made a list of ideas for parents and teachers to use when disciplining and teaching children. Marcus had made copies and was passing them out to the parents while Shante explained them.

"Let's look at Number Three," she said. "It has to do with your child's self esteem. Praise your children when they do something good, or when they try a new task. It could be anything. It could be . . . gluing one piece of paper to another. If they show you their work, talk to them about it. Ask open-ended questions."

One parent raised her hand.

"Yes?" Shante said.

"My son got the glue everywhere. It was all over my hardwood floors. All I had to say was, why? There was paper stuck to the floor. It was a mess. Is that the kind of open-ended question you're talking about?"

Shante smiled, then spoke. "As you know, children are very sensitive. Their little self-esteems can be crushed over what we adults may not even notice. Make sure you take the time to look at his or her little face when you reprimand or express disappointment . . ."

As Marcus listened, he thought about his father and how he wished things could have been different for them. He smiled at Shante in appreciation for all she did for Ashley and other children. He nodded in agreement as Shante continued.

"I suggest you pause, take a deep breath, and then focus on the effect your words could have on your child—not only at that time, but also when he or she goes out into the world as an adult. Ask yourself, will what I'm about to say enable my child to achieve—to believe that he can do or be anything? Will he love or even like himself? Will she believe that she is just as good as anyone else? You can say to your child something like: this is creative, original, interesting or beautiful, colorful. Then ask him or her to tell you about it—it's shape, texture, features, function, what it means to him, what it represents, and so on and so forth."

The same parent raised her hand again.

"You want us to ask our children to tell us about two pieces of paper glued together, when there is glue all over the floor." A few parents giggled.

"I'm not standing up here claiming to be perfect," Shante said. "Parenting is not an easy job for anyone who attempts to do it right. But to answer your question, yes, I do. These questions help stimulate your child to grow cognitively. When asked these questions, children expand on and think more in depth about what they have done. You want to learn how and what your child was thinking when he or she was doing the project. Then encourage him to keep up the good work. As far as the messes are concerned, that's part of growing up. But, you as a parent are responsible for setting rules and limits and making sure those rules are followed. Your child will need and appreciate your consistency and guidance in this area as well. I know it's hard sometimes, but do it in a positive way, and always with love."

"I do," one parent said.

"Good," Shante said. "I'm sure you all are good parents, but none of us know everything. That's why Marcus and I like to have these workshops. It gives us an opportunity to support one another and the children. And remember, if you have any suggestions or concerns, we always want to hear them. Now let's look at Suggestion Number Four."

Nikki and Malik went to see a movie. They stepped out of the theater arm in arm, both wearing blue jeans. Nikki rarely wore jeans. She always said they made her ample behind all too noticeable. But since Malik seemed to admire her rear end, she was becoming more accepting of it too.

"Did you like the movie?" he asked as they walked along.

"Yeah, it was pretty good."

"Me, too. Samuel L. Jackson can act his butt off."

They stopped walking and gave each other a kiss and a hug.

"Hey, give me some to-o-o," a man driving by in a white car yelled.

Nikki and Malik shook their heads and resumed walking arm in arm to his truck.

❖

Thirty-three

I t was almost November and a light snow fell from the sky. Serena hesitantly got out of bed this morning. Julian had already left for work.

"Why?" she said to herself. "I don't want to go to work today." Serena longed to stay in her warm home and not have to drive in the snow. But she felt guilty if she missed a day of work even every once in a while. She had only missed work a few times in her now seven years of performing in New York City. If she was scheduled to perform, she was there on time, and ready to go. One day she didn't feel like going to work. She called Ollie. He told her, "Stay home, it's no problem." But she worried about it so much that she said she would have been better off going in. She spent half the day on the phone calling friends, asking them how they felt about her not going to work. She asked Nikki and Shante questions like: "Do you think they're mad at me for calling in? What do you think they thought when I called in? Do you think they believed me? Do you think they're okay without me?" Then after all the questions, she would give a lengthy analysis of the subject, in an attempt to convince herself that everything would be fine. Caroline used to worry about what other people thought too. "I hope they don't get mad at me for not coming to the church program. I just was too tired," she'd say. Like Caroline, Serena could be overly conscientious and concerned about inconveniencing people. Fortunately, she was beginning to realize this and starting to change—some.

"Why," Serena said again. "I have no business driving in the snow. But as they say, the show must go on. Besides, I don't want to let anyone down."

Serena showered, got dressed and bundled up in a big black wool coat with matching gloves and a hat, only to discover that her car, which was in the garage, would not start.

"What's wrong with this car?" she asked herself.

She went back in the house and called Julian. "Hi, Julian, my car won't start."

"What's wrong with it?" he asked.

"I don't know. I just got in it like I normally do. I tried to start it and it wouldn't start."

"Try it again."

"I did try it again, and again—before I called you."

"I hope you didn't flood it."

"I didn't flood it," she said. "I'll have to drive your old Ford. Where are the keys?"

"Can't you just stay home today?"

"I wish."

"Well, stay home then."

"I can't, Julian. I need to go to work."

"The keys are in the garage on the second shelf by the paper towels. Drive carefully."

Oh, he's concerned about me, she thought, that's nice. "I will," she said.

"Those car parts are hard to find, not to mention expensive," he said.

"Good-bye, Julian." I should have known he was worried

about the car and not me, she thought to herself as she was locating the keys.

After Serena returned home that evening, she prepared a luscious dinner of roast chicken with lemons and a Caesar salad with shavings of Parmesan cheese. As she set the table, she pulled out two wine glasses and a bottle of 1989 Chateau Haut-Brian. She filled both glasses. She usually drank a non-alcoholic concoction of her own, but tonight she decided to please Julian and have a glass of wine with him.

She started a fire in the fireplace. Then she went upstairs and put on an elegant, red, off-the-shoulder dress that clung to her body and drew attention to her gorgeous figure.

Julian arrived home minutes later, hungry and eager to sit down to dinner. He kissed Serena. "You look sexy," he said.

During dinner Julian said "Umm, this is good Serena."

"Thank you,"she said. *A compliment—and it wasn't followed by a negative comment or suggestion.*

"Let's take our wine and sit by the fire," she said upon their finishing the meal.

They settled on the sofa in front of the fireplace. Serena looked amazing as her skin glowed in the firelight. Julian set his glass of wine on the coffee table. Then he started rubbing Serena's legs.

"Oh. Oh, baby," he said. "Look at those sexy legs."

Am I supposed to be excited? she wondered.

He moved his hand up her waist and began caressing her breast. He kissed her neck, over and over again.

"Wait, Julian. I have a glass of wine in my hand."

"Well, set it down," he said.

"Please wait, Julian."

He stopped, secretly rolled his eyes and took a deep breath.

She looked seriously at him. "I want to talk."

"We can talk later, Serena."

She set her glass of wine on the coffee table. Then she opened a book that was on the end table. Taking out two airline tickets to Florida, she handed them to him. She picked up her glass of wine and started drinking again.

"What's this?" he asked.

"I thought a Christmas in Miami Beach would be fun. We can get started on a family. I'm ready to have a baby."

This caught Julian by surprise. "Right now? I have a beautiful wife, a big house, a career I like. Hey, my life is great the way it is. And you, you're doing what you've always loved to do, and that's perform. How are you going to perform if you're pregnant, and when do I have time for a child? And you said that you didn't want children until we could communicate better."

"Julian, it's been just you and me for six years. I need more than this." She stared pleadingly at him. "You're not a talker. I can live with that. I realize that this is who you are, and I need to accept it."

"That's good," Julian said. "But I talk. I just don't like to talk about things that aren't important."

Serena thought that Julian probably didn't mean what he said. And that he didn't realize how cruel it sounded. Julian was Julian, she thought, and he had no interest in most subjects.

"Okay, Julian. So, what do you say? Can we take this trip together and just concentrate on having a baby?"

"Serena, I don't want to have a baby."

"What!" She dropped her glass, spilling wine all over his expensive trousers.

"Hey," he said angrily in a high-pitched squeal. "Watch what you're doin'!"

He stood up, walked into the kitchen and came back out with a towel. He swiped at his pants, frowning.

"Before we were married, you said that we could have children as long as we discussed it before I got pregnant," she said, with a quivering voice.

"I was younger then. I would have said anything to —"

"To get what you wanted." She glared at him. She suddenly realized that the reason Julian always wore a condom, even though she was on the pill, was to make sure she didn't get pregnant.

He sneered at her.

Serena felt like the world's biggest fool. Her eyes grew teary as she climbed the stairs and left Julian downstairs to worry about his pants. He was so upset about the wine on his pants, he didn't notice or care how hurt she was.

Serena went into the bedroom and locked the door. She lay on the bed weeping and thinking about how the last six years had been a lie—nothing more than a front. She thought of Nathan and how she had turned him away.

"If he could hold me in his arms right now, everything would be okay," she muttered.

Julian went upstairs and tried to open the bedroom door. He rattled the knob. "Serena, unlock the door."

"Julian, I need some privacy."

"Not in my bedroom you don't! If you don't open the door, I'm going to open it myself."

Serena turned over on her back, put a pillow up against the headboard, and lay there, belligerent, with her chin bent against her chest and her legs stretched slightly apart. Her eyes narrowed as they zeroed in on the center of the door. How is he going to get in here? she wondered.

"You're being so damn selfish, Serena."

"Me, selfish!" she said in astonishment. She sat up on the bed, her mouth wide open as she glared at the door.

She got up, grabbed her pillow off the bed, and proceeded toward the door. She jerked it open. Julian tumbled to the bedroom floor.

She stepped over him and walked into the hall. She spun around and looked at Julian still sitting on the floor.

"I married you," she said angrily, "and that was *totally* unselfish." She tossed her head and stepped into the bedroom across the hall.

Julian was baffled. "Is she trying to insult me?"

Later that night, Julian left his bedroom and joined Serena in the guest room. She got up and went back into their bedroom. He followed her there. She felt like her face was breaking out, she was so angry. She left again.

When Serena woke up the next morning, she was downstairs on the sofa, exhausted, with a wicked headache. "Oh," she said in a tired voice, running her hands threw her wild hair, "at least I didn't sleep with him."

As Serena was going up the stairs, Julian was coming down. "I'll see you this evening, Serena," he said, adjusting his tie.

Serena knew there was no point in trying to discuss the argument with Julian. She knew that Julian probably felt like he hadn't done much wrong. Plus, he was on his way to work, and that always came first. "Okay, Julian," she said, looking down at the stairs as she climbed them.

While Serena was showering, she thought of Nathan. She remembered that his birthday was in a few days. She wanted to call him, but she decided to send him a card instead.

Thirty-four

Brandi and Justice invited a small group of friends over to celebrate Nathan's birthday.

Nathan took the opportunity to tell Monique that James was interested in her. "You have an admirer," Nathan said to Monique as they stood talking in Brandi's living room. She looked over at James, who was standing across the room talking to Brandi and Justice.

"He's kind of cute," she said. "I remember him from the party." She looked him up and down and smiled. James smiled and waved at her.

Monique used her pointer finger and signaled for James to come to her.

"Excuse me," Nathan said to Monique as James happily approached her. Nathan walked over to Brandi and Justice. He folded his arms across his chest and grinned as he briefly watched Monique and James, who seemed to be enjoying each other's company.

When Nathan arrived home, that evening, he checked his mailbox and was thrilled to see a card from Serena. It read: "Thinking of you on your birthday, and always, Serena."

Nathan leaned back against the sofa, laid the card on his chest, and closed his eyes.

The next day he called Serena at work.

They talked for a few minutes and then he said, "You remembered my birthday. Thank you. The card was very nice. It means so much to me."

"You're welcome," she said.

"Can I see you again?" he asked.

"I don't want you to misunderstand my intentions," she said. "I'm married. I don't want you to come, expecting something I can't give." Serena wanted to see Nathan more than anything, but her strict up-bringing made her feel like it was forbidden, unless she could convince herself that they were just friends. In addition, she had hurt him before, a long time ago, and was determined not to hurt him again by leading him to believe that he had a chance. She didn't want to make any promises she couldn't keep.

Nathan didn't like what he was hearing, but wanted to see her nonetheless. "I'm so happy when I'm with you," he said. "I understand what you're telling me. I just want to enjoy your company, okay? I'll fly up and spend a few days in New York City."

"Okay," Serena agreed.

Later that week, Serena met Nathan in front of a theater on Broadway where they had agreed to meet to see *Ragtime*. They greeted each other with a hug before entering the theater. Serena looked pretty in her long, eggplant-colored velvet dress and matching cardigan. Nathan looked like he had just stepped off the pages of "GQ Magazine" in his dark brown wool suit.

As they sat in the dark theater, Nathan thought Serena smelled so good he wanted to kiss her right there. He reached over and held her hand.

I'm really bold, she thought. What if someone she knew saw her sitting in here holding hands with Nathan. Her parents would think she had lost her mind if they knew. But this feels so nice, she thought. Just like it used to.

She's not resisting, he mused.

"Great show," Nathan commented at the end.

"Yes, it was." She clapped and looked up at the stage as the cast members took a final bow. "See the guy on the end and the two girls in the middle," she whispered.

"Yes," Nathan said.

"I know them. I can't wait to tell them how fantastic they were."

As they were leaving the theatre, Nathan asked, "I know it's late, but would you like to have dinner? There's a cafe down the street." He pointed. "We could walk."

"I really must go now." She signaled for a taxi.

"Then I'll ride with you home," he said, holding out his hand to flag down a cab.

"That's not a very good idea, either," she said, looking into the bustling traffic. "Julian is there." She waved her arm again. "He might think something is going on."

"We can't have that, can we?" Nathan said, looking away sadly.

Serena glanced at him. A cab stopped for her. "No, we can't," she answered, stepping toward the cab.

Nathan opened the door for her.

"I'll call you in the morning," she said.

Nathan watched the cab until it was out of sight.

The next morning, Serena called Nathan and gave him directions to Ollie's horse ranch in Westchester County. Nathan had rented a car, and he agreed to meet her there at 10:00 a.m.

An occasional morning spent riding provided an enjoyable and much-needed escape from her usual life in the limelight.

She felt happy whenever she got a chance to ride in the fresh air with the sound of nature all around. It reminded her of being back home in Georgia, so unlike the busy streets of Manhattan.

Nathan had never been on a horse in his life. He didn't know how to ride, but he wanted to try. He had difficulty getting on. The first time he tried, his foot slipped off the stirrup.

Serena laughed. "We'll take it very slowly," she said, in a comforting voice.

"This is kind of fun," he said, once he got used to being on a horse. "I'm pretty good at this," he bragged as their horses walked along.

"Yes, you are." Bless his heart, she thought. "When I ride, I feel so relaxed and exhilarated. When I was little, Mom used to take me to the horse show once a year. My favorite horse was the Tennessee Walker."

"I don't think I've ever seen one," Nathan said.

"Oh, you haven't?" Serena told Nathan that she liked the graceful way they cantered, lifting their feet high. She told him she liked their beautiful form, too. "I used to tell Mom that, when I grew up, I was going to have a ranch with Tennessee Walkers. I only get to ride occasionally, and there are no Tennessee Walkers here, but I still enjoy coming here and riding. It's so quiet. Listen."

"I could get used to this," Nathan said, feeling secure and quite capable of riding after being on the horse thirty minutes. "We can go a little faster."

"That would be lovely," she said. "But are you sure?"

"Yeah. I'm sure." Serena smiled and looked carefully at him. "I can handle it," he said, their horses still walking.

Serena was itching to get one good run in. The horses started to canter.

"Don't try to keep up with me," she said, as her horse cantered just ahead of Nathan's.

Serena heard Nathan's horse neigh. Then she heard a

thump. She whirled around to see what was the matter. Nathan had been thrown from the horse, but somehow, he'd managed to land on his feet, leaning backwards. Serena had never seen anything quite like it.

"Are you okay, Nathan," she asked, getting down from her horse.

He looked at Serena and saw her smiling from ear to ear. "Oh . . . am I okay?" he said. "Yes, I'm okay."

"I'm sorry." This time her smile wasn't quite as noticeable.

"It's okay," he said. "I just got the big head. I tried to keep up with you after you told me not to. This has been fun, though. I like a new challenge. Maybe we can do this again sometime."

They remounted their horses and rode back to the stables. She walked Nathan to his car and agreed to meet him for dinner that evening, knowing that Julian would be having dinner with some business associates. Then she remounted her horse. She wanted to get in one swift ride—alone, before leaving.

❖

Thirty-five

$\mathcal{S}$erena arrived at the Plaza hotel wearing an elegant black, one-shoulder evening dress and a beautiful emerald necklace and matching earrings. She thought perhaps they were going to have dinner in the Oak Room, the Palm Court, or one of the other restaurants, but Nathan had spent much of the afternoon making sure that the concierge reserved a private dining room.

As they entered, Serena was thrilled to see lovely floral arrangements all around the room. There were lilies, roses of every color, and orchids. Serena's eyes sparkled like the brilliant crystal that decorated the dinner table.

"This is so beautiful," she said, as the attendant took her black silk coat. "I can't believe this. This is so nice."

She stood in awe for a few moments. She felt a little uncomfortable—as if the private dining room were too much. But then she thought of Julian, and how he took his friends to dinner now and then. She recalled the time Julian took a female college friend of his out to lunch. And she was sure Julian talked to her during their meeting—something he rarely did with Serena. So she said,

"You're so sweet Nathan." Nathan smiled.

As the waiter described the menu, Nathan and Serena gazed lovingly into each other's eyes. "Thank you," Nathan said to the waiter. "We'll need a few more minutes before we're ready to order."

"Take as much time as you need. Your tea will be served momentarily."

Nathan had another surprise for Serena. He had hired a saxophonist to play for them. After dinner, Nathan glanced at Serena's plate. He noticed that she had eaten her entire meal. He knew that Serena never cleared her plate unless something was bothering her. Nathan remembered everything about Serena. He recalled the time he took her out to dinner the night her parents' divorce became final. She ate everything on her plate. He had never seen her do that until that night.

"Serena, is something wrong?" he asked.

She took a deep breath. "No," she said, exhaling.

"I can tell something's troubling you." Staring into her eyes, he felt her sadness. "You don't have to tell me what's wrong, but I want you to know you can trust me, no matter what it is."

He reached out and held her hand.

Serena said, "Julian just told me after over six years of marriage that he doesn't want any children." Nathan listened with sympathy as she went on. "You know, I believe he knew all along, but didn't tell me." Her voice quivered. "It is so incomprehensible how someone could lead you to believe something that wasn't true, and for so long. I mean especially when they're supposed to care about you. I'm so naive! How can I still be so naive? I'm thirty years old. I'm not eighteen anymore. I should have figured this out a long time ago."

"I don't think you're naive. You believed him. It's not like he was a stranger. He told you something, and you trusted him. That's who you are, Serena. You're a sweet, trusting person. If everyone were like you, there would be peace on earth."

"Thanks, Nathan. You're so wonderful."

"I mean it, you're all that and much more."

"I know you do," she said.

Serena suddenly felt the desire to make love to him, to feel him close to her, to show him how much he really meant to her. "This is so wonderful Nathan. Being with you anywhere, is just the best thing."

"Serena, when I'm with you, I feel like I can do or be anything. I love you now and forever."

"Nathan," she said.

He could tell she wanted to say the words. He reached in the pocket of his suit coat and handed her a poem he had recently written for her entitled, "Missing You." The saxophonist began playing Richard Elliot's version of "Bridge Over Troubled Waters."

As she silently read the poem, a tear rolled down her face. This is the most moving poem I've ever read, she thought—this entire evening has been incredible. Her body began to pulsate with the warmth of his words. Every verse was a sweet melody to her soul.

"I need a tissue," she said.

Nathan jumped up and came back with a box of tissues. Serena pulled out a few and wiped her eyes.

Nathan wanted so badly to make love to her. He needed her right now. His eyes burned with desire.

"You're still writing beautiful poetry," she told him.

"Only for you, Serena. Will you dance with me?" He reached for her hand as she nodded yes.

They held each other with intense passion as the sensual sounds of the saxophone filled the room. Serena felt Nathan's hard body against her as they swayed back and forth.

I wish this could last forever, she thought.

"You're so soft," he whispered. Then he gently kissed her neck.

Serena knew that if she didn't leave now, it would be too late. She would no longer be able to control herself—her feeling for Nathan. "It wasn't a good idea for us to be alone like this. I really must go," she said as she pushed away from him.

"I promise, Serena. I won't touch you again."

She dashed to the table to retrieve her black satin purse, then rushed toward the attendant. "I need my coat, please" she said.

Nathan followed her.

"It's not your fault, it's mine," she said as Nathan pleaded for her to stay. She hurried past him.

"Wait!" he called.

As Serena rushed out the door, the waiter walked in with the dessert tray.

Nathan felt like he'd been pierced by the world's largest arrow. "How could I be so selfish?" he said as he walked back to the table and sat down. "No, thank you," he said to the waiter. "You may leave," he told the saxophonist.

She'll never see me again now, he thought. I have to let her go. He looked down and noticed that the poem was still on the table. He picked it up and read the title. A tear fell from his eye onto the paper. He folded the poem and tucked it back inside his jacket pocket.

Later that night, Serena called Nathan to wish him a safe trip back to Washington, and to say a proper goodbye.

"I'm so glad you called," he said. "I'm sorry about this evening."

"It's not you fault, Nathan. I wanted you just as much as you wanted me."

Nathan was once again aroused. He closed his eyes and imagined being inside Serena over and over again. "I still want you, Serena. I know I'm being selfish, but it's not my fault for loving you. You nurtured our love long ago, and it's out of our hands."

Serena wanted so desperately to make him happy.

"Our love will never go away," he continued. "It will stay in your heart and soul, just as it does mine, and it will continuously remind you."

"Please, Nathan. We can't do anything about this right now, maybe never."

Nathan's eyes filled with tears as he sat on the edge of his bed and Serena sat on the edge of hers.

Serena felt like her heart was breaking into tiny fragments, but she knew she had to tell him to move on. "Just find someone to love you the way you deserve to be loved," she said.

"That's no good, Serena. There will always be you. I can never love anyone the way I love you. I never have and I never will. Besides," he said, "you don't mean it, anyway. When I held you tonight, every inch of your body was calling my name."

At that moment, Julian entered the house. "Serena," he called.

"Coming," she said. To Nathan, she said, "I have to go. Goodbye."

"What were you doing?" Julian asked as Serena walked down the stairs to greet him.

"I was on the telephone," she answered.

"So how was your day?"

"Good," he said.

Nathan sat frozen in place in the dark hotel room, holding his head in his hands.

Thirty-six

The next day Serena was in the exercise room, stretching, when Julian yelled from his office." Turn that music down!" Serena got up and lowered the volume on the stereo.

"Turn it down some more," he said.

"If I turn it down any more, I won't be able to hear it, Julian."

"Yes, you will."

Serena frowned and kept stretching.

Julian came into the room and turned the music down to a whisper. Serena got up and turned the music off.

"Julian, don't forget, we're going to my mother's house for Thanksgiving." She looked at him with daring eyes. He seemed uninterested. Serena felt herself getting brave. "And if you say you're not going with me, you can just get out right now."

Serena had never talked to Julian that way before.

"This is my house too, Serena."

"Gee, thanks for reminding me," she said, leaving the room.

She went upstairs, showered and changed into a comfortable cream sweater, a long brown skirt and a pair of tall brown leather boots. Then she went back downstairs.

"Julian," she called. "I'll be back shortly. I'm going to visit Shante." She stood in his office doorway.

"Oh, you're leaving," he said.

"Yes."

Julian didn't say anything in response.

Serena shrugged and said, "Okay, I'll see you later," as she found her purse.

It was cold outside. As Serena started down I- 95, she realized that she should have left earlier. Noisy trucks, exhaust from the vehicles, and people blowing their horns were all converged in a huge traffic jam. It took her an extra hour to get to Shante's place, but she didn't mind. She spent that time thinking of Nathan. Now she stood on her friends' doorstep and rang the bell.

"I'll get it." Marcus jogged to the door to meet Serena. "Hey, baby," he said cheerfully.

"Hey, honey," she said. "I hope I'm not interrupting anything."

"No, you know you can't interrupt us—you're family. Here, let me help you with your coat."

"Where's Shante?" she asked.

"Hi, Serena," Shante said, emerging from the kitchen. "Come in the bedroom. I want to show you the shoes I bought for the wedding."

Serena sat down on the bed while Shante retrieved the shoes from the closet.

"Those are perfect," Serena said. "Marcus is going to flip when he sees you walking down that aisle."

Shante put the shoes on and modeled them for Serena. "Do they look good on me?" she asked. Shante knew they did, but she wanted to hear Serena agree.

"Yes," Serena said. "They look so pretty on your feet."

"In a few more weeks, I'll be Mrs. Marcus Elder." Shante strutted around for a few minutes before taking the shoes off and putting them back in the box. "Marcus moved out of his apartment. We're looking for a house."

"Oh, you are?" Serena said.

"Serena, what's wrong? You look sad, and so preoccupied."

"I'm in love with Nathan," Serena answered.

"Serena, how much longer are you going to torture yourself in that marriage?"

"When I married Julian, I promised not only him, but myself, that I would take this commitment seriously."

Serena realized that even though Julian could be self-centered and sometimes arrogant, he might be dealing with some internal conflicts and self-esteem problems—perhaps in his unconscious mind. Maybe he knew he had these insecurities, and was over-compensating through his actions.

She sighed. "There's still some hope for us. We've been married for almost seven years, and I just can't pretend like it didn't happen."

Shante was frustrated. "Serena, you're living a lie. Are you willing to keep doing that?"

"No. I'm saying that in time I can grow to love him again if he would only treat me the way he did the first year of our marriage."

"Nikki said the first year of your marriage wasn't that good. She said Julian was acting."

"Nikki says that about all men."

After a short silence, Shante spoke again. "I'm sorry. I'm not being very understanding, am I?" Shante suddenly realized that this was more difficult for Serena than it would be for her. She remembered that Serena's parents never had the kind of relationship hers had, the kind that was a shining example of the way love is supposed to feel. "I just want you to be as happy as I am. If you believe you can have happiness with Julian, then so be it. You're smart, Serena." She sat on the bed and put her arm around Serena's shoulder. "You'll find your way through this, and you'll emerge having made the right decision. I think you already know what to do, but you feel the need to make sure, to study things carefully. That's the way you are, and that's not a bad characteristic. You just want to make sure that you have done the best you can, and that you come to the right conclusion. You'll figure it out. Hey . . . and I do understand. I know it's not easy."

Serena smiled wanly. "Thanks," she said, and they hugged.

This same night, Marcus gathered his blankets and pillow and made his bed on the sofa. Shante bent down and kissed him goodnight before going into the bedroom.

Marcus was lying down and just getting comfortable when Shante went back into the living room and sat on the edge of the sofa.

"Marcus."

"Yes, dear."

"My heart breaks for Serena."

"Why?"

"She's so loyal to Julian, and she hasn't been happy for years."

"That's sad," he said. "Why is she so unhappy? Wait, I think I know why. That man is all into himself."

"That's it in a nutshell," Shante said.

"Why doesn't she just leave?"

"You know Serena. She doesn't want to let anybody down."

"Yeah, that's Serena."

"She has tried for so long to make that marriage work," Shante said. "Julian hardly talks. He barely listens to her. Personally, I believe he thinks he doesn't have to listen any more. She's his wife now. The hunt's over. He hit the bull's-eye." Shante paused. "You're not gonna try and pull that, are you?"

Marcus chuckled. "No-o-o. Come on now, you know me better than that."

"Yeah, I do." Shante smiled, leaned forward and kissed him on the lips. "Serena told me that she's beginning to realize that it feeds Julian's ego to hear her desperately try to communicate with him—as long as she doesn't try for more than a few minutes. If she does, then he gets irritated. She said she never understood that before now because she thought he would appreciate her efforts to communicate in order to help their marriage."

Marcus shook his head as he listened thoughtfully. "That's a difficult situation to be in."

"No doubt. I love you so much, Marcus."

"I love you too, angel," he said. "Give me some suga." They kissed. "Well, Shante, you better get back in bed now darlin', it's getting late."

"Uh, mmm, well." She didn't want to go to bed without him. She kissed him again.

"Thank ya, suga pie."

"Come, let's go to bed." She reached for his hand and he sat up on the sofa.

"Whoa, wait a minute. It's only a few more weeks before we're married. I thought you wanted to wait."

"I don't want to wait anymore," she said as Marcus studied her. "I really need you to hold me tonight. I miss you."

"O-o-o-k-a-a-a-y," he said, "but you have to promise me something."

"What?"

They stood. Marcus gave her a peck on the lips.

"No more waiting," he said playfully. "Not tonight"—peck— "not tomorrow"—peck— "not the next day . . . ." Shante giggled with each kiss, all the way to the bedroom.

Thirty-seven

At noon on Thanksgiving Day, Serena and Julian arrived at her mother's house just outside Columbus. Caroline was standing in the yard before they could even get out of the car.

"John, they're here," Caroline yelled into the house.

"Hi, Mom," Serena said as they hugged.

"Hey, Serena, I'm so glad to see you. Come over here so I can hug your neck, Julian."

"How are you?" Julian asked Caroline.

"I'm not complaining. Actually, I'm doing well," Caroline answered.

"Ah, there she is," John said just before hugging Serena. Then he shook Julian's hand.

"Ya'll come on in the house," Caroline said. "You look good, Serena."

"So do you, Mom."

"Julian, it looks like you're taking good care of Serena," Caroline said.

Please, Serena thought.

"Got to," Julian replied.

"It looks like she's taking pretty good care of you, too, Julian. You look good," Caroline noted.

"Thank you."

"Julian," John said, "let's go in the den and watch the game."

"Sounds good," Julian agreed.

"Mom, this floor is creaking mighty loud," Serena said as they crossed the living room. She looked down at the wooden floor and pressed both feet firmly against it, giving it a test.

"Ah," Caroline said, "you're just used to that fancy house of yours."

"Mom, this is a nice house," Serena said of the three bedroom brick split-level.

Serena went in the kitchen to help prepare dinner. "We stopped by Daddy's on the way here," she told Caroline.

"Oh, you did?"

"Yeah, we've been in town for a couple of hours."

"How's he doing?" Caroline asked.

"He seemed to be doing just fine. They had a crowd over there. Bertha's three boys were there with their families."

Serena canvassed the kitchen counter and stove. "You have cooked everything known to man, Mama. And it looks so good. I can't wait to dig in." She rubbed her hands together.

Even though Serena considered herself a good cook, there was nothing she enjoyed more than her mother's Thanksgiving dinner. Caroline had prepared sweet potato casserole with pecans, collard greens, potato salad, dressing, rolls, turkey, ham, pintos, corn bread, green beans and corn on the cob. For dessert, she had made pound cake, pecan pie, sweet potato pie, and banana pudding.

"Who's going to eat all this food, Mom?"

"I'm gonna send some of it home with you and Julian, and some I'm gonna take to the sick and shut-in church members. They so enjoy my cooking. Some of them can barely get around, if they can get around at all."

"That's nice, Mom."

"Oh, and I made your favorite tea."

"Thanks."

Serena was suddenly deep in thought.

"What are you thinking about, Serena?" Caroline said. "Come on, let's sit down and talk for a few minutes." They sat at the honey-colored kitchen table. "What's on your mind?"

"Mom, I don't mean to bring this up after all this time, but since you asked . . ."

"Yes?"

"I still don't understand why you and Daddy got divorced. I mean, obviously it was because you didn't want to be together any more, but I never saw you two argue. Well, maybe a couple of times."

"That's because your father would always walk away. How can you argue with someone who's always walking away? He would say his piece, and that would be the end of the conversation. I never liked to argue, anyway, so it was easier to just let it rest. He'd leave and go back to the body shop and work past dinner."

"When I was little, you told me that marriage was forever."

"Yeah, that's what my folks told me, so that's what I told you."

"Well, even when you took me to church, the preacher said divorce was wrong, and that you'd be committing adultery if you married again."

"That's one reason why I stayed with your father as long as I did. I wasn't happy with him. Well, the first ten years, I was fairly content. There was hope, or so I thought. I had gotten used to being ignored and feeling worthless. The next ten years I knew there was no hope for us. Twenty years I spent like that. He had been taught that a woman's opinion wasn't much use. Did I ever tell you that I wanted more children?"

"No."

"He didn't want any more children, so we had only you. Can

you believe it? He didn't want me to have any more children, but he married somebody with three." Caroline paused and then continued. "I used to feel so sorry for you growing up all alone."

Serena looked surprised. "I was okay." She thought of her childhood pet, an African Basenji hound dog named Jambo. "I had Jambo, and I had friends." Then Serena remembered that there *were* times when she wished she had a brother or sister, times when she *had* felt a little lonely.

"I know, Serena, but my point is, your father was so controlling—and stingy, too. He didn't even want me to work. When you were about three years old, I got a part-time job as a receptionist at Dr. Sullivan's office."

"The dentist on Main Street?"

"Yeah. I took you to Aunt Lucy's house while I worked."

"I think I remember that," Serena said.

"I was so proud of myself," said Caroline. "I had a little money of my own and I didn't have to ask your father for everything. I worked for two weeks, and the whole time he was complaining. Do you know that he came to my job and made me leave? He wouldn't even let me finish that day out. He cursed at Dr. Sullivan."

Serena gasped. "Daddy cursed!"

"Yeah, Serena, your Daddy cursed," she said matter-of- factly. "Then he said, 'You must be going with the man. You don't have any receptionist skills, you don't know what you're doing.' "

"Daddy said that!"

"Yeah, Serena, your daddy said that . . . I was never so humiliated in my life."

"Why didn't you tell me any of this before?"

"Because, in your eyes, your father could do no wrong. And I didn't want to ruin that for you. You loved your daddy so much. I didn't want to break your spirit. I still don't feel comfortable talking negatively to you about your father. He was not, and is not, a bad person. He just had some ways that were too difficult for me to bear."

"I know this is hard for you, Mom. You never did talk bad about Daddy."

"When you were ten, I decided that I should get out of the marriage. Everything I did or tried to do seemed to put a frown on your father's face. Then I thought about it some more and I changed my mind. I decided to stay, to keep the family together. I told myself that if I was still unhappy when you graduated from high school, I would leave then."

Serena's eyes began to water.

"You were my life, Serena. You were my joy. You gave me the only happiness I knew at the time." Serena smiled softly, her eyes misty. "When you started getting bigger and bigger, you didn't need me so much any more. I was lonely. You were off with your friends most of the time. Your life was beginning to sprout. You blossomed into the most beautiful young lady. When I saw you and Nathan, and the way he looked at you, I knew you two were in love. I said to myself, 'My little girl is not my little girl anymore.' "

Caroline's eyes welled with emotion. "I missed that feeling—the feeling of being in love. Your father hadn't touched me in years at that point. I didn't feel even remotely like a woman."

"Mom, you were a beautiful woman, you still are—everybody told you that. More than that, you're a wonderful person."

"Knowing it and feeling it are two entirely different things. I didn't feel pretty. Ah, the heck with pretty. True beauty is in a person's heart and spirit. It's in their qualities. I didn't feel like I had any qualities. I didn't feel smart, worthy—I didn't feel anything other than sadness."

Serena knew exactly how her mother felt. She began to see that she was emulating her mother's actions by staying married to Julian.

"Serena?"

"Yeah, Mom?"

"Honestly, I would rather have lived alone. When I left, the guilt was unbearable. The longer you stay with someone, the harder it is to leave. After I left, I was sorry I didn't leave years before. It would have been easier for both of us if I had.

"During that first year after we separated, I refused to date anyone. I thought I had to punish myself for leaving. John asked me to go out with him on many occasions. I turned him down every time that year. Do you know that, while I was busy feeling guilty, your father was busy planning his wedding? When I knew for sure he had somebody, I finally agreed to go out with John. And I'm glad I did." She smiled. "I'm glad he persevered. He understood me. He was so patient. I think that's what charmed me the most. I don't have any regrets where John is concerned. The past ten years with John have been happier than I could have ever imagined. I feel like a woman. Like I'm cherished. I am cherished. I prayed to God for a love before dying, and he gave me John."

Tears streamed down Serena's face.

"I love you, Mom."

"I love you too, Serena."

Serena cleared her eyes as John came into the kitchen. Caroline prepared to stand, a little stiff from the arthritis that had set in even though she was only fifty-one. John carefully placed his hands around her waist, helping her stand, though she could manage on her own. Then he kissed her on the cheek.

Serena smiled. She finally understood completely why her parents divorced. And for the first time in her life, she felt glad it happened.

Thirty-eight

*I*t was the week after Thanksgiving. Serena and Julian were talking less and less these days. Julian seemed happy with the situation. As long as Serena was there, he was fine. She often sat and watched as he arrogantly strolled about the house. She no longer bothered to bring up the subject of starting a family. The idea of having children with Julian had lost its charm.

"Serena?" Julian called from upstairs.

"Yes, Julian."

"Have you seen my black bag?"

"It's in the hallway closet."

She went to the window and looked out. It was a beautiful, clear, cold day. She realized that she needed to practice for the wedding. She sat down at the piano and started practicing "The Wind Beneath My Wings," and a few other songs.

"Serena!" Julian yelled again as he shaved.

Serena couldn't hear him because she was playing so loudly. Her fingers danced quickly up and down the keyboard.

Julian cut himself with the razor. "Damn," he said. He grabbed some tissues and wiped the blood from his face.

Serena played on as the hall clock struck six.

At 6:01 p.m., Nikki was shopping for shoes to wear in the wedding. She decided to pay a surprise visit to Malik at his job. She parked her car and started walking toward the construction site.

She turned the corner and was about to approach Malik when she saw him hugging a young woman. She stepped back around the corner and against the wall. She closed her eyes, before peering around the corner. Malik and the woman were still embracing. Then he kissed her.

Nikki ran back to her car and forgot all about shopping for shoes. She felt like a rag doll. Some of her threads were unraveling, others were being yanked out. She tried to keep her eyes clear as she drove, but the tears kept coming—tears as blinding as the sun in her eyes. She slammed on the brakes to avoid hitting another car.

Marcus and Shante were leaving Brooklyn, on their way to premarital counseling at their church near Mt. Vernon, when Marcus saw a homeless man sitting on the sidewalk. The wind had picked up and the man was shivering. His hair was blowing in the wind. He had no blanket. Marcus pulled his car against the curb on the opposite side of the street.

"Why are we stopping?" Shante asked, glancing at Marcus. She had been looking at a bridal magazine.

Marcus grabbed a blanket that he kept in the back of his jeep. He crossed the street and gave it to the homeless man.

Shante saw Marcus kneel down and talk to the man. She smiled and kept looking through her magazine. Marcus reached in his pocket and gave the man a few dollars.

As he turned to walk back to the jeep, he saw two men wearing ski masks. One man jumped into the driver's seat of the jeep, while the other slid into the back. Shante screamed and tried to get out, but the first man yanked her back by her hair. Shante tried unsuccessfully to remove the keys from the ignition.

Marcus ran toward the jeep. "Hey!" he screamed.

The first man started the engine.

"Shante!" Marcus called. "Let her go! You can have the truck—just let her go!"

Shante managed to get her door open slightly and Marcus flung it open the rest of the way, his adrenaline pumping like never before. Leaning into the jeep, he struggled with the men. He pressed his back against the window frame and dug his shoes into the ground, trying to keep the jeep from starting off as the lead carjacker slammed the gear into first.

"Jump, Shante! Get out of the car!" Marcus yelled.

Shante was able to get out before the jeep picked up speed, but Marcus was trapped. His sweater and canvas belt got caught on the seat lever. He tried to free himself, but as the car moved faster and faster, he was dragged. Then his sweater tore, his belt snapped and he was tossed into the air and—slammed to the ground.

Shante stood in the street, screaming, as she saw Marcus's head hit the pavement. She ran over to him and blocked traffic so no other cars would hit him. *"Somebody call an ambulance, please!"* she screamed.

Crying uncontrollably, she cradled his upper body in her arms. Her hands and clothes were soaked with blood.

Marcus tried to say something.

"Forever, Marcus," she said.

"For e-ter-ni-ty," he said, struggling to pronounce every syllable.

"Yes, Marcus, yes—for eternity."

Marcus lost consciousness.

By now, a crowd had gathered around. "Oh, my God!" one woman said. Others gasped and muttered. Their voices were drowned out by the growing sound of the sirens.

When the ambulance pulled up, Shante was mumbling like a child lost in the wilderness. This cannot be happening, she thought. She felt like she was having a nightmare, and she told herself that she would wake up any minute. "I just know I am, I just know I am," she cried out. "No. I just know I am, I just know I am . . . ."

"What, ma'am?" a paramedic asked.

"She doesn't realize what she's saying," another paramedic told him. "She's in shock."

When they arrived at the hospital, Marcus was fighting for his life. "He's not going to make it," the doctor told Shante before permitting her to enter the intensive care unit.

Leaning over his bed, Shante said, "I love you so much, Marcus. I will always love you. And I promise, I will always take care of Ashley." Marcus looked at Shante as she talked. He wasn't able to speak, but he was able to hear.

"Squeeze my hand if you understand what I'm saying." He squeezed her hand firmly for a few moments. Then his grip relaxed, and he closed his eyes.

Shante thought she had fallen into a deep pit and she was scratching to find her way out. But no matter how hard she tried, the pit kept getting deeper and deeper, wider and wider, and the air less and less plentiful, until she became the pit. It filled with tears and submerged her.

Shante asked the hospital staff to call Lillie Mae and Serena. She knew she wasn't able to make it home on her own. The doctor prescribed some tranquilizers to help calm her.

Serena was visibly distraught when she arrived at the hospital. Lillie Mae was numb with grief as she walked through the hospital doors in a trance. Shante looked at her and said, "How are we going to tell Ashley?"

Meanwhile, the phone at Shante's apartment was ringing. It was Marcus's dad. He left a message on the machine saying that he wanted to see Marcus.

Thirty-nine

*I*n the cold drizzle, Serena and Nikki rode to the funeral together. Shante was in the limousine, along with Lillie Mae, Ralph, Ashley, Marcus's half-brother and sister, and some of his cousins.

At the church, Reverend Alexander gave a sterling tribute to Marcus's life. "Marcus was a courageous man," he said. "He worked tirelessly on behalf of people less fortunate than himself. He was a compassionate friend, a loving father, and a man of peace who reached out to anyone in need. His heart was pure and his soul was meek. He spoke for world peace and against discrimination and violence, yet it was violence that took his precious life."

As Reverend Alexander spoke, Shante flashbacked to her childhood ...

She saw herself lying in the middle of the street. A car was speeding toward her, but she couldn't move. She was hypnotized by the glare from the headlights. She had her Halloween candy in one hand. She had fallen while trying to cross the street.

Her mother screamed from the parked car alongside the road. Marcus was in the back seat. He jumped out of the car, scattering his candy all over the ground. He scooped Shante out of the street just before the car reached them ...

"Oh," Shante gasped.

Until that moment, She had forgotten about the night she and Marcus had gone trick or treating. "He saved my life. He saved my life," she cried as Lillie Mae hugged her.

Nikki and Serena whimpered. Serena looked at Ashley sitting next to Lillie Mae. She looks so sad, Serena thought.

"And in his death," Reverend Alexander continued, "he was just as courageous. He had stopped along the road to help a homeless man. He will be remembered for helping and caring for others. That will be his legacy. You know, he came to me not too long ago to express his desire to become a deacon in the church. He told me that he was getting married to the most wonderful woman in the world. He talked about his daughter Ashley, and how much he wanted to be the best father he could be. He talked about his mother, and how loving she had always been, and how she had raised him by herself. He wanted to make the right decisions in his life, and he did, he did. He will rest in peace forever. We must take comfort in knowing that."

Shante knew that Marcus would always be with her. She felt his warmth all around her.

Shante stayed the next week at Lillie Mae's house. She wanted to be near Ashley and she didn't want to be alone. Serena and Nikki visited daily. They and many others brought food so that Lillie Mae and Shante wouldn't have to cook.

After that week at Lillie Mae's, Shante summoned the strength to go back to her apartment and face the fact that Marcus would never be there again. She hesitated before unlocking the door. She entered slowly.

Once inside, she looked at all the places Marcus used to sit and stand. She saw him greet her with a cheery smile. She looked at the desk and saw him sitting there, writing a speech. She looked in the kitchen and saw him cramming a sandwich in his mouth. Tears rolled down her cheeks. She scanned around the room at the various objects he used to touch. She saw his note pad on the coffee table. She saw all these things, but heard nothing.

She walked into the bedroom. She looked at her wedding dress hanging in the closet. She sat on the floor and cried for help—for someone to make the pain go away. "*Please help me!*" she screamed.

Fourty

For the first time, Serena called Ollie and told him that she needed some time off. "Take as much time as you want," he said.

She packed a few clothes in an overnight bag. She thought about Marcus, and how he was here one day and gone the next. Then she thought about the years she had spent in an unhappy marriage. Her marriage to Julian made her feel sad and hopeless, and she now realized that nothing was ever going to change. She left a note for Julian saying that she was going to spend the night with Shante.

On the drive to Shante's apartment, Serena thought about how close she and Marcus had been. She felt like she had known Marcus all her life. When Shante first introduced Marcus to Serena, Marcus had told Serena that he was glad Shante had met her. Marcus and Shante were still only friends at that time, and Marcus had felt relieved that Shante was adjusting to life in New York and making great friends like Serena and Nikki.

Marcus and Nikki liked each other, but he and Serena seemed to have an innate understanding of one another. Serena loved the way Marcus kidded around. She thought he was adorable. Serena wiped her teary eyes and thought, he was a blessing sent from God. I have to get control of myself. I have to help Shante.

Meanwhile Nikki lay face down on her sofa, listening to the many messages from Malik. "Nikki, this is Malik. Yo, where are you? I've been workin my butt off. I guess you have, too. I have to go. Talk to you later."

"Yeah, I bet you do have to go," she said. She refused to answer any of his messages. "I'm going to see Shante," she muttered. This was not the time for her to feel sorry for herself.

It was supposed to be Shante's wedding day. She was on her bed crying when she heard the doorbell ring. It was Serena.

"Hi, Shante." They hugged. Serena left her bag by the door, and they sat together on the sofa.

"Are you okay?" Serena asked.

Shante looked dazed. "Yes."

"Hey, listen," Serena said. "I have two tickets to Florida. I invited Julian, but he can't go. I'd like you to go with me. I think it would be good for you to get away."

"I'm spending Christmas with my family in California," Shante said.

"We'll be back before Christmas."

"If I go, I'll probably fly straight from Florida to California. How long will we be there?"

"A week," Serena answered.

"I'll go," Shante said, "but I won't be able to stay the whole time."

"That's fine. I may not stay the entire week myself."

Moments later the phone rang. Shante acted as if she wasn't going to answer it. "Do you want me to get it?" Serena asked.

"That's okay. I'll get it."

Shante walked over to the desk. "Hello, Daddy," she said. "No, you don't need to come. I'm fine, Daddy. I have a bat, and some mace. I got rid of the gun. I didn't feel comfortable with it in the apartment. I'll be home soon. I love you, too. Tell Mom I love her and I'll see her Christmas. Goodbye."

Shante hung up the phone. "Would you like something to eat or drink, Serena?"

"No, I'm not hungry. Thanks. How's Ashley doing?"

"She's staying with Lillie Mae. Cindy's spending a little more time with her than she usually does. They were over here earlier today."

"Who, Cindy and Ashley?" Serena asked.

"No, Ashley and Lillie Mae." Shante looked and sounded exhausted. "Serena, will you go by the toy store and get Ashley something for Christmas? I really don't feel like shopping this year."

"Sure, I'd be happy to."

"Thanks, Serena. I'll ask Lillie Mae to bring her over here, and I'll give it to her before we leave for Florida."

"Why don't you get out of the apartment and go for a walk?" Serena suggested.

"I walk to get the mail. That's all I feel like doing. I'm so tired."

Serena patted her hand. "I know you are."

Nikki arrived thirty minutes later. Her hair was piled on top of her head and she wasn't wearing any make-up. Her eyes looked naked and tired. The three of them sat around in their gloom for the rest of the evening, but being together gave them a small measure of hope.

❖

Fourty-one

erena left early the next morning to do last-minute Christmas shopping. She immediately found something for Ashley. It was a collectible doll dressed like an angel. Serena also bought Ashley an airplane because she knew how much she liked toys with engines. When Serena returned with the gifts, she showed them to Shante before wrapping them.

"Thanks, Serena, these are perfect for Ashley. You know how Ashley is, don't you?"

"Yeah, I do."

"Her best friend is a little boy named Jason," Shante said. "He introduced her to the trucks, cars, and airplanes, and she acts like she likes them better than her dolls. You should see them playing together. They remind me of Marcus and me when we were little."

Shante started to whimper. "Excuse me," she said. She went in the bathroom to clear her face, then returned. Serena was still at the desk wrapping gifts.

"Have you packed yet?" Serena asked.

"Yes," Shante said. "I'm only taking one suitcase."

"I haven't packed, so I'm going to leave now."

"Okay. I'll see you later."

When Serena got home, she started packing for the trip to Florida. "I need a change of climate—bad," she said under her breath.

As she walked down the stairs, Julian came out of the kitchen with a drink in his hand. "How's Shante?" he asked.

"She's having a difficult time, as I'm sure you can imagine. She's coming with me to Florida."

"Oh," Julian said, with raised eyebrows. "I thought maybe you would just stay here, since I'm not going."

I don't get him at all, she thought, stay here for what? She said, "I'll be back before Christmas. You're going to be working a lot anyway, aren't you?"

"Yeah," he replied. "Well, not a lot, but I'll be working. So tell me, Serena, what are you going to do in Florida? Why don't you just stay here? Why do you have to go to Florida?"

"I don't have to go. But if you'll recall, I bought two tickets so we could both go. When you decided you couldn't, I decided to ask Shante to go with me. I want to enjoy the warm weather and relax."

Serena went back upstairs to the sitting room. She called it her Victorian room because it was elegantly filled with Victorian-style furnishings. She especially liked the beautiful Victorian swan chaise, abracadabra chest made of wood and wicker, and the Tiffany style lamps. But it was the color scheme of light blue, sage, coral, light green, and ivory that always lifted her spirits when she walked into the room. She got a magazine off the swan-legged table, sat in her armchair and began to read. Resting her head against the back of the chair, she closed her eyes.

Lillie Mae and Ashley arrived at Shante's house later that day. Shante tried not to look upset, for Ashley's sake, but it was obvious to Lillie Mae that Shante was not doing well. The first thing Lillie Mae noticed were the dark circles under Shante's eyes, and her weary face.

Shante reached on top of the desk and got the two gifts Serena had wrapped for Ashley. "Here, Ashley. These are for you, for Christmas."

"Thank you. Can I open them?" she asked.

"Wait until Christmas, okay?" Shante said.

"Okay."

"Give me a hug," Shante said. She knelt down to Ashley's level. "O-o-h, that feels so good. Lillie Mae, would you like some coffee?"

"Yes, dear, but I'll get it myself. You look like you're about to pass out. You sit down, and I'll fix us both a cup."

"Okay," Shante mumbled as she put Ashley's favorite Winnie the Pooh video into the VCR.

Lillie Mae handed Shante a cup of coffee. "Here you go." They sat, taking little sips of coffee as Ashley knelt on the floor, watching the video.

"This is good," Shante said tiredly. "Thank you." She looked at Ashley. "How is she doing?"

"She had a nightmare last night," Lillie Mae said.

Shante's eyes squeezed shut. She opened them slowly and said, "Was it because of Marcus's death?"

"Yes. She dreamed that she fell off the school bus during a field trip, and she was wandering around lost and couldn't find the bus. Then she said her daddy came and found her and made her happy again."

Shante and Lillie Mae sobbed quietly. They wiped their eyes so that Ashley would not see them crying.

Ashley ran over to them. "Will God let Daddy come back for my birthday, and Christmas? I don't want anything. I just want to see Daddy."

Lillie Mae got up and went into the bathroom.

"I need another hug." Shante didn't want Ashley to see her tears, so she held her close until she could regain her composure.

"Marcus is in heaven now," Shante explained. "He's with God and he is safe. He loves you very much, just like he did when he was here. He will always love us. He can't come back to earth, but nothing can ever hurt him again, and one day, we will be with him. Until then, he helps watch over us from heaven. You can talk to him every night, as you pray. He'll be listening with love and understanding, and his warmth will be all around you. Okay?"

"Okay, Shante." Ashley ran and sat back down in front of the television as Lillie Mae came out of the bathroom.

Lillie Mae sat beside Shante. "This has been such a shock, hasn't it?

"Yes. It hurts so bad I can't even begin to tell you. But I'm sure you know."

"I know how much you loved my son. I want to thank you for giving him happiness while he was here."

"I love him still," Shante said, shaking her head in disbelief at the fact that Marcus was no longer here.

"Shante, a love like yours and Marcus's is hard to find. Years ago I reached a point in my life where loving myself was enough. I suppose I could have married. But the right one just never came along. And I didn't wanna just settle for any old body. Every once in a while I'll give myself a flower. Sometimes I look in the mirror and say, 'I love you Lillie Mae.' Those small things I do for myself make me feel good."

After a few moments of silence, Lillie Mae spoke again. "Shante, Marcus would not want you to be depressed or unhappy. He loved you so much. You were his world."

"I know," Shante said with a fatigued smile.

"I'll never forget ya'll growing up. Ya'll just about worried us to death." Shante giggled and a tear dropped from her right eye. Lillie Mae went on. "The minute we bathed ya'll, you were filthy again. And Ashley took straight after ya'll. Now I know she's not yours biologically, but she's the spitting image of how you and Marcus used to be. If we lived in the country, we would not be able to find that child."

"Well, she's mine in my heart," Shante said, her voice crack-
ing. She looked over at Ashley. "I want you to know that I will
always help take care of Ashley. I love her like she's my own
child. You and Ashley are all I have left of Marcus. I don't want
to lose you, too."

As they hugged each other, Ashley walked over and stretched
her arms around them. Shante kissed Ashley on the head and
said, "I love you, Ashley."

"I Love you," Ashley told her. "I love you, too, Grandma Lillie
Mae."

"I love you, Ashley," Lillie Mae said.

Fourty-two

Malik barged into Nikki's office at WOZN unannounced. "Where in the world have you been?" he said in a soft, firm voice. "I've been trying to contact you for two weeks."

He paced back and forth. Nikki sat watching, with her arms folded. "Why didn't you return my calls?" Malik stopped pacing, faced Nikki and waited for an answer. He stretched his hands out as he waited for her to speak. Then he frowned. "Were you out of town?"

Nikki had stopped answering her telephone at home. "It's not working between us."

Malik held his left hand behind his ear and leaned his head forward. "What?"

"I believe you heard me," Nikki said. She was calm on the outside but fuming on the inside.

Malik could not believe what he was hearing. This is crazy, he thought. But it was even more painful for him than strange. Then he spoke up. "Just like that?" he said, crossing his arms.

"Yes," Nikki's voice cracked as she held back her tears.

Malik felt like his heart was being crushed. "Why, Nikki? I deserve to know why, don't I? Do you think I've been ignoring you or something? Is that it? I've been working overtime, but I called you several times. I even came by your place but you weren't home."

Nikki glared angrily at Malik. "You insist on lying to me."

Malik blinked hard and shook his head. "I can't believe what I'm hearing."

Nikki suddenly broke into tears.

"Nikki," Malik said softly. He walked over to her and knelt down. "What's wrong?"

"I saw you," she said. Her body jerked as she reached for a tissue from the box on her desk. She blew her nose loudly. "I know this is not very attractive," she sniffed. "But, I don't care." She grabbed another tissue.

"Tell me what you think I've done," he said.

She took a deep breath and sighed. Mascara was smeared all around her eyes. She decided to lie about what she had seen, just to see if he would admit to it. "I saw you making love to another woman." She couldn't believe how immature she was acting. But she was angry and didn't give a damn.

Malik rose to his feet with his hand on his chin as if he was about to solve some mystery. He knew he had not slept with anyone, so he began to think that Nikki was testing him. *What kind of game is she playing?*

"Oh, I see," he said. "Your private investigator's at work again, is he?"

"Yes," she answered.

"This is so childish, Nikki. I haven't been with anyone in that way since I met you. Except you, of course. And I don't want to be with anyone but you. I have no idea what this is all about, but I wish you would come clean."

"Okay. Okay. Fine. A couple weeks ago I stopped by your job to pay you a little surprise visit. I ended up being the one who got surprised. So there."

Malik blew in exasperation. He pulled up a chair and sat,

REFLECTIONS OF CHERISHED LOVE

folding his arms and resting one hand on his right cheek. He sat in silence, staring at Nikki.

Nikki looked back like a betrayed little girl.

" 'So there' what, Nikki?"

"I saw you laughing and talking to a woman. I saw you kiss her and hold her."

"Hold her," he said under his breath. He tried to figure out what Nikki was talking about.

"Don't tell me she's your sister, because you don't have one. Remember, you're an only child."

"Oh. Oh, yeah," he said. "Why didn't you come up to us and say something?"

"I'd seen enough. I didn't need to come up to you and say anything."

"I remember now! That was my cousin Daniela. She's like a sister to me."

Nikki's stared incredulously.

"I'm telling you the truth. I hadn't seen her in twelve years, because she married a serviceman and they've been overseas."

Nikki looked both confused and hopeful. "Really?"

"Yes, and I'll prove it to you. I'll introduce you to her and show you some pictures of us growing up. In fact, I've been want-ing to introduce you to her, but I couldn't get in touch with you. Now I know why."

"Malik, I want to believe you, but I don't. What are you go-ing to try to do, get her to go along with your lie? I can't believe you. I'm not going to let you manipulate me."

"Nikki, I'm telling you the truth. Look, she was about your size, right?"

"Yes."

"Did you see her hair? It was cut short, in layers in the back."

"Yes, it was, but I don't want to talk about this right now. I want you leave."

Malik rose from the chair and said, "Give me the phone." He slid Nikki's phone to the edge of her desk. He dialed his grandmother's number. "Hello, Grandma. Will you tell Nikki who

Daniela is and describe what she looks like . . ."

Nikki felt embarrassed. She waived her hands, trying to get Malik to change the conversation.

Malik kept talking to his grandmother, then he handed Nikki the receiver. "She wants to talk to you."

Nikki frowned at Malik, then spoke into the receiver. "Hi, ma'am. Yes ma'am. I don't know why he called you. Is she. At the construction site. Yes, that was her. Oh, sure, I'll come over and see the pictures. I'd like to meet her, too. Tonight? Okay. Yes, Malik told me they were close. Bye now."

Nikki looked at Malik and said, "Okay." She felt so stupid. She had tortured herself and had been angry with Malik for no reason.

"Oh, baby, I'm so sorry." He walked over to her. She stood and hugged him. He held her as if he would never let go. He stroked her hair. He kissed her pouty lips. "Oh, you scared me," he said, "I thought I had lost you, babe." They kissed some more. Malik's fear was now gone and he felt relieved.

"Do you still love me?" she asked shamefully.

"More and more every day. But don't ask me how that's possible."

"I love you so much," she said. He cupped her derriere with one hand. She moved his hand back up to her waist.

Logan walked past Nikki's office and looked in. "Nikki," he called, "this is not the Motel 6."

Nikki had to laugh.

"No, he didn't," Malik said. "Cut us some slack."

"It looks like you cut yourselves quite a bit," Logan teased.

"You better go," she said.

"I'll call you tonight," he said.

Fourty-three

$\mathcal{T}$wo days passed before Serena was able to persuade Shante to sit on the beach. All they had done since they had arrived in Miami was order room service, sit by the pool, and relax in the Jacuzzi.

Serena pointed to a distant pier. "Let's walk down to that pier and back."

Shante was silent as they walked. Serena was deep in thought. Two handsome young men walked by and whistled at them. Serena was wearing a tan bikini. Shante wore a black sheer at the waist, one piece. The men stopped and tried to make conversation, but Shante and Serena said nothing. They waved but did not focus their eyes on the men. They just kept walking.

"Shante," Serena said. "When I get back home, I'm going to ask Julian for a divorce."

Shante looked amazed. "Are you serious?"

"Yes. I'm not in love with him, and I'm only cheating both of us if I stay."

"Is this because of Nathan?"

"No. Nathan is probably seeing someone else now, especially after what happened the last time I saw him."

"What happened?"

"He came to New York, early November. I told him that we couldn't be together. I told him to find someone who could give him everything he deserves."

"Maybe it's not too late," Shante said.

"Maybe not, but I don't want to contact him until I've told Julian about my plans to end our marriage."

They walked along in silence. Serena knew that Shante didn't feel like talking much. "The weather is beautiful isn't it?" Serena commented.

Shante took in the fresh smell of the sea. "Yes, it is."

It was a warm, breezy day, the ocean a beautiful azure. They saw pelicans on the pier as they approached. Shante sat on a pier bench, watching as Serena talked to a lady feeding the pelicans. The lady gave Serena some of her fish. Serena tossed them into the water.

Serena smiled as she watched the pelicans dive down with their huge bills stretched wide open, scooping the fish into their pouches. Then she noticed a fisherman frowning angrily at the lady with the fish. "I'd better stay out of this," she thought. She stopped feeding the pelicans and leaned against the pier, looking far out into the Atlantic Ocean. Then she sat next to Shante. The sun was shining just enough to keep them warm as the wind blew Serena's hair all over her head.

"I really like your haircut," Serena said. "It just falls right back into place when the wind blows."

"Thank you," Shante said.

Shante wasn't talking much, but Serena was happy that she had been able to get her out of the hotel.

"Let's walk back," Shante said.

"Sure," Serena said, looking attentively at Shante and studying her mood.

Shante stared at her fingernails and rubbed them together while she walked. "Only five more days until Christmas. You'll be back home in four days. Are you going to tell him that you want a divorce on Christmas Eve?"

"No. I'm going to wait until the week after Christmas. Not that it really matters. Julian doesn't really get into Christmas all that much. He hates shopping for gifts, and he doesn't like to take the time out of his schedule to help put up a tree and decorate it. As you know, Marcus would always help me get my tree up, remember?"

Shante nodded, and Serena's eyes teared. "I always had the biggest trees. He would say 'Leave it to Serena to find the biggest tree in the forest.' I'd say 'Marcus, now you know you don't have to do this.' "

Shante gave a fleeting smile. Serena continued. "He'd say, 'I do-o-o-n't? You mean I've been doing it all this time and I didn't have to?' Then he'd say, 'Baby, just hush!' Then we'd all start laughing."

Their eyes teared as they recalled the times spent with Marcus.

"I haven't even decorated the tree," Serena went on. "I wonder if Julian will do it while I'm gone."

Shante shrugged. "Maybe."

They approached the hotel. Minutes later, they were back in their adjoining rooms. Shante lay down to rest and Serena went to take a shower. Just as she stepped into the shower, her phone began to ring. "Where is she?" Julian asked himself as he stood in the living room of their home.

When Serena stepped out of the shower, the phone started ringing again. She wrapped a towel around her and rushed to answer it.

"Hello," Nathan said.

Serena's eyes widened with surprise. "Nathan."

"I called your job. Ollie gave me this number. He said he thought it would be okay if I called."

Go, Ollie, Serena thought, giving a thumbs up.

"I just wanted to apologize again for kissing you," he said.

"It's okay, really," she said. "I'm glad you called."

Feeling relieved, Nathan exhaled. "It's good to hear your voice. It's the holiday season and I just wanted to talk to you so badly. I'll have a much better Christmas now."

"Oh." She was too touched for words.

"Here I go again," he said. "I don't have the right to do this. I'm going to go now."

"Wait," Serena said.

Did she say wait?

"Are you still there?"

"Yes, I'm here."

"I'm going to be here for a few more nights," she said.

"You are?"

"Yes. My friend Shante is with me now, but she's leaving tomorrow. So, you can call me here for the next few days, if you want to."

"If I want to. Do you want me to come there?"

"Well, it's such a short notice," she said.

"I'll be there tomorrow. I just want to see you so badly," he said.

"I want to see you too," she said, her entire body tingled, "but I . . ."

"I know. You're married. I promise I won't try anything. I just want to see your face. I've been off work all week, and all I've been able to do is think about you."

That's so sweet, she thought. Then she told him where she was staying.

"I'll see you tomorrow," he said.

"Goodbye." Serena fell back onto the bed and closed her eyes.

An instant later, she sat up and dialed Shante's room. "Guess who's coming here tomorrow?"

"I'll be right there."

When Shante entered Serena's room, she could tell by the smile on Serena's face who was coming. "Let me see," Shante teased, tapping her lips with her finger. "Nathan?"

Serena smiled. "Yes."

Shante smiled, as well. It was the first tearless smile Serena had seen since Marcus's death.

"I finally get to see him in person," Shante said.

Fourty-four

athan arrived in Florida the next afternoon. Shante was in Serena's room waiting to meet him when they heard three knocks on the door. "That's him." Serena blushed with excitement.

Shante raised her eyebrows in anticipation, and she pressed her lips together. "Let him in, Serena."

Serena took a deep breath, then opened the door. "Hi, Nathan. Come on in." The two of them hugged.

He really loves her, Shante thought. She could tell by the way he looked at her.

Serena introduced them. "Hello, Shante," Nathan said, extending his hand.

"It's very nice to meet you, Nathan. I feel like I know you already. Serena has always spoken fondly of you."

Nathan's smile beamed. "That's very nice to hear."

"Well, I'm sure we'll see each other again, but right now I need to go. I'm catching a cab to the airport."

Serena said, "No, Shante, I hired a limousine to take you. It's waiting downstairs. I wish you would let me and Nathan ride with you."

"No, no. That's not necessary." Shante insisted that a cab would have been fine. The airport wasn't far away, and she only had one bag. She said her goodbyes, hugging Serena and waving at Nathan.

"Have a safe trip and tell your family I said hello," Serena said.

Serena had made reservations at the Mai Kai, a dimly lit Polynesian restaurant decorated with ceremonial masks, and other western and Asian art.

They arrived early so they could sit up front near the stage and order dinner before the show began. They were settled at their table, with their orders placed, when the show began with some authentic Polynesian musicians and singers. Some of the big, tan men in the band wore grass skirts and no shirts. Others wore colorful aloha shirts and shorts. When the male and female dancers came out, the musicians played and introduced the dancers as being from Fiji, Tahiti, and Hawaii.

Initially, the female dancers came out wearing holomuus, with leis around their necks. For their second performance, they wore aloha skirts. Finally, they changed into grass skirts. They told stories and described the breathtaking scenery of the islands while performing traditional dances accompanied by drums and chants. One of the dancers changed into a lovely wedding gown. Then they performed a romantic wedding story.

"The dancers are pretty aren't they?" Serena commented.

"Not as beautiful as you," said Nathan.

He seems so sincere, she thought. "I like their costumes," she said.

"Yes, I do, too."

As the waiter served their meals, Serena looked at Nathan and wondered how in the world she had been able to resist all this time. "The food is good, isn't it?" she said. "Yours looks even better than mine."

Nathan slid his plate closer to Serena. "I'll be happy to share."

"I'll give you half of mine, and I'll just take a little bit of yours."

Nathan laughed.

"What?" she said.

"This is starting to be like old times," he said. "You'd order something, and then you'd want to trade yours for mine."

"Oh. I'm sorry." She was suddenly bashful.

"Don't be." He looked lovingly into her eyes. "You're just being Serena."

She smiled as she transferred a little of his food onto her plate.

"If I want more, I'll just order more," he said.

"I didn't do that all the time, did I?"

"No, but when you didn't, you usually ate like a bird." Then he laughed. "Do you still sit with a pillow between your thighs?"

Serena hadn't really thought about that until he mentioned it. Gosh, she thought, he remembers everything about me. "Sometimes," she answered, before giving her full attention to the magnificent stage performance.

As Serena watched the fire dancing, Nathan studied her. The light and warmth from the stage shone brilliantly upon her radiant face. Her brown eyes sparkled like the sun shimmering on a beautiful smoky quartz. Thank you, God, he thought. Thank you for giving me this night. Dear Lord, if you give Serena back to me, I promise to always cherish her, for I know what it's like not to hold her in my arms. I know what it's like not to have her in my life. If it's Your will, please help us be together. I don't know everything about her marriage, but I don't think she's happy. If she's not, help her face the truth.

Serena started clapping. "That was excellent, wasn't it?"

"Yes." Nathan looked back at the stage.

"I need a volunteer," a slender male dancer said. He wore a grass skirt and no shirt. He stepped down from the stage. "How about this beautiful lady?" He took Serena's hand. "Doesn't she look beautiful, everyone? What's your name?"

"Serena."

"This is Serena, everybody. Let's give her a hand for being so brave."

Everyone clapped. Nathan smiled. Serena agreed to go on stage and do a brief hula dance.

Nathan watched with pleasure as Serena gracefully swayed her hips from side to side and waved her arms to the rhythm. Serena had been imitating hula dancers since she was a child, and the audience had no idea that she was a Broadway performer.

Later that night, when they arrived back at the hotel, Serena gave Nathan the key to Shante's room. "It's already paid for," she told him.

As they stood in the hallway outside their rooms, Serena leaned forward and kissed Nathan on his cheek. "Thank you so much for coming."

"I'm happy you wanted me to come. When I'm with you, I'm the happiest man in the world."

Serena swelled with desire.

She's got that look, he thought. But he didn't want to take advantage of the situation. He was afraid she might not agree to see him again. "I'm going . . . to my room now. I'll see you tomorrow."

Serena unlocked the door to her room. "Come inside for a minute, I want to tell you something."

As they entered, the telephone was ringing. She answered it, waving Nathan further into the room.

"Hello? Oh, hi, Julian. I'll be home in a couple of days." She turned on the lamp.

"Where did you go?" Julian asked.

"To dinner. The Mai Kai."

Nathan waited for Serena's conversation with Julian to end. He hated hearing her talk to Julian, but he managed to hide his feelings.

"I'll be home soon," she said. "Goodbye, Julian."

She hung up, then asked Nathan to sit down. Nathan pulled a chair from the desk and sat.

Serena stood in front of him. "I'm going to ask Julian for a divorce after Christmas. It's not much of a marriage to me. I haven't been happy for years. We're more like housemates."

Nathan couldn't believe what he was hearing. He felt like he was having the most incredible dream. Serena went on. "I've tried, and there's nothing else I can do. I made a mistake by marring Julian before I knew him well, before I knew myself well. I don't believe I should punish myself for the rest of my life because of it."

Nathan was in a daze. He heard her, but it didn't seem real.

"Nathan . . . Nathan . . ," she said. "Are you okay?"

Nathan shook his head to clear his mind as chills rippled through his body. "Thank God." He sprang to his feet and reached out for her. She walked into his arms and he held her close. "I'm sorry, Serena. I don't mean to seem so happy. I know this is difficult for you, but I've prayed that if we were meant to be together, to please let it be."

"I understand," she said, as their lips met for a soft, and passionate kiss.

"Oh Serena, I want you so bad."

"I want you too, Nathan." She turned away from him. "But we have to wait until I've ended it with Julian. We have to do what's right."

"You're right," he agreed. Tears of happiness filled his eyes. He felt like the weight of the world had been lifted from his shoulders.

"I'll see you in the morning," she said.

"Goodnight," he said just before entering his room.

Serena and Nathan laid awake in their separate rooms, but were in ecstasy knowing that they were near each other and would soon be together—forever.

❖

Fourty-five

*S*erena grabbed a handful of brochures from the hotel lobby and they spent the next day sight seeing. There was so much to do and so little time, but they finally decided to go on a cruise of the Intracoastal Waterway.

As they boarded the cruise boat *Jungle Queen*, Serena smiled and waved at some of the other passengers. Then they stopped and posed for a young gentleman who asked if he could take their picture. Just as the boat was leaving its dock, the narrator began to speak. "Welcome on board the *Jungle Queen*. The *Jungle Queen* will take you through the Intracoastal Waterway, also known as the Venice of America. In about one hour we'll stop off at a Seminole Indian village. Looking to your right, this mansion is owned by . . ."

It was a perfect day. The humidity was low, the sun was shining, and the temperature was about eighty degrees. "The mansions are beautiful, aren't they?" Serena said.

"Yes, they're very nice. Look at that one over there." Nathan pointed to their far left.

About an hour into the cruise, the boat stopped at an Indian village where they saw exotic birds and monkeys, and watched alligator wrestling. "Do you want to get some ice cream?" Nathan asked as they walked around looking at the various crafts on sale.

"Not right now, maybe later," Serena said.

Nathan got himself a cone and Serena smiled as she watched him eat it. He finished it just as the boat was preparing to leave. He started to toss the napkin in the trash when Serena asked for it. She wiped the corners of his mouth and then his shirt. "Thank you," he said. "It never fails. I always make a mess if I'm not at a table."

"I remember," she said.

The young photographer passed out the pictures he had taken of everyone. Nathan bought two, one for himself and one for Serena. Minutes later, the *Jungle Queen* stopped at Marketplace Mall. Serena and Nathan listened to a Caribbean band play reggae music, then separated briefly so they could buy each other a Christmas gift.

After the cruise, they stepped off the boat and walked a few yards to Burt's seafood restaurant. Afterwards, they spent a few hours walking along the street, dipping in and out of various stores. Serena told Nathan that she wanted to get some tomatoes and oranges. She especially liked fresh tomatoes. While growing up, she used to pick them from the garden. Then she'd run home, rinse off the fruit and sprinkle salt on them before devouring them.

As they strolled along, they stopped at a fresh fruit and vegetable stand. "I'm going to make some tomato sandwiches," she said.

That's so cute, Nathan thought. You can take the girl out of the country, but you can't take the country out of the girl. He felt happy as he watched Serena pick a bag full of fruit. Being with her felt so natural to him—just like old times. Like they had never been apart.

Serena was serious about the tomato sandwiches. She and Nathan went straight to the grocery store and bought bread, mayonnaise, salt, pepper and two colas. She rarely drank sodas because they made her skin blotchy and she'd gain weight, but she always made an exception when she ate tomato sandwiches.

They went to a nearby park and had a picnic. "This is so good," Serena said as she ate. "Sometimes the simplest things taste the best."

"Yeah, they do," Nathan said.

The two spent the next day on the beach. They swam and played in the water like children, ate at a seafood restaurant along the shore, and later strolled for miles, stopping along the way for ice cream. Then they sat on the beach. Serena played in the sand with her feet and Nathan felt the urge to reach out and massage them the way he used to. But he knew he had to be patient. Soon, he thought, soon.

Then a big wave came ashore, and they backed up to avoid getting wet. When they did, Nathan shifted his eyes from Serena's feet to her thighs. He smiled and focused for a few moments on her small brown birthmark shaped like ocean waves. He recalled how Serena had always thought it had a special meaning. Today, he was willing to believe it.

Moments later, Serena started telling Nathan about Marcus, and how devastated Shante was. "We were very close," she said. "From the moment I met Shante and Marcus, it was like we had grown up together or something. Their love was so amazing. I don't know if she'll ever be the same after losing him."

Nathan suspected that something was bothering Serena. He thought she might have felt guilty because of spending time with him. "I'm so sorry, Serena." He ached for her loss of a dear friend.

As they sat on the beach watching the sunset, Nathan wrapped his muscular arms around her. Within them, she felt a peaceful, secure warmth. "You know, Nathan, Shante and Marcus loved each other so much. I learned so much from them. I learned that if you're not happy with someone, you're with the wrong someone. I'm stronger than I used to be. I won't live like that ever again."

Nathan rubbed her shoulder. "I'm so happy to be here with you," she said.

"Not nearly as happy as I am," he said. "I don't ever want to lose you again. I will never make the mistakes I made before. I was young then, but my love was solid. That's why it never faded. But now I know what it takes to keep you, and I'm certain you will always want to stay."

"We both made mistakes," she said, "but we've been given a miracle—another chance."

The next morning, before leaving for the airport, they exchanged Christmas gifts. Nathan gave Serena an exquisite diamond bracelet and earrings. She gave him a gold watch. She also gave him the athletic wear and soccer ball she had bought for Devan.

On their way to the airport, Serena said, "Nathan, I'm going to need some time to settle things with Julian."

"I understand," he said. "Do you want me to come to New York?"

"No. No."

"I don't want you to handle this by yourself." Nathan didn't want Serena to go back to New York. He wanted her to come straight to Washington with him. He knew Julian might try to talk her out of leaving. And if she stayed, his heart would be crushed once again.

"I'll be okay," she said. "I can handle it. I just need to get through Christmas. I'll call you in a few weeks."

"A few weeks." His breath was taken away, like someone had punched him in the stomach.

"I'm not going to tell him until after Christmas," she said.

Nathan felt sick with worry. "How do you think he's going to take it?"

"Not good," she said. "But I'm sure he'll get used to the idea, and accept it, in time. I know this is the right thing to do."

They both looked worried as they waved goodbye and boarded their separate flights.

❖

Fourty-six

$\mathcal{N}$ikki and Malik picked up Serena at the airport. Serena was happy to meet Malik and even more pleased to see Nikki dating after so many years alone.

"He seems really nice," She whispered to Nikki as Malik helped her with her luggage.

"He is."

"Nikki, it's so good to see you this happy." They hugged as Malik loaded Serena's luggage into Nikki's car.

When they got to Serena's house, Malik helped her take her luggage to the front door. "It was nice to meet you," he said.

"I'm certainly impressed with you," Serena said. "I'm sure you know what I mean."

"Yeah," Malik said. "She was hard to get. And now that I got her, I'm gonna keep her."

Serena smiled. "Keep her happy. Goodbye."

Nikki and Malik waved goodbye and drove away.

Serena was surprised to see that Julian had decorated the Christmas tree. She thought of Marcus and visualized him bringing the tree inside and helping her set it up. Then she took a deep breath as Julian came to greet her with outstretched arms. She gave a quick hug, a pat on the back and moved on.

They spent a quiet Christmas Eve together. He made a fire in the fireplace and Serena baked some cookies and an apple pie. In fact, Serena stayed in the kitchen as much as possible over the holiday season. She wanted to avoid any intimate encounters with Julian.

Serena got up early Christmas morning. Still dressed in her pajamas, she went downstairs and looked out the window. It was a white Christmas and Serena thought it was beautiful. She went in the kitchen and fixed herself a cup of hot chocolate with marshmallows. Then she went back into the living room. "Good morning," she said to Julian as he came down the stairs. "Merry Christmas."

"Merry Christmas, Serena."

They exchanged gifts minutes later. Serena opened hers to find a brown wool coat with a matching scarf and gloves. Inside Julian's box was a suit and an additional pair of slacks, like the ones Serena had spilled wine on. They thanked each other, then went into the kitchen to sample the various dishes and desserts Serena had made.

In California, Shante was glad to spend Christmas with her family. Her twin brothers, both law students at UCLA, were there. But she missed Ashley and Lillie Mae even more than she thought she would. While her family ate dinner, she went in the living room and called Lillie Mae.

When Lillie Mae told her that Cindy hadn't shown up twice when she was supposed to, Shante guessed that Cindy had slipped back into her old patterns of unreliable and inconsistent behavior. Shante decided to cut her trip short. She had planned to stay in California through New Year's; instead, she flew back to New York on the Twenty-seventh.

She drove straight to Lillie Mae's house from the airport. Ashley came running out with her arms wide open. Shante knelt and hugged her as Lillie Mae stood in the doorway smiling at them.

"I'm home, Ashley," Shante said, a tear in the corner of her eye. "I'm so happy to see you. I love you with all my heart."

"I love you too, Shante. I missed you."

"I missed you too, Ashley. Hey, listen. I'm not going out of town again any time soon unless you're with me, okay?"

"Okay." Ashley smiled.

Malik and Nikki flew to New Orleans to bring in the New Year with her family. They rented a car at the airport and Nikki drove.

"We're here," she said as she pulled into the long gravel drive-way. She looked at the one-story white clapboard house where she had grown up. A German Shepherd and a Doberman Pinscher ran up to the car, barking hysterically.

"Is it safe to get out?" Malik asked.

"Yes. They won't bite," she said as she stepped out of the car.

Malik thought, am I supposed to believe her, and just happily bounce out of the car? Then he eased out the door. The brown Doberman jumped up on him with muddy front paws. "This is definitely a country Doberman," Malik said.

Nikki laughed.

Nikki could have brought home just about anyone; her family was happy to see somebody of the male gender with her at the door. They had always believed that she was lonely and would not admit it to herself—or anyone else. When Nikki's mom, Olivia, saw Malik at the door, the first thing she said was, "Get in here, son." Then she wrapped her arms around him, swinging him to the left and right as she did. Malik's animated expressions provided a laugh for Nikki and her younger sisters. Nikki, however, was uncomfortable with her mother referring to Malik as "son."

Her mother knew that Malik had to be something wonderful. "Have a seat," Olivia told him. Then she grabbed Nikki's hand and led her into another room to talk privately for a few minutes.

As Malik sat in the sofa chair, Nikki's sisters sat across from him on the sofa, staring at him. They were trying to figure out how he had been able to convince Nikki to become involved with him. They stared so hard that he began to feel like a fair freak. I guess they're waiting for me to perform some kind of magic trick or voodoo or something, he thought as he tapped his fingers on his knees.

He pointed to the sister sitting on the right. "So you're Kileigh, right?"

"Right," she said.

"And you're Yasmin," he said.

Yasmin nodded yes and smiled.

"You're the youngest—twenty, right?" Malik asked.

"Yeah," Yasmin said, still staring.

"It's really nice to meet you girls," he said.

They kept staring.

They're not very talkative, he thought, but they sure like to stare.

Malik decided not to look at them any longer—at least until they got their fill of looking at him. He was tired from the flight and from working long hours the day before. He turned his head toward the foyer and surveyed the art, the old black and white photographs on the walls, and the artificial floral arrangement on the table beneath the art.

When Nikki came back into the room, she noticed that Malik looked a little uncomfortable. She realized that she needed to break the ice. She told her sisters how she met Malik. "I was reporting on an accident at a construction site in Manhattan. He came to my job the next day. He was so persistent . . ."

"Oh, oh," her sisters nodded in unison as they listened attentively.

"Now, you can stop staring at him so hard," Nikki said. "He's a real man, I promise you that."

Malik smiled. Yasmin and Kileigh started giggling.

Malik sighed in relief. I'm glad she told them, he thought.

"Who's that?" Malik pointed to a picture of a Native American man standing proudly with his arms folded across his abdomen.

"That's my grandfather," Nikki said. "My mother's father. He died before I was born."

"Oh, I'm sorry," Malik said.

"That's my mom's mother," she said, pointing to a picture of a beautiful, dark-skinned black woman. Then she pointed to a picture of a light-brown skinned man. "And that's my dad."

Kileigh and Yasmin watched Nikki and Malik walk around the house holding hands.

Nikki's mom cooked a blend of Spanish and French dishes, and Malik enjoyed her Creole cooking. He was beginning to feel right at home. Later that evening, they laughed, talked, and played Spades. "Your mother is so nice," Malik told Nikki.

"Malik, can I get you something else to eat?" Olivia asked.

"No thank you, ma'am. I'm full. I couldn't eat another bite."

They spent two nights there. Malik slept rather uncomfortably on the sofa. Nonetheless, he had a wonderful time being with Nikki and meeting her family.

Fourty-seven

Serena managed to get through New Year's without telling Julian she wanted a divorce. She knew there would be an argument when she did tell him and she didn't want to argue during the holiday season. She also believed that Julian did love her in his own way. And though he loved himself much more, she knew that part of their problem was simply their incompatibility.

By the first week in January, Serena was ready to tell Julian that their marriage was over. That evening, when he arrived home from work, she was waiting for him in the living room.

"Julian, sit down, please. I want to talk to you."

"What is it, Serena? I'm busy right now."

"I want a divorce," she said.

Julian chuckled vaguely. He thought Serena was just trying to get attention.

"Julian, this is no joke. I mean it."

Once Julian realized she was serious, Serena saw a side of

him that she had never seen before. She had never seen him so angry.

"I've given you everything," he said sternly. "Plenty of women would be glad to have me."

Serena listened tensely as he began asking her, "Why?" She suddenly realized that Julian must have been convinced that she felt so privileged to have a man—successful and nice looking—that she would never in a million years leave him.

"Do you know that there are far more available women out there than there are men?" he asked.

She was dumbfounded. "Did you think I stayed in this marriage because of the percentage of available men? I stayed with you because I wanted our marriage to work. I believed that there was hope for us. I've learned a great deal about myself lately, Julian."

"What's that, Serena?" he said in a nasty tone.

"I've learned that I'd rather be alone, than to settle for unhappiness in a relationship with someone else. I'm a strong woman, Julian, I can stand alone."

"Is that why you went traipsing off to Africa last year? To prove to me that you were this strong woman?"

With those words, it all made sense. Serena now knew why she had gone to Africa. It had been to face her fear of traveling alone. And she had learned that it was okay to be alone—that you're never really alone. But now she realized that the trip had even deeper meaning. She said, "No, Julian. It was to prove to *me* that I'm a strong woman. I had the strength all along. It was just lost inside of me." And her trip had been the beginning of her search to find it.

"Why aren't you happy? What have I done to you?"

"Julian, like you always say, we've had this conversation twenty times."

"Is there someone else?"

"The reason I want a divorce is not someone else. I want a divorce because I've done the best I can in this marriage. I've tried. At some point, I had to accept the fact that we are not compatible, and never will be, in terms of a marriage. I like you. I have loved you. But I just don't want to be in this marriage any longer."

Julian stood with his hands on his hips, blowing hard in frustration. "So, after seven years, you just casually say it was a mistake."

"Julian, why now? My feelings never mattered to you before. Now that it's over, you want to discuss something in depth?"

"You're not going to find anyone like me," he shouted. "And I hope you don't think you're getting the house. Where are you gonna stay?"

Julian was unaware that Serena had not put most of her money in the same bank account with his. And he thought she had spent most of what she had left on clothes. After a few years of unhappiness, she had wised-up and started keeping some of her money in a separate account.

"This is interesting," Serena said. "Did you think that I would put up with anything just to stay in this house?"

"No. I'm saying that since you're the one who wants the divorce, you shouldn't expect to receive anything from it."

Now he's trying to scare me with the idea of financial hardship, she thought. It won't work. "Julian, I'm not really concerned about any of that. I'm sure we can agree on something. I have no hard feelings towards you. I can see, however, that is not the way you feel about me."

Nothing Julian said seemed to be affecting Serena the way he wanted it to.

"I'll leave first thing in the morning," she said. "I'll stay with Shante or Nikki until I find an apartment. I think it would be best if we settle everything between us without a bunch of lawyers. But if we can't, I'll have mine call yours next week."

Julian was hurting. He realized that his anger seemed to make Serena more determined to leave.

Serena started up the stairs.

"Wait!" Julian called. He decided to try a different strategy. "Sit down. I want to talk to you."

Serena had never heard *those* words before. She felt emotionally drained, but she sat next to him on the sofa anyway.

He took her hand and held it in his. "Serena, please."

Oh, now he's nice, she thought.

She felt sad and terribly guilty, but she was sure she was doing the right thing. "Julian, I'm sorry. I respect you and everything you've accomplished. I just can't live like this any longer. Your idea of what a marriage should be is totally opposite from mine. A woman needs more than a house, and a husband to wait on and have sex with. Now I know you think I'm supposed to get my happiness from making you happy. And the truth is, I enjoyed waiting on you and fulfilling your needs, but you never seemed to be concerned about me and my needs."

"My mama would have been glad to have a house like this, Serena. She used to wait on my father hand and foot, and she never once complained."

"I'm not your mama, Julian. And it's not about the house."

"I still can't see why you're not happy," he said.

"Julian, I've been telling you why for six years now."

"Stay for a few months. Give it some time. Please. I can't believe this bullshit. I think I deserve at least *that*." Julian thought that if Serena gave it some time, she would calm down and change her mind. He felt desperate. "If you stay for a few months, we can settle things without a lengthy legal battle . . ."

Serena's mind was made up. But because she felt guilty, and cared about Julian's feelings, she thought perhaps she'd stay for a few weeks.

Then she looked at Julian and how angry he was. She thought about how busy her work schedule was going to be for the next two months. She knew she would need more than a few weeks to move some of her belongings — things Julian wouldn't notice — without having him standing over her making life difficult. Would he try to lock her out of the house before she had a chance to handle her affairs? She didn't put it past him the way he was acting. "I'll stay for a few months," she said.

When Julian left for work the next morning, Serena called Nathan and explained the situation to him.

"I'm coming up there," he said.

"No," she told him. "That would be a disaster. I don't want a dragged out fight with Julian and his lawyer. We'll work things out civilized."

"I don't want you to go through this alone. He's going to try and convince you to stay."

"Nathan, if I don't give him at least this, it's going to make things much worse. I have to go right now, I'll be late for work. We'll have to stop talking for a while, because Julian is watching everything I do now that I've asked for a divorce. I'm sorry, but it won't be long."

"I love you," Nathan said.

"I love you, too," she said.

The more Nathan thought about Serena's situation, the more anxious he became. What if she changes her mind, he thought. What if Julian pressures her into staying? He stood in his living room with his hands on his hips and his eye twitching. "Damn it, that's exactly what he's doing," he said.

That evening Nathan called Serena.

"Nathan, please don't call here like this. If Julian finds out about you, things will become even more difficult than they already are. I'm going to stay here for three months like I promised. That's the least I can do."

"I hear you telling me this, Serena, but it hurts. What if you decide you want to stay with him? I can't stand the thought of him touching you."

"It won't happen," she said. "I have to go now, he's coming."

"Please don't forget our love," Nathan said.

"I couldn't if I tried, Nathan. Goodbye."

As Nathan said, "I love you," Serena hung up.

Fourty-eight

he next three months seemed like forever. But Serena had honored Julian's wishes. When she announced she was leaving, he said, "Don't leave. Give it some more time."

"No, Julian. This is not going to work, and you know it as well as I do." Julian had spent the three months trying to manipulate Serena into staying. But she was not fooled by his cajolery, his many acts and different faces. She knew he was the same man she had lived with for the past seven years.

When Julian realized that nothing was going to change Serena's mind, he confessed to having had a brief fling while she was in Africa. "It was only one night and it didn't mean anything," he admitted bitterly.

Serena wondered why he was confessing now that their relationship was over. Either he was confessing to relieve her of her guilt for wanting a divorce, or he was trying to hurt her or gain her attention. She wanted to believe it was the first, but in her heart, she knew it was just an attempt to upset her. She knew that if she told him about her feelings for Nathan, he would explode and the divorce agreement would be tossed in the fire. "Julian, your fling doesn't matter to me now. I just want you to be happy. And I want you to consider the happiness of the person you choose to be with next." I'm so glad he confessed, she thought. A load of guilt had been lifted from her.

"I'm keeping the house," he said.

Although Serena loved her house, she agreed that he could keep it. "That's fine, Julian. You've been happier here than I have."

Serena was financially comfortable. She had saved and invested wisely and was making good money as a performer. She also received a share of the profits from some of Julian's real estate investments. That wasn't the most important thing to her, though. What was significant was the feeling she had when she walked out the door. She felt like she was in charge of her life for the first time in years, in control of her own happiness and self worth. She felt free, and knew that she would never allow herself to remain in a relationship where she was taken for granted. She would never stay in a bad relationship again.

When Serena walked out, Julian stood with his head down and his hand pressed against the closed door. "She's gone," he said, and a tear rolled down his face. Even as his arrogance filled with grief, he held his head high and slowly climbed the stairs.

Serena moved in with Nikki until she could find a place to rent. She spent the next week having her art, piano, and other possessions put into storage. Nikki and Shante helped her move some of her things while Julian was at work each day.

As Serena filled the last box with personal belongings, she stopped and looked around the big house. "There's just one more thing I have to do," she said to herself.

Fourty-nine

*N*athan sat on a bench near the Reflecting Pool on a beautiful spring day. He felt defeated once more. Had he lost Serena again? It was his fault, he thought. He wanted her too much. Did she realize she couldn't leave her marriage? Would he ever have her? Was it just a dream—a magnificent dream? He visualized Serena standing near the Reflecting Pool, the way she had exactly one year before. No. She said she would never forget. He had to keep believing that.

The sky suddenly turned dark. It looked as if a storm was approaching. "I better go," he said.

Suddenly the sun shone again. The sky brightened. As Nathan started to leave, he heard a voice.

"Nathan."

He turned around, his heart pounding. Tears sprang to his eyes.

"Am I too late?" Serena asked. The spring breeze blew her hair and tan silk dress.

"Never," he said.

"I don't want to lose any more time," she said. "I want us to be together forever. So, what do you say?"

"Yes! Oh, God, yes! This is what I have always wanted." He walked up to her and put his arms around her. "You have made me the happiest man in the world. I couldn't stop believing. I didn't even want to try. I promise, I'll never stop loving you."

They kissed.

"I'll always be faithful to you, Serena. I'll support you, listen to you, respect you, and I'll cherish you for the rest of my life." They kissed again.

"I trust you completely," she said. "I just hope I'm really everything you need. I'm not perfect."

"You are, you always were, and you always will be my Serena Hope, my shining star, and that's everything I need you to be."

As they embraced, they received the smiles of tourists and curious passers-by.

Two hours later, Nathan and Serena entered his apartment. He had taken her to a quiet restaurant to talk and get a bite to eat. Now, as they stood in the living room, he found himself wishing he had fixed the place up and put some pictures on the wall.

"This is a nice apartment," Serena commented as she looked around. "I like your rug."

"Thank you," he said, feeling embarrassed as he turned on the lamp, giving the dusk darkened room a little more light. "I'm sorry I haven't done much decorating."

"Everything looks fine," she said. "Looks like we made it just in time." She pointed at the window toward the rain coming down.

"Yes, we did."

Noticing the many compact discs, she walked over to the entertainment center. He studied her as she bent to read the titles. He could nearly see through her dress as the thin silk gripped the soft curves of her buttocks.

"Do you mind?" she asked, choosing romantic jazz recordings by David Beoit.

"No, ahh, go ahead," he managed to say in a strained voice.

She turned up the music as Nathan walked toward her. He slowly reached his arm around her, showing her where to find more jazz. When he did, she caught the fresh, sensual scent of his cologne for the second time today. She turned to face him, gazing into his eyes.

"I feel like I'm dreaming," he said. "Please tell me it's not a dream."

"I have a better idea." She reached for his hand, kissed the palm and trailed her hand down the shape of his face. The warm moisture of her lips and the touch of her hand sent a wave of pleasure through him and he gasped. He pulled her against him and they slowly began to grind to the jazzy sound of the saxophone, creating choreography as smooth as the music itself. April showers fell outside, giving a cozy, warm atmosphere to the room as they nuzzled together. The light from the lamp set her face aglow, enhancing her soft bronze skin and the shimmer in her bright eyes. "Oh, Serena," Nathan said in a whisper and feeling weak in the knees. "I missed you so much."

"I missed you too, Nathan." Serena began unbuttoning her dress, revealing her gold lace bra and bikini panties. When she did, Nathan could take it no longer. She kissed his neck and moaned and that was it. Trembling, he lifted her in his arms, carried her into the bedroom and closed the door.

Later that night, the rain had stopped, the music had played out, and they lay nestled in each other's arms. They listened to the crickets chirping outside Nathan's bedroom window. Then Nathan spoke. "Thank you, Serena. Thank you for the most beautiful love I have ever known."

"Thank you for loving me so much Nathan, and so well."

"It's so easy to love you. It's an honor."

Nathan could not hold back his tears of happiness as they lay awake holding each other and making love into the wee hours of the morning. And it was everything they had dreamed it would be.

"You're so beautiful," he whispered at one point. "I don't ever want to lose you again."

"You won't," she said. And she raised her head and sealed their future with a kiss.

Fifty

*S*erena spent the next week in Washington. Nathan introduced her to Brandi and Justice. Serena and Brandi liked each other immediately, and Nathan wasn't surprised. He smiled when Brandi said, "Serena, I'm *so* glad you're here."

Serena hadn't seen James since college, so Nathan invited him over one evening. James was happy to see Serena and even happier to report to Nathan that he and Monique were getting serious. "I believe I'm ready to settle down and become an honest man," he said to Nathan with a broad grin.

Serena and Nathan also attended one of Devan's soccer games that week. Devan was all smiles as Serena cheered and showed enthusiasm over his part in the game. While Serena and Nathan cuddled up on the bench, Nathan felt like he was floating on a cloud of dreams come true. In between cheers, Serena rested her head on his neck.

After the game, Devan rushed up to Nathan and whispered in his ear. "I like her, Daddy."

"Good, son, because I do, too." They smiled.

Before Serena flew back to New York, she and Nathan made plans to commute regularly to see one another.

Nathan began to wonder how he could move closer to Serena and still keep joint custody of Devan. That's it, he thought, I'll ask Alysse if she's still interested in moving to New Jersey.

One weekend he flew to New York to discuss the matter with Serena, and to ask her to be his wife. They went to a four star restaurant in Manhattan. She wore a lilac lace dress that clung to her body.

He had another poem for her this night, entitled, "If You'll Be My Wife." On his knees, he presented her with a two-carat flawless diamond. "Will you be my wife, Serena?" he asked.

She answered without hesitation. "Yes." They were so overcome with emotion that they left the restaurant without eating.

Later that night, as they sat in his hotel room, Nathan told Serena about the custody situation with Devan. "It would be easier for Devan if I moved to Washington," she said.

"I don't want you to leave your career because of me," Nathan said.

"I can continue my career in Washington," she said. "And I'll still work in New York from time to time. This is what I want to do, Nathan."

Fifty-one

As soon as Serena's divorce was final, she married Nathan back in her hometown in Georgia. When Nathan saw Serena walking down the aisle, he wanted to shout his happiness to everyone. Instead, tears of love filled his eyes.

Serena wore a stunning, Victorian, ivory wedding gown with her hair romantically swept atop her head. Nikki and Shante were her bridesmaids. They wore antique rose dresses with black satin trim. Devan was the ring bearer and Ashley the flower girl. Devan and Nathan both wore ivory tuxedos. Ashley wore a pretty ivory lace dress that flared out at the hips.

The church was adorned with roses, lilies, orchids, and gladioli. A saxophonist and pianist played romantic music.

Ollie and Daria came to the wedding. Both Serena's parents and step-parents and Nathan's family were there. Justice and Brandi, and about one hundred other guests—including some of Serena's and Nathan's high school friends—attended, as well.

Serena was happier than she had been in years, but when she looked at Shante, her heart ached. It had been well over a year Since Marcus's death, and Shante still grieved heavily. Serena could tell that Shante was thinking of Marcus and the plans they had made to be wed.

After a glorious honeymoon in Hilton Head, South Carolina, Serena and Nathan bought a beautiful brick house in Fairfax County, Virginia. It had a stunning carved stairway in the foyer and enormous back-to-back living and dining rooms. Serena continued performing, mostly at the Kennedy Center and the National Theater. She made occasional trips to New York to perform and to visit Shante, Nikki, and Ollie—usually staying a few weeks at a time. She also spent a hefty amount of time talking to them on the telephone, long distance. They enjoyed coming to Washington to visit her on occasion.

Serena continued writing her musical, a little at a time, and she and Devan became very close. She often told Nathan and Alysse that they had done a remarkable job raising Devan. Serena flattered Alysse so much that Alysse couldn't help but like her.

Nathan and Serena had been settled into their home for a week when Serena heard the screen door slam. "Serena, love—I'm home."

She greeted him with the usual warm embrace and kiss. "You're early."

He took her hand. "Let's go. Keep your eyes closed—I have a surprise." Nathan shut the door behind them and helped her into the car. "You have to keep your eyes closed until I tell you to open them," he said.

Serena closed her eyes and covered them with her hands. Nathan glanced at her to make sure she wasn't peeping.

"I'm not dressed for anything fancy, Nathan."

"You're beautiful," he said.

About three miles and three minutes later, Serena heard the sound of gravel under their tires. Where am I, she thought. Then Nathan slowed down, and she could tell he was parking the car.

"Keep your eyes closed," Nathan said. He got out of the car, walked around to Serena's door and opened it. "Okay, you can open your eyes."

She caught her breath, and her face lit with enthusiasm. "Oh Nathan," she said.

Straight ahead was a wooden fence. Beyond the fence were two Tennessee Walking Horses. One horse had a shiny black coat; the other was pecan brown, with black mane and tail. "They are so beautiful," Serena said.

In the field stood a man wearing a cowboy hat. It appeared to Serena that the man was checking the horses' shoes to make sure they were fitted properly. Minutes later the man mounted of the horses and Serena watched as it lifted its slender legs high in the air. Tears dampened her lashes.

"This is all ours," Nathan said. "The ranch, the horses." They looked at all the land surrounding them. "One horse is for you, and one is for me, so I can ride alongside you for the rest of our lives." She leaned against him and he held her close.

The man with the cowboy hat signaled for Serena to come ride. Nathan was filled with pleasure as he watched her mount and gallop happily into the sun.

Fifty-two

One summer evening, as Serena sat on the front porch writing and watching Nathan and Devan kick a soccer ball, she thought of Shante and Nikki and decided to give them a call. She dialed Nikki's number first.

After they exchanged pleasantries, Serena asked, "How's Shante?"

"When she's not teaching, she's with Ashley and Lillie Mae," Nikki said.

"Is she seeing anyone?"

"No. And I don't think she has any intentions of ever doing so. She says it's no fun without Marcus. Malik and I have tried to talk to her. We told her that Marcus wouldn't want her to go on grieving this way. She hides it pretty well when she's with Ashley."

"I think she's feeling guilty," Serena said.

"Why?"

"Because Marcus got hurt trying to protect her. She could be feeling like it's her fault that he died."

"I don't know, Serena, it's possible. I just figured it was because they were always so close."

"Of course that's the main reason. Has she been going to church?"

"I don't know," Nikki said.

"I'm going to call her. I'll talk to you later."

Serena hung up and then dialed Shante's number.

"Oh, hi, Serena. How are you?"

"Everything is wonderful here," Serena said. "How are you doing?"

"I'm fine."

"Have you been going to church?" Serena asked.

"Yes, but not regularly," Shante answered.

"Have you talked to Reverend Alexander lately?"

"No, not lately."

"Promise me you'll talk to him about Marcus. He's so supportive. I used to talk to him about Julian. You should ask him to pray for you. You can't carry these burdens alone. I know Ashley and Lillie Mae are there, and that's great, but I think you need all the support you can get. Mom always told me to lean on the Lord."

"You're right Serena. Thanks for opening my eyes once again."

"Hey, it wasn't too long ago that you helped open mine. I love you."

"I love you, too, Serena. Goodbye."

That same evening, Malik took Nikki on a dinner cruise along the Hudson. Nikki wore a peach-colored dress suit with a draped collar. Malik looked incredibly handsome in a beige pinstriped suit he had bought for this special evening. Malik had planned everything. The band would stop playing in the middle of a song and ask for a volunteer to come up and sing.

When Nikki saw Malik raise his hand, she couldn't believe her eyes. His singing is even worse than mine, she thought. She began to wonder who had lied and told him he could sing.

As the band started to play, Malik cleared his throat. "Let the show begin," he yelled. Then he launched into song.

Nikki closed her eyes for a few seconds, then slowly opened them. She looked on with squinted eyes and a skeptical smile. Her tension showed on her forehead. Oh, my goodness, she thought, covering her mouth with her hand. And everyone knows he's with me. He's such a clown. I might as well grin and bear this.

A minute into the song, Malik began singing the final verse: " 'Then I met a girl, her name is Nikki Campbell.' "

"Oh, gosh," she said under her breath. She smiled timidly.

" 'I hope she'll be my wife, so we can roll and ramble.' "

He's such a nut, she thought. Then—What did he say? Did he say marry me?

Everyone was clapping and smiling at her.

"Oh, my gosh." She started to tremble.

Malik left the stage and approached her. He dropped to one knee. "Will you marry me?" he asked. "I promise I'll be your dream come true forever. I won't let you down, babe. I love you." He removed a diamond ring from his pocket.

Nikki was so choked up, she couldn't answer. She just shook and cried and looked down at the ring.

"Easy babe . . . easy," he said. "I need an answer. My knobby knees are hurtin', and my pants are gettin' dirty."

Nikki started laughing and crying at the same time.

"Yes," she said.

Everyone clapped and one man whistled.

Nikki and Malik married three months later, in October. It was a small wedding. Nikki's family came from New Orleans. Malik's grandparents, his cousin Daniela and her husband, and a few of his friends were there. Shante, Serena, Nathan, Logan and about twenty other guests came. Serena sang, "Looking Through The Eyes Of Love."

Nikki wore an elegant white satin dress. Malik wore a white Nehru-style jacket and black pants. Malik and Nikki had just bought a white, three-bedroom house with a basement in

Norwalk, Connecticut. They had the ceremony in their beautifully landscaped backyard. The green grass and plants were well kept and a few yellow roses still bloomed in the yard. Nikki had never seen roses bloom that late in the year, but it had been unseasonably warm lately. Nikki had no floral decorations other than her bouquet. She said the fall foliage was all the flowers she needed, and the photographer agreed. It provided lovely scenery.

After the ceremony, there was a catered, buffet-style dinner outside. Nikki made her way around the yard, hugging all the guests.

Logan was so happy for Nikki that his eyes grew teary. He and Nikki gave each other a warm hug. Nikki said, "Thanks for being my friend, Logan. I know it wasn't easy."

"You're right, it wasn't," he said. "It was terrible." They laughed.

It had been almost two years since Marcus's death, and Shante was still not involved with anyone. But Serena and Nikki noticed that the farway, empty look in her eyes was gone.

Serena took her plate and sat next to Shante at the picnic table. "Shante, what have you been up to lately?"

"I'm not dating, if that's what you want to know."

"Oh," Serena said.

"It's okay. I appreciate your concern, I really do. I've been going to church every Sunday. Reverend Alexander has helped me a lot. I can't say enough about him. You know, he was very fond of Marcus," Shante said. "Sometimes we just sit and laugh, and talk about Marcus."

"Really." This is good, Serena thought. This is very good. She needs this. She needs someone who has the gift of discernment—someone wise, compassionate, patient, and someone with love in his heart—someone just like Reverend Alexander. He's a God-send. If anyone can bring her back, it's him.

Fifty-three

Exactly one month after her wedding, Nikki called Serena in Washington with good news.

"I'm going to have a baby."

"Congratulations!" Serena was almost as delighted as Nikki.

Over the next eight months, Nikki and Malik enjoyed spending their weekends shopping for baby clothes and equipment and decorating the nursery and crib in pale green and white with white lamb designs.

When they were finally finished decorating—nine months into the pregnancy—Nikki dialed Shante's number, excited and wanting her to see what she and Malik had done to the nursery.

But Shante wasn't at home. She was at church where she had been spending a considerable amount of time lately. She and Reverend Alexander were becoming good friends. He began to confide in Shante about his ex-wife, who had left him seven years before because of religious differences that arose when she became a Jehovah's Witness. He also spoke about his son, Reggie, who was a student at N.C. Agricultural and Technical State University. He and his ex had no hard feelings towards each other, though. And they had raised a terrific son, despite the fact that their marriage had ended when Reggie was fourteen.

Shante had a great deal of respect for Reverend Alexander. She found him to be a very honorable man. She also appreciated the fact that he had always respected and admired Marcus, even when Marcus was struggling with alcoholism.

One day, a few months back, when Nikki and Shante had gotten together for lunch, Nikki had noticed that Shante was referring to Reverend Alexander as "Guy."

As soon as Nikki put the receiver back in the cradle, she felt a sharp pain. "Malik!" she yelled.

Malik ran into the nursery. "What, baby."

"I think it's time."

"Okay babe, let's go," he said and they left for the hospital.

Five hours later, Nikki gave birth to a beautiful baby boy. They named him Daniel Lear. He had a head full of black curly hair, and he looked just like Nikki.

Fifty-four

*S*erena had been trying to become pregnant ever since Nikki's wedding. After a year and three months of trying, she discovered that she was indeed pregnant.

She was so happy that she flew to the door to greet Nathan when he came home from work that evening. As Serena jumped up and down like a cheerleader, Nathan watched happily. She bounced herself right into his arms. "I'm so excited," she shouted. Then she pecked him on the lips.

"I still feel like I'm dreaming," Nathan said, "but it's real. It's, oh, so real." They kissed again and Nathan carried Serena upstairs and made love to her.

The following day, she called Nikki to tell her the good news.

"I'm pregnant!" Serena said.

"Oh, that's great, Serena! I'm so glad you are, too!"

"What?" Serena asked. "Who else is pregnant?"

"I'm pregnant again," Nikki said.

"Congratulations!" Serena said, with a surprised smile on her face.

Later that same day, Shante agreed to meet Reverend Alexander at the church. His secretary had been out sick for two weeks and he needed help in the office.

"Guy," she called as she stepped inside the empty church. She peered into the sanctuary and saw him kneeling before the altar. She entered quietly and waited for him to finish.

He stood and looked at his watch. Realizing it was time for Shante to arrive, he turned around. There she stood. He took a deep breath and walked toward her. "Shante, thank you for coming."

"Oh sure. What is it exactly that you need me to do?" she asked.

He reached for her hands and tenderly held them in his.

Shante was a little surprised. Other than an occasional friendly hug after church, he had never touched her before.

"Please sit down for a few minutes," he said, extending his hand toward the pews. "That's a pretty sweater."

She looked down at her sweater and felt its fabric. "Thank you. I knitted it myself." I hope he's not sick, she thought. He's acting strange. She watched as he anxiously played with his mustache. *He looks healthy. Well, he does look a little peaked.* "Is something wrong?" Shante asked.

"I don't think so," he said nervously. "I don't know. It depends."

Shante was confused. She'd never seen him so hesitant. "It depends on what?"

Oh those eyes, he thought. Those beautiful eyes and those lips. That skin.

As Reverend Alexander sat fantasizing, Shante debated whether to take his temperature. She frowned as she watched him study her face.

"Oh," he said, snapping back into reality. "Shante, I've known you for a long time now. I've . . ." He swallowed hard. "I've always felt like there was something special about you."

"Oh. I've always thought you were special, too, Reverend Alexander."

"Guy," he, reminded her.

"Yes. Guy. Of course."

He looked down at her soft hands as he held them. "I have been trying to hold back these feelings I have for you, but it's becoming increasingly difficult. You have come to me for guidance and support, and it's my responsibility as your pastor not to violate that trust. I want you to know that this has never happened to me before. But . . . the flesh is weak, Shante." He looked like he was in agony. Shante listened carefully.

"You've never, in all the years I've known you, disrespected me in any way," she said.

"I guess what I'm trying to say is that, because of our friendship, your trust in me, and my responsibility to you as a member of my church, I have tried to fight these feelings that I have for you. But now it's gone beyond that for me. I have fallen in love with you."

Shante took a deep breath. She couldn't believe what she was hearing. She was even more surprised when she realized that she didn't mind hearing it.

Guy was choked up with emotion. "I can't stop thinking of you, Shante, and it's becoming a struggle for me to see you walk away. Now, I know you're not over Marcus. I realize that you'll always love him. I respect and understand that, and I always will . . ."

Shante's heart was suddenly filled with love for Guy as she listened to his passionate and genuine words.

"Shante, if you will consider being my wife, I will make you very happy for the rest of my life. Now if you say no, I will understand, and I won't try to pressure you. I don't want to disappoint you or lose our special bond, or your respect."

Shante was touched beyond words. She leaned forward and gave him a hug and a peck on the lips.

"Oh, thank you, Lord," Guy said, under his breath.

"I need some time to think about this," she said. "It's still very difficult at times. I think about Marcus every day."

"And that's okay! I understand. If time is all you need, it's yours." He felt relieved and now hopeful. He had been afraid that if he told Shante how he felt, she would say no and stop seeing him altogether.

Over the next few weeks, Shante considered Reverand Alexander's proposal and everything he had said to her. She went back to the church and gave him her decision.

"We can date," she said, "but I'm not ready to marry."

"Thank you, Shante," he said, gladly accepting her conditions.

Fifty-five

Seven months later, Nikki gave birth to another precious baby boy. Malik was as proud as a father could be. He danced around the hospital holding two fingers in the air and boasting. "I've got two boys now. I've got two boys now."

Serena and Nathan were just as proud as Nikki and Malik. Exactly one day later, Serena gave birth to a beautiful baby girl. As she lay in the hospital bed, she held her daughter close. She couldn't take her eyes off the baby. Nathan sat next to Serena and gazed at her with endless love for her and their baby.

Devan sat on Serena's other side. "I can't believe I have a sister," he said happily. He softly stroked his sister's leg and gently patted the bottom of her foot as if she were a fragile little angel.

"Can I have a kiss?" Serena asked Devan. Devan leaned forward and they kissed each other on the cheeks.

Nathan smiled as chills ran through his body.

"Daddy, can I go get a snack from the vending machine?" Devan asked.

"Yes." Nathan handed him some change.

Nathan could easily see how much Serena loved Devan. She had even brought gifts to the hospital so she could give them to Devan: one from her, one from Nathan and one from the new baby.

"She has your eyes," Nathan told Serena. "In fact, she looks just like you. I'm so blessed."

Serena smiled. "I think she has your eyes, but, yes, the rest is me." Serena sounded a bit smug and Nathan thought it was adorable.

"What shall we name her?" he asked.

"How about Cherish?" Serena suggested.

"That's beautiful."

"Cherish Taylor Whitaker," Serena said.

He leaned forward and kissed them both on their foreheads.

Serena and Nikki weren't the only ones enjoying the pleasures of being new moms. Brandi gave birth to a cute little boy three weeks later. She and Justice named him Brandon. They were enormously happy.

Four months later, Shante accepted Guy's marriage proposal.

Serena, Nathan and their children flew to New York. Serena was the matron of honor. Nikki was a bridesmaid and Ashley, now nine, was the flower girl. Shante's parents and younger brothers came from California. Lillie Mae was there, though her health was failing her some. She suffered from high blood pressure. While Nikki participated in the wedding, Malik had his hands full with their two sons.

Shante's wedding was very elegant. The bridesmaids wore satin and lace royal-blue dresses. The groomsmen and the groom wore black and royal blue tuxedos with white shirts. Shante wore a breathtaking, off the shoulder, white gown with long lace sleeves and a flowing organza skirt with a cathedral train and a trailing veil. The church was decorated with white roses, mums, and carnations. Serena sang "How Beautiful Is The Body Of Christ."

Reverend Alexander walked around greeting everyone like he had just won the lottery.

After the ceremony, they posed for pictures and then walked straight to the church reception hall. There, Nikki and Serena doted over each other's children.

"This is our latest addition. His name is Joel Ryan," Nikki said.

"They are so adorable," Serena said. "He looks like Malik, and Daniel Lear looks like you."

"Yeah, that's what everyone says," Nikki told her. "Cherish is so beautiful, Serena. She looks just like you. But I think she has Nathan's eyes. And Devan, you're just as handsome as ever."

Devan blushed. "Thank you."

"Guess what, Serena?" Nikki said in confidence.

"What Nikki?"

"I'm going to have another baby."

Serena's eyes widened. "U-u-u-u-h. Oh, really. Congratulations," Serena said with a strained smile on her face. She tried to look happy, but she was actually concerned about Nikki having so many children so close together.

Nikki leaned forward and whispered in Serena's ear. "Malik had a vasectomy last week."

"Congratulations?" Serena said, relieved yet questioning her feeling.

"Oh, Serena, stop." Nikki laughed and slapped Serena gently on the back of her shoulders. Serena swallowed hard.

❖

Fifty-six

hante and Guy had been married and living in their two-story house in New Rochelle for exactly one month. She prepared an extra special dinner that night. Her mother had always told her that good cooking was the way to a man's heart. That, and a little cleavage.

"This is very good, Shante," Guy said just before filling his mouth with roast beef.

"Thank you," she said. "I have something serious I want to talk to you about."

He put his fork down, wiped his mustache with his napkin and listened attentively.

"Lillie Mae is not in good health. Cindy is a little more reliable than she used to be, but it's still nothing to brag about."

"Yes," he said, nodding.

"I want us to adopt Ashley, if we can. If not, I want to at least raise her. I want Lillie Mae to know that, regardless of Cindy's inconsistencies, Ashley will always be taken care of and loved. I figured that Cindy can still see Ashley whenever she wants to. I want to ask Ashley how she feels about this idea. We're together so much anyway."

Guy smiled. "I think that's a great idea."

Shante sprang from her seat, squeezed his cheeks, and kissed him, almost knocking off his glasses as she did. He smiled happily.

The next day, Shante went to Lillie Mae's house to discuss her desire to adopt Ashley. Lillie Mae was overjoyed. "There is no one I'd rather have raise Ashley than you, Shante."

"I want you to know that I'm not trying to take her away from you," Shante said.

"I know that." Lillie Mae said stressing each word. "You can see I'm not in the best of health, and you're just trying to do what's best for everybody."

"You know we'll be over often, very often. And Ashley can spend the night here sometimes, just like when Marcus was here. I'll make sure Cindy sees Ashley just as much as she does now."

"I don't know how to thank you, Shante. Whenever I do leave this earth, I know I can certainly rest in peace."

Shante still enjoyed her career as a schoolteacher. She and Guy continued their volunteer work at the community center. They took Ashley to the center and Shante explained to her how she and Marcus had founded the center in 1995. They told Ashley about all of Marcus's accomplishments. They named the center the Marcus Elder Center for Positive Growth and Guidance. As they drove away, Shante looked at Marcus's name on the building. She felt inspired. And at that very instant, she thought it would be a good idea to open more centers in memory of Marcus. And so, months later, with the support of friends and the community, she did just that.

Shante's marriage to Guy was a happy one, though she always had loving memories of Marcus, and who better to share them with than Ashley and Reverend Alexander.

Nikki gave birth to a third son. She named him Malik, Jr. Malik continued to do most of the cooking and was an excellent father. Nikki landed a job as an early morning anchor for ABC News. Her mother and sisters came to visit often. They were always eager to help with the boys. Nikki adored her boys and her husband. They treasured her too. She told Serena, "There is something special about being the only female in a house filled with males." She learned more and more every day that "all men are not the same, not by any means."

Serena finished writing her musical, which eventually made it to Broadway.

One day she and Nathan took Cherish and Devan on a family tour of Washington. Cherish was walking now, and looked just like Serena. She had long curly brown hair and Serena had her dressed in a denim dress and matching hat. Devan was a doting big brother.

When they walked by the Reflecting Pool, Serena and Nathan told them what had happened there years before.

"And your dad looked up," Serena explained to Devan.

Nathan knelt beside Cherish and pointed. "You see, Mommy was standing right over there."

❖

About the Author

Darlene Davis grew up in North Carolina, and holds a B.S. from North Carolina Agricultural & Technical State University. She is a human rights advocate, a former pre-school director, and has worked in various other professions. Her most rewarding work has been raising her two sons. She has the utmost respect and appreciation for stay-at-home mothers and those who work outside the home. She lives in Virginia where she enjoys singing and other hobbies, and is at work on her second novel.

If you would like to write to the author with comments, please send letters to:

Ingenuity Publishing
P.O. Box 42055
Fredericksburg, Virginia 22404

To order copies of Reflections of Cherished Love, contact your local bookstore, visit our website at www.IngenuityPublishing.com, or write us at P.O. Box 42055, Fredericksburg, VA 22404